THE RIDDLE OF
THREE-WAY CREEK

THE RIDDLE OF THREE-WAY CREEK

RIDGWELL CULLUM

WILDSIDE PRESS

Originally published in 1925.
Published by Wildside Press LLC.
wildsidpress.com

CHAPTER I
Loyalty

THE trail fell away to the heart of a valley, which nursed in its bosom a watercourse that was frozen solid to its bed. The hummocks of the foothills rose up in every direction. Many of the hills were sheer slopes of tawny, sun-scorched grass that had lost the last of its summer hue. Some were barren crags; others, again, were covered with woodland bluffs of spruce, and pine, and the generous poplar, whose dead foliage lay thick upon the ground, stripped from parent boughs by the wintry breath of the late season.

It was a grim enough prospect. No snow had as yet fallen, but the air was cold and crisp; the grey sky was heavily charged with snow-clouds; and the stark arms of deciduous trees were sharply outlined against the skyline.

Two horsemen were moving down the frozen trail. They were riding at that distance-devouring lope which is native to the Canadian broncho. Both were clad in sheepskin coats and fur caps. And through the fog of steam that rose from the bodies of the sweating horses, on the head of one of them the yellow flash of a mounted policeman's cap badge stood out strikingly. Corporal Andrew McFardell was escorting a prisoner to his headquarters at Calford, which lay some fifty odd miles to the south.

The policeman was in a hurry. Ten miles farther on lay Rock Point, a small farming settlement, which was to afford him a camping-ground for the night. There was little more than an hour of daylight left, and the banking snow-clouds left him anxious. It was a bad region in which to get snowbound.

McFardell was taking a chance. He had abandoned the old fur trail which was the highway from Greenwood to Calford for a short cut through the wilderness of the foothills. He knew every inch of the territory through which he was riding, but he also knew the peril of a blinding snowstorm in that confusion of hills.

They reached the depths of the valley in silence. They urged their horses to greater efforts along the level bank of the frozen stream. Then, as they faced the ascent beyond, the animals were permitted to drop back to a walk. McFardell transferred the leading-rein of his prisoner's horse to the horn of his saddle and began to fill his pipe.

His companion observed him with eyes that smiled good-humouredly, in spite of the frigid bite of the steel shackles set fast upon his wrists. Then, as his custodian struck a match and lit his pipe, he turned his gaze alertly to the frowning sky.

"Here she comes."

The prisoner spoke without a shadow of apprehension. It was the voice and accent of an educated man. His smiling eyes were regarding the lolling snowflakes with which the air had suddenly filled.

"We'll get it plenty in a while," he went on a moment later, with a pleasant, deep-throated chuckle. "You reckon it's ten miles this way to Rock Point? It's going to shorten our trail by five and more?" He shook his head. "Well, if this storm is going to be the thing it looks, why, I guess it might just as well be fifty miles to Rock Point. We shan't make it this night—through these hills."

The policeman was regarding the skyline. He, too, shook his head, but in denial.

"You think that?" he said sharply, with a quick, scornful flash of his jet-black eyes. "You're wrong. Guess this is my territory. There's not a hill, or bush, or creek to it I don't know better than my prayers. There's a top stretch up there of a mile and a half," he went on, indicating the hill they were ascending. "Then we drop right down to Clearwater River, and pass by Joe Lark's horse ranch. After that we pick up the old fur trail again, which you couldn't lose in the worst blizzard that ever blew. I'm not worried a thing."

The prisoner laughed.

"It's good not to get worried when you're in the hills, with the snow falling and night getting around. She's coming thicker, so there's no need for argument," he added drily. "You police boys are bright on the trail. I've mostly had five years of Alaska, where they know a deal about snow. I claim fifty-fifty with you on that subject."

The man's laugh was good to hear. It was a laugh of reckless indifference, of a heart devoid of fear.

Andy McFardell made no reply. He stared straight out into the falling snow. He was a good-looking, black-haired, black-eyed

6

man of about twenty-eight years. But his good looks had nothing of the frank openness and smiling good-nature of his prisoner. The two men were in sharp contrast. The whole cast of Andy McFardell's face had something of the narrow sleekness of a fox, with a mouth hidden under a carefully trimmed black moustache that was heavy-lipped and ugly. It was a face to inspire confidence in the work that was his. But the best tribute his associates in the Police cared to pay him was an unanimous opinion that he was surely marked out for promotion.

His prisoner was a larger man in every sense. His furs only left visible a strong face, and the light of philosophical good-humour that looked out of his eyes. And this for all he was on his way to Calford to serve five years' hard labour in the penitentiary.

As they reached the top of the hill, Andy McFardell turned to his companion again.

"You know I can't get a boy like you, anyway," he said, in a tone of frank impatience. "What in hell! Five years' hard pan up in Alaska. Five years' sweating blood to collect a bunch of dust that's to hand you all the things you've ever dreamed about. Five years of a climate that's calculated to freeze the vitals of a brass image. Then you pull out. And the first thing you do is to pitch everything to the devil by hitting up against the law. You've done worse than five years' penitentiary up there in Alaska, and collected a big fortune; and now you've got five years' real penitentiary ahead of you while your gold rots. Why? For the fool notion of helping a boy who didn't need your help. Say, there's times I reckon human nature's the darnedest fool thing God A'mighty ever created."

"Is it?"

Jim Pryse's reply came with perfect good-temper. He was one of those blessed creatures who can always contrive to find a smile lurking in the worst tragedy with which they are beset.

"Take a hunch man," he went on amiably. "The only fool thing God ever created is the white-livered coyote that wants to snivel its way through life, instead of getting a grip on the throat of things. I knew just the thing I was doing. You see, that boy was my brother, and the best feller I know. The skunk he'd killed was the feller who'd robbed him of a wife, and done the unholiest thing any low-down bum can do by any woman, married or single. Well, I was with him, just as though my two hands had choked the life out of that skunk instead of his. Was I going to risk seeing that boy the centre of a hanging bee? Not on your life.

I held you boys off while that kid feller got away. And I held you good. And I'd have shot to kill rather than you should have laid hands on him. He's got clear away. And, for all the law doesn't reckon to let up once it camps on a feller's trail, you'll never get him. The gold you reckon is going to rot will see to that. That boy was no murderer. His act was sheer justice. I didn't butt in. No, boy, it was better than that."

"Man, you're plumb crazy!" McFardell urged his horse on under his impatience. "No, no. Life's a pretty tough proposition, anyway. And it's only a crazy man sets out to make it tougher, whether it's for a brother or anybody else. I s'pose there's folks would call that sort of junk 'loyalty.' I guess they need to get a fresh focus. 'Duty' I know. Duty's the thing demanded of us boys in my calling. That's all right. It's always within the law, and if you carry on, and keep an eye well skinned, it's going to help you to the sort of things we all worry for. But the other stuff is a crazy notion, that's as liable as not to get you hanged. I tell you you were dead wrong. You were butting in like some fool kid. That boy would never have hanged if he could have proved his case. It was the Unwritten Law, and he'd have got clear away with it. And you—you wouldn't be riding these darned hills in a snowstorm."

The policeman's view only had the effect of deepening his prisoner's smile. And the blue eyes watched the officer tolerantly as he brushed the snow from about his fur collar.

"Maybe he'd have got away with it," Pryse said quietly, emulating his companion, wiping the snow from about his eyes with his mitted and shackled hands. "I don't know, and I'm not worried. He's away now, and I'm feeling good about it. Five years in penitentiary is going to hand me an elegant spell for quiet reflection, and maybe I'll be able to locate where our viewpoints are wrong. Just now it seems to me that duty's a sort of human-made notion that mainly has self for its principal calculation. Loyalty, as you choose to call it, seems to me to be something we can't help. Maybe it's built in us, the same as the things that set us crazy for the dame that seems good to us. I'm not yearning to worry it out, anyway. The thing I know is, Eddie boy is clear beyond the reach of any Mounted Police Patrol, and, that being so, I feel as good as a skipping lamb in springtime. Alaska handed me a deal better than a million dollars, and, if necessary, the whole of that bunch of dust will go to say you boys are nothing to give that boy a headache. I——Hold up, you!"

Jim Pryse's final exclamation was flung at his floundering

broncho. For one moment the creature seemed to be about to crash headlong. Then the lead-rein securing it to the horn of the policeman's saddle snapped and released it, and, under the tremendous effort of its rider's shackled hands, it recovered itself.

The whole catastrophe was wrought on the instant. At one moment both horses were loping leisurely over the virgin carpet of snow, with ears pricked alertly as they peered out into the grey twilight of the storm. The next the policeman's horse had gone down like a stone, and its rider lay inert, still, a huddled fur-coated heap upon the hard-frozen ground. It was the old story of thawing snow balling in the creature's hoofs.

* * * *

The twilight was deepening. It was no longer merely the sombre grey of the snowstorm. It was the gradual passing of the last of the day. The surrounding world was almost blotted out. Here and there were faint outlines, barely perceptible, to mark some woodland bluff in the immediate vicinity; but beyond that there was nothing—nothing but a grey, impenetrable pall of falling snow lolling silently upon the breathless air.

The horses were standing apart. They had no concern for the thing that had happened. They had turned away from the drift of the storm, and stood gently rubbing their frost-rimed muzzles against each other's sweating sides.

A few yards away Jim Pryse stood with shackled hands, gazing down at the prone figure of the man who had been conveying him to the penitentiary at Calford. There was no sign of life in the fallen man. He lay unmoving, just where he had been hurled from the saddle, and the flakes of falling snow were rapidly obscuring the black outline of his fur-clad body.

For some time the convict's scrutiny continued. Then, of a sudden, he dropped to his knees and ran his hands over the man's body. His movements were clumsy by reason of the shackles that held his wrists, but he persisted in his task slowly and deliberately. After a while he stood up. And his hands were grasping the cartridge belt and side-arms he had removed from about the policeman's body. With much difficulty he bestowed the revolver in the pocket of his fur coat and proceeded to remove the cartridges from the belt. These he stowed away in another pocket. Then he dropped the belt and holster in the snow.

Again he bent over the fallen man. This time it was for the purpose of ascertaining the extent of the latter's injuries.

9

But he need not have concerned himself. Corporal McFardell raised his head and looked up at him.

Quick as a flash the convict was on his feet and standing clear.

"It was a bad fall boy," he said, and for all the twilight hid his expression there was a smile behind his words. "Guess it knocked you out. Maybe it found your head softer than the trail. There's nothing broken?"

McFardell gazed about him a little dazedly in the failing light. Then his limbs moved. He drew up his legs and straightened them out. Then he sought to raise himself on his elbow. It was his reply to the other's question.

Jim Pryse nodded quickly.

"That's all right, boy. You aren't hurt, and I'm glad. Your head'll clear in a while, and you'll be able to get back into the saddle and make Rock Point. But don't do it now. Don't move a hand or foot. You see, your gun's in my hands," he went on, producing the policeman's loaded revolver, "and for they're all shackled tight I can still pull a trigger and see straight over the sight. Maybe you've a key to these bracelets. But I'm not going to worry you for it. It might cause argument and a clinch, and, though I've your gun, I'm ready to admit you'd have the best of it in the circumstances—in a clinch. No. Just lie there, if you aren't a fool, while I climb into my saddle. And you'll lie there just as long as I'm within gun-range. For, sure as God, if you don't I'll shoot you like a dog. Do you get it? I'm getting away. Providence has handed me a chance I'm grabbing with both hands. It's a tough chance all right, but I haven't a grouch. Now, lie quite still till I quit."

He backed away to the waiting horses. He paused beside his own animal, and his eyes were steadily observing the policeman who lay watching him. Then, quite suddenly, the discomfited officer was treated to an exhibition of horsemanship he was wholly unprepared for. The convict raised his fettered hands to the horn of his saddle, and, in an instant, vaulted on to his horse's back without touching a stirrup. The threatening gun, supported in both the man's hands still, held the prone figure covered.

Jim Pryse chuckled gleefully.

"You've got sense, boy," he cried, as the other made no movement. "You certainly have. You know your duty, sure—when the drop is on you. Well, so long. I can't wait. Now, get up quick and grab your horse. He won't stand when mine moves off, and I haven't a wish to leave you out here in the snow."

He moved away, and McFardell leapt to his feet and ran to his horse. The threatening gun held him covered.

He stood for a moment holding his horse, while the outline of the moving horseman became more and more indistinct in the twilight of the storm. Then suddenly his voice sounded harshly in the dead silence of the world about him.

"You fool! Do you think you can get away? Not on your life! Take your dog's chance! Take it! But you'll serve those five years—and more—if the coyotes don't feed your carcase when the storm's through with you."

CHAPTER II
The Marton Homestead

MOLLY MARTON was standing in the storm doorway of her home. She was gazing out at the magnificence of the winter sunset blazing on the crystal peaks of the far-off mountains. The hour of the evening meal was approaching, and the savoury odours of simple cooking pervaded the warm interior behind her. In less than an hour the glory of the sunset would have passed, and the purpling twilight would reduce the snowbound world to the bleak prospect of the reality of the season.

The girl was awaiting her father's return from his day's work in the timber belt. It was the time of the early winter labours, when the haulage of cordwood for the fuel store was the chief consideration. He would be along soon now, and everything was in readiness for his comfort.

Molly's devotion to her father was almost a passion. Her mother had been dead for many years, and in all her eighteen years the girl had never known a moment when her sturdy father had not been the whole of everything to her.

The Marton homestead was far enough beyond such civilisation as city or township afforded. It was set in the heart of the lesser foothills of the Rockies. Its nearest human neighbour was an Irishman of ill-repute, Dan Quinlan, who boasted some sort of a mixed ranch about twenty-five miles farther up in the hills, and the nearest township was that of Hartspool, some twenty-odd miles to the east, where the hills came down to the prairie lands, and the waters of Whale River flooded its banks every time the spring freshet broke.

Molly loved her home, and the hard, free life of it. She knew every trick and turn of Nature's whim in the progress of the seasons. She asked nothing better; she knew nothing better. The sturdy life of it was hers. She had been born, and bred, and deeply inured to its hardships, and she would not have changed one moment of it for the narrower delights of city life.

Of hardships there were plenty, of privations none. The fierce winters of the hill country were no easy thing to face. But every coming of the perfect summers saw an increasing yield of the abundant fruitfulness of the earth which the thrifty mind of her French-Canadian father taught him so well how to foster.

The homestead was a whole section of land, with practically unlimited grazing rights. It consisted of a log-built and thatched home, with barns and out-buildings similarly constructed. There were corrals rudely but strongly set up, and nearly one hundred acres lay under the plough. There was a water-front on a nameless mountain creek, and a stretch of prairie feed that was pretty well inexhaustible. In short, there was everything a good farmer could need to make life reasonably prosperous and endurable in a climate that knew little of moderation.

The delight died out of Molly's grey eyes with the passing of the sunset. And she turned her gaze in the direction where the snow-trail vanished round a bluff of woodland. It was from that direction her father would come, and she looked for him now.

She was pretty and attractive in her neat, home-made clothing, that was more calculated to resist the onslaught of the elements than add charm to the delightful figure it concealed. She was dark, in an essentially French-Canadian fashion, but her eyes were merry, and her strong young body was tall and vigorous, after the manner of the Anglo-Saxon mother she scarcely remembered. She was full of an easy patience that robbed her not one whit of a wholesome joy of life. Animal spirits were always surging in her, and helped her to discover happiness in the unlikeliest moments of the life that was hers.

Movement down at the barn distracted her watch on the distant trail. It was the hired man bearing a bucket of fresh milk, steaming in the wintry air. He was a tall, lean creature of an age he would have been reluctant to admit. He wore a chin-whisker that was almost as white as the snow that overlaid the world. And he came up to the house at a gait the vigor of which suggested a youth he could never hope to see again.

"She's runnin' slack," he said, in a tone that jarred harshly on the still air. "But I 'low she's a swell beast, and she's made a good winter feed for herself. There's a good haf-gallon of juice that'll be solid cream by morning."

"Jessie's surely a good cow, Lightning," Molly smiled. Then her smile broadened into a laugh. "Say, it's queer how our feelings bubble over when we get the thing we want. Jessie hands us gallons more milk in the year than any of the others. So she's a swell beast, and we pat her, and make a fuss of her, and give her an extra dope of feed. If she gave us less, why, she'd just be any ordinary old thing, from a fool cow to something worse. It's the way of things, eh? When folks hand us all we ask we purr over them like a bunch of cats when you stroke them right."

The lean face of Lightning Rogers distorted itself into a grin. He loved to hear his young mistress "say things." Often enough he failed to get the meaning underlying her laughing comments, but his twisted smile was a never-failing response.

Lightning was a derelict of a strenuous past. He had, like many another of his kind, passed through a disreputable life, to settle down to an old age that was completely occupied with the attempt to supply his old body with sufficient fuel to keep burning the smouldering fires of such life as remained to him. Maybe the hot spirit of early days had lost something of its volcanic nature, but there were still flashes of it to be discovered by those who knew him well enough. He still prided himself on his skill with his ancient guns, which, in his early cattle days, had earned him the sobriquet of "Two-gun" Rogers. He still delighted in the thought that he could take his liquor like a man, and not want to shoot up more than one town at a time when the red light of Rye whisky flooded his bemused brain. He still found satisfaction in a flow of anathema that had never yet failed him. For all his sixty years, he was still a creature of extraordinary vigor of mind and body. And nothing on earth could dissuade him from working from sun-up to sun-down, whether in the height of summer or the depth of winter.

Molly had known him as her father's hired man nearly as long as she could remember. And even now there still remained something of the fascination for his tattered chin-whisker, which, in her early childhood, had made her love to claw it with both hands whenever she could find a position of reasonable security on a lap that somehow never seemed to have been built for the accommodation of any human body.

Lightning went off into a guffaw of laughter.

"Cats! That's what we are," he cried. "Full of claw's an' meanness if you don't stroke us right. That's how it was, Molly gal, when I shot the glass of Rye right out of the hand of Jim Cluer when he said my paw must ha' bin a Dago 'cos I guessed to the whole saloon I'd a big hunch for a feed of spaghetti. It sure is a mean thing to rob a boy of his liquor. I——"

14

"That's enough of your bad old past, Lightning," Molly cried, with another laugh. "I can stand for your talk of other days till you get inside the saloons. You see," she added slily, "the saloons are still only twenty-odd miles away, and I haven't heard that twenty-odd miles worries you a thing with a Rye highball at the other end of it. Are you through with the chores?"

The man's grin passed, and a look of uncertainty clouded his snapping eyes. He was afraid lest the girl was really offended.

"I'm makin' the crik for a bar'l of water," he said. "Then I'm through, I guess."

Molly nodded and smiled, and the man's look of doubt passed.

"Good. Food's mostly ready, and father's just coming round the bluff. I'll take that milk right in."

She took the pail from the man and passed back into the house. And Lightning hurried off to the barn to hook up a team to the water sled.

* * * *

It was still daylight when the farmer's team drew up at the cordwood stack. The pile of winter fuel was stored against the log walls of the corral, which was nearly three parts surrounded by a dense bluff of spruce. The intervening barns and sheds cut it off from all view of the house, where Molly was busy with the evening meal.

George Marton climbed down from his seat on the load, and stood beating warmth into his mitted hands. He stood thus for a moment, his gaze upon the tuckered flanks of his steaming team. He was a stocky creature of a year or two over forty, with a keen, dark face that was partly enveloped in a close-cut, pointed black beard that matched his hair and eyes.

After a moment he brushed away the icicles accumulated about his mouth and passed around his team. He examined their fetlocks for abrasures. He knew the damage that was possible on the snow-trail from the sharp calks with which the beasts were "roughed." He was very careful of his team.

Satisfied with their well-being, he started to unhook the horses. The sled load would remain where it was for the night, but the team must be well and carefully tended. The tugs released, he passed on to the creatures' heads to lead them to the barn. But he halted half-way, and a curious, startled rigidity seemed to grip his body. He stood there quite unmoving and obviously listening, an

15

alert figure of tense-strung energy in the thick bulk of his heavy clothing.

It was a sound. It was an unusual sound that broke sharply from within the adjacent bluff. It came with the snapping of breaking brush. Then, in a moment, it ceased with the lumping sound of a falling body.

Just for an instant it was in the man's mind to move out and investigate. But the thought passed. He remained where he was, and turning gave a sharp word of command to his patient team, which promptly moved off in the direction of the barn.

There was no doubt in the farmer's mind; there was also no undue concern. But as his horses moved off he removed the fur mitt from his right hand, and plunged it deeply into the pocket of his capacious leather coat. It was a movement of instinct. It was a movement that was the outcome of existence in a territory where survival depended upon the capacity of the individual in defence. His muscular hand was gripping the gun that he never failed to carry somewhere secreted about his person.

The silent moments prolonged. Then the sound broke again.

The next instant George Marton found himself gazing upon the unkempt, haggard face of a fellow-creature. The face was peering out, framed by the boughs of snow-laden spruce which had been thrust aside. And a pair of hungry blue eyes were staring at him out of deep, hollow sockets.

"Well? What's the game?" Marton spoke quietly, but there was an incisive note in his challenge. "You're covered. Move hand or foot till I say, an' you're surely a dead man."

The stranger's reply was a laugh. But he obeyed very literally.

"Well? I'm waiting."

Marton had not moved a muscle. But the understanding behind the stranger's wild eyes was plain enough. The man in the bluff knew the farmer's gun was levelled at him in the depths of his pocket.

It was a wofully hoarse voice that replied as the laugh died out.

"I'm lost. I'm starving. Another night in the open without a feed and I'll be dead."

Marton's reply was instant.

"Put your hands right up over your head and come out of that bluff. Your hands up first."

He was obeyed without demur, and the farmer beheld the steel handcuffs that were set about lacerated wrists.

"Now come right out."

The farmer's tone had changed ever so slightly. Maybe the sight of the lacerated wrists had excited his pity. Perhaps there was relief that the man was defenceless. At any rate, the tone had less sharpness and more humanity in it.

* * * *

They stood face to face, and within two yards of each other. The stranger was the taller. He was clad in the black sheepskin coat of the police. His fur cap was pressed low down over his fairish face. There was a stubble of beard and whisker disfiguring the lower part of his face; and, on his cheekbones, and on the end of his nose, were great blisters of frost-bite. But it was the man's hungry eyes that held the well-fed farmer.

"What's your name?" he demanded.

"James Pryse."

"What are those irons doing there?"

"I made a getaway from the police patrol taking me down to Calford penitentiary for five years."

"For cattle?" The question came backed by a fierce light in the black eyes.

The stranger shook his head.

"No. My brother killed a man who'd robbed him of a wife and seduced her. I held up the police while he made his getaway."

"Is that the truth?"

"God's truth."

"And the patrol?"

"Guess he's hunting me right now."

"He—wasn't hurt?"

"Not a hair of his head."

Marton nodded.

"Then come right along. I'll do what I can."

CHAPTER III
A Real Samaritan

IT was the dim-lit interior of a lean-to built against the big barn. It was the farmer's workshop, littered with the tools that served his simple needs. Marton was propped against a sturdy, home-made table that also served the purposes of a bench. He was gazing down in the yellow lamplight at the famished creature squatting beside the small wood-stove on an up-turned box.

It was a painful spectacle. He had realised from his brief catechism that the man was educated. Yet he sat there devouring a great platter of hot stew at a speed and in a fashion such as he had never before witnessed in any human creature. The wolfishness of it was terrible. The man was literally starving.

Marton was a man of swift decision. And his decision had long since been taken. The stranger had spoken truth when he said that another night in the open without food would be his last. He had committed a crime against the law, and had been sentenced for it. And now he had made a getaway. Well, that crime by no means found the farmer on the side of the law. On the contrary, it found him on the side of this poor, starving wreck. And he meant to help him all he knew. That is, if subsequent talk failed to inspire doubt.

So he had brought him to this little workshop, where the stove was still alight, and had released him from the lacerating shackles. He had sought out Lightning and warned him not to intrude. Then he had forthwith passed on to the house, and told Molly just sufficient to account for his demand for the necessary food with which to restore the convict to some semblance of well-being. But in all this he gave no clue to the feelings which the encounter had inspired.

The convict cleared up the last of the gravy by wiping the platter out with bread. He devoured the last crumb of the bread, and took a long drink from the pannikin of steaming tea that was on the ground beside him. Then he looked up with an irresistible smile in his eyes.

"Gee! That's swell!" he said. "The liquor doesn't count so much, except it's hot. Snow-water's poor sort of stuff, but it's drink. I'll never forget you gave me that feed, whoever you are. I hadn't eaten for seven days and seven nights."

Then his gaze lowered to the hideous lacerations of his wrists.

"They've been frozen again and again," he said.

"And they'll rot if you ain't careful."

"I s'pose they will."

Marton bestirred himself. He drew out of a pocket the bandages and ointments he had procured from Molly.

"We best not try to heal 'em," he said. "You'll get worse trouble that way. This dope'll maybe save 'em from gangrene, and the bandages'll keep the frost out of 'em—and the dirt. It's the best I know. Here, we'll wash 'em first."

For ten minutes or so the farmer worked with the skill of long experience in frost-bites. He worked in silence, and his patient offered neither comment, nor protest, nor expression of pain. Then, when the operation was completed, Marton sent him back to his seat and returned to his position on the bench. He lit his pipe.

"Well?" he said, in that meaning fashion so comprehensive in difficult circumstances.

The convict shook his head.

"What're you going to do?"

The blue eyes were smiling, but a shadow of anxiety was looking out of them.

"If I hand you feed and loan you a broncho, can you make a clear getaway without involving me with the Police?"

"D'you mean that?"

The smile in the convict's eyes was radiant.

Marton still gave no sign of any feeling. He smoked on heavily, his eyes coldly expressionless.

"I don't say things without meaning 'em, I guess," he said, in the same even tone, which never seemed to vary very much. "Ther's just two things I can do. One's hold you right here till the Police get around and relieve me of you. The other's to help you beat it to a place of safety—that ain't the penitentiary. Anyway, I've a hunch for the man who can kill his wife's seducer, and for those that helped him."

The man at the stove drew a deep breath. His condition was utterly forgotten. The thought of all that might still lie ahead of him when he again set out on the winter trail gave him not a tremor of disquiet. He was thinking only of the heavily built creature smoking his pipe against the table, and wondering. The sphinx-like face was impossible to read.

After a few silent moments he stirred.

"Won't you hand me your name?" he asked almost diffidently.

"Sure. George Marton. Do you feel like talking?"

* * * *

For some moments Jim Pryse gazed up silently into the face of the stranger who had so unexpectedly become his benefactor. His emotion was such that for awhile the talk he had been bidden to seemed impossible. It was all a miracle—a veritable miracle. A few short hours ago the last shadow of hope had been extinguished. For days he had been wandering about interminable hills, with the thermometer more than ten below zero. His horse had long since been foundered and abandoned, while he essayed to reach some sort of shelter on foot. Oh, he had made his escape from Corporal McFardell surely enough, but the hell he had endured as the price of that escape had been something he had never thought that human body could endure.

The short days, the desperately long nights; no matches to kindle a fire, no blankets, nothing but the merciful sheepskin coat which the police had provided him with; no food of any sort, and only snow-water to drink; nothing, nothing but his will to flounder on through a world of snow and ice and a maddening sea of uninhabited hills. The terror of those last days had been almost insupportable. And only was it a sort of grim philosophy which had kept him going. A hundred times he could have lain down and let the temperature lull his weary, starving body and mind to that final peace which would have saved him from his agony. But he had kept to his weary feet, that, as he had told himself through his clenched teeth, he might go down fighting.

And now, now that was all behind him. The scars of it all were there. Those manacles. The bite of the frost upon his face and hands. Then the dreadful sense of bodily weariness. Even now he felt that the only thing he desired was sleep—just sleep. And yet——

No, there was no sleep yet. This man, this queer, unsmiling creature had offered him help, had given him food and had named no price. God! There was no price adequate that he could pay him. What was it? Where was the sign of this silent creature's humanity? He passed a bandaged hand over his forehead and thrust his fur cap back.

Then he began to talk, and with talking the desire for sleep passed away. He talked to the man who sucked silently at his pipe and offered never a word of comment. And his talk was of that queer history which had brought him to the gates of the penitentiary. He told everything without any reservation, even to the fact of the great wealth he had accumulated during his five years up in the gold country of Alaska. He felt in his wave of gratitude that he could do no less.

"You see," he finished up, "I'm handing you all this because I don't fancy leaving you with a shadow of doubt. I'm a mighty rich man. So rich I don't fancy you can guess. But I'm not the sort that figures to offer you a thing for what you reckon to do for me. But I want to say this, and I mean it all; there just isn't a thing I wouldn't raise hell to do for you or yours any old time, and for just as long as I live. You've handed me life and hope. Hope! You don't know what it means till you've lost it. Hope! Think of life without it. No, you couldn't. No one could. Death a thousand times sooner—without hope. Gee, I'm tired!"

Suddenly he thrust his elbows on his knees and dropped his chin into the palms of his bandaged hands.

The farmer bestirred himself. He knocked out his pipe, and, moving over to a small pile of wood, replenished the stove. Then he stood up, and, for the first time, the convict beheld a twinkle in the keen black eyes.

"I wanted that story, Pryse," he said, addressing the other by name for the first time. "And you've told it good. I'm not left guessing. Well, boy, I'm going right up to the house now. I'll be back along with blankets in awhile. There's wood right here that'll keep the frost out of your bones. You're welcome to it all. Then you can sleep good. I'll have my gal, Molly, pack you up a big bunch of food by morning. I'll hand you dollars to pay your way with, in case that wealth of yours has been left behind. And you can have a broncho that'll worry the trail a month without let-up, and live on the dead grass it can scrape from under the snow. If you can make your getaway with that outfit you're welcome to it. If you fancy it, there's a shot-gun and some shells that'll maybe help you to pick up some feed. That's about all I can see to do. And you'll have to make that getaway after you've eaten good in the morning. You won't see a soul but me till you've quit here. I'll hand you the best trail to make. That's all. Now I'll get along to my supper."

He moved towards the door, but paused at the sound of the voice of the weary creature beside the stove.

"Say, I want—I want——"

Pryse broke off lamentably, and Marton beheld the piteous spectacle of a strong man with hot tears welling up into his eyes.

"Don't say a word, boy," the farmer said, in his curious, even tone. "Not a word. I know how it feels. Forget it."

And a radiant light in the twinkling eyes entirely transformed the unsmiling expression to which the convict had grown accustomed.

George Marton turned again to the door and passed out. And as he went there was a picture in his mind of a pair of fine blue eyes that gazed after him through a veil of hot tears of which the man was unashamed.

CHAPTER IV
A Stroke of Fate

THE hush of the woods was undisturbed by the rhythmic clip of the farmer's axe. The cloak of winter seemed to muffle the whole world, and transform it into a dour desolation, fit only to harbour the timber wolves and the coyotes which haunted the foothills.

A foot and more of snow lay everywhere in the open. Mounting snowdrifts were driven against every obstruction. The pine bluffs were laden with a roofing of crystal whiteness, and the greater hills had become a world of snow, which would remain unchanging throughout the winter.

But George Marton was without concern for Nature's desperate moods. He knew she was a simple blusterer, governed by laws she had no power to defy. She might rage or smile. It was only the weakling she could ever hope to bluff. No, he never permitted himself an anxious thought in the life that was his. He moved on with machine-like precision, and his undisturbed methods brought him a slowly but steadily rising measure of success.

For days now he had been labouring in the timber belt, hewing, splitting, without pause for aught but those scheduled moments when the needs of his stout body must be ministered to. And thus the stack of cordwood stored at his homestead had risen to the proportions which experience had taught him were necessary.

The sun had already set, and in something over an hour darkness would have fallen. His day's tally of cordwood was stacked on his double-bob sleigh, and his team stood ready and eager for the journey that would terminate at their snug barn.

Ordinarily he would have set out forthwith, and left the next day's work for the day to which it belonged. But for once in his life he had decided to prolong his labours. The reason was that less than a week ago he had lost half a day's work because of his charity to an escaping convict, and his spirit rebelled against that loss. So he turned again to the standing timber, determined to employ the last hour of daylight, and make the homeward journey in the darkness.

So the gleaming axe, with its razor edge, kept on at its work of destruction. And in that hour twenty more of the youth of the forest lay sprawled in the clearing. With the fall of the twentieth the tireless man glanced up at the western sky. Already the starry sheen of night was looking down at him.

But he turned back at once to a standing trunk that was a good deal larger than those he had already felled. He measured its height with a swift, upward glance, and ran his thumb over the edge of his axe. Then he hunched himself, and flung his weapon at the work.

It was a strange scene in the growing darkness. The swing of the axe was faultless. There was not an ounce of wasted strength in the blows which fell on the rapidly widening cut at the base of the trunk. There was not a single blow that fell other than where it was intended. Each cut told, and each cut came nearer and nearer to the soft heart of precious white timber. Just for an instant there was a pause, to measure again the fall of the tree. Then he spat on his hands and returned to his work.

The axe swung aloft and descended into the heart of the tree. It rose again. Again it fell. Again and again the cutting edge hewed out the flying chips. Then, in a moment, the snowy crest of foliage swung over, and the tearing of uncut wood crashed sharply. The man stepped to move clear. And then—and then——

It was done in less than a flash of the falling axe. The disaster came before the doomed man could utter a sound. That step back, which had been made a thousand times in the work he knew so well, should have carried him to safety. But the darkness robbed him of that certainty of vision that was always his.

His foot struck heavily against a prone log. It struck with sufficient force to upset his balance. He sought to recover himself and jump clear. It was too late. The falling tree crashed to the ground, bearing him with it. And he lay pinned beneath it, face downwards, with the great trunk crushing his shoulders and chest under its enormous weight.

* * * *

Night had descended upon the farm, and the lamplight of the living-room threw into relief the slight figure of Molly as she stood in the open doorway. She was talking to Lightning, and her tone was anxious. There was no smile in her eyes. She was urgent, and the trouble in her mind was something which, in all her eighteen years, she had never known before.

"It's no use, Lightning," she said at last. "Father's never been late like this. It's been dark more than two hours, and the bluff isn't more than a half-hour away. Ther's not a thing to keep him. Jane and Blue Pete should have hauled him to home nearly two hours ago. I just can't stand it. That's all. Beat it and hook up the cutter. Hook up my pinto. She'll get us out to the bluff quicker than the other beasts. Get a great big move on. I—I—can't stand waiting around. And his supper's baking itself to death."

"Won't you give him another haf-hour, Molly gal?" Lightning urged. "I can't ever see reason to jump in till you need. Your father'll raise hell with us. Guess he's a hunch for folks keeping tight to their own business, an' not buttin' in wher' they ain't needed. Won't——"

Molly's gaze came back abruptly from the dark direction of the invisible snow-trail. And there was a cold look in her eyes which silenced the man instantly.

"Beat it, Lightning, an' do as I say," she cried sharply. "Get your old fur coat on, and a robe. You'll need to come along. I'll fix the rest I need."

The man offered no further protest. He realised something which before he had not rightly understood. This girl was in a complete state of panic. Had he been more imaginative he would perhaps have understood. George Marton should have returned to his supper at the proper hour. Never within his daughter's memory had he failed to do so before.

Lightning went off in a hurry, and this lean, queer creature's hurry was something astonishing. He was back at the door of the homestead with the pinto mare and the cutter before Molly had completed her preparations.

She came to the door carrying a small wicker basket. She stood clad in a long beaver coat, with a fur cap pressed low down over her ears. Her storm collar was turned up and secured about her neck by a long woollen scarf, and with her darkly-fringed grey eyes anxiously peering out into the night, she was a vision that warmed the old choreman's heart under his tattered buffalo coat.

"No sign?" she said a little hopelessly. "Still no sign." Then she sighed deeply. "Something's happened, Lightning. I just know it."

Lightning cleared his throat.

"I'm not worrying, Molly, gal," he said, with a poor attempt to restore the smile to her anxious eyes. "But I sure am feeling bad about the thing he's goin' to hand us when we meet him on the trail."

The girl climbed into the driving-seat and took the lines from the man.

"We aren't going to meet him on the trail," she said, in a low, significant tone, as she eased her hand to the impatient mare.

* * * *

Out of a cloudless sky a myriad of coldly winking stars peered down upon the snowbound earth. No breath of wind came to stir the snow-laden tree-tops. The cold was intense, and zero had long since been left behind by the sinking mercury.

The clearing in the timber belt was littered with sprawling trunks. They lay still—so still. Near by to them, drawn up in the shelter of standing timber, was the team still hitched to its load of cordwood. The horses stood in their harness quite unmoving, their great heads drooping in sleep. They had waited and waited for the sharp tones of the voice they knew, and then, with equine philosophy, had permitted their dream world to overwhelm them.

Drawn up near by stood the dim outline of a cutter, with its single pinto mare. The mare had been driven hard, but tied fast to a sapling, and wrapped in the comfort of a fur robe, she, too, was resting quietly, with down-drooped head.

In the starlight two darkly-outlined figures crouched about the heavy end of a fallen tree. Near to them lay the shining head of an axe where it had fallen from the grasp of the man who had used it so indefatigably. The two figures uttered no sound as they laboured. Both were prying the log with improvised levers, which were tree-limbs of stout proportions.

It was Lightning who had made the terrible discovery. In the half-light he had literally tripped over the body of the crushed farmer. It was a hideous moment for both. But for Molly it was a time of complete despair. One look at the position of the fallen man had confirmed her worst fears, and, with a cry of agony, she had flung herself upon her knees, embracing the remains of the sturdy parent who had been her all in life.

The loyal Lightning had proved himself the man he was in emergency. With harsh words and rough hands he had forced the girl to abandon her wild demonstration of grief. Then his practical mind had shown her the thing that must be done.

26

Now his plan was being operated. It was terribly hazardous if life yet remained beneath that log. They worked silently at their levers, and inch by inch the log was lifted, and blocked up with carefully placed tree-limbs. At last the reward they were seeking came to them. The log was sufficiently raised to free the crushed body.

Slowly, and with infinite care, the still form of George Marton was drawn clear of the tree. But no sound escaped the injured man as they moved him. And the omen of it shattered the girl's last shadow of hope. She crouched on her knees beside him, passing one hand tenderly over the crushed and broken body in a vain endeavour to estimate the damage. And the while Lightning had gone back to the cutter for her basket of remedies.

When the man returned with the basket, Molly had abandoned her examination. She gazed up at the tall, shadowy figure standing over her. The expression of her despairing eyes was hidden in the darkness. But the tone of her voice smote the loyal creature to the depths of his old heart.

"He's—dead," she cried. "Oh, Lightning, he's dead. And he was all I had."

CHAPTER V
The Sentence

THE cold fabric of discipline at the Police Headquarters at Calford had been shocked into a flutter of excited interest and anticipation. The machine-like routine of police life had, for a moment, reacted to a more human aspect of itself. Interested comment passed from lip to lip, and widely conflicting were the opinions expressed. But, curiously enough, there was pretty general unanimity amongst the lower ranks of the Force in a feeling of quiet satisfaction. Corporal Andrew McFardell had been placed under arrest, and, at "Orderly-Room" that morning, he would be tried and sentenced for permitting the escape of his prisoner while on escort duty from Greenwood to Calford.

Alone in his barrack-room, which had been his charge for so long, Corporal McFardell was more than sick at heart. But over and above everything else he was smarting under a sense of intolerable injustice.

It was four days since he had returned to barracks. And before that he had driven himself and his horse well-nigh to death for ten days, scouring the snowy desolation of the hill country in search of the man who had tricked him so badly in his moment of helplessness. The man had vanished; completely and utterly disappeared. He had made good an escape which McFardell had deemed impossible. The man was a stranger to the country; he was shackled; his horse was none too fresh. How was it possible?

McFardell had expected to discover his frozen body at least. But his ten days of superhuman effort had left him unrewarded. So he had been driven to return to Calford, his horse well-nigh foundered, and himself in little better case, to make his report, and to be promptly placed under arrest for his pains. Then he had been forced to place himself on the sick list, to be attended for the frost which had bitten him almost to the bone. And now, rested and recovered, he was awaiting that brazen summons of the bugle for the thing that was yet to come.

28

It was curious. As the man lolled upon the brown blankets of his bed his resentment and bitterness were in no way directed against the prisoner who was the cause of his disaster. It was anger, furious anger, against the authority which took practically no cognisance of any circumstance in a case of failure amongst those who acknowledged it.

For years he had laboured and schemed, sacrificing everything to "duty." Step by step he had gained his advancement by sound, patient work, until now he stood first on the roll of seniority for his sergeant's stripes. Now he knew that all that record would have to go by the board. It would count for practically nothing. He must face a cold tribunal, governed only by police regulations, which were devoid of all human sentiment. He must accept the last ounce of punishment for the loss of his prisoner for which they happened to call. He would be punished in just the same degree as any other whose record was incomparable with his. The injustice of it maddened him. In his bitterness he claimed the right to treatment in accordance with his record of years of good work.

But that was the Andrew McFardell whom his associates knew. That was the man who, for all his good police work, had failed to inspire any warmth of regard amongst those with whom he worked. That was why there was excitement, and anticipation, and a sense of quiet satisfaction in the thought of the trial that was to take place that morning.

Andrew McFardell took no thought for anything or anybody but himself.

As the last harsh note of the bugle died out on the crisp winter air McFardell sprang alertly from his bunk. He set his fur cap on his head and buttoned the shining buttons of his red jacket. Then, with a swift glance round the deserted room, he passed hurriedly out in response to the summons.

* * * *

On the wooden side-walk just outside the Superintendent's office Corporal McFardell sprang to "Attention" in response to the Sergeant-Major's barking order. He felt that a hundred pairs of eyes were peering out at him, prompted by a curiosity that had little friendliness in it. He was under no illusion. Popularity with his comrades was a thing he had treated with quiet contempt. He had never concerned himself with their opinion. The only good opinion he had sought had been of those in authority over him. And now he knew he was about to learn the true value of the favour of the gods he had set up. He pulled himself together, and thrust every other thought aside, concentrating upon the task of combating regulations whose cold framing left him so little hope.

As the little procession lined up facing Superintendent Leedham Branch's desk the Sergeant-Major snatched the fur cap from the prisoner's head. It was a further indignity demanded by regulations.

The Superintendent was contemplating the charge sheet before him. He did not even glance at the prisoner. On either side of him and slightly behind his chair, stood the two Inspectors of his command. They were very definitely regarding the prisoner, but in that cold sphinx-like, unrecognising fashion which the discipline governing them all had taught them.

It was a bare, uninteresting room, with calsomined walls and a flooring of bare boards. There was just sufficient furnishing to meet the needs of administration. The Superintendent's desk was a simple whitewood table, and the chair he occupied behind it was of bentwood. Immediately behind him stood a fireproof safe, and, distributed about, where necessary, stood other whitewood tables and bentwood chairs for the use of Inspectors and staff. The whole atmosphere of the place epitomised the lives of these men, who spared themselves as little as the criminals it was their work to deal with.

Superintendent Branch seemed in no hurry to deal with the case. Perhaps his attitude was calculated. He continued his reading, while McFardell regarded him with anxiously speculative eyes.

At last the man behind the desk spoke, without looking up. He was a clean-cut, clean-shaven creature, with fair hair and pale blue eyes. He was possibly forty. He was tall, slight, and his whole appearance suggested energy and capacity.

"Corporal McFardell, the charge against you is one of gross neglect of duty," he said, in a quiet, colourless voice. "On November 8th you permitted the escape of the prisoner, James Pryse, sentenced to five years' imprisonment with hard labour, while on escort duty from Greenwood to Calford. You are further charged with absenting yourself from duty from November 8th to the 18th, contrary to General Order 9075A2 governing the escort of prisoners by trail. What have you to say? Are you guilty or not guilty?"

"Guilty on both charges, sir."

McFardell's reply came on the instant. He knew he had no alternative. There was, however, a sharpness in his tone that gave some indication of the alertness, the readiness to defend, that lay behind his words.

"Sergeant-Major Ironside."

The man at the desk looked up interrogatively at the first witness. And the Sergeant-Major cleared his throat.

"Sir, on the morning of the 18th Corporal McFardell rode into barracks and reported the loss of the prisoner, James Pryse. He stated that the date of the man's escape was the 8th. When I questioned him as to the delay of his return to barracks he explained he had been riding the hill country in an attempt to recapture the escaped prisoner, who, he believed, could not have made a clear getaway in the snowstorm that was prevailing at the time of his escape. The Corporal's horse was in bad shape, and the Veterinary Sergeant reports that he had been pretty well ridden to death. I placed Corporal McFardell under arrest, and reported at once to the Orderly Officer of the day."

The Sergeant-Major's evidence was given in the unemotional manner of an automaton. He had given the outline of the facts in the manner his duty demanded. There was no exaggeration; there was no softening. Superintendent Branch turned to the prisoner.

"Have you any question to ask Sergeant-Major Ironside?"

"None, sir."

Forthwith the Superintendent turned to Inspector Kalton.

"You were Orderly Officer on the 18th, Mr. Kalton?"

The Inspector also gave a slight clearing of the throat. Then, very briefly, he corroborated his subordinate's evidence. As the prisoner had no questions to put, for a few reflective moments, Superintendent Branch gazed steadily up into his face.

"You have heard the evidence, Corporal," he said at last, in that cold fashion that was so desperately discouraging. "What have you to say in your defence?"

Not a detail of the manner in which Orderly-Room cases were dealt with was new to Corporal McFardell. He knew the whole ritual by heart. His years of experience had brought him into contact with it often enough. But this was the first time he had occupied the central place as the prisoner. His whole concern at that moment was how far he might hope to escape the full penalty due to him as laid down by General Orders. He pinned his last hope to the extenuating nature of the circumstances of his disaster. He believed that no one would have fared better under his conditions. And, furthermore, he felt he had done all he knew to recover the escaped man. He had striven till the last of his bodily resources were exhausted. He felt that his case was good. Superintendent Branch was a just man.

He knew that the extreme penalty for his crime against regulations was reduction to the ranks, imprisonment, and dismissal from the Force without character. If he could escape with reduction to the ranks he would be happy. If imprisonment were added he would not despair. Dismissal from the Force was the thing he dreaded most of all. It would be the end of all things for him. For he had looked to make the Force the whole of his career. A "bobtail" discharge was the nightmare of the mounted policeman. So he, like those others, cleared his throat before speaking, and hurled himself to his defence.

"Sir," he began, a little hoarsely as he passed his tongue across his thick lips to moisten them, "I've no sort of defence to offer beyond the letter of the report which I addressed to you as my commanding officer on my return to barracks on the 18th. You'll have read it before this, sir, and I want to say that every word I wrote there is just the God's truth. I was knocked out cold by my horse falling, through the balling snow in his hoofs. And I guess there was no power in the world to prevent the man getting the drop on me while I was unconscious. When I woke up he'd got me covered, so I couldn't do a thing. I just had to lie there while he got clear away in the half-light of the snowstorm. The moment I had the chance I was on my horse and after him. And I didn't let up till my horse was done, and I couldn't sit a saddle right. I've been through hell to recover that prisoner, sir. Give me a chance, sir, to get after that feller again. I don't ask to escape punishment. I know I'll lose my stripes, and maybe I'll go to the guard-room for a spell. But for God's sake, sir, don't discharge me from the Force. It's the only way I can hope to get after that feller right. Hand me the chance to get after him. It's all I ask. It's him and me, sir. Whatever happens, it's that way just as long as I live. If you keep me in the Force I can do it right. It's my one big chance. That's all, sir."

The passionate sincerity of McFardell's appeal was wholly convincing. His words came hotly, and regardless of the usual formalities. But there was no sign of the relenting he looked for in the eyes observing him so coldly. With his last word there came an ominous shake of the head from the man behind the table.

"I've read your report very carefully, Corporal," he said coldly. "I'm quite convinced that it is the whole truth, and you are to be commended that that is so. But, unfortunately, for you the truth is very damning to your case. Your horse fell and threw you, and you were rendered unconscious. No one can blame you for that. Had the prisoner made his getaway while you were unconscious I should have dismissed the charges laid against you. But he did not do so. He apparently only had time to disarm you before you came to, which suggests you were only momentarily stunned. Then, when he held you covered, you made no resistance. You apparently did nothing. In fear of your life you *let* him get away. Do you understand my meaning? There is the moral charge of cowardice preferred against you. Your report condemns you so flagrantly that I shall inflict the maximum penalty. You are reduced to the ranks. You will be confined to the guard-room for two months, with hard labour. And—your case will go up to the Commissioner with a recommendation that you be dismissed from the Force."

"Right turn! Quick march!"

The Sergeant-Major's commands rang out. It was like the hideous toll of the prison bell after an execution.

* * * *

Superintendent Branch, his officers, and Sergeant-Major Ironside had been discussing the escape of James Pryse. Orderly-Room was over. Trooper McFardell was already in the charge of the guard, and about to begin his two months of hard labour. His case was already relegated to the orders of the day. And, in so far as he was concerned, the matter was dismissed from the minds of his superiors. They had no thought for the career which their discipline had devastated.

"You know, Sergeant-Major, it's a far more serious matter than I can say," Superintendent Branch declared at the conclusion of the discussion, with an emphasis which his associates recognised as his most profound danger-signal. "Were this man, Pryse, an ordinary criminal, it would leave me less disturbed. Through him the Police prestige has suffered a double blow. Think back. What is the position? A murder is committed—a clear, frank, deliberate shooting by a man who, maybe, felt justified. That's all right. His brother, this Pryse, fresh from Alaska, is staying in his house in Greenwood. The murderer has no thought of a get-away. He knows our people are coming for him, and he reckons to stand his trial. We know all that. Meanwhile this wild man, James Pryse, gets at him. He plans his escape and prepares. When our men come along, the house is transformed into a veritable fortress, and we are forced to storm it. Well, eventually we get in, and what do we find? This man, James Pryse, simply laughing at us. Which means that the whole of the town of Greenwood was laughing with him. It was all a game. Our man had been got away before we came. And the whole pantomime of barricading the house was performed to give him added time, and delay our ultimate pursuit. That all came out at Pryse's trial. That's bad enough. But now this later escape of Pryse himself is ten times worse. We've lost so much ground I simply daren't think of it. We shall have the Commissioner here to investigate our discipline and efficiency. And very rightly so. Things have got to be jerked up, and at once. I shall hold myself responsible that this is so. And I shall hold my officers no less responsible, and you, too, Sergeant-Major."

"Yes, sir."

The Sergeant-Major's face reflected the storm which the other's words had set boiling behind his hard grey eyes. His superiors all knew his swift methods of passing any reprimand he might receive on to the troops under him.

A grim light was shining in the eyes that regarded the rugged face of the harshest Sergeant-Major in the Police Force.

"Now, let there be no mistake, Sergeant-Major. No mistake whatever," the man at the desk went on, in a carefully calculated tone. "The prisoner, Pryse, has to be recaptured. If there is any further failure, you will have to answer for it. Do you understand me? How many patrols have you got out?"

"Three, Sir."

"Three? You will treble that number. You will treble it, if you have to return half the staff to duty. You must go through the territory within a hundred and fifty miles of this post with a fine comb, and any failure in efficiency in the work will be dealt with in the most rigorous fashion. See to it. These patrols must be on the trail by noon. That will do."

CHAPTER VI
The Gateway of Hope

A WORLD of smiling hope looked out of the man's tired blue eyes. The sky was brilliant, and flecked with fine-weather cloud. The air was full of a warmth that was increasing with each passing day. The whole world about him was bursting with renewed life. He felt that the battle had been fought out. At long last the prospect of ultimate victory was infinitely more than a vain hope.

His face and body were painfully thin. But the full ravages, induced by the privations he had suffered during the desperate months of winter, were largely concealed under a thick growth of grey beard and whisker. His hair was long, with scarcely a streak of its original colour remaining. And its white strands reached to the decayed collar of a coat that would have ill-become the body of a "hoboe." His nether garments were worn and patched, and painfully soil-stained. But his thin body was unbowed, and the spirit looking out of his eyes was undismayed.

Near by his horse, in little better shape than himself, was hungrily devouring the new-born shoots of sweet grass. Its long winter coat was heavily matted and mud-discoloured. There were the disfiguring scars of saddle-galls about its withers and under its forelegs. And its whole condition was illuminating as to the part the wretched creature had played in the desperate battle for existence which they had fought out together.

Just behind the man, in a shelter of a pinewood bluff, stood a crazy habitation. It was a patched ruin which must have been set up many years ago by some other wanderer seeking hiding within the mountain world. It was log-built and box-like, without windows or smoke-stack. It was just a shelter against the storms of winter, with sufficient space in its hovel-like interior to admit of accommodation for horse as well as man. A small fire was spluttering before the doorway, and a cooking-pot stood steaming over it.

The man had reached that condition of endurance when bodily comfort no longer concerned him. The smiling sun, the warm rains that had swept the snows of winter from the face of an earth that was lusting to produce, the stirring life that was in full evidence about him—these were the things which preoccupied him, to the exclusion of everything, and afforded him an answer to the question that had dogged his every thought for months.

Jim Pryse had christened his hiding-place the Valley of Hope. And, in the weary months he had spent within its shelter, he had buoyed himself by planning a dream world within its bosom—a whimsical, fantastic world that satisfied a quiet sense of humour that never wholly deserted him.

But this had been at a time when he knew not from day to day the fate that was in store for him. This had been when storm and blizzard buried the world about him feet deep in snow, when the depths below zero ate into his bones, and such fire as he possessed was insufficient to thaw the frost rime that whitened the whole interior of his quarters.

Now his dream had become a real, vital purpose to him. Now it was altogether different. Now the great gateway of the valley stood wide open in the brilliant spring sunlight, and revealed the wonder of the world within. It was a glorious, fertile plain of sweet grass, that reached so far out towards the warming south that its confines lay beyond the reach of human eyes.

It was a radiant picture, alive with a busy, fussing, mating, feathered concourse. It was dotted with woodland bluffs of spruce, and pine, and poplar, and tamarack, and a wealth of undergrowth already bursting into full leaf. There were wide pools of snow-water standing in the troughs which lay between the rollers of new-born grass, a happy feeding and playing ground for the swarming geese and mallard. Splitting it down the centre, winding a crazy course over the line of least resistance, a surging mountain torrent tore joyously at its muddied banks in a mad desire to release its flooding waters. East and west the limits of the valley were frowning with dark forest-belts that came down from the mountain slopes. Southward the gateway revealed nothing but a broad, sunlit highway.

The gateway itself was marked by two sheer cliffs, black with the weathering of ages. Standing half a mile apart, and rising to immense heights, they embraced between them a spread of dense forest, which, in turn, concealed the cascading torrent whose source was the world of eternal snow above. The meaning of the gateway was simple of explanation. Beyond a doubt the great cliffs were all that remained of a saddle of hill, linking twin mountains, which had ultimately yielded to the fierce erosion to which the melting snows had subjected it.

Beyond the northern confines of the valley, somewhere behind a barrier of lesser hills, one great snowy head reared itself to the clouds. Similarly, to the south-west another stood up at a height that could not have been less than twelve thousand feet. Then, to the east, there were two others. They were monsters whose purpose was clearly that of cradle posts for the valley they sheltered between them.

It was all far-hidden by the secret approach up Three-Way Creek from the east. It was all even deeper lost to the hill and forest country of British Columbia, to the west. Devoid of any highway approach, it suggested the hiding-place it had become. It was one of Nature's remotenesses completely disguised at the moment of furious labour when the world was born.

Pryse bestirred himself. Food and drink were aflood in this home that was his. And food and drink summed up his needs at the moment. He moved out into the full sunlight, and the dripping soil oozed under his ill-shod feet.

At his first movement his horse flung up its head. Its ears were pricked with all the alertness of its well-being. Its eyes were full and bright, for all its body was little better than skin and bone. There was inquiry in the soft-gazing depths. To the man it almost seemed as if they contained reproach.

"Don't worry, old feller," he said, as though speaking to a well-loved companion whose comprehension was beyond question. "Get right on with your feed. Eat it all. I'd like to see you so pot-bellied I couldn't get the cinchas around you right."

He moved on till he stood close up to the animal. Then he laid a caressing hand upon its attenuated neck.

"There's no saddle to-day," he went on. "Dan's coming along, if he doesn't get held up by a wash-out. He's bringing tobacco, and matches, and tea, and a bunch of cartridges, so we can shoot up some of those dandy mallards. Maybe he's bringing us news, too. And if it's good news it's liable to lead us to a place where there's a bunch of oats for you, and something that'll likely help me to look more like a man. We've waited and stuck it out, old feller, you and me. And I sort of feel there's a good time coming. I'll just get right along and haul up the lines in the creek, and see what sort of eat I'll make."

The horse rubbed its shaggy head against his thread-bare coat. No doubt it meant nothing. Yet it almost seemed as if the creature understood the feelings lying behind the smiling words. Pryse moved away.

He hurried out across the moist grass, and his step was light and vigorous. At that moment the world looked good to him. He was hungry. He was always hungry. And he knew from past experience, ever since the thaw had come, that it would be only a question of how many fish his night-lines had collected.

He reached the undergrowth at the river bank and disappeared within it. And only the sound of breaking bush came back as he thrust his way. He was gone for nearly half an hour. And when he reappeared, it was to be greeted by the hail of a horseman waiting for him at the edge of the woods that contained his winter home.

"Say, thanks be to the Holy Mackinaw this is going to be the last trip I'm makin' up Three-Way Creek," the man bellowed across at him, in a tone and accent that was unmistakably Irish. "I've beat it through muskeg that had me right up to the cinchas. There's enough flood water by the way to drown a whole darn world, and the skitters are crazy for good Irish blood. Say, boy, I come along to tell you you're going to get out right away."

Jim Pryse hurried across to his visitor with his bunch of strung trout. He looked up into eyes as blue as his own. The man was infinitely bigger than himself. He was a weather-stained creature round about forty, clad in the hard clothing of the prairie. And his big horse was well fed and cared for.

Dan Quinlan swung out of the saddle, and began to unship a pair of bulging saddle-bags.

Pryse watched him.

"Do you mean all that, Dan? About my going, I mean?" he asked, in a voice that was not quite steady.

The Irishman answered him over his shoulder while he tugged at the rawhide lashings.

"Mean it? Faith, I do that, man," he said, in his big-voiced way. Then, the saddle-bags released, he held them out. "Beat it, and empty that truck right out. Ther's soap there. But for the love of St. Patrick I can't get your need of it. There's a razor, too. Maybe it's a shade better than a hay mower, which would seem to be just an elegant proposition for that carpet hanging to your face. Ther's tobac an' lucifers, a flask of Rye, and all the junk we folks reckon fits our bellies better than hay. Just empty it right out, and bring that flask of the stuff back. We'll sit around awhile, so you ken roast them measly trout and eat. And we ken yarn. I got things fixed the way you asked and the police boys have quit your trail."

Jim Pryse made no reply. He offered no word of thanks. But the thing shining in his sunken eyes was all sufficient for the Irishman. He took the saddle-bags from his benefactor and obeyed him implicitly. When he returned with them empty, and bearing a pannikin and the flask of Rye, he indicated a large log beside the spluttering fire.

"Will you sit, Dan?"

Pryse's invitation was quiet in contrast with the other's larger manner. And the Irishman turned abruptly from his contemplation of the flood of snow-water teeming with legions of wild-fowl.

"Sure, boy," he said. Then he indicated the scene with a broad gesture of an out-flung arm. "Can you beat it? Get a look. Ther's millions of 'em. Gee! This would be one hell of a swell place to fix a homestead."

"That's what I've decided to do."

Pryse smiled as the other swung round and stared at him. Then he sat down on the log, and Dan Quinlan took up his position beside him.

Pryse poured out a tot of the Rye and offered it to his benefactor. But the man thrust it aside.

"Get to it yourself, boy," he said, with a rough laugh. "I take a deal too much of that belly-wash. It's a curse on me. You're needing it. I guess you're needing it bad. Drink up, boy, and set the rest aside. One's all you need now to set life into your tired grey head. Two would set you crazy. And you don't need any craziness just now. What d'you mean about that—homestead?"

Pryse drank down the raw Rye, and the scorch of the spirit made him gasp. Then he carefully re-corked the bottle, and set it on the ground beside him, and sat gazing into the fire. Dan Quinlan lit his pipe, and diving into a pocket, produced a second. He held it out.

"It's a new one," he said. "I went right into Hartspool for it. Smoke."

Pryse accepted the thoughtful present, and the warming spirit brightened his eyes.

"Say," he ejaculated, with sudden urgency, "I'm going to talk a whole long piece, Dan. Will you listen while I roast these trout over the fire? It's all I've got to offer you for feed. There's a big bunch of them, and they've just come out of the creek. Will you share? And I'll boil up some of the tea you've brought me. And there's the sugar. I haven't tasted sugar for days. Not since I finished the last you brought me."

Dan nodded his rough head.

"I ken mostly eat anything. Get on with that talk."

"Did you hear from my sister?"

"Sure. I got this registered mail when I went into Hartspool."

The Irishman held out a bulging envelope.

Pryse set his fish to roast on the hot ashes and took the mail. He looked at it. Then he looked into the eyes of the man who had passed it to him.

"You haven't opened it and—it's addressed to you."

Dan laughed.

"It ain't a way I have looking into other folk's affairs," he said. "That's from your sister in answer to the letter I put through for you. That bunch is for you. It's not for me."

"Yes. I know that. But—say, Dan Quinlan, you're a big feller and a swell friend. Why?" Pryse shook his head. "Because your heart's mostly as big as your fool body. There are things to life I can't get a grip on. Here are you, living away up in the hills with no one near you for twenty-five miles. You got a poor sort of ranch homestead, and a bunch of stock that couldn't hand you more than a bare existence. Why? Are you a hunter? Do you just love the crazy hills, with their storms, and snow, and cold? No. It's not that. And I'm not going to ask things. I'm just going to say it's a God's mercy for me that you do live that way. If it hadn't been that I fell into your place last fall, by a chance I can't ever account for, I shouldn't be alive and talking now. You've done for me what no ordinary fellow—but just one other, I know of—would have done for me. You showed me Three-Way Creek and found me this hiding-place when the Police got smelling around. And you've handed me feed and things at intervals ever since, like the ravens did for that boy in the Bible. You've done that for me I can never repay you for. And you've done it on my own story, without ever a question. And now you've completed your good work by getting me in touch with my sister."

"Best get on with it, hadn't you?"

The Irishman's grinning eyes were full of beaming good-nature. But he had not come there to listen to any expression of gratitude.

Pryse tore open the envelope. He drew out a roll of money folded inside a long letter. Dan Quinlan stared. The outer bill he could see was for one hundred dollars. And inside it there looked to be at least fifty more of a similar denomination. But the other gave the money no heed. He was hungrily devouring the contents of the letter. Dan stooped and turned the roasting fish, amazed at the thing he had beheld.

Pryse looked up from his letter.

"Let's eat, and I'll fix the tea. I can talk as we eat."

It was that talk Dan wanted to hear. Pryse passed into the hut, and returned with the limits of his household utensils—one plate of enameled iron. He knocked the ashes from the roasted fish, and piled them on the plate. Then he set the pot to boil, and threw a small handful of tea into it. Then he sat on the log again, and Dan possessed himself of a fish.

"You don't know me, Dan, except the police are yearning to set me to hard labour," Pryse began, while he ate the hot fish he, too, had picked up in his fingers. "You know what for, but that's all. The thing you don't know is I'm a pretty rich man as gold goes. My sister's got charge of my stuff, and she's living down in New York. She's sent me the stuff I need to make my getaway. You've given me the news the Police have quit my trail. And so, with the summer coming, and maybe your further help, the way lies open for me. That all looks pretty good to me after the thing I've gone through. But I want to tell you I've fixed it to come right back again."

"To set up that—homestead?"

The Irishman's eyes were no longer grinning.

"That's it, Dan. And I want you to help me. I want you to be partners in it with me. Oh, it's going to be a crazy proposition. It's crazy enough to suit an Irishman like you. It's going to be a homestead like you've never heard of before. And the notion of it got right into my mind from the moment I christened this queer stretch of Nature the 'Valley of Hope.' It's been that way for me, and I want to make it that way for others. Don't get the notion I'm crazy. I'm not, boy. First one great fellow, and now you, have taught me something I can never forget. You folks have taught me there's no feller so down and out there isn't a shadow of hope for him somewhere in this tough old world. Well, my notion is, with you a partner, to collect that hope, and hand it to the folks needing it. Are you on, if I tell you about it? You'll be my partner? I'll find the stuff and organise. And you'll come in on my profits without taking a chance."

The Irishman guffawed loudly. But it was a laugh intended to disguise the feelings the other had stirred in his emotional heart.

"Sounds a swell proposition for me," he said. "I'd like it a deal better for some of the chances lying around. But get to it, boy," he went on, helping himself to another of the trout. "Ladle it out. Hand me the whole darn fancy, an', short of murder, I haven't a scruple. If ther's a fight to it I'll be glad. You see, it's only when I'm up against things I can keep off the liquor. Give me something to help me dodge the liquor, and I'll call down all the saints to bless the day, or night, you blew into my shack in a snowstorm."

The two men sat on talking while the sun rose higher, and the stirring flies and mosquitoes advanced to the attack. They talked and ate, and drank tea with sugar, discussing all the details of a proposition that looked to be wild enough to satisfy even so reckless a creature as Dan Quinlan.

And Dan fell headlong for the whole thing. He questioned closely. He argued points all along the line. And Pryse realised something of the extent of the latent ability he possessed. But in the end full agreement was arrived at between them. And when the time came for Dan's departure, and his horse was saddled, and he was ready to lift his huge body into its seat, a great change had been wrought in their relations. For Pryse, Dan Quinlan had suddenly become a shrewd, long-headed creature, with a great capacity and foresight; and for Dan, Pryse was no longer a fugitive from justice, but a creature of infinite sympathy, whom he asked nothing better than to serve and support.

Dan leaned down from his saddle and gripped the lean hand held out to him.

"Say boy, I want to tell you something," he cried, with one of his boisterous laughs. "You got me plumb in the vitals with this thing. Same as if you'd pushed a gun there. You can count me for it body and soul."

Pryse smiled up in response.

"So long, Dan," he said. "A week of this grass'll see my poor old plug fit, and I'll be down along by your shanty. Get those things in train I told you about. You can't ever tell. This thing has come out of my own selfish need. It looks like I'll be more glad of it than—anybody else. You see, I was condemned to five years' hard labour. And until those years of penitentiary have been served they're always hanging over me. So long. May the saints of your queer old country bless you."

CHAPTER VII
In New York

MOST of New York—that is, all those more fortunate individuals who were not actually tied to the city by the necessities of business, were somewhere on the seashore, or up in the hills, seeking cool, bracing air with which to sooth their jaded nerves. The heat was torrid. The noise and the city odours burdened life to an almost insupportable extent. There was no shade anywhere that could help things, and not a breath of air, except that set in motion by artificial means in the dwellings, was stirring to make things easier. The sun scorched down on the immaculate streets from early dawn to late evening. And even as late as nearing midnight the furious mercury registered anything up to eighty degrees of humid heat.

It was the one time in the year when the bustle and rush of the great hotels was at its lowest ebb. The telephone boys had time to sweat at leisure. The head-porters had breathing space from their everlasting task of booking railroad "reservations" for their transient custom. Even the waiters were able to give a personal touch of interest to their guests. But for all the greater ease of service the leisure thus obtained was more than counter-balanced by the discomfort of the appalling humidity.

At the Seraphim Hotel the oval of the great dining-hall was almost empty. An army of waiters stood ready to advance upon their customers. But the customers were few, and many of the beautifully appointed tables had remained unoccupied for the day's lunch. On the raised amphitheatre which circled the outer extremities of the hall only about half a dozen tables were occupied, while in the central space one solitary couple sat lunching.

It was a man and a woman. The girl was exquisitely gowned in a quiet, unassuming fashion. A woman might have appraised the costliness of her equipment at its true value. To a man she appeared to be just well turned out in something that was sufficiently diaphanous for the temperature all must endure in July in New

York. But her hat—well, even a man could not have made any miscalculation as to her hat. It was exquisite, and added a wealth of charm to the beautiful, smiling face beneath it.

She was regarding her companion with almost hungry interest. Her blue eyes were gravely smiling, for all a certain anxiety was gazing out of them. She was eyeing his well-barbered, snow-white hair that was a never-ending source of admiring concern for her. Then, too, the deeply-lined, clean-shaven face left her not a little troubled. He was dressed well in well-cut summer suiting, and his broad shoulders and strong, shapely hands told of work they could never have encountered in New York.

The man had been talking for some time in a tone which was never permitted to reach beyond his companion's ears, and the twinkle of a smile lit eyes that were twin in colour to those he was gazing into.

He had been recounting the details of a long story that held his companion completely enthralled. There were moments when he had to break off to remind her of the food that no longer made any claim upon her appetite. And as he finished a deep sigh proclaimed the breathless interest in which the girl had been held.

"It's all amazing, dreadful," she breathed, in a suppressed tone. "If it weren't you, Jim, sitting there telling me I could never have believed it. I just hadn't a notion when I got your letter asking for those five thousand dollars. You never gave me an inkling. You never said a thing. And now you tell me all this."

She made a gesture that expressed her amazement.

"Eddie hunted for killing the man who had broken up his home-life. Poor, dear, weak, foolish Mary gone—goodness knows where. And you, my dear old brother and best of all playmates, convicted and sentenced for—for—as a price for that fool loyalty which has always been your besetting curse. The disaster of it is unspeakable. It's—it's dreadful. And look at you," she went on, with that final touch of the woman which she found impossible to resist. "Your hair snow-white, and not a single curl remaining. Your poor thin face lined like a man of more than twice your years. And you have come here with—with a price on your head. Jim—Jim, you must get away. You must get away to a place of safety. Your money's been safe with me. I'll hand it over. And you must get away."

Jim Pryse's eyes twinkled humorously.

"That's what I came here for."

"That's why you came here—for safety?" The girl's eyes

44

widened. "You must be crazy."

Jim shook his head.

"Not a thing. But smile, Blanche. Get that look of worry out of your dandy eyes. There are waiters around."

The girl shrugged her shoulders a little helplessly. But she smiled. And somehow the smile was unforced.

"Oh, Jim, you're just the same. Just the same—what shall I say?—devil-may-care you've always been. You've told me enough to make me realise something of the awful thing you've been through. And your beautiful white hair, and those cruel lines down around your mouth and cheeks, tell of what you have not told. What are you going to do?"

"Do?"

Jim sat back in his chair and laughed happily as the waiter approached with two *pêches Melbas*. He continued to smile while the man removed the plates and set the sweets before them. Then, as he withdrew, his smile resolved itself into that twinkle which was his natural expression of good-humour.

"Why, I guess there's a whole heap of things I could do," he went on quietly. "But I'm only going to do just one of 'em. You know, Blanche, it's a pretty terrible thing when a feller gets bug on notions of the welfare of his fellow-man. It's the sort of craziness that sets a boy yearning to get after folks and things with a club. He sort of sees red most every time he hears some fool kid won't eat its bottle right, and the birch in a school-house is liable to set him shooting up Presidents. Which mostly means the bottom's dropped right out of his sense of proportion, and his backbone's disintegrated in the juices of a mess of sloppy sympathy. Well, there's nothing much wrong with my backbone yet, and my sense of proportion seems in decent shape. All that's happened is that I've got a notion, and, if *you* feel good about it, I'm going to work it out. If it works good I'll be mighty pleased, and'll be feeling like some commercial philanthropist who reads a news-sheet's account of his good works. If it doesn't, why, I'll throw in my hand, and start a fresh deal with the same deck of cards."

The man paused for a moment, and his sister shook her head admonishingly.

"I don't think I'll ever understand you, Jim, any more than I shall ever understand our Eddie," Blanche said. "Maybe I lack a sense of humour. Maybe, being a woman, I haven't a notion beyond the things I was raised to. Why—why had you two boys to quit business right here in New York and get out to the—tough countries? You had ample here. Our folks left us all three the same. And the business was good. No, you sell up and get out. I know you've made a big fortune in gold, and Eddie was doing well in Greenwood. But—but all this terrible disaster could have been avoided. All this——"

"No, it couldn't, Sis." Jim shook his head and laughed. "If we'd stayed around we'd have got mixed up with things, anyway. These things don't happen because. They happen anyway. A feller's going to get the marked-out tally someway. Fate's got just so many kicks for every feller born. And he's going to get 'em. Do you fancy hearing my plan?"

"Of course I do, Jim. I've been waiting. And I want you to know that there isn't a thing in the world you can ask me that I won't do for you."

The man chuckled softly as he ate the last of his sweet.

"Fine," he cried. "That fool loyalty again. Only it's you this time, Sis."

The girl smiled back at him.

"Don't be absurd," she said gently. "Get on with the thing I want to hear."

"Well, for all I've got a million or so gold in my bank-roll I guess I was right down and out after getting clear of that red-coated boy, and looked like leaving my miserable bones feed for the coyotes. It was then I found it—in those two boys. One was a pretty tough, straight-thinking French-Canadian farmer, and the other was a broth of an Irish boy, whose only worry in life seemed to be he was scared to death of liquor, and scared worse that some time prohibition would make him have to live dry. Those two boys knew me for an escaped convict. Yet they kept me alive, fed me, and helped me all they knew to make a getaway. And they both did it for nix, and under threat of penitentiary for themselves. Say, those boys had a cargo of sheer sympathy and humanity aboard them enough to stock a heavenly department store, and the whole thing has given me a hunch. That hunch says I'm going to stake my last ounce of gold to help other 'down-and-outs' the same as they helped me. And I've come along now because I kind of hope you'll help me. You see, a boy can do ordinary things. But when it comes to the real good things of life the girl's got him beat out of sight."

"There isn't need to ask me, Jim," the girl said, in a voice in which emotion came near to robbing it of steadiness. Then she laughed in self-defence. "You see, I'm one of those fool women who haven't a notion beyond the men-folk belonging to them. My brothers have always been first with me. And now I sort of feel they're more first than ever."

Jim sat silent for a moment. His eyes were hidden as he contemplated the table. However he had been hit by the humanity and sympathy of those others, the utter and complete self-sacrifice of this sister, who dwelt in all the comfort and even luxury of her great home city, left him speechless for the moment.

At last he looked up. And when he did so the humour had faded out of his eyes. It had been replaced by a smile that was full of a world of tender gratitude.

"That makes me feel good, Sis," he said quietly. "It also makes me feel bad. You see, you don't know the thing I'm going to ask you."

He glanced about the room. Then his gaze came back to the fair-haired creature who was only midway between twenty and thirty, and who he proposed to expose to a life the roughness of which would test her to the uttermost.

"Not ask, Jim."

The smile accompanying her denial was dazzling.

"No."

Suddenly Jim spread out his strong hands.

"How would you fancy coming right out West to the heart of the Canadian Rockies?" he began. "How'd you fancy setting up a swell home with me there? There's no stores or subways there. There's no Fifth Avenue, or theatres, or bridge parties, or dances. The only noise and bustle you'll get there is when the wind howls down off the glaciers. There won't be a thing to worry over but the cold, and snows, and blizzards in winter, and the storms and wash-outs in summer. Then there'll be the buzzy flies, and the crazy skitters, and the voice of the timber wolves, and the yowl of the coyotes who missed feeding my bones. Maybe you won't locate Eddie there, but there'll be other folk who aren't yearning for the sun of civilisation to shine on them. There won't be any steam heat, and lots of other things you're used to. But there'll be cattle, and horses, and a real live trade, and work that'll leave you with a joy of life and health you can't ever get in a city. I've got to do something for the 'down-and-outs.' I'm filled right up to the neck with a yearning to help the way I was helped. I've found the wonderful, sweet grass Valley of Hope. And I want to set its gateway wide open for those folk who haven't found it. Will you come along, Sis?"

"Why, I'm crazy to."

The man turned abruptly and hailed the waiter. When the bill was settled he pushed back his chair.

"Come along, Sis," he said, in a tone that thanked the girl infinitely better than words could have done. "It's hot enough here with the fans going. Maybe Central Park'll be a foretaste of hell about now. Any way, we'll chance it. We'll take a crawl out there in the open, with that great old sun beating us over the head, and I'll tell you all the details of the thing I've set my heart upon. And we'll plan it out together."

CHAPTER VIII
Two Years Later

TWO years had passed since the calamity at the Marton home-stead. Molly's eyes were smiling again, and all signs of her grief had been swept out of them, driven headlong by the spirit of youth, and the merciful healing which time brings to the aid of all human grief. Her cheeks had lost none of their bloom, her eyes none of their brightness. The life that was hers once more claimed her to the full.

It had not been so for long weeks after the tragic discovery in the woodland belt. The process of recovery had been slow. But gradually the sun of her life had emerged from behind the clouds, and, when once reaction had set in, the speed of the girl's trans-formation had been something almost magical.

Now the labours of the seasons had again assumed their due importance, and were no longer useless, burdensome tasks, with-out real significance, and only calculated to further depress the spirit. Now the air that came down from the eternal snows im-parted to nerves and mind, and the springs of human emotion that sense of well-being that gilds all youthful yearning, and sets old age desperately clinging to the ebb-tide of life.

But the change, the recovery, had been subtle. Molly herself had known nothing of it. Even when the time came when she found it natural to turn her thoughts back to the dead man in deep, abiding, but calm regret, she was left unaware of the meta-morphosis. Nevertheless, she found it possible to feel gratitude to Fate, and draw real consolation, that her dead father had been spared all suffering of mind and body. Death she knew had been instantaneous. And she was glad that he had gone to his rest with-out a moment of anxiety for the daughter he had left behind.

But Lightning Rogers had no such thought or feeling for the man he had served. This lean, grey-whiskered remains of an un-savoury past was wholly a product of the hard life he had lived. He was desperately human, and his service for George Marton had been solely for wages. He had been wholly uninterested in the man.

But his attitude towards Molly was different. In her case his service was something no wages could have bought. It was the manhood in him—the primitive. Molly had proved an anchorage for all the affection that was parental in him. She was of the other sex, and her eyes were bright and smiling, and her femininity was something that carried memory back to those far-off moments when his pulses had quickened more easily. To him Molly was the beginning and end of his vision of his remaining years. When her father had been struck down horror had leapt upon him. But it was not for the fact of the girl's disaster. It was for the possibility which the disaster might have for him. He feared lest, as a result, Molly herself might pass out of his life.

He had bethought him heavily on that drive home from the woods. And decision had come on the instant. He spoke no word of comfort to the departing girl, feeling that such an attitude would be the best expression of consummate delicacy. Besides, he had no idea of what might be the suitable thing to say. But, once back at the homestead, he lost not a moment in taking charge of the situation.

He took the already frozen body of the dead man and laid it out in the parlour in such state as seemed to him befitting. Then he returned to the kitchen, where the stewing supper was as Molly had originally left it. Without a word to the girl, sitting huddled in her grief over the stove, he prepared a meal for her. Then, with an assumption of grave authority, he stood over her with the firm intention of seeing that she ate it. His philosophy taught him that the surest, the only support at a time of grief was a good, round feed of beans and sow-belly.

The girl had looked up at his bidding. It was only one momentary glance, but the old man beheld in it such a look of repulsion for the food that he edged hastily away to the table, and sought to restore his suddenly lost confidence by devouring it himself.

With a return of courage he essayed another magnificent effort. This time, in seeking to enforce the necessary authority, his voice, which was rarely gentle, became unduly harsh.

"You best beat it to your bunk, Molly, gal," he said. "You best make your blankets right away. Hev a good cry. Ther' ain't nothin' for a dandy gal like a bunch of tears you couldn't swab right in a week. Susie Larks allus reckoned that way. You ain't heard tell of Susie Larks, the li'l dancin' gal o' Moss Crik, down Arizony way. If things got amiss she just used to cry like hell till they came right, an'—— Eh?"

Again the girl had looked up, and the whole of her tragedy was there, looking back at him out of eyes which were gazing in horrified, tearless amazement. She said no word. She gave no other sign. And, after one apprehensive glance, Lightning had shuffled off out of the room and betaken himself to the lean-to workshop, where he forthwith set the stove going.

The efforts of his brain amounted to something little short of storm that night. He planned, and smoked, and swore. And he swore, and smoked, and planned. And by daylight a tangle of ineptitude completely befogged him. The only clear idea that gripped him was a settled determination that he was going to see "Molly, gal" through her troubles, if it used up his stock of brainpower and left him with nothing over for himself.

With daylight, however, he was free to act, which, in Lightning, was a wholly different proposition. His motives for the things he did that day were never at any moment clear to him. Something impelled him to ride into Hartspool. He took money with him, feeling that at such a time he might need it. He may have been right. At any rate, he contrived to leave it behind him in the town, having exchanged it for a subdued, drunken melancholy.

But he had obtained other results. First a Mounted Policeman appeared at the homestead. He was closely followed by a doctor. And, finally, a man who was known to be a carpenter in Hartspool made his appearance. He interviewed them all, and sternly headed them off from the stricken Molly.

A few days later, Lightning took another trip into Hartspool. He had no money which he could take with him. This time he drove the heavy team and the double-bob sleigh, which usually hauled cordwood. His trip was rapid, for his burden was light. The latter was just one long box of unpolished wood.

He had feared that Molly would accompany him, but, to his extreme satisfaction, the girl completely broke down at the last moment, and the wife of the carpenter, who was a kindly creature, who usually aided her man in that work which was not intended for the living, volunteered to remain and look after her until Lightning's return.

And now, with the passing of time, and the return of the girl's smile, Lightning gazed back on those painful days, and took full credit to himself for her recovery. He felt himself more than entitled. His little vanities peeped out from amidst his sterling qualities like blemishes dotting pure, crude metal.

Oh, yes. He had done well. He was glad. And, to his credit, no thought of thanks concerned him. The girl's smile and well-being were more than sufficient reward for anything he had done. She was the farmer in place of her father. And he had achieved the thing he had desired.

It was a perfect spring morning. The air was fresh, and the sky, ablaze with golden beauty of dawn, was studded, with wind-tossed, swift-moving cloud-flecks. It was a morning to stir the pulses of the old ranchman, and set the sturdy tide of his vigorous life in full flood. He stood for a moment in the doorway of the log shack, which was his sleeping quarters, and breathed deeply of the mountain air. Then, with a characteristic hunch of his shoulders, he passed out to begin his day's work.

He moved down to the corral, where, now that the warming spring days had come, the milch cows were housed for the night. His first task was to hay and milk them. But for once his task remained unfulfilled. The bars of the corral were down, and the place stood empty.

For some moments he stared stupidly. To him the discovery was incredible. It was even staggering to his self-confidence. The cows, that were his work to shut up for the night, had got out. It never occurred to him that the bars might have been set up carelessly. It never occurred to him that he could have made any mistake. The cows had been set in their corral overnight. They should still be there in the morning.

His study became active. He looked at the fallen bars. He looked at the cloven hoof-prints in the still soft soil about the entrance. Then his eyes hardened and narrowed and a curious thrust took possession of his bewhiskered chin. He had become a victim of one of his hasty, obstinate opinions that came so easily. He passed to the log barn and saddled up his horse.

After that he hurried up to the house.

Then came an exhibition of the man's regard for the girl. He said no word of the thing that preoccupied his mind, but contented himself with warning her that the cows had strayed.

"They broke out," he declared, implying no blame to himself. "They made a getaway. I'll jest git a sip of your swell coffee, Molly, gal, an' beat it after 'em."

Molly, in the midst of her cooking, looked round from the stove.

"Sure you will, Lightning," she said. "And you'll get your feed with it. An empty stomach's no sort of thing to chase up 'strays' on. Just sit around while I fix things."

The man obeyed. He took his place at the spotless table set with homely ware for two. And in less than two minutes he was noisily devouring the bacon and beans, of which, in all his years, he had never yet grown tired.

Molly went on steadily with the work of her home while Lightning ate his food. And when he had finished she speeded him on his journey.

"I'll make a big seeding while you're gone," she said, from the doorway. "Maybe you'll be quite awhile. You can't ever guess where those crazy creatures will make. I'd try the sweet-grass flats."

Lightning shook his head.

"Maybe I will. You just can't tell," he added, with a tightening of his thin lips.

Molly watched him go, his tall figure lurching with that peculiar gait which, with advancing years, seems to become ever more marked in men of great height. She knew the man for what he was—a hard ruffian utterly devoid of any graces or refinements, but a creature with a heart of unalloyed gold. She knew how great was the debt she owed him. She knew how much his goodwill meant to her. But beyond all question of self-interest there was real affection in her heart for him. She loved the simple, foolish, headlong nature that seemed beyond his power to control. She laughed at his vanities, his inadequate reasoning. Sometimes, even, she found pity for him. But this was only rarely. No one knew better than she how little pity was needed. He lived his life full to the brim of supreme contentment.

She went back to her kitchen and her own breakfast.

CHAPTER IX
Suspicion

LIGHTNING did not return until sundown, and when he reappeared the hard light of his eyes had deepened, and the thrust of his chin had become more aggressive. Molly realised these ominous signs when she encountered him at the barn, where she had just stabled her team after a long day's seeding.

"Well?" she inquired.

The old man shook his head, and the storm leaped into his eyes.

"Not a sight of 'em," he declared harshly. Then he turned a swift, malevolent glance in the direction of the hills to the southwest. "An' we ain't gettin' a sight of 'em anyway. Our six prime cows in full milk. It ain't no sort o' use chasin' these hills fer strays with—hoss thieves around."

Molly's smile changed to a look of incredulity.

"Horse thieves?" she echoed. Then she shook her head. "They surely would look for a territory where there's stock to steal. Why, there isn't fifty head between Dan Quinlan, up in the hills, and us, and that poor boy, Andy McFardell, on the road to Hartspool, with his miserable half section he's trying to make look like a homestead. And there's no one else within fifty miles of us, except Hartspool way."

The choreman slid out of the saddle. He loosened the cinchas of the saddle and flung it on the ground. Then he clapped his mare on the quarters, and watched her move off for that roll which a horseman knows means so much.

"It's only reasonable fer you thinkin' that way," Lightning admitted with unintentional patronising. "I guess you argue like the dandy gal you are, an' not like a hoss thief tough." He gazed thoughtfully down at the girl's slim figure in its simple homemade clothing, that was so carefully planned to leave freedom for her work. "But I ain't told you all the stuff I got in my head. I tell you my eyes and ears, an' nose are all wide open. I'm wise to a whole heap of doings about these hills. Them cows is gone. Plumb gone. They ain't within a ten-mile range of us. I've rode every yard this day. An' six milch cows full of milk couldn't have made ten miles in the night grazin'. They've been drove. Them bars at the corral hev been taken down. When I set 'em in place ther's no buzzy cows ken make a getaway."

Molly's smile broke out.

"I fixed them last night," she corrected. "You were busy getting the seeder right for me. Don't you remember?"

The man stared.

"I'd fergot," he said shortly.

"Maybe I didn't fix them right," Molly went on quickly, in an endeavour to make things easier. "It was nearly dark. But—best come right up to the house. I'll fix supper, and you can tell me about—horse thieves."

Molly went off to the house. But Lightning made no move to accompany her. A day wasted scouring the hills left him with a heavy leeway of chores to make up. It was upwards of an hour, and darkness had closed down, before he appeared at the house for the meal the girl had prepared. Molly made no attempt to question him further till the man's needs had been amply supplied. She knew too well the value of a comforted stomach in men-folk.

After she, too, had eaten, Molly sat with her elbows planted on the table, and her cheeks supported in the palms of her sunbrowned hands. She was thoughtfully watching Lightning devour the last of his third portion of baked hash. They were in the neat kitchen. It was plain and scrupulously simple in its furnishings, much of which had been home-made. But they were ample for the needs of their no less simple lives.

Lightning washed down his supper with a noisy draught of tea from an enamelled beaker. And as he did so Molly withdrew from the table to replenish it.

"Light your old pipe," she said, as she passed the teapot back to the stove. "Then you can tell me about—horse thieves."

"It's—Dan Quinlan."

Lightning's statement was an explosion.

"Dan Quinlan?"

Molly came again to her chair, and sat down in a hurry. She was genuinely startled.

"Why, Dan Quinlan's been up in the hills years," she went on, recovering herself. "I remember him when I was a kiddie." She shook her head. "I'd say you've made a bad guess."

"Hev I?"

The old man's eyes widened. And Molly saw the old "Two-gun" Rogers glaring out of them.

"Oh, yes, maybe I hev. Maybe I'm a bad guesser, anyway," he cried sarcastically. Then, with sudden ferocity: "But I'm right! It's Dan Quinlan!"

After that he sat back in his chair and lit his pipe.

"Say, Molly, gal, you'd jest hate to think bad of Dan Quinlan, 'cos you'd hate to think bad of any feller," he went on sharply. "I ain't seen you raised from a squallin' bundle of fancy fixin's without gettin' wise to the things lying back of your dandy eyes. You don't ever get near Dan Quinlan. Twenty-five miles of bad hill territory an' muskeg is quite a piece, even to folk like us. But if you knew him you wouldn't be feelin' good about him same as you do fer that darn gopher, McFardell, the Police set adrift without a 'brief' to say the boy he was. Dan Quinlan's a drunken Irish bum, the sort that's dead sure to get on the cross when it suits him. I know his sort. I met a heap of his sort in the old Texas days. I——"

"But why? What makes you think he's on the cross? Because our cows have strayed?"

Molly had recognised the reminiscent tone. In a moment the old man was flaring again.

"Them beasts was—drove!" he cried fiercely. Then he removed his pipe and flourished it at the girl. "How do I know? Why, I've rode our territory fer ten miles around. Who's drove 'em? Dan Quinlan. How do I know? Dan Quinlan's shippin' a bunch of yearlings he couldn't have raised honest out of the ten fool cows he starves around his bum layout. He's no sort of ranch-man, an' a no-account feller, who's fixed his place right there twenty-fi' miles south-west of us, up in the hills where folks an' the police boys ain't like to worry around. Last year he registered his brand. 'Lazy K'—that's his brand. An' I'd surely guess it's suitable. An' last summer he shipped into the Calford market, an' through Hartspool, a hundred an' fifty beasts risin' two-year-old. It can't be done on his cows. An' all that I got from Hartspool, wher' the folks are guessin' hard about it."

Just for a moment the girl was impressed. Then she shook her head in quick decision.

"It surely sounds queer, Lightning," she said, the more gently for the denial she was about to make, "but there's something missing. Dan Quinlan hasn't a neighbour but us, and we're twenty-five miles away. Who's he duffed his breeding cows from? We haven't lost even a calf ever before. And you say he's traded a hundred an' fifty? No. That doesn't answer whose stolen our cows."

Lightning stirred irritably. His argument had been all sufficient for him. But the girl's reason worried him.

"I'm goin' right up there, anyway," he declared. "An' I'll shoot his vitals to coyote feed, but I'll get them beasties back."

Molly realised the danger-signal.

"I shouldn't," she said. "Let's get so sure there can't be a mistake."

"I tell you I'm goin'." The man's hasty anger was stirring again. "An' I'm goin' farther. We've sat around a deal too long. I'm goin' all through this territory. Ther's folk gettin' around, like that boy, McFardell. An' we got to know jest how things are. We can't stand fer neighbours acting queer. With boys raising stock out of cows they ain't got, an' throw-outs from the Police squattin' on the land under pretence of raising a farm, an' spendin' most of his time bucking the game, an' shooting craps in Hartspool, we need to keep tab of things with a brace of guns in our belts. I surely am goin' right up to that Irishman's layout right away."

Molly reached out and laid a pacifying hand on the old ruffian's shoulder.

"No, don't you do it, Lightning," she said almost pleadingly. "I know just how you're feeling. And, in a way, I surely feel the same. But let's take another day. Then I'll be right with you in anything you do. I'll take my pony and chase up the creeks to-morrow. I'll peek around, and I won't leave a blade of sweet grass unturned. You stop right here till I get back, and after that, if I haven't located those cows—why, we'll just get right after the Police in Calford."

"You're givin' him time, gal, an' I don't like it," Lightning protested. "He'll get nigh three days to hide up them beasties in the hills. That ain't my way. Git right after 'em quick. Guns is the only thing fer hoss thieves."

"Sure it is. All the time," Molly agreed, her eyes twinkling. "But let me have it my way this time. It makes me feel real bad suspecting folk—till——"

A wide grin spread over the choreman's gaunt features.

"That's it, gal," he cried, slapping the table in sudden glee. "What did I say? You'd hate to think bad of a jack-rabbit. Sure.

We'll act your way—to-morrow. After that—my way."

Molly nodded.

"You're good to me, Lightning," she said warmly. "I guess I'll be all wrong, and you'll be right, as you mostly are. Still, I don't see you need be worried about that boy Andy McFardell, though. I sort of feel good about him. I'd say any boy who takes up land is a swell tryer. Can you wonder he gets into Hartspool to buck a game? Why, think. He's right on his lonesome there. Not a soul to pass a hand to him. He's mighty little money, and he's got to fix it all up himself. I'd go crazy that way—if there wasn't some sort of game around to buck. Then to get fired from the Police. My, that's awful. I haven't heard why, and he never talks, but I often see a deal of worry in his swell eyes. We shouldn't think hardly of him."

"No. You've a hunch fer that boy."

Lightning's smile had passed. Molly looked squarely into the eyes behind the smoke of his pipe. Hers were unsmiling, too.

"When disaster hits a man, and he's the courage to start up in decency, it gets a hunch from me all the time," she said coldly. "Life's tough in these foothills, Lightning. I've been bred to it. The man who can jump into it, and face it right, seems to me my best notion of a—man."

"Sure. If he's on the straight."

Molly drew a deep breath. A quick sparkle lit her eyes. "Andy McFardell's on the straight," she said quietly, as she rose to clear the supper-table.

* * * *

Lightning passed out of the house to the blankets awaiting him at his bunk-house.

As he passed along to his quarters audible expressions of disgust and anger broke from him. The cows were forgotten. Dan Quinlan was forgotten. All his bitterness was turned against the man the mention of whose name had stirred Molly to a rebuke that had hurt him in a fashion of which she was wholly unaware.

Horse thieves were anathema to Lightning Rogers, whose life had been wholly spent in cattle countries. His hatred of them was something traditional rather than personal. He believed it was the right of every citizen to shoot to kill "on sight" where cattle thieves were concerned. There could be no extenuation. They were the wolf-pack to which no mercy should be shown, to which no quarter should be given. But the man, Andrew McFardell, who had come into their lives something under two years ago, was on a different plane.

He hated the man. He hated his dark good looks and foxy face. He hated his easy, pleasant manners. He hated the thought that he had come to set up his homestead on the trail to Hartspool, within ten miles of the farm. He hated him because of Molly's liking for him. So, for once he rolled into his blankets and lay awake for hours searching his mind for the answer to the threat which he believed to be overshadowing the child of whom he had become the self-constituted guardian.

Lightning had no illusions. He had no false sentiments. Molly was the owner of a farm that had been amply prosperous in her father's lifetime. It still afforded her a livelihood. She had good stock, and ample buildings. She had a stout home, and knew the business in all its phases. Furthermore, she was strong and capable, and a pretty girl of twenty; and as simple as the hills that had bred her.

Now, almost immediately after her father's death, this "bobtail" policeman had come into her life. Why? Why of all places had he chosen the foothills for the setting up of his homestead?

To Lightning's method of reasoning there was only one answer to the question. He saw the time coming when Andrew McFardell's pretence of a homestead would be completely abandoned, and he himself would be asked to serve under a master instead of a mistress. And it would be a master who was a "throwout" from the Police Force.

More than half the night was endured in angry thought. And when, at last, his stertorous breathing proclaimed his sleep, it was only after his mind had been completely made up as to the line of action he intended to follow on the morrow.

Molly had retired to bed in the firm belief that she had effectually steadied her loyal friend. She was certain that she would discover the precious cows calmly grazing, tucked away in some secret, sweet-grass slough in which the hill country abounded. She anticipated a day in the saddle, perhaps; a day of hill-ranging, with her saddle-mare's eager body thrilling under her. She would strike out north and east along the creek in the direction of Whale River, into which it flowed. It was sweet grass all the way. It was on the way to Hartspool, but she had no intention of doing the whole journey. She would not go farther than Andy McFardell's homestead. If the cows were not in that direction she would strike out on a fresh line that afternoon.

Molly was at that age when self-deception is the most natural thing in the world. It never occurred to her to doubt her sincerity in selecting the direction of McFardell's homestead for her first search. But, having decided her course, she lay there between the snowy sheets contemplating a picture of the dark-faced, dark-eyed man she had first learned to pity for the hardships confronting him; whose courage she applauded.

Lightning was right. For all her twenty years Molly was an innocent child. Love as yet meant nothing to her. But even so, as she dropped off to sleep at last, it was with a ravishing feeling that to-morrow would be a day of unusual pleasure. And the pleasure of it had no relation to her search for her missing cows.

CHAPTER X
The "Throw-Out"

WHALE RIVER meandered pleasantly down the middle of a valley. It was wood and grass from end to end, and the reed and willow banks of the river completed a picture of luxuriant fertility.

Andy McFardell had selected the valley of Whale River for the setting of his homestead without hesitation. In his police days he had come to know the place, and had pondered the thought that some day it would surely shelter a thriving homestead if only a sufficiently hardy settler should chance upon it. Often he had urged that only ignorance and something approaching superstition kept the homesteaders to the prairie lands. These people were obsessed by the openness of the plains, and, all unsheltered, preferred to face their winter storms rather than grapple fearlessly with their awe of the mystery world of the hills. But never in his dreams had he visualised himself as the first settler in Whale River valley.

Utterly dispirited, bitter and desperate, he had passed out of Calford barracks at the end of his term of imprisonment with but the vaguest plans for his future. Like many another, he had given himself up completely to police life, and regarded his calling as settled for the full extent of his working life. He had contemplated due promotion. He had contemplated a slow upward moving, which, at the end, should open for him the road to some form of official appointment which would afford him the comfortable old age he knew to be attainable. But he had reckoned without the machine. He had reckoned without those chances and accidents with which the machine dealt so mercilessly. And so he found himself adrift, with a thousand or so dollars in his pocket, and without any training or equipment for the civil life in which his future lay.

So it came that he had recourse to the fall-back which Canada holds out to everybody. There was land. There was Whale River valley, which he had so often pictured as sheltering a sturdy homestead. And he forthwith set out for it as the only possibility presenting itself.

But his suitability for the life had yet to be proved. It was all so very different from the shepherded life of the Police Force. Discipline, as a servant, he understood. It was an easy thing, provided temperament was right. He had even come to love the simple process of obeying the last order. And then, as a Corporal, he had had the appeal of inflicting orders upon others. Now the position was altogether different. He had become his own machine as well as its servant. Was he morally equal to the dual capacity?

For the first season he had worked with an enthusiasm that looked to be carrying all before it. His capital was spare, and he husbanded it carefully. With a few tools he built himself a shanty of green logs, and thatched it with reeds cut from the bosom of Whale River. The whole thing cost him no more than the labour, and he felt good about it, and settled his kit into it with no little satisfaction. Then he built his barn for the team he had acquired during his police days. And all the time in the work of it he was widening a clearing in the woodland bluff he had decided should shelter his homestead.

With the summer no more than half spent he set to work on the corral for his two cows, and a second small barn for their winter shelter. Then he embarked upon his first real expenditure. It was for the wire with which to fence in a twenty-acre pasture of sweet grass upon the river bank. It was all a wonderful exhibition of single-handed labour. But, then, his mood was bitter, and lent him artificial courage. It drove him hard. He was a "throw-out" from the Police, and he wanted to prove to the world the fierce injustice with which he had been treated.

At midsummer he passed into Hartspool, with its saloon, and store, and its freight of mixed human nature. The place caught him on the rebound, as it were. He had achieved amazingly, and felt a reasonable satisfaction. He felt himself to be a man of some sort of property. He felt he could afford to hold his head up with those others. He felt, alas! that he must loosen the strings of his purse, and show these folk that he knew the game he had only just embarked upon. He fell headlong into the pitfall awaiting every unwary settler. The implement and machinery agent was at his elbow, and pleasant evenings at the saloon helped towards his undoing.

He bought plough, and harrow, and seeder, and hayer, and

binder, and a dozen and one other implements on the mortgage plan. It was so easy—so very easy. The future would pay for them—the crops he was going to grow. And Barney Lake, from behind his bar, watched the smiling dark eyes, and observed the confident attitude of the new man as he handled a deck of cards in the evening, or shook the crap dice with the men of substance who had built up large agricultural interests in the neighbourhood. And his mental reservations were decided and sharply pointed.

McFardell went back to his farm with his new possessions. And when winter closed down he had fifty acres under the plough. It was a tremendous feat.

It was during that first summer that Molly Marton became aware of her neighbour. For three months McFardell had been at work in Whale River valley before the girl discovered him, or the watchful Lightning became aware of his existence.

It happened on one of the girl's periodical trips on domestic errands into Hartspool. As she rode down the valley over the grass-trail she beheld the smoke of a camp-fire curling above the tree-tops. Then she beheld the fencing down on the river flats where the grass was abundant. Then had come the final revelation, when she had looked into the clearing McFardell had cut in the shelter of the forest. The man was at work then on the finish of his log-built corral.

At sight of him her imagination was completely captured. His appeal was enormous. She beheld a muscular, good-looking man clad in an undershirt and trousers, and with queer, stout moccasins on his feet, waging a lonely battle with all the elements of the world she knew to be so fierce. Single-handed he was grappling with his colossal task, and the sight thrilled the hill-bred girl with its courage.

Beyond doubt McFardell was good to look upon. His eyes smiled pleasantly into hers, and the stubble of whisker about his cheeks and chin, and his black moustache, all helped to hide that curious ugliness of mouth which, even had she noticed it, Molly could hardly have read aright. That was the beginning of an intercourse that had never been allowed to die out. Intimacy leapt. She was a simple child, and he—he beheld a sweet, dark face, with fine grey eyes that were too honest to conceal her woman's admiration.

Molly remained faithful to the picture of her first discovery. There was never any reason for her to do otherwise. Since that meeting she had seen him many times—far more frequently than she permitted Lightning to become aware of. And she always saw him in the same setting, battling with the labour of his primitive homestead in a fashion that never failed to provoke her admiration. But it was left to Lightning to nose out the things that helped to foster his unreasoning dislike, which he never attempted to conceal. And these things came in the short days and long nights of the first winter.

Winter was Lightning's playtime. It had always been so during George Marton's life, and Molly was content. Lightning would snatch days and nights in Hartspool. A fifty-mile ride or drive was nothing to the old sinner, if a reasonable soak of "hooch" was to be acquired as a result. And it was on these trips that he learned the depth of McFardell's weakness.

The fierce loneliness of the hills in winter quickly proved intolerable to the ex-policeman. His homestead was snowed up. Whale River was solid to its bed. And the storms roaring down the valley, and the cruel depths of cold, left him with his thoughts flung back to the police canteen, with its roaring stove and pleasant companionship. He resisted temptation for a period. Then he yielded. By far the greater part of his first winter was spent in Hartspool, and his visits seriously ate into his capital, but they made far deeper inroads into such store of moral resolve as he possessed.

Barney Lake nodded reflectively over the thing he beheld, and his dictum remained uncontroverted.

"It ain't no sort o' use," he said, for the enlightenment of Lightning and a group of his winter custom lounging about his office stove. "You can't raise wheat enough to pay the machine agent settin' around a cyard parlour all winter. I'd say winter's mostly a bad time fer folks in general. Fer a tenderfoot, yearnin' to look like a mossback, it's just about all the hell he needs. But there's a heap a feller ken do around winter, and he needs to do it if he's goin' to make good. You can't sit around half soused, shootin' craps fer a wad that wouldn't attract a Hebrew-Chink," he declared, spitting copiously into the stove. "That boy, Mc-Fardell, ain't better'n the ord'nary police 'throw-out.'"

* * * *

The signs of McFardell's weakening must have been apparent to any close observer as he stood in the doorway of his shanty gazing out upon the litter of his clearing. His eyes were unsmiling, and discontent looked out of them. He had no right to be standing there. He knew that. But his head ached, and he was hating the thought of work more than he had ever believed himself capable of hating it. His horses were in the barn, where he had put them somewhere about midnight. They were unbrushed, and unfed or watered. His two cows were at the corral bars bellowing for the milker and the feed they knew themselves entitled to. Then there was that seeding that should have been completed to-day. And now, in an hour or so, it would be noon. He felt tough. But——

He dived his hands into the pockets of his trousers. Then he searched his hip pocket. The result was a few silver coins and two bills of small denomination. He gazed at them awhile, and a feeling of sickness, which had nothing to do with the whisky he had consumed overnight, pervaded his stomach. He was thinking hard, and remembered he had "shot craps" to a late hour. Two dollars and a half was the change out of the fifty good dollars with which he had visited Hartspool the day before.

He thrust the dollars back into his pocket. Then he moved out into the sunlight.

"Gee! I must have been soused," he muttered.

His heavy gaze surveyed the scene while the cows continued their clamour. It was a poor enough place, typical of its kind. The whole thing was haphazard. It was slipshod. Maybe the buildings were stout enough. It was the best that could be said of them. There was inexperience, carelessness, even indifference, in every detail of them. The thatch upon the barn was loose and wind-blown; the corral, snugged against the sheltering woods at the far side of the clearing, looked to have been constructed with regard to haste rather than stability; the near-by hay-stack of last year's hay was a hopeless, wasteful litter. So, too, was the extravagant assortment of expensive implements, already rusted and paint-worn, which it would take him years to pay for.

He disregarded it all. At the moment his only concern was for the bad day he had had in Hartspool, and his complete disinclination for the arrears of work he knew to be awaiting him.

He passed down to the corral and cursed the clamouring cows. And later he returned with a bucket of none-too-clean milk, which, regardless of the swarming flies that descended upon it, he deposited just within the doorway of his shanty. Then, his mood improving with activity, he went on to the barn to tend his neglected team.

As he passed into the miserable building the whinny of gladness that greeted him was lost upon McFardell. All the years of

65

his association with horseflesh had failed to inspire a shadow of appreciation. Horses had their uses, and, for him, that was all sufficient. And just now his only thought was to be done with irksome labours. The brush and curry-comb were things he had learned to hate in the days of his police life.

By the time he had rushed through the bare necessities of his team his mind was made up. There would be no seeding that day. It could wait until the morrow. He condemned himself for over-sleeping. He knew that he had been half-drunk overnight. He had lost money at "craps" he could not afford. But he would straighten up. Yes. That was it. He would cut out Hartspool for awhile—at least till that big farmers' dance which would take place in about two weeks. Hartspool was no use to him. He would stick to his work now the spring had come. So, for the rest of the day he would overhaul his machinery, and get it into good shape. He——

He looked up in the act of dipping corn from his iron bin, and stood listening. Then a shadowy smile crept into his eyes. He passed the feed to his horses while he listened to the sounds of someone approaching, and suddenly a girlish voice, hailing him by name, set him moving quickly to the doorway of the barn. His tongue moistened his thick lips behind the screen of his moustache.

"Ho! Andy!"

Molly Marton's call was full of joyous greeting. She had just leapt from her saddle as McFardell appeared in the doorway. Her face was alight and smiling as she gazed into the man's. She noted his stained, moleskin trousers, belted at the waist. She observed the business-like cotton shirt, with its sleeves rolled up to the elbows. She saw the muscular, sunburnt arms, and drew conclusions that satisfied her.

"Fixing your team for midday?" she said.

McFardell lied without hesitation.

"Sure," he cried. "They done a big morning. But say, this is just great. I hadn't thought you'd be along. It's two weeks since—since—— It's tough you living so far away, Molly. I sort of count the time between seeing you around."

A quick flush mounted to the girl's cheeks, and somehow she found herself interested in the cows feeding their hay down at the corral.

Molly stood with her reins linked over her arm. Her tall, gently rounded figure was full of appeal to the covetous gaze of the man. Her divided skirt was sufficiently attractive and business-like for all it was home-made, and of her own design. Her feet were well shod in soft tan riding-boots that were adequately spurred. Her half-length jacket over a white shirt-waist, and the wide-brimmed prairie hat securely strapped under the coil of hair at the back of her neck, completed a picture that stirred the man and banished the last of his heavy morning mood.

"It's a real great time when we start seeding," Molly cried impulsively, with a little laugh of excited spirits. "Doesn't it make you feel glad? Seeding, I mean. It's a good time for us folk." She nodded wisely. "You see, we're all looking ahead. The sun's full of promise after winter. The birds an' things are making ready, too. And the earth. Yes, everything's just looking ahead. I love seeding. How many acres have you put down?"

McFardell lied again.

"Twenty so far," he said. Then he reached out to take the reins from her arm. "You'll stay and eat?" he went on eagerly. "I'll just fix your mare, and we'll go right up and eat. The beans are ready, and I've a swell piece of imported bacon I brought out from Hartspool last night."

"Were you to Hartspool yesterday?"

The man's smile passed abruptly as thought flung back.

"Yes," he said, and laughed without mirth. "But I'm glad to be out again. As you say, it's good with spring around."

Molly was thinking of Lightning. She remembered his expressed contempt of this man. And her smile passed.

"You go right up and fix things," she said quietly. "Sure I'll be glad to eat. I'll fix Rachel," she went on. "I always fix her. She needs hobbling, and I guess I'll set her out on the grass. You see, I'm out after our cows that have strayed. I left Lightning back there cursing cattle thieves and folk like that. He never reckons our cows can stray." She laughed. "Lightning would hate to think they hadn't been driven by cattle thieves."

McFardell nodded.

"I see," he said seriously. Then he added thoughtfully: "But I'm not so sure about Lightning being crazy that way. You know there's a lot of young stock coming down out of these hills. The folk in Hartspool are guessing about it. A boy named Dan Quinlan, somewhere away above your place, has set them all wondering. And being folk who're interested, and easily disturbed, all sorts of queer hints and looks are passing amongst 'em. Anyway, I'll go fix the food while you pass your mare all she needs."

Molly was sitting on a box just outside the doorway of the man's shanty. McFardell was facing her on an up-turned bucket. And between them, on the ground, was the remains of their repast of beans and the boasted imported bacon.

Their tin platters had been laid aside, and each was in possession of a beaker of tea, which had just been dipped from the simmering camp kettle. The man was smoking his first pipe of the day and regarding the girl with that curious, burning smile which her innocence would never have permitted her to interpret aright. Frank admiration was looking out of Molly's eyes. To an onlooker the truth must have been all apparent. The girl was in love. And the man with the curiously ugly mouth was contemplating her with no great purity of thought behind his eyes.

But McFardell held himself under restraint. He had come to know something of Molly's courage and independence. He realised, too, the innocence of her mind. Her beauty was unusual. Her shapeliness was something that ravished him. So he did his best to hide up the feelings she stirred in him.

"You know, Molly, it's a mighty tough life, this homesteading," he said, with the air of a man contemplating affairs in the abstract. "It beats me, the way you get through on your lonesome."

"But I've got Lightning."

The man laughed contemptuously.

"Lightning?" He shook his head. "The fag end of a misspent life."

Molly's smile died on the instant.

"You think that?" she cried, a flush mounting to her cheeks. "You needn't. You surely needn't. He's no 'fag end,' and never will be. He'll be 'Two-gun Rogers' to the day he dies. A reckless, headlong creature, who'd as soon fight as eat. Sooner. I couldn't get along without him. He knows the game from A to Z, and puts it through. Besides, he's more than that. Since father got broke up, he's been a sort of father to me. He's got all the courage when I weaken."

"Sure. But—do you ever weaken?" McFardell asked, a little hastily.

Molly's smile returned at once.

"You don't get things. Weaken?" she cried. "Why, surely I do. I weaken most all the time. I don't know. I love my life. I just love our poor farm. There isn't a beast or a stick on it I don't love, but—but—oh, I don't know," she went on, spreading out her hands. "It's the same. Always the same. The seasons come an' go. The whole round. An' each season has its work. Sometimes——" She sighed a little hopelessly. Then she laughed. "But I'm not grumbling. Sure. Sure. It's spring now. And the sun's fine, and the birds are nesting. There's mallard and geese in the sloughs. And—and I just feel glad about everything. Why, I'm not worried a thing about our six cows. I just can't worry in springtime."

The man pressed the tobacco down in the bowl of his pipe. His eyes were hidden.

"I know," he said. "It's the way I feel. Most folks feel good when spring starts life moving again. You don't ever get to the cities?"

Molly's eyes widened as she shook her head.

"Only Hartspool for dry goods."

"It's a poor sort of settlement. But it isn't that."

"What d'you mean?"

"You know, Molly, folk just can't live alone always," McFardell went on, his eyes on the litter of his homestead. "That's the thing. We're human, and all that that means. We're not machines to work like—like a thresher. We need companionship—our own kind and age. We want things to laugh at, or get mad about. We want things over which we can exercise all those moods and feelings Nature gave us. You're feeling that way and don't know it, or maybe your grit won't let you admit it."

The girl was just a little frightened. She knew that Andy had put into words something of her own secret thoughts.

"Maybe that's so," she hesitated, while she wondered admiringly at his penetration. "You know, Andy, it's real ungrateful of us to feel that way. Get a look around. There's nigh everything we folk need. There's sweet grass you couldn't find anywhere else. There's the rivers full of fish. There's shelter the Almighty set for us. There's the wonderful, wonderful sun, and an earth ready to grow us the things we ask it. There's——"

"Always that crazy human feeling we just can't help." McFardell nodded. "That's why I went into Hartspool yesterday—to buy that bit of—bacon."

They both laughed. Then Molly fell serious again as she watched Andy refill his pipe.

"But I wish it wasn't that way," she said.

"Why?"

"Oh, I don't know. Father never felt the need of—playtime."

"He was more than twice your years, I guess."

Andy re-lit his pipe.

"You mean when he was young?"

"Surely." Andy nodded. "Don't you reckon he ever hit up a joytime?" he asked. "Don't you guess he and your mother made out at parties an' dances? Maybe," he smiled, "he even found the inside of a saloon better than the outside. I tell you we all need to get joy or—burst."

"Yes. I feel that."

"Why, you can even get joy in Hartspool."

"Hartspool? How?"

"A party. A swell dance."

"A party? A—dance?"

Molly echoed the words with a deep breath of ecstasy. Then she shook her head.

"I've—I've never been to a—party," she said dejectedly.

Andy nodded and laughed. And his eyes were hotly regarding this child of the hills who was like clay in his hands.

"Will you go to this one? It's the swell farmers' dance that they hold when seeding's through. There's two weeks yet. I'm going. I guess I wouldn't miss it for a deal. Say, I haven't always been a farmer like you. I couldn't go right on here from year to year without a break. I'd go crazy. You come with me to it. I'll fix the tickets. It don't mean a thing but a good time. And for you a fifty-mile drive. Will you do it, Molly? Say, I'd be mighty glad and proud. You'd be the belle of that dance, and I'd be——"

"I don't know," Molly demurred. "Lightning would be real mad. He'd——"

"Oh, to hell with Lightning. He's your hired man. You'll come?"

"But I haven't a party gown," Molly cried, in sudden dismay.

"I said there's two weeks yet."

"You mean I could—fix one?"

The light in the girl's eyes told the man all he wanted to know. She was a little overwhelmed, but wholly yielding. Her excitement was apparent in the rise and fall of her gently swelling bosom. He pressed her the more surely.

"Surely you could. There's all the elegant stuff you need in Mike's store in Hartspool. Make a trip in after you get your cows back—if the cattle thieves haven't got 'em," he said with a laugh. "Say, Molly, promise. You will?" he urged, leaning forward and suddenly reaching out for possession of her hands. "Promise," he cried. "You must come. I—I———"

But the girl had risen from her seat. Perhaps it was those reaching hands she wished to avoid. Perhaps— Something was stirring within her, a feeling she had never known before. Quite suddenly she found herself impelled to flee from the sight of those appealing eyes, beyond the reach of those outheld hands. For one moment her cheeks had paled. Then, in an instant, a deep flush suffused them right up to the temples, and the broad, low forehead, shaded by the wide brim of her hat. She glanced quickly out over the clearing. Then she laughed. It was a forced laugh she was almost unconscious of.

"I—I won't promise, Andy. I'll just—think about it."

The man urged her no further. He was content. He knew.

"All right, Molly," he said, rising from his bucket. "That's fixed."

His confidence passed all unheeded. Molly was lost in the new, strange sensations of the moment. Quite suddenly and almost sharply she declared her intention of going.

"I'll saddle up right away," she cried. "Look! Look where the sun is! I must have sat here more than an hour!"

CHAPTER XI
Lightning Operates His Plan

LIGHTNING had reached the summit of a "saddle" between two considerable hills. The hills themselves were wood-clad, but the "saddle" between them was grass-grown and open, and a wide view of the valley of Whale River spread out before him.

The old man had reined in his horse, and sat meditatively munching his tobacco as he searched for the thing he expected to find. He was looking for McFardell's newly-enclosed pasture somewhere there down on the river bank. He found it quickly. Yes, it was there, away to the east about a mile. And beyond that, just above the tree-tops, he beheld the drift of smoke which indicated his clearing.

Lightning had left the farm and struck out as the crow flies. That was the way of the man. He had avoided all trails, lest chance should bring about an encounter with Molly in search of the lost cows. Just now she was the last person he desired to meet. And the way he had chosen of reaching McFardell's homestead seemed to be the best possible in the circumstances.

His satisfaction was considerable. It was now only a question of the best point at which to cross the river itself. He knew Whale River as he knew most of the region of the foothills. It was quite as treacherous as were the mountain rivers generally. But there were two fords. One was directly opposite McFardell's homestead, and the other——

A mounted figure had suddenly appeared on the far side of the valley. It had just left the ex-policeman's homestead, and was moving straight for the river ford he had been contemplating. In a moment the cattleman's easy confidence was shattered, and replaced by a spasm of agitation. He had recognised the rider. He had recognised the sorrel and white of the pinto mare. It was Molly.

Lightning was badly shocked. But he remained where he was. There was no fear that Molly would discover him. She was at least a mile away, and her way lay over a trail that crossed the river and pressed straight on up the slope and out of the valley.

So he watched the girl till she entered the bush that lined the river, and the while sat nursing his feelings in furious silence. Once out of view, he knew she would not reappear. He would need to give her time to get away. That was all.

He calculated the time carefully. Not for a moment did he permit his feelings to jeopardise his plans. Storm was raging behind his shining eyes, but it had no effect on his purpose. At last he stabbed the rowels of his spurs into his horse's sides and moved on down towards the river.

* * * *

When Lightning was disturbed he was like the threat of an active volcano, and just as liable to break out into violence. On the other hand, he had unique powers of dissimulation when his passions were sufficiently under control. In his crude way he was as cunning as an old dog fox.

It was like that now as he sat on the box outside McFardell's doorway. It was the same box which had so recently supported the more delicate burden of Molly. A bland smiling amiability had apparently replaced his recent furious mood.

McFardell was again occupying the up-turned bucket, from which he had gazed so hotly upon the appealing figure of Molly. He had made no attempt, in the interim between the coming and going of his visitors, to proceed with his promised chorework. For all his antipathy to the man he had even found excuse in Lightning's visit.

The old man's announcement on arrival had been carefully considered, and the manner of it had possessed a calculated sarcasm.

"We're out after 'strays,'" he declared, with a laugh. "Molly's out one way, an' I'm out another. Our cows is missin'. Molly guesses they're 'stray.' Guess you ain't picked up a bunch around this valley?"

McFardell shook his head, while he searched the other's grinning face.

"Not a sign," he said.

Meanwhile Lightning had dismounted and loosened the cinchas of his saddle, which was his way of forcing the other to offer hospitality.

"Have you eaten?" McFardell inquired without enthusiasm.

"Surely." Lightning lied deliberately. He had no desire to eat under this man's roof. "But I'll sit awhile," he added quickly. "You see, I ain't on any party visit, an' I ain't guessin' to locate them cows around this valley. I've come right along to yarn some."

McFardell turned and led the way across to his hut.

"Then we don't need to waste time," he said coldly.

Now they had settled down for their talk, with the drift of smoke from the fire doing its best to counter the onslaught of newly-hatched mosquitoes, and dispel the hordes of sticky cattle flies.

Lightning was talking expansively. He was talking with all the graphic elaboration he was capable of. He was striving to create an atmosphere of friendliness between them, which neither had the least genuine desire for. McFardell saw through the other's manner instantly, and wondered. But he listened the more intently in consequence.

"You see, boy," the old man grated, in his harsh way, "them cows is no more strayed than you an' me. I'm dead wise to the things goin' on around these hills, an' you bein' a police boy that was, I guessed I need to hand you the stuff I got in my head. Molly, gal, jest don't know a thing. An', anyway, she'd hate to think ther' was cattle thieves around. But there is. By gee! Ther' surely is. An' they're at work right here around us."

McFardell removed his pipe from his heavy mouth.

"I see," he observed. And his manner had swiftly fallen back to that acquired in his police days. "What's lying behind this, Lightning?" he demanded sharply.

"Guess you haven't ridden ten miles just to hand me—with my two cows—warning. Well?"

The suddenness of his challenge suited Lightning's more direct methods, and, as a result, the questioner improved several places in his estimation.

"It's easy," he said at once, chewing vigorously. "Dan Quinlan, up there above us in the hills, has run a hundred an' fifty yearlings last year into Hartspool an' Calford. Well, you can't grow a hundred an' fifty yearlings out of ten mean cows that must have quit milking when you couldn't raise a crop of chin-whisker. Not in the same year, anyway. Say, he runs a registered brand, too. 'Lazy K.'"

McFardell glanced out over his clearing. His machinery held his gaze.

"I've heard about his shipments in Hartspool," he said meditatively.

"You'd need to be deaf if you ain't."

"Yes. What then?"

McFardell's eyes were levelled on the other's, with a searching half-smile. Lightning sustained the regard with superlative blandness.

"It's police work," he said meaningly.

"I'm no longer a policeman. I'm a farmer—like you."

"You quit 'em—yes."

"I was—'fired.'"

"That don't cut any ice. You know the play."

McFardell shook his head, and Lightning saw the ominous snapping of his eyes.

"Why should I help out police work?" he said. "Guess I haven't a thing to lose through cattle thieves." He laughed. "Why, my stock wouldn't mean a thing to the craziest bunch of rustlers ever rode the prairie. Anyway, I don't see where Dan Quinlan's duffing his yearlings."

"Yet he's passed in a hundred an' fifty in one year an' registered a brand. Say"—Lightning's eyes were just a shade anxious—"a boy don't need to register a brand if he ain't keepin' right to the business. Maybe this year he'll pass in more. Wher' do they come from? I'd say they don't grow on the hill-tops, an' you surely can't fish 'em in the criks."

"No."

McFardell smoked on thoughtfully for some moments. Lightning's rough argument was not without its effect upon a mind that had been carefully police trained. But there was something else puzzling. Was the cattleman genuine in his anxiety in coming to discuss the situation with him?

"Maybe it's as you say, Lightning," he said after awhile. "I've heard all this before in Hartspool. At least, I've heard them talking. But I don't fancy jumping in to worry out things for other folk. Why should I? I got all the work, an' more than I need, right here. No. It's police work, and I'm not yearning to help the Police." Suddenly his eyes lit with a feeling that swept him along with it. "No, by God, I owe the Police nothing. Not a thing. You know there's things a man can never forget. You're a cattleman. You gave your whole life up to—cattle. I was a policeman, and gave my whole life up to the job. Guess I'd sooner do police work than anything I know. If I may say so, I'm dead cut out for it. I did it for years, and made good all along the line. I'd a name for good work, and saw Easy Street coming my way as a result. I allow I wanted nothing better. Then came bad luck—plumb bad luck and nothing else. No fault of mine. Just luck. In a moment discipline got busy. I—— Psha! It don't matter. Here I am—'fired.' And with a 'bobtail' discharge. I'm sore on the Police, boy. I wouldn't do a thing to help their work, unless—unless——"

"You could get back to 'em with—a clean slate."

Lightning was smiling fiercely, and his whiskered jaws broke into renewed activity upon his tobacco. He took full credit to himself for the channel into which he believed he had headed their talk.

"That's how I'd feel," he said insinuatingly. "Say, it's sort of hittin' the other fellow a boost plumb in the neck. But I'd say it would be mighty elegant settin' the Police Commissioner squealin'." He laughed, and watched a smile dawn in McFardell's eyes. "It would be a real swell play to be able to roll in to Calford with a stacked deck of cyards in your pocket. 'See right here, Commish, I ken lay my hands right on a bunch of hoss thieves, and pass 'em down to penitentiary. Do you need 'em? Well, play the game. Set me right back where I was, and wipe out the darn thing you got against me. I'd say that's a play that looks a'mighty good to me. Gee, it would be elegant!'"

The old man's glee was consummate acting, and its very crudity carried conviction. McFardell was completely deceived, and the thought took hold of him against his better judgment. It was helped tremendously by the long winter, most of which he had passed in Hartspool, and the knowledge of the growing depletion of his finances, and the laborious prospects which the coming summer opened up. But he shook his head at the man who was tempting him.

"It's surely all you say, but I can't see putting it over," he said a little reluctantly.

"Not if you passed 'em the rustlers, an' a right story to send 'em to penitentiary?"

"Oh, yes, that way."

McFardell knocked out his pipe, and put it away deliberately. The hint was obvious, and Lightning was ready enough to accept it. He stood up, and his lean figure towered over the other, who had risen from his bucket.

"Wal," he said, "mebbe it ain't worth the worry. I guess you got an elegant valley of sweet grass around you, an' a swell outfit

76

of machinery to trim this place into a right farm. It's tough work, but good. You ought to be showin' yourself a wage after the first five years. It ain't a deal of time when a boy's young. Then you're your own boss, an' if you fancy a time, why, you ken jest take it, an' to hell with work. An' your machinery ain't a worry so long as the season hands you a right crop. If it don't them boys'll hit your trail good. Still, you got a good patch of ploughing. Maybe you'll get another fifty acres broke this year. Gee, us mossbacks ain't never through," he finished up with a laugh.

He moved away towards his horse feeding hay beside the corral, and McFardell accompanied him.

"Guess I'll get along," he went on. "I jest felt I had to get around. Dan Quinlan's turned rustler, an' by the looks of things our bum stock don't come amiss to him, I'd say you'll need to keep an eye for your team. There it is. The folks are talkin' P'lice in Hartspool, and if they get around I can't help the notion it's goin' to be dead easy for 'em."

They reached the corral, and McFardell thoughtfully watched the old prairie man tighten up the cinchas of his saddle. Then, as the lean figure leapt into the saddle, he nodded a casual farewell.

"Dan Quinlan's quite a piece up in the hills south of you?" he inquired.

Lightning's interest quickened.

"Twenty-fi' south-west," he said.

McFardell nodded.

"Maybe I'll get a look around that way when I'm through seeding."

"Mebbe it'll pay you—feelin' the way you do."

Lightning picked up his reins, and his horse raised its head. Then he nodded at the dark-faced man he disliked even more intensely than any cattle rustlers.

"So long," he grated, and swung his horse about.

"So long."

McFardell watched the queer figure as it rode out of his clearing. Then he went back to his fire, and the work of sorting his machinery was no longer considered. Instead, he sat pondering the thing which Lightning had just put into his head. So the afternoon passed, and he prepared his supper. Then he hurriedly attended his horses and cows, and, when the barest necessities had been seen to, he returned again to his shanty.

Before he turned into his blankets that night, which remained just as he had arisen from them that morning, his brain was seething with the new idea. There was a chance, as Lightning had suggested. There was hope. And the moment he admitted it the prospect grew to the proportions of certainty.

Yes. He would certainly look into this thing up at Quinlan's, and then—and then—God, how he hated the prospect of breaking another fifty acres!

CHAPTER XII
Dan Quinlan

IN the years of Lightning's service at the Marton farm he had only penetrated the greater foothills to the south-west as far as Dan Quinlan's homestead on two or three occasions.

His real reason for avoiding Dan Quinlan was his cold opinion that the man was unfit for white man's association. The thing that was anathema to his ideas of manhood was that Dan lived with a squaw. There were always to be found loafing about his place a number of his wife's coloured relations; and then there were off-spring which he claimed no white man had the right to bring into the world—little dusky, happy, laughing, wild creatures, with all the potentialities for evil resulting from the mixture of colour.

Then his farm was such as no white man need take joy in. A log dug-out on a hillside, overlooking a poor corral that was just sufficient for his ten mean cows; a ramshackle barn which stabled a small bunch of saddle choyeuses; and a patch of ploughing that barely provided sufficient feed, with a few cabbages, and a supply of potatoes thrown in. And, added to the rest, the whole place was completely overrun by savage trail dogs.

In Lightning's view, whatever he might choose to call himself, there was only one designation to which Dan Quinlan was enti-tled. The man lived by trapping and pelt-hunting, and any other means that offered itself. He had become a white Indian. In short, he had "taken the blanket," and was no longer entitled to asso-ciate with white men or claim their respect. Lightning's opinion was characteristic, and in consequence of it he had not been near the Irishman since the death of George Marton.

Had he done so, the scene he would have discovered would still have been, to all outward appearance, much about the same. There stood the dishevelled dug-out, that was sufficiently stout, and supplied all the man's needs and those of his dusky family. The barn looked to have been slightly enlarged, but had gained nothing else by the change. The corral still accommodated the ten mean cows which grazed over the flat of grass which filled the valley below. The wolfish dog pack still beset the place.

But the change was there, and he would no doubt have discovered it. It lay within the forest which clothed the whole hillside about the dug-out. Less than half a mile from the Irishman's home a clearing had been made. It had a winding roadway cut through the trees. Four ring corrals had been set up, and in connection with them was all the paraphernalia of the cattle-raiser. There was the branding "pinch." There was the smith's forge, and the searing-irons. There were great stackings of hay for feed. And several soundly built huts of log and thatch dotted the outer ring of the clearing for use in the work amongst the cattle.

The place was basking under a blaze of spring sunshine that was only little short of the full heat of summer. The forest had already set forth its paler shades of green, and the stark arms of deciduous trees were donning their delicate spring costumes. The mountain stream, in the heart of the valley, was a boisterous, rushing torrent, and the grass in the open was leaping by inches with every passing day.

Two men were standing near by, overlooking the work of branding the cattle with which the corrals were teeming. The men in the corrals, and at the forge, and working the cumbersome "pinch," were not ordinary cattlemen. They were not even white men. They were relatives of Cama, the wife of Dan Quinlan, and the Irishman had pressed them into his service without scruple.

Standing with his white-haired companion, Dan's eyes were alight with humour. His big body was clad in the buckskin which the faithful Cama prepared for it. The only thing with which to distinguish him from his dusky relatives by marriage was his white face, rugged and weather-beaten, his enormous size, his mass of curling, fair hair, and his laughing blue eyes.

"Say, Jim," he cried, as he watched one of his many "in-laws" struggling furiously with a roped steer, "I want to laff. I surely do. Say, look at that guy hanging to that pore critter's stumps of horns. Now, how in hell does he guess that beast's to reckon he wants it to move ahead while he's smotherin' its fool head with his darn sight more foolish body? Can you beat it?"

He moved off on the run, and laid a hand on the top bar of the corral opening. The next moment he had vaulted it, and became lost amidst the teeming throng.

Jim Pryse smilingly awaited his return. The Irishman amused him almost as much as did his "in-laws." And when Dan came back to him his face was beaming with good-nature.

"Gee! They're an outfit!" he cried, with a great laugh. "Did you ever see such a play? They got a Dago bull-fight skinned to death. Get a look at 'em. They're the whole darn tally of Cama's brothers, an' cousins, an' uncles. I feed the bunch, an' talk Black-foot to 'em from daylight to dark. They'd eat that bunch of steers in a week, but it takes their whole darn combination o' brain to handle 'em right. I surely want to laff. They guess they're show-ing the white man. They're the queerest crowd of darn-foolish-ness you could locate outside a bughouse."

Pryse laughed delightedly.

"It's no wonder they're a dying race," he said.

Dan nodded and chuckled.

"They're Reserve-raised," he said significantly. "They know all about doctors' dope an' pie-faced religion. They can talk and read 'white.' They can count dollars to beat the band, but cents better. They got a hell of a notion for soap they fancy looking at, but 'ud hate to use. But set em to the work their old folk reck-oned was natural to 'em, an you've got 'em hatin' it like the devil hates holy water. But they're a good crew, an' I've got no kick comin'. They'd commit murder fer me, an' I sort o' feel they're like a bunch of silly kids that need beating over the head with a club when they do wrong. Ther' it is. It's the civilisin' play of our races—the old dames who sit around in steam heat figgerin' out the best med'cine fer their own useless souls. I'm tryin' to make men of 'em. But it's mighty hard work after the missioners are through with 'em. I tell you, civilisation beats out of a boy all those things God A'mighty set out as right fer him. An' it drives home a bunch of sloppy junk that any man worth the name gets worryin' around to lose quick."

"It was something of that set me yearning for Alaska seven or eight years back," Pryse chuckled quietly. "But you couldn't lose it there. The townships, even there, are up to their necks in au-tomobiles, and 'phones, and wireless, and all the rest. Why, they got societies up there for every darn thing, from a Chink Labour Union to an Anti-Natural Fur Society. I guess the anti-fur bunch has tough work ahead in Alaska."

Dan drew a deep breath, and his eyes sobered.

"Give me these hills," he cried. "It's peace here, Jim. It's peace an'—if you ain't yearning for fancy feeding—plenty. We're out of it all, an' up against all the things God A'mighty reckoned was good fer us. Taste the mountain air, look at the sun, see the

81

grass grow, an' the woods packed with every pelt and feed a boy needs. There's no by-your-leave here. Ther's no crazy say-so. Act the man or go plumb under. If ther's any kickin' get after it quick. It's peace here, the only peace I've ever known. Ther's folks in Hartspool an' Calford, when I get around with cattle, pass a whisper all the time. I know it. I bin told. I've 'taken the blanket.' I'm 'white Injun.' An' all because I married Cama right, an' she's raised a dandy bunch of kids to me. I don't care a curse. Why shouldn't I? Ain't haf the whole world mongrels of colour? If they ain't they were oncet. Psha! I ain't lookin' fer no halo. I got some three-score an' ten to put in on this crazy old earth, an' I'm goin' to do it the best way that suits me. I ken scratch a livin' right here fer myself an' my whole bunch. I got Cama, an' I'm happy. Ther' ain't a saloon fer miles, which is God's blessin' to a crazy Irishman like me. An' then, things bein' so, I'll go down when the time comes singin' thanks to the good God who's passed me the peace an' happiness I never found under the electric sky signs of civilisation. Say, I'll hold up this bunch till fall, an' then run 'em right over the border into Montana without making any pow-wow with the United States border folk. We got to go slow Calford way. Folks there are pushing their noses our way."

Pryse's interest in the branding had passed. Dan Quinlan had absorbed it all. The man's philosophy suited his own mood. Somehow he felt that deep inside that burly ruffian dwelt a great, strong, human spirit—a reckless, untamed spirit, whose genuine good almost completely smothered the weakness he sometimes saw peeping out.

"I was wondering that way, Dan," he said quietly. "The curiosity of folk was one of the things I didn't search closely enough. Yes, we must surely spread our market. I've been thinking hard. Our bluff isn't all it needs to be. We've got to bluff harder. You've got your brand registered. That's all right. Now we must play right up to it with a 'full house.' Do you get me? We got to set up a swell sort of ranch place right here for you, and your Cama, and her folk to live in. It must be big and good. And we'll need bloodstock ranging this valley. Then, when folks get around, as they surely will, they'll see the meaning of things as we want 'em to see. You've built yourself into a swell stock-raising proposition. Then they'll rub their foolish eyes and forget their talk of 'taking the blanket,' and they'll lift their hats to Dan Quinlan, and we can trade our stock all we please down at Calford and Hartspool."

Dan hawked and spat. He was watching an Indian approaching the "pinch" from the forge. The man was flourishing a nearly white-hot branding-iron. He let out a shout.

"What in hell?" he cried. "Quit it, Ash-te! Quit it, you seven sorts of darn fool! Are you lookin' to roast the poor crittur? Cool it down, you crazy son of a goat. Fer the sake of Holy Mary! Ah, to hell wid ye!"

His moment of angry disgust passed, and his smile broke out at once. And, as the Indian scuttled back to the forge, he turned again to the man beside him.

"Sure an' you're right, Jim," he cried, with a laugh. "You'll set Cama crazy fer joy building her a swell home. And these boys, too. Gee! I wish I could lick 'em into the things they were before the missioner got after 'em," he added regretfully. Then: "How's things going inside?"

Pryse laughed.

"Why, fine," he said. Then he added significantly: "I got more hands than I can pass work to. They come from the cities east, and west, and south. They're all sorts, from crook politicians right down to the boys who've skidded on the main trail. It's just wonderful. There's a great estate there, and well-nigh a settlement. And I've just had to case-harden myself to hold a discipline of sheer steel. We'll be shipping grain this year as well as stock. And if nothing goes amiss I'd say it'll come in a flood. I must get right back now. It needs me all the time."

"Yep. I guess that's so. Well, so long, Jim," Dan said, as the other turned to go. "I'll start right in building—out in the open. We can't be too quick with it. I'll stop right here now. I can't leave these fool boys. You'll look in on Cama an' the kids before you quit?"

"I surely will. So long Dan."

"So long."

Dan watched the white-haired figure till it was swallowed up by the forest. Then he turned again to his hopeless task of guiding, instructing, and blaspheming his dark-skinned relatives.

CHAPTER XIII
Silver-Thatch

MOLLY MARTON sat leaning over the horn of her saddle. One elbow was propped upon it, while her brown hand supported her chin. The other hand was reaching down holding her mare's reins, while the thirsty creature buried its muzzle in the speeding waters of the creek.

The afternoon was well advanced, and the sun was already approaching the crystal peaks of the more distant hills. Molly calculated there was a good three hours to complete darkness yet, and she could reasonably expect to reach home in less time than that. So far her search had been fruitless. She had discovered no sign of her missing cows. But she was quite undisturbed, and not a whit nearer agreement with Lightning as to the meaning of her loss.

The excuse of her search, however, had served Molly well enough. Ranging these hills, with Nature bursting into renewed life, was a joy that never failed in its appeal. Molly loved it all with a youthful passion. She loved the radiant sunlight—the immensity, the complete solitude, of this world of forest, and hill, and sheltered valley.

The scented spruce came right down to the grass-grown banks of the creek. Where she had entered the water was a boulder-strewn gap. It was clearly the bed of one of those swiftly passing spring torrents. Now it was almost dry, and had served as her approach to the shallow ford.

The happy waters surged about Rachel's sturdy legs. Beyond, across the creek, the hills rose sharply, clad with a woven pattern in every shade of green. Molly had no intention of crossing the creek. Her homeward way lay back over her tracks, and down through the endless woods which lined almost the entire course of the creek.

But the girl had no thought just now for the beauty of her surroundings, or the business of returning home, or even the object of her search. She was all unconcerned that she had some fifteen miles to cover before she again saw her snug homestead. She was thinking of the dark, good-looking face of the man who had offered himself as her escort to a real dance.

For long weeks, and even months, thought of Andy McFardell had preoccupied her. There had been times when she had had no realisation of how deep was the appeal he made to her. Then there had been other times when she knew, and the youthful blood had swiftly swept to her head, and a sort of delirium of longing had left her a little horrified and ashamed.

There had been moments of doubt, when she had longed for the father who was dead. But all these emotions had been passing, lost in her healthy-mindedness. But now it seemed to her as if the whole combined strength and weakness of those past moments had descended upon her in an overwhelming rush. A passionate love for Andy McFardell was sweeping through her. And she knew and understood the wonderful thing that had befallen.

She knew none of the old earlier shame now. The woman in her had suddenly become dominant. In a wondrous revelation, all the innocence of childhood had been swept away like some obscuring mist, yielding in its place that splendid spectacle of a golden love wherein every emotion, every hope, every purpose in life, becomes definitely focused upon one single glorified human creature.

Molly gazed out upon this vision while her pinto drank. A deep emotion held her. Her unseeing gaze was upon the water-race. Her ears were deaf to everything, but the rush of happy thought passing headlong through her brain. She was ecstatically absorbed in her love for the man, with his warm, dark eyes, his splendid courage in adversity, and she longed for him. There were no reservations. In Molly there could be none. At that moment no less could satisfy her than to yield everything to him—everything that was hers, everything she herself might be.

The clatter of hoofs upon the boulders behind her left her wholly unaware of any approach, and it was not till her mare flung up her head that she awoke to realities. Rachel had quenched her thirst, and the girl reluctantly turned her about to regain the bank.

Molly sat like a statue on her unmoving mare. Her dream had tumbled headlong. She was alert and searching as she gazed upon the white-haired figure of a horseman in the act of watering his horse a few yards away.

She took the man in from head to foot, even to the last detail of the splendid, coal-black horse he was riding. And the man returned her stare with smiling interest. His wide-brimmed prairie hat cast a shadow over his eyes, and so hid something of the strength that looked out of them. Molly beheld the broad pattern of his tweed jacket, and the cord riding-breeches which terminated in his soft-topped boots. She noted that he was wearing a waistcoat; and, curiously enough, this was the thing that perhaps attracted her most. Right across it stretched the yellow links of a gold watch-chain.

Just for an instant a flutter of very natural apprehension disturbed her. She was alone. She was still miles from her home in the heart of the hills. Then she remembered. After all, these hills were her home. She had been born and bred to them. A stranger, clad in garments such as she associated with a city, need only excite her interest. Besides, there was something very pleasant looking out of his eyes.

* * * *

Jim Pryse had seen Molly as he approached the water on his way from Dan Quinlan's; but he had failed to recognise her sex until she turned her pinto to return to the river bank. For a moment he had hesitated, doubtful of the wisdom of revealing himself. Then he had dismissed the thought. His horse must be watered, and this was the only suitable place along the whole of the densely wooded river. So he had passed on down to the ford.

Molly's surprise as she faced him was no greater than that of the man. Jim could scarcely believe his senses as he gazed into the pretty face, with its big, grey, innocent eyes. He had been prepared for some rough cattleman; he had expected such. In the coated, divided riding-suit he had never for a moment looked for a girl. A white girl alone in these hills was a thought that had never entered his head. Now he was glad he had flung caution to the winds.

It was Molly who offered greeting, and it came in an impulsive expression of surprise.

"Why," she exclaimed, "I just hadn't a notion——" And she broke off in a little laugh of embarrassment.

"It doesn't seem I had either, till—you turned your pinto around."

Both were laughing. To Molly the man's tone matched the expression of his eyes. It was deep and resonant, and reminded her of the organ she remembered to have heard at the Catholic church in Hartspool when she used to visit it during her father's life. To the man the moment was one of sheer enjoyment. Beyond his sister, and the dusky wife of Dan Quinlan, he had not encountered a woman in many months.

His horse flung up its head and investigated the pinto. In a moment the man was forgotten in Molly's admiration of the horse he was riding.

"My!" she cried. "What a lovely, lovely beast."

Pryse leant over and patted the sweat-dried neck of his horse.

"Beelzebub's quite a dandy," he admitted, with smiling pride. "He was raised on a race-track down Kentucky way. But say, they've both finished watering, and the creek's ice-cold."

Molly nodded and urged her mare. And they both passed up the boulder-littered bed of the mountain torrent.

Molly led the way, her sure-footed mare infinitely more nimble than the other amongst the boulders. Neither spoke a word. Both were thinking hard. Molly was quietly making up her mind to ascertain the stranger's identity, and then leave him while she continued her way alone. Jim Pryse was, on the other hand, deliberately intent upon riding with her just as far as she would permit him.

The girl drew rein at the edge of the forest, and Beelzebub gallantly came to a halt beside the pinto and rubbed his muzzle against her white neck.

"My way lies east," she said quietly, as again she encountered the smile of the man.

"Mine, too, for a mile or so," Jim said casually. "Then I break west up Three-Way Creek. There's no get-out of this valley before that. We best ride on. We're mostly lonesome folk. Company's swell when we happen on it."

Molly's resolve was scattered to the winds. The man's smile was irresistible. Besides, there could be no harm. And, anyway, what he said was perfectly true. This valley went on with only a break here and there right down to her home. The creek was the same that supplied the water-front on her farm, miles away on. If he were riding east, it would be simply churlish to refuse to ride with him.

"You know," she said, with a frank laugh, "I'd just fixed it in my mind to quit you right here. You see, you're a stranger."

Jim nodded, watching the light in her eyes.

"That's dead right, too," he said. And then his eyes sobered admonishingly. "It doesn't do riding around these hills with stranger men. Now you can't tell. Maybe I'm a 'hold-up,' looking around for young gals on the 'stray.' Maybe I'm a 'two-gun' man. Or a cattle thief. Maybe I get around eating up any old thing in the human way all the time. You surely can't tell. The more I think of all the things I might be the tougher it makes me feel. Now, say, hadn't you best make me ride ahead of you, and hand out my talk over my shoulder, while you keep a gun pushed up against my spine? It 'ud help make things safe—for you."

Molly broke into a peal of happy laughter.

"I like fool talk," she cried. "But you hit things right in a way, too. Still, my gun, which is right here in my coat pocket, can stay where it is, and we can ride aside each other. Let's get on. I need to make home by sundown. There's all of fifteen miles of this valley to make. And I haven't located a sight of my fool cows yet."

"Your cows?" Jim asked curiously, as his horse moved along beside the sedate mare.

Molly's gaze searched the distance through the tree-trunks as they loped over the rotting underlay of the woods.

"Yes. I'm out after 'strays,'" she said, in explanation. "They got away two days back. The fool dears didn't know better than to quit our corral for the open and the timber wolves. It makes you reckon they got no sort of sense," she laughed. "Here we're doing the best we know for them; we're handing them feed, and shelter, and water. Then—do you reckon they're thankful an' pleased? No. It's sure like us human folk, isn't it? We just must do the things we want, an' not what's good for us. Lightning guesses they've been stole by rustlers. But——"

Jim listened to the girl's explanation in wonder, and broke in as she hesitated.

"Do you live hereabouts?" he asked quickly. "You got a farm? I hadn't a notion there was a soul around this valley but Dan Quinlan, away back there where I've just come from."

Molly turned, soberly speculative as she studied the face beside her.

"Then you surely must be quite a stranger," she said. "Marton's farm has stood right down at the mouth of this valley twenty years. I was born on it, and I'm twenty," she concluded in her precise fashion.

Jim soothed the impatient Beelzebub with a restraining hand. As the beast modified its gait he looked round.

"Marton's farm?" he inquired, with an effort to conceal the excitement he was labouring under.

Molly nodded.

"Yes," she said. "That's my name. Molly Marton. You see," she added, "father's dead. He's been dead two years now. I run the farm with Lightning. He's my hired man. At least, he calls himself that way. But he's more than that. He's a queer old tough. He's been a cattleman all his life. He's getting very old, but—he's good to me. An'—an' I guess I couldn't run the farm right without him."

But Jim was paying no heed to Molly's eulogy of Lightning. In a moment his mind had leapt back to a time in his life when the name of Marton had meant complete salvation to him.

"I hadn't a notion," he muttered. Then, as they galloped silently down an incline towards a wide break in the forest that lay ahead, he bestirred himself under the girl's scrutiny and laughed. "And you are Molly Marton?" he said. "And your father was George Marton a—a French-Canadian?"

"Then you do know us?" Molly swung her mare wide to avoid a fallen tree-trunk. But Beelzebub took it in his stride, and the girl noted the ease of the man's seat in the saddle. As they came together again she went on. "Yes. He was my father," she said, and waited.

Jim shook his head, and the silver whiteness of his bushy hair fascinated the girl.

"It beats everything," he said. "I'd forgotten George Marton had a daughter. And yet I shouldn't have," he added, with an enigmatic smile. "But I only saw your father once. I hadn't a ghost of an idea his farm was hereabouts."

"Where did you know him?"

"That's what I've been asking myself—months. It was somewhere around this hill country. But the particular locality?" He laughed and shrugged. "You can search me."

Molly accepted his reply with all the trust of her unsuspicious nature. She nodded.

"That's the way of things," she said. "We meet folks, and pass right on. Don't we? Then, when they happen into our lives again, we—we—just sit an' wonder, an' guess we must be dreaming. Maybe even you didn't meet him in these hills at all. Maybe it was Hartspool, or—or—Calford. He used to go there."

"Maybe."

Jim drew a deep breath. They were nearing the edge of a wide break in the forest. Beyond lay a stretch of grass. Away beyond that the forest continued, but there was a definite change in its nature. It was low and sparse. Then away to the right of them lay the creek down which they had been riding. Silver stretches of water showed up. The valley was changing its course eastwards. Just behind an abutment of hill ahead was the opening that would take him westwards. Jim knew that the moment of parting was drawing near.

As they rode into the open Beelzebub strove fiercely to break into a race. But the man held him down.

In this fashion they rode on in silence. Jim was absorbed in the memory of a time when his fortunes had been at their lowest ebb, and he had been running a neck-and-neck race with disaster, and even death. His more spectacular association with Dan Quinlan had claimed his interest to the exclusion of that other. And yet he knew he owed just as deep a debt of gratitude to George Marton. This girl was his daughter—this child, with her innocent eyes, her pretty, dark face. It was she who had packed up that food that had kept him from sheer starvation for days.

Again they were in full sunlight, which transformed the valley, and the blue grass they were riding over, into something very wonderful. To the man it was like an omen—an omen of delight. He abruptly checked his horse, so that Molly came abreast of him.

"You know, Molly," he said, using her first name without realising it, "it's queer the tricks life plays about us. You've told me something I'm more glad about than I can say."

"You mean—about father? Why?"

"Why?" Jim echoed. Then he shook his head. "No. It's too long a yarn now." He pointed out ahead at the break in the hillside, where Three-Way Creek debouched. "There lies my way now. Yours is ahead down the valley. The sun's dropping fast, and we'll both need to hustle or get benighted. Some time I'll—— Say, look right down there amongst those spruce bluffs at the river. What's that moving? It's—say, there's one—two—three—four—five—six. And they're Pole-Angus cows. Were yours Pole-Angus?"

Molly turned in the direction he was pointing. And instantly her face became radiant.

"Why, say!" she cried. "Look at them! The foolish old dears! They've handed me a nightmare. And there they are gawking around like a bunch of foolishness eating stray grass in a spruce bluff when there's all this swell feed right here. No, they've no sense. They just haven't. Lightning'll be crazy mad to think there's no rustler around."

Molly was alone with her truant cows. She was herding them before her along the creek bank. She had driven them across the stream that came out of the westerly gap with the aid of the white-haired man on his black horse. Then, at her bidding, the stranger had taken himself off.

In the moment of the discovery of her lost cows the girl had forgotten everything else. There had been the perverse work of rounding them up, which mainly devolved upon her. Beelzebub had missed all that sort of thing in his education. Then had come the passage of the creek. And then a hurried farewell. It was not until she had lost sight of the stranger that she remembered her unfulfilled purpose. She had let him go. And she knew no more whence he came, or his name, or whither he was going, than she had at the moment of their meeting at the water-hole.

It was absurd. It was something outrageous. She was angry with herself, and not without resentment against him. For a moment she had thought to recall him. But she restrained the impulse. No. Why should she? She had been a fool. And he—he might at least have enlightened her in exchange for the enlightenment she had so foolishly afforded him. Evidently he could not have wanted to do so. Evidently he had no desire to discover himself. Well, let him go, with his coal-black horse and his queer white hair.

Her cows preoccupied her, and quickly enough her ill-humour passed in the business of driving the foolish, hornless creatures, whose antics so often made her want to laugh. Anyway, her long day had been more than successful, and as the valley opened out, and the woods gave way to the broad open as she drew near her home, the cows seemed to realise whither they were being herded, and to welcome a return to the shelter of their familiar corral. They hurried along almost frantically.

As she neared the end of her journey Molly's thoughts were no longer dominated by the all-absorbing emotions which had been inspired by the man McFardell. It was not that they had undergone any change. On the contrary. It was simply the natural claim of the life that was hers. The solitude of the hills had been broken for her. A fresh interest had suddenly tumbled headlong into it. And she found herself thinking of the white-haired creature on his coal-black horse.

How came it that the stranger's hair was so white? He was

young—quite young. She was certain of that. She had heard that trouble sometimes whitened the hair. Yet there was no trouble in his smiling eyes. It was all very strange. It was—— What wonderful hair! It was like silver—polished silver. And as thick as a thatch.

She laughed aloud as she came in sight of the smoke rising from the chimney of her homestead. A sudden thought had flashed through her mind. It was a childish thought, that pleased her immensely. He had refused to reveal his identity. Well, it was of no consequence. She would very likely never see him again, and, anyway, she had coined a name for him. It was a good name, too—better than he deserved—Silver-Thatch.

CHAPTER XIV
The Heart of the Hills

JIM PRYSE was leaning against one of the verandah posts of his home in the Valley of Hope. And, just behind him, lounging in a low-seated chair, was a red-headed creature, freckled, clean-shaven. He was a man of perhaps thirty years. Certainly not more. And he was dressed in somewhat similar fashion to Pryse himself. The difference lay in the fact that he wore no coat or waistcoat over the yellowish silk shirt, whose sleeves were rolled up to the elbow, and revealed forearms which suggested tremendous physical strength.

"Talk it out, Larry," Jim said, as the other broke off from his half-laughing, wholly serious protest, and helped himself to a drink from the Rye whisky and water that stood on the small table close beside him. "Notions stick with me when I get 'em into my fool head. They take a deal of shifting. Still, I always reckon there's things other folks can see that I'm mostly blind to, and I like to know about 'em."

He gazed out over the shadowed, evening scene. It was as though the wand of some magician had passed over the valley he had known some two years back, when Hope and Despair had fought out their long battle in his half-starved soul.

The mighty background of it all was unchanged. There lay the shadowed forests sweeping up and about the giant hill-slopes, which helped to hold secret the sweet grass pastures which flooded the heart of the valley. There lay the calm, silvery winding path of the river that had once provided him with his principal means of life. There lay the unending pastures that had first inspired his imagination. It was all there, just as he had known it in the days when Dan Quinlan's ministering visits had meant his moral as well as physical salvation. But it was no longer simply a splendid picture of Nature's handiwork. A complete transformation had been wrought.

The outline of it all was still clearly visible in the last of the daylight. Night shadows were gathering, and a few twinkling lights dotted the fringe of the forest beyond the river. There were buildings in almost every direction within half a mile of where he stood. They were low, squat buildings of green logs and skilful thatch, and represented human habitations for the unfortunate freight that had come to people the valley. Nearer by stood a number of larger buildings. They were barns standing in the vicinity of the corrals, which were many and stout. Beyond these lay the rectangular outlines of fenced pastures, which seemed to extend so far into the distance that they became completely lost to view. Beyond that were several hundred acres of fenced ploughing that were beyond his view.

The lowing of cattle came back to him from the corrals and the far pastures. The night sounds of the river, where the frog chorus was unceasing, no longer emphasised the desolation he had once known. The whole valley was alive with all that which the human mind delights in. There were occasional echoes stirred by human voices, and the friendly yelp of dogs. And then there, where he was standing, was his own beautiful log-built home, furnished as civilisation demands, and full of human companionship.

His had been the controlling mind that had brought it all about. His had been the wealth that had made it possible. And in the work of it all he had been supported without stint by the loyalty of his sister, and this cheerful, freckled creature who was revelling in one of his occasional cautionary protests.

Laurence Manford laughed as he set his glass back on the table and lit a fresh cigar.

"It's not a deal of use, Jim," he declared. "I haven't a thing to say against the notion of it all. It's the sort of notion any feller who knows you right would look for. It seems to me there's boys born into this pretty swell old world of ours with most of the juice you ought to find in their heads running around the valves of their foolish hearts. It's not reasonable to figger a feller's heart can think right with the things inside it that don't belong there. That's your trouble. Guess you were born with a heart that's short-circuited your thinking machine. Now, I'm the other way about. I start in to think at the right end of me, and, when anything else butts in, just beat it over the head till it quits. Being that way, I got a pretty wide view of this enterprise of yours, and find myself guessing darn hard about the way it's going to end. We got forty crooks around this layout," he finished up significantly, "and some of 'em are pretty tough."

"Well?"

Jim moved back to a chair and sat himself opposite his fiery-headed friend. He was smiling contentiously, and Larry recognised that he must make good his argument.

"If I know a thing, that's just what it isn't," he said, sending the ash of his cigar sprawling. "The forty-first blew in to-day with the record of a sewer."

"But we don't take in folks with that sort of record," Jim protested. "Who sent him?"

"Your man in Vancouver."

"Richards?"

"Sure."

"What's his trouble?"

"Smuggling Chinks. And with that goes the dope trade, if I know a thing, though he don't admit it. Then he beat the boy who arrested him over the head with a lead pipe, and made his get-away. He didn't kill the feller, but—it wasn't his fault. Richards reckoned because he hadn't killed him he could send him along. It looks like Richards stretched a point in this boy's case. And when that sort of thing happens it seems to me there's an ugly look in it. Do you get me? This boy's a real tough. You'll see him in awhile."

Pryse remained silent, and Larry went on. He pointed out across the valley where the twinkling lights were shining.

"I took a walk around those bunk-houses just after the dinner hour, and happened on some knife-play. You know that boy, Dago Naudin? Reckons he's French, 'an stinks of sage brush. He'd chewed off Slattery's right ear, and was yearning to disembowel him with a ten-inch knife that I'll swear has tasted the job before. Here's the knife."

He drew a vicious-looking weapon out of a sheath slung at the back of his belt, and touched the edge of it with his thumb. It was horn handled, and studded with inlays of what looked like gold and silver.

"Mexican," he said, passing it across to the other. "And I guess that's his country, too. I jumped in to save murder, and nearly broke his wrist to get that knife. He cursed me and mine, and you and yours, in bastard Spanish. We're going to get trouble with that tough. And Slattery's not a deal better. Say, did you ever figger just how we stand right here? Do you ever remember Blanche? Oh, yes, I know. We got boys around here who're mighty glad and pleased to be here. They're boys we can count on good, in a way. There's the Doc—Peter Lennox. There's that boy Lovell Taylor, who tripped up in his bank in Toronto, and has hated himself for it ever since. There's Jock Smith, who did what he did to save a woman from the husband who reckoned to kill her. There's that queer soul Fingers, who, if he's a crook at all, is a merry son-of-a-gun, anyway. Oh, yes. There's boys who deserve all we can do for them. But there's others——" He spread out his hands. "Dago Naudin's the worst of the bunch. And Slattery's darn bad, too."

"And what d'you think they can do?"

"Why, every sort of old devilment you ever heard of, from giving this layout away to highway robbery, and murder of one Jim Pryse. And—there's your sister, Blanche."

"And what are we doing when that play starts?"

"Why, bucking a game, with the chances ten and more to one with the other feller."

Pryse shook his white head, and smiled derisively.

"You know, Larry, one of the reasons—only one, mind—I was so almighty glad when you wouldn't stand for me running this layout without taking a hand in the play yourself was that you're the sort that looks all round and through a thing, and, having looked that way, makes up his mind and never shifts it. You've got a faculty I don't know a deal about, and I'm glad to have you hand out the things that faculty suggests to you. But I want to say right here you're seeing things just now I can't get a glimpse of. There's going to be no highway robbery and murder, with me for the victim. When it comes to that, I guess I've a real good hand to play. And I'll play it to the limit. But you're not thinking of Jim Pryse, boy. You're just about as certain as I am that I can beat the game at a show-down, especially with Larry Manford at my elbow. It's Blanche you got on your mind."

Larry nodded, and there was no laughter in his eyes.

"I know," Jim went on earnestly, "and I think the more of you for it. Blanche is dead game to the bone, and—and she's worth the love of the best man in the world. And I want to say right here that when you and she fix things to get married you'll get nothing in the world from me but my best goodwill and any old thing I can do to make things the way you'd have 'em. I allow there's quite a big chance that we're taking for Blanche. I saw that from the start—or, anyway, when I saw, and began to realise, the make-up of the crook. Now I'm ready, with you, to persuade her to beat it back to our home city. Do you guess she'll quit us? Not if we both wear out our knee-caps crawling at her feet. She's red-hot on this thing, and we've got to take the whole darn blame if things should turn amiss for her. You can't impress me a thing more than I am impressed on this. I'm guessing all the time. And with men like Dago, and Slattery, and this new boy you tell me of, your best warning isn't any too much. Knowing Blanche the way I know her, we've just got to do the best we both know."

Larry re-lit the cigar he had permitted to go out and finished his drink.

"Sometimes I thought you didn't realise, Jim," he said. "You haven't said a deal before. But you do, and I'm glad. You're right. But for Blanche the worst of 'em wouldn't matter a whoop in hell. But I'm crazy for Blanche, an' I'd go stark, raving mad if things happened to her. No," he finished up regretfully. "She wouldn't quit. That's the worst of it. That's what——"

"Sets you so almighty crazy for the greatest woman I've ever known."

Larry's eyes shone responsively as Jim stood up. He pulled out his watch and looked at it. Then he, too, stood up, and for a moment gazed out into the twilit valley.

"I'll round up that 'stray' for you, Jim," he said, and stepped off the verandah.

* * * *

Now a swinging oil lantern was shedding its warm light on the verandah. Jim Pryse was sitting at the table which the whisky decanter had recently occupied. A book like a ledger lay open before him. And Larry Manford was in occupation of a chair near by.

A shortish, stocky man, clad in a city suit, was standing before the table. He was black-eyed, with nearly a month's growth of dark beard and whisker on his face. His eyes were small and narrow, and twinkled alertly, but without any amiability of expression.

"Name?" Pryse prepared to write. Then he added: "You don't need to hand any name but that by which you wish to be known."

"It don't matter a curse, boss," the man retorted sharply. "If this is the right joint folk reckon, names don't need to worry. Richards knows me, anyway. Pike—Jack Pike. That's the name I've carried fer most of ten years."

"Wanted for?"

The man laughed softly.

"Yeller traffic, an' spreadin' out the cop who jumped in on me."

"Richards sent you along?"

"Sure. He told me to make these hills, where I'd find the shelter I needed fer awhile. I hoofed the railroad to Raeburn, as the feller said, an' waited around. Then I picked up a boy who put me wise."

"Yes. Picked you up outside the depôt."

"By the water-tank. That was how Richards said. I went there each day at noon till he came."

Jim took down the details, and the crook looked on with a shade of anxiety.

"Say, what's the game?" he asked sharply, eyeing the book and the man beyond it without friendliness. "Ther' ain't no trick in this? If ther's cross work, I guess——"

"There's no trickery." Jim looked squarely into the man's eyes, which shone fiercely in the lamplight. His own were smiling without warmth. There was something very compelling in them, and the man calmed at once under their regard. "You best understand just how things are here. Any man who's up against the law in an ordinary way can get shelter here for just as long as he fancies—under conditions. There's crimes I guess this place is no shelter for. Yours, as Richards has warned me, don't rank with those crimes. This book is a roaster of the folks who come along. If you need our shelter—and you're free to come or go when you choose—you've got to work for your keep, and will be paid for that work at the ordinary rate of pay. It's farm and ranch work, cattle raising and grain. If you need to hide years you can stop right here on those terms. If you choose to quit to-morrow you'll be guided clear, after being blindfold, same as you were brought here. You can go east or west or across the United States border. You'll have to part with those two guns you've got in your pants if you fancy stopping around, though. There's no need for guns here."

The crook was on the point of sharp protest, but Jim's voice anticipated him.

"There's no argument. You can't shelter here one night with those guns in your pants. Further, you'll need to convince us you've no weapon of offence on you. That's all."

"If I hand 'em over, will I get 'em again when I quit?"

"Surely. This is a shelter for boys like you, not a 'hold up.'"

The stranger reluctantly drew a pair of heavy automatic pis-

tols from the two hip-pockets of his trousers, and still more reluctantly passed them across the table, butt first. The latter detail
had a significance by no means lost upon those watching him. Jim
took possession of them, and placed them in the drawer of the
table.

"That's all right," he said. "Now, just oblige by showing me
the linings of all your pockets—unless you are willing for my
friend here to go through them. We take no chances."

The man laughed bitterly.

"No, you surely don't."

"No," agreed Jim calmly. "Those pockets?"

The man turned them out. There was nothing it was necessary
to relieve him of, except some cartridge clips for his pistols. And
he returned his goods to their places, his narrow eyes twinkling
with something intended for a smile. As the last of the collection
was replaced Larry cleared his throat.

"You best unfasten your vest, boy, and hand over that knife,"
he said quietly.

The man turned like a tiger on the red-headed man, whom he
had almost forgotten.

"What d'you mean?" he cried.

"Just what I say. That knife," Larry said, without moving.

"Do you think I'm going to herd around with a bunch like you
got here without——"

"We need that knife."

Larry had risen from the chair, and the newcomer measured
him with no friendly eyes. Then, as though his estimate was con-
clusive argument, he opened his cloth vest and produced a long
sheath-knife and laid it on the table, hilt towards Jim.

Jim nodded and glanced across at Larry. Perhaps there was a
sign passed between them. At any rate, Jim turned on the crook.

"I think we're through. My man Despard'll pass you on to
your right bunk-house, and see you get the blankets, and feed, and
anything in reason you need. You can buy smoke and most anything else you need from him. Even a certain limit of booze. Work
starts at daylight. You're welcome here so long as you behave like
a reasonable citizen. And if any danger from outside comes along,
you'll get ample warning. I want you to get this, and get it good.
This layout is run dead right. It's a sheer shelter from the things
that worry you outside. We guarantee that. We call it the 'Valley
of Hope' because it gives folks like you a chance of a getaway
from what's chasing you, and the chance of a fresh start. What

we ask in return is work, and that you can act the reasonable man while you're here. If you don't, we can deal with any breaking of our rules. Stop around as long as you fancy, and you're welcome."

Completely disarmed, Pike's whole attitude seemed to undergo a change. He drew a deep breath, and glanced from Jim's snow-white head to the fiery red of Larry Manford. And quite suddenly his eyes twinkled with genuine good-nature.

"You two guys are pretty bright," he grinned, "an' someways I don't feel sore about it. Well, you got me wher' you need. I don't guess I could put up a scrap worth callin' with a skippin' lamb. I'm to get right after mossbackin'. I'm goin' to run a binder, an' cut hay, an' cordwood. Gee! Me! I want to laff. But it's good, too. It surely is to a boy whose spent most of his time in the dark corners of the city, and only works overtime when there's no moonlight to worry with. I'm only lookin' fer shelter till the noise dies down. Then I'll beat it over the United States border. Meanwhile I'll chew those reg'lations good, an' put 'em through. I'm surely goin' to be a real peaceful mossback in this layout. Say——"

Jim waited. He wanted the man to talk. The psychology of the crook was a never-failing source of interest to him. The man flung out an arm, and the gesture was comprehensive.

"It kind of leaves me guessing, this," he declared, and his eyes took in the wide, single-storied house, and passed on to the remotenesses of the valley. "You boys ain't any religious bunch. You don't seem the kind of junk them queer folks who run fancy societies are made of. This gent here," he went on, indicating Larry, who was still standing, "looks the sort that belongs around a prize-ring. I've seen a deal worse'n him in a first-class sluggin' match." He chuckled in his throat. "I'd surely need all that knife, an' them guns, if I got up agin' him." He shook his bullet head. "No. It beats me. You ain't askin' dollars. Only work. An' you reckon to pay for that right. Well, what then? You got a swell ranch place. I've seen it in daylight. I guess it's a business proposition of sorts."

"Yes. It's a sheer business proposition, and needs to pay."

"Then why in hell get boys on the crook around to run it?"

The man's question came sharply. Jim smiled up into the furtive eyes.

"That's our business," he said. "Your concern is, it's a safe shelter just when you need one. You'll be up with the daylight and in your blankets before ten o'clock. And you'll be well paid for the work you do. You'll eat good, and just live the way you feel, and, after awhile, the air and work'll have cleaned out your vitals and made life seem good to you. For the rest, it doesn't matter to you. There's Despard waiting behind you. I'll say good-night."

Jack Pike glanced over his shoulder and discovered a burly white man standing immediately behind him. He had approached without a sound, and the stranger was unpleasantly startled at the vision. He looked into the man's face, studying him with suspicion uppermost. But he said no word. Then he turned back to the man at the table, and his eyes were full of unvoiced questioning. He glanced round at the silent vision of the red-headed Larry. Then he shrugged his shoulders.

"So long," he said curtly. And to the man behind him; "Lead the way, boy. This is the queerest joint I've lit on in years. But it don't matter."

CHAPTER XV
Brother and Sister

IT was a delightful apartment, lit by carefully-shaded lamps. It was furnished and draped with the inspiration of a cultured woman labouring under the difficulty of remoteness. The walls and ceiling were of polished red pine and the floor was of narrow-cut, polished hardwood. The whole scheme was clearly that of a woman's boudoir, with the reservation that men-folk would share in its comforts.

There was a characteristic display of carefully-selected bric-a-brac. The floor was carpeted with expensive rugs and skins. The chairs were well upholstered, covered, and flounced, low-seated vehicles of comfort, and there were two deep rockers capable of resting the bodies of large men. In one corner of the room stood a modern piano in an ebony case, and, in another, a specially designed wood-stove.

Brother and sister were seated before the latter, which was radiating a pleasant warmth in the chill of the mountain evening. They were alone. Larry was somewhere out on the ranch administering the discipline under which the enterprise was carried on, and of which his was the chief control. Blanche was engaged upon a piece of simple fancy-work. It was part of her evening habit.

Jim was lounging in the biggest rocker. He was smoking a large briar pipe which by no means seemed to fit with his surroundings. Then his feet were thrust up on the polished steel rail of the stove in an attitude of sheer comfort. His half-closed eyes were watching the movement of the girl's nimble fingers.

Blanche looked up, and surveyed the snow-white head.

"I guess you're tired, Jim," she said, with more than usual feeling. "You two boys never seem to get rest in this thing you're doing. You've been out in the hills all day, and——"

"I wouldn't have missed this day's work for a whole bunch of rest," Jim broke in, with a laugh of deep satisfaction. "It's been the best day since we came to this valley."

Blanche's interest quickened. And because of it she bent over her work again, and her needle laboured on.

"You were up at Dan's, weren't you?" she asked.

"Ye-es."

Jim thoughtfully pressed the charred tobacco down into the bowl of his pipe.

"How's Dan making out? And Cama and the kiddies?" Blanche laughed softly. "You know, I want to laugh every time I think of those dusky little creatures, with their beautiful mother, and that queer, crazy thing, their father. My, they're just sweet!" She sighed. "But they're half-breeds. And—and they'll grow up like all—half-breeds. It makes me more sorry than I can say."

Jim shook his head.

"Don't worry for them, Blanche," he said seriously. "Does it matter? They're plumb happy. They'll grow up men and women. Life'll be to them just what life is anyway. What more can they ask? It's we folk who're wrong, feeling the way we do about half-breeds. They're just as much an expression of Nature as we are, and anything else is. The world's no better or worse for their happening. I love those queer darn kiddies. I love 'em for themselves, and I love 'em for Dan's sake. And even Cama's. I wasn't thinking of them, though. Something like a miracle happened to-day. And, as usual, I want you to help me out."

The girl laughed.

"That's what I like to hear," she said contentedly.

"What? I want you to help me out?" Jim asked. "That's the way of it, isn't it? We men are all mighty clever. But I notice most all the time we're wanting some women to help us out. First it's our mothers. Then it's our sisters. Then, later, it's some other feller's sister. But I surely need your help right now. You know about Dan, who helped me in my bad time. You'll remember there was another boy who did all he knew for me. Marton—George Marton."

Blanche laid her work aside.

"Yes. I remember," she said. "You happened on him on his farm, and——"

Jim nodded.

"Hadn't a notion where I was," he said. "You see, I'd been wandering these hills more than haf dead."

"Yes." Blanche sighed. The terror of his story of that time still had power to affect her deeply.

"Well, that boy's dead. I'll never locate him now."

Blanche's gaze was searching.

"I seem to remember there was someone else there. He hadn't a wife. It was a daughter. She fixed some food for you."

"Which kept me alive more than a week."

"Yes. I remember."

"Well, his farm's about forty miles from here as the birds fly. It's down at the mouth of the valley where Dan's place is. Only he's twenty-five miles higher up in the hills. Since George Marton died his girl's alone on that farm with a choreman she calls Lightning. She's alone—running that farm to scratch a living. Do you get all that means? A young girl, as pretty as a picture. Then think of all I owe him—her."

"You've seen—her?"

Blanche's instinct stirred.

"Yes."

"Tell me of her."

Jim bestirred himself. He sat up, and leant forward in his rocker. His pipe had been removed from his mouth.

"She was down at a water-hole on the creek," he said, speaking deliberately, and with obvious appreciation. "She was riding a pinto pony. Sorrel and white. She was fixed in a riding-suit of brown, and rode astride her pony as dapper and neat a sight as you could wish for."

He paused. Then he drew a deep breath, which the girl interrupted in her own fashion.

"When she turned and I saw her face, say—— It was roundish, and tanned with the weather. It was fresh as the russet of a beautiful apple, and studded with a pair of big, grey, laughing eyes, all fringed with dark lashes. She had dark hair and—and—— My, Sis, she was just as elegant as a swell ripe peach. And that girl helped to save my life."

"And you talked with her?"

Blanche's interest had become consuming. Her eyes were alight with a smile. Here was the thing she had always looked forward to. In all the years of her life she never remembered to have listened to the glowing description of a girl from Jim.

Jim's eyes widened.

"Talked? I should say I did. I talked with her, and rode with her, and helped her round up her lost cows."

Then a deep note of concern crept into his voice.

"Say, Sis, she's poor and struggling. She's dead poor, and fighting a battle only fit for a strong man. She didn't say it. No.

She's grit. But I could see it. It was lying back of all she said. I want to help her. I want you to help me help her. Say, that girl's life's got to be made easy. And—and I'm going to make it that way."

Blanche laughed softly. She was sitting with her hands clasped in her lap. Never in her life had she enjoyed herself as she was enjoying herself now. A little tender raillery shone in the eyes that were gazing so affectionately upon her brother.

"You're going to do more than that, Jim," she cried triumphantly. "If I know you, I know what your help means. You've fallen for this 'prairie flower'—or should I say 'mountain flower'? You're going to marry her." She shook her head as the man's eyes widened at her challenge. "It's no use, boy. You can't deceive me. I—I know the signs too well."

Jim laughed a little self-consciously.

"Can you beat it?" he inquired, appealing to the stove. "Isn't that a woman all over? Tell her of a girl, another girl; show her you're interested, and mighty grateful, and want to help her; and right away you're plumb in love, and mean to marry her. Say!"

"Deny it, boy," Blanche cried teasingly. "Deny it, and I'll believe you."

Jim shook his head, and refilled and lit his pipe.

"I'll deny nothing, Sis. I won't hand you that satisfaction. But you're going to tell me right here and now that you'll help me to help Molly Marton."

"Molly Marton? So that's her name." Blanche laughed again. "Oh, I'll get all the story directly. Molly. I like the name." Then, quite suddenly, her teasing passed and her eyes sobered.

"Jim, dear, there's not a thing in the world I wouldn't do to help pass you the happiness you deserve. Molly Marton shall get all the friendliness I know how to show her. And if she's the girl you reckon her to be, I shan't regret a thing of our time in these hills. Say, this is the most exciting thing I've known in years. Help? You've only got to start me right. Just tell me the thing you need me to do. And I'll do it—to the limit."

Jim smiled and glanced around as the door opened to admit the red-headed figure of Larry Manford. Then his eyes came back to the girl who had risen to welcome the late-comer.

"I knew you would, Blanche. Thanks."

CHAPTER XVI
Two Women

IT was a well-sheltered patch of ploughing. To the south a fringe of woodland bounded it. Then came a narrow opening. And then again, on the eastern side, a wooded hill rose up to protect it from the bitter east and north-east. To the north stood an extensive stretch of tamarack and pine woods, beyond which lay the farm, while its western boundary was formed by the creek which watered the farm. There were approximately two hundred acres of open, and the last of the ploughing had just been harrowed down.

Lightning stood beside his team gazing over his completed work. The man's fringe of whisker was thrust aggressively. His eyes were unsmiling. His gnarled, brown hands were thrust in the top of his soil-stained trousers.

He was regarding his work with a curious contempt. It was the contempt of the cattleman for the industry of the simple farmer. He was nursing his memories of past glories, when his skill with both rope and gun, and in the saddle, were bywords with the men who were as ready to fight as drink themselves to death. How he regretted those wonderful days!

Blue Pete flung up his fiddle head, and Jane was gazing out to the south-west. Lightning spoke a sharp word in the harsh tone the beasts knew so well. And the break in his thought brought him back to the meaning of the things about him.

Oh, yes. Those days were past, and he had no real right to complain. They were days of irresponsibility. Now it was all different. Responsibility was with him, and something more. He knew that. And he was glad. He regretted the cattle days, but his work now was for Molly. And Molly needed all the help he could give her.

For all she had returned home the night before with the lost cows he still retained his obstinate conviction that there were cattle thieves about. Who was the white-haired man she had told him she had met? The man had learned all the information she had to supply, and had given her in return no inkling of whence he came, or his business in the hills, or even of his name.

Then she had told him the man was riding a coal-black horse from the race-tracks of Kentucky. That sort of thing was by no means new to him. Every cattle thief prided himself on his horse-flesh. Doubtless the horse had been stolen. Then his city clothes. That was sheer bluff, only to deceive a simpleton. Disguised as a city man! Why, it was a game that was a good deal older than he was.

No. The facts remained. She was surrounded on the one hand by a bunch of cattle thieves who were located around Dan Quinlan's, and on the other lay the threat of a good-looker bad lot, who had somehow contrived to dazzle her innocent mind. She certainly needed all the help he could give her.

He made a sound in his throat like a chuckle. He felt he had by no means done badly by Mister Andy McFardell. He had sown the ground well, he felt. Set him after the cattle-thieving bunch up at Dan Quinlan's, get him playing the police game which belonged to him, with the prospect of getting back into the Force as a result. The thing would get right hold of him, and, if it succeeded, it might well rid the neighbourhood of his detested presence. Then Molly would forget him.

But would she? Women were queer. He remembered Sadie Long, who once chased him half-way across the States. Anyway——

His reflections were interrupted, and he thrust up a hand to push the loose brim of his hat clear from his eyes. His startled gaze was fixed on the approach of a horseman on a big, raking sorrel. He was emerging from a gap in the bush lining the bank of the creek, which he had apparently only just crossed. In his quick way Lightning also realised that the horseman must have come from somewhere out of the south-west. Maybe from—Dan Quinlan's!

But as the horse came on an ejaculation of surprise broke from him. It was not a horseman at all. The rider was a woman! A woman clad in city clothing, and riding on a man's saddle, with the horn and leggaderos and stirrups which he recognised at once as of Californian make!

Blanche Pryse reined up sharply. And her greeting came with a disarming smile. Lightning's hat was torn from his head, to reveal the shock of grey hair which looked never to have known the use of a comb.

"I'm looking for some place I can get feed for my horse," Blanche cried, "and a bite of something to eat for myself. You see, I came further than I ought, and—and got rather mazed up with the hills around here. I saw you with your team, and reckoned you must have a homestead near abouts."

Lightning's grinning face was transparently reassuring. Had the stranger been a man, there would have been a difference. He cleared his throat, and, out of respect for a woman who was obviously a lady, and a stranger, he spat out his chew of tobacco, and trod the result underfoot.

"I'm real glad you come along, ma'am," he said cordially. "You surely hev come to the right place fer feed. The barn's back o' them woods," he added, pointing in a northerly direction. "An' Molly gal's right to home, an'll feel good if you'll eat with her. I'm just quittin' fer feed myself, an' making home, an' I'll be mighty pleased to give you a lead."

Lightning's effort was in his best manner, for he was gazing up into a face which, even to his suspicious mind, could have no association with cattle thieves.

"Why, that's real kind of you, and—and I'm very grateful."

Blanche gazed interestedly down upon the tall creature. She knew him at once. There could be no mistake. This was the Marton farm. So this queer, grey-whiskered creature must be "Lightning" she had been told about. The man impressed her. There was something tremendously purposeful in the hard lines of his weather-beaten face. There was something compelling in his eyes, and in the aquilinity of his nose. Then there were his old guns on the belt at his waist. He was startlingly picturesque.

"You're the owner of this farm?" Blanche suggested shrewdly.

"Hired man, ma'am."

"Oh. Then Molly's not your daughter?"

Lightning shook his head, and his gaze wandered regretfully towards the farm.

"Can't just say she is, ma'am," he said. "I work for her. She hires me. But if you'll kindly foller right along I'll lead the way to the farm, where Molly gal'll be right glad to welcome you."

* * * *

Molly saw Lightning and the stranger approach from the doorway of the house. She was washing out some garments, revelling in the wonderful spring sunshine. There were already a number of articles drying on the near-by bushes, and the iron bath, over which she was standing, was a-froth with a lather of soap-suds.

She left her work at once and came down to the barn. The impulse was irresistible. The sleeves of her shirt-waist were rolled up, displaying a pair of beautifully rounded arms, and a linen sun-bonnet enveloped her neat, dark head.

Curiosity and amazement were struggling for place in her mind. Even at a distance she had recognised the stranger was a woman. Then, too, her horse was so different from the bronchos she was accustomed to. And instantly her thoughts flung back to the white-haired, city-clad man on his black thoroughbred. Could this woman by any chance be connected with Silver-Thatch? It must be. Where else could she have come from?

Her eyes were full of the questions in her mind as she gazed into the stranger's face.

"Howdy."

A curious awkwardness had taken possession of Molly. She wanted to say something cordial. But, strangely enough, the best she was capable of at the moment was a simple, almost meaning-less "Howdy."

A mental reservation warned Blanche that Jim's description of Molly Marton had by no means been a man's exaggeration. The sweet, shy face gazing out of the sun-bonnet at her struck her as a picture such as she had never before beheld.

"I'm just dying to eat, and so is Pedro," she said with a laugh, patting her horse. "You're Molly Marton. He told me your name," she went on, indicating Lightning still waiting in the background. "Mine's Pryse—Blanche Pryse—and I guess I've ridden farther than I ought. May I off-saddle?"

Molly thrust out a brown hand. She felt that the girl's introduction demanded it. And, in a moment, it was clasped in the two gauntleted palms with which Blanche took possession of it.

"Why, surely," Molly cried, all her shyness suddenly swept away before the frank manner of the city woman. "But you don't need——"

She broke off. Lightning was already at the cinchas of Pedro's saddle. In a moment the saddle was on the ground, while the old man passed an appreciative hand over the creature's back.

"That's a rare bit o' hossflesh, ma'am," he commented shrewdly, as Blanche turned about to him. "He's the bellows of a forge. Legs? Gee! They're elegant, an' as clean as young saplings.

That plug can beat a hell of a gait, or I ain't wise. Look at them pasterns. An' he's ribbed, too. Short-backed an' ribbed to his quarters. You could ride the prairie all day an' night fer a week, an' he wouldn't blow a lucifer out when you're through."

Molly laughed quietly.

"He'll hand out that stuff all day if you listen to Lightning," she said. "There's just one thing he's crazy about. Don't worry for your Pedro. Lightning'll treat him like a babe. Will you come right up to the house? Food's most ready. There's nothing fancy. The beans are right, an' there's good dry hash. But it's not too bad if you feel like eating."

All the warmth her greeting had lacked was in Molly's invitation. And Blanche stepped towards her, and linked an arm under the girl's, and let her fingers clasp themselves on the forearm which the rolled sleeves left bare.

"My dear," she cried, as they moved off together, "you don't need to worry a thing. Food's food. And the food that's filled out your pretty cheeks, and built up the swell muscles of this arm, is more than good enough for a woman like me. Laundering?"

Molly nodded. A sudden feeling of interest and liking for Blanche was already stirring. The way she had of saying things was quite irresistible.

"Yes," she said. "I've been at the wash most all morning."

Blanche laughed happily.

"You know, I'm crazy over a wash-day. It's been that way always. Why, when I lived home in New York City there were times when you just couldn't take a bath for the laundry I'd got drying in the bathroom. My brothers used to get mad, and bundle things out of the way, and hide them. There isn't a week goes by but I have an elegant laundry."

Molly laughed.

"Now?" she cried, eyeing the quality of the girl's riding-suit. Then she raised her other hand and touched the fingers clasped about her arm. There were rings on them containing beautiful stones. The fingers were tapering, and carefully manicured, and she felt ashamed of the roughness of her own beside them. "With these hands?" she asked incredulously.

Blanche released the girl's arm and spread out her hand, palm upwards. For all their condition of care there were lines indicating utility in them.

"Surely. And they're strong, too. Nearly as strong as yours. Oh, yes. I never let them get afraid of work."

Molly sighed.

"They're real beautiful," she said. "Oh, I'd just love my hands to be like yours. But they aren't, an' never will be. You can't plough, an' milk, an' fork hay, an' do the chores of the farm, an' keep swell hands. But, my," she went on, with a little firm setting of her lips, "it doesn't matter. Those things don't really matter, do they? You've got to make good in these hills, and you can't do that right without using the hands God gave you." She laughed a little self-consciously. "You know, I never used to think about hands, and feet, and pretty fixings. I can't think why I do now."

They were nearing the house, which Blanche was regarding interestedly. But now she turned, and her eyes contained all the twinkling humour of her brother's.

"When a girl suddenly gets worried about those things she hadn't bothered with before there's mostly—a beau around," she said slily.

Molly half halted, and turned her startled eyes upon her companion.

"How—how? I never thought that way. I——"

"Then there is a beau?"

Molly linked her arm through the other's again and squeezed it.

"I—I like you, ma'am," she cried impulsively. "But," she added, with a note of real regret, "you don't belong around here."

* * * *

Blanche was lounging in the old frame rocker, with its rawhide seat, which, years ago, George Marton had designed for his own comfort. It was capacious beyond her needs, for all she was tall and of shapely proportions. Molly had insisted. She had set Blanche there while she went about her business preparing the meal which stood ready on the cook-stove. Molly was happy. A sense of delight in this woman's presence thrilled her. And she chattered and laughed as she went about her preparations, with a light-heartedness that entirely captivated the other.

Ordinarily Lightning would have shared the meal with the girl. But, in the circumstances, Molly knew the old man would not put in an appearance if he waited for his food till the evening supper. The cattleman had definite notions about eating as he had about most things. He disliked the observation of strangers. Perhaps he realised that years of bunk-house life had by no means added to his limited stock of table manners. And Molly was re-

111

lieved and glad.

Blanche surveyed the simple furnishings of Molly's living-room, and sought to learn something of the girl from her surroundings. It was Molly she had come to see. And for the moment nothing and nobody else mattered.

The smell of cooking was appetising. The sight of a boiling kettle on the stove, and the warming teapot beside it, were a positive joy to Blanche. And, rocking herself leisurely, and listening to the girl's chatter, she contemplated the thing she had yet to do. She knew that in a few moments she must resort to subterfuge. It was worse than that. It was downright lying. And to her frank nature it was an outrage. The more so that the victim of it was a girl of such transparent simplicity. But it could not be helped.

Molly had passed over to the stove to ladle out the hash and beans into the hot dish prepared for them.

"You haven't asked me yet where I come from, Molly," Blanche said gently. "Maybe you're not interested. Is that so?"

Molly turned hastily. She wondered if she had displeased.

"I surely am interested," she protested. Then the colour mounted to her cheeks. "I just didn't feel I'd a right to ask. You hadn't said."

Blanche experienced a further feeling of contrition. But she smiled and shook her head.

"Say," she cried, "if I lived around this farm I shouldn't have such scruples. I'd be scared to death of strange faces. I certainly should. Do you know, Molly, I should always have a gun tucked somewhere handy in my skirts. And when a strange face got peeking around I should 'draw' quick. It would be 'Name!' right away. 'Where from?' and 'Why?' Now, if you'd acted that way to me I should have told you my piece like answers to a catechism. I'd have told you I was stopping around on a visit to friends the other side of Hartspool. That I was on a holiday trip from New York, my home city, and a place I get sick to death of, and am ready to quit most any time. I should have said I had all the things a woman mostly needs except a husband, and that these hills are so fascinating I don't even worry about that. That I've been riding around gawking like a personally conducted tour, and didn't guess how far I'd come till I got yearning for dry hash and those beans you're fixing for us. Doesn't it all sound dreadful? I just can't keep my thoughts from food. But there it is, and I guess it's mostly human."

Molly joined in the laugh with which Blanche finished up,

while her eyes twinkled slily.

"I knew you weren't married," she said.

Blanche noted the prim pursing of her lips.

"How did you know that?" she humoured her.

Molly set her dishes on the immaculate table, and glanced over it to see that everything had been provided for.

"Guess ther' isn't a wedding-ring on your left hand," she smiled triumphantly. "Only beautiful, beautiful diamonds."

"Well, say! Did you guess anything else?"

Molly set the chairs ready, and stood grasping the back of one of them. Just for a moment there was hesitation.

"I—I thought someway you belonged to—to Silver-Thatch," she said.

"Silver-Thatch? Who's Silver-Thatch?"

Molly laughed at the look of surprise she beheld in the other's eyes.

"Oh, it's just my fancy," she said. "The name, I mean. You see, he didn't hand me his name, an' I felt mean about it. So I called him 'Silver-Thatch' to myself, just to punish him."

Blanche stood up. Her eyes were smiling very softly.

"You queer child!" she said. "Tell me about him."

"Oh, it's just nothing. I was out after my fool cows yesterday. They'd strayed, and Lightning guessed the cattle thieves had them. I was at a water-hole along the creek, away up towards Dan Quinlan's. While I was there a man came to water his horse. He looked like a city man, an' he'd a gold watch-chain, an' a check coat and vest, an' riding-pants, an' boots, and—and the whitest hair you've ever seen. It was just too lovely. And he'd blue eyes that—that smiled like yours. Well, he rode a piece with me, and when I'd located the cows he passed me a hand rounding them up. And—and then he quit up into the hills westward. And then I remembered I'd handed out my talk to him like a fool kid, and he just hadn't said a thing of himself. So—so I got mad to myself and called him 'Silver-Thatch.' But he didn't know."

Blanche took her seat at the table, and her eyes regarded the meal set ready.

"Silver-Thatch," she said. "It's—a pretty name. Why, Molly," she laughed, "I guess your notion of punishment would have delighted him."

"Oh, it wouldn't if he'd known how mad I was with myself."

Molly helped her guest with a lavish hand. And Blanche set to work with a will to reduce her overflowing plate. She felt it was no moment for protest. She had no desire to upset this girl's ideas of hospitality. Besides, she was really hungry.

For some moments the two ate in silence. Then Molly poured out tea, and her eagerness would no longer be denied.

"You're the first girl I've seen sitting at this table, ma'am," she said, as she passed a cup to Blanche, and set milk and sugar near to her hand.

Blanche looked up.

"My name's Blanche," she said.

Molly blushed.

"It seems queer saying 'Blanche' to you."

"But you must. I called you 'Molly' right away."

"But it's diff'rent."

"Is it?" Blanche shook her head. "It isn't. You and I are going to be friends. Good friends. I shall certainly be around all summer, and maybe longer. And I'm going to see you whenever I can. So I'm 'Blanche' to you, and only the other to folks I don't know and don't care about."

Molly's eyes lit with delight.

"You're goin' to be around all summer—Blanche?"

"I certainly am—Molly."

Both laughed happily, and Molly went on:

"Then maybe you'll be at the swell farmers' dance in Hartspool?"

"Dance? What dance? I—hadn't heard."

"Why, it's the annual dance," Molly cried, with a little dash of awe. "It's—it's awful swell. Folks come in from all around to it. They have a big supper—a real sit-down supper, with ice-creams, and—and everything. I'm going to it. I—I made up my mind yesterday. Oh, I do hope you'll go. My, you'd be the belle of the ball. You just would."

Blanche shook her head.

"Not with Molly Marton there," she said. Again she saw the colour mount to the girl's cheeks. "But it's a long way for you. What is it? Twenty miles?"

Molly had finished eating, and sat with elbows on the table. She was gazing out of the window, through which the noon sun poured on to the whiteness of the cotton tablecloth. A surge of excitement was driving through her young body. She was thinking of Andy McFardell, and an irresistible desire was urging her to tell this wonderful new friend the story of the thing that had just come into her life. She yielded to the impulse. She flung discretion to the winds. She—she must tell someone. And Lightning, the only other person, was denied her by reason of his hatred of Andy.

"I'm not going alone," she said quickly. "I'm—I'm——"

She broke off in confusion, and Blanche urged her gently. "Yes?"

"Andy's promised to take me. He'll drive me in, and drive me out again. He's——"

"Yes?"

There was no smile in Blanche's eyes now. They were urgent, and something of their calm had gone. She was thinking of Jim. She was thinking of the possible meaning of this man, Andy, who-ever he was, driving Molly into the dance.

But just on the brink Molly drew back. That which she had been about to say remained unspoken. Instead she laughed.

"Oh, Andy's a neighbour. He's ten miles down the creek on Whale River. He's only just started his homestead about two years. He's a great worker, and he'll make good. You know, Blanche, the boy who's got the grit to start right up on bare ground, without capital, an' make good farming, gets all my no-tions of a man. Think of it. These hills. The awful, awful winter. It's us folk know what it means. You don't; you're a visitor. My it's—it's just ter'ble."

The girl's effort at concealment was sheer revelation.

"I must try and get to that dance," Blanche said, avoiding the subject of the man deliberately. "I'd just love to see you all fixed up in your party frock. What'll it be? Let's see, you're dark. And those grey eyes of yours. You mustn't wear white. It's too ordi-nary for you. Pink? No," she went on critically. "It mustn't be dark, either. I should rather think the palest of pale blue. You can't go wrong that way. Say, have you a nice frock?"

Molly's face was a study. While Blanche was talking it passed from happy laughter to the gravest trouble. And as the older woman put her final question she shook her head almost deject-edly.

"I've never been to a—real party," she said.

"No. You live so far away from a town."

"Oh, it wasn't that. You see, father didn't just think dancin' was right. An' then there was always the farm. Mother died when I was a small kid. But I got my Sunday suit," she added, bright-ening. "Maybe that would be too heavy, though. It's black, and it isn't a party frock. Then I thought of a skirt and a waist. I could

115

fix up a waist. I got one that's real silk. Only that's black, too."

A thrill of intense pity flooded Blanche's heart. To her the pathos of the thing she was listening to was beyond words. Their meal was finished. They were only sitting over their tea. Suddenly she stood up, and a joyous smile lit her eyes.

"Here, Molly," she cried, "stand up, and let's measure. I believe we're the same height."

The girl obeyed her with a wondering smile. They stood back to back, and Blanche measured with her hand.

"Exactly," she cried. Then she turned and studied the girl for some critical moments. "Yes, and just about the same build. Here," she hurried on, "put your foot against mine. That's it."

"Sure, sure," Blanche exclaimed, as the two feet came into contact. "My shoes will fit you, too. Oh, this is bully. My word, but you shall be the belle of that farmers' ball, I promise you. Sit down, my dear, and I'll tell you about it."

Blanche sat again, and they gazed across the table at each other. Molly was all smiling hope and expectation, and Blanche was happy in the opportunity which chance had afforded her.

"Listen, Molly. I've got the sweetest forget-me-not blue dance frock you've ever dreamed about," she cried impressively. "It's just the latest thing, made by a swell New York house. I've—never even worn it. I got shoes to match, and lovely, lovely silk stockings that'll set all the other women crazy with envy. My, you'll just look sweet in it. And then I've a beautiful fur-lined wrap. You can wear that on your journey, under a coat. Now, when's the dance?"

"Why soon—very soon. When seeding's through. But——"

Blanche was in no mood to listen to any protest. She had come to see Molly because Jim had asked her. The thing she had in mind now was out of her own impulsive liking for the girl herself.

"It's useless, my dear," she laughed. "My mind's quite made up. You're going to the dance in that frock, if I have to come and dress you myself."

The light in Molly's eyes was ecstatic.

"But—but if I muss it?" she cried, in sudden alarm.

"Muss it? Why, you dear, simple child, that's right up to you. It's a—a present, silk stockings, and shoes, and wrap, and all—with my best love."

* * * *

Lightning and Molly were standing together down by the

116

barn. The door stood wide open. Blanche had just ridden off on her Pedro. The old man was observing the creature's gait with all the admiration of a real horseman. The rider interested him far less.

Molly, too, was gazing after the departing visitor. But the horse held none of her interest. She was thinking of Blanche. She was contemplating again those smiling eyes. And a great joy was surging in her heart. The whole thing seemed to her like some fairy-story, or some happy dream from which she would surely wake up.

She drew a profound sigh, and Lightning promptly withdrew his fascinated gaze from the departing horse.

"Ther' ain't nothing better'n the whole darn world than them four legs, an' a bar'l like that," he said. "That plug's worth fi' thousand dollars."

Molly's smile searched the old man's eyes.

"An' the girl on its back's worth—a million," she said decidedly.

Lightning spat.

"She's surely an upstander," he admitted. "But she ain't a circumstance beside her plug. I ain't ever seen a human that could be. Ther' ain't nothin' better. Not in the world."

He spat again to emphasise his opinion.

"I know something better."

The girl's eyes were dancing with delight. She was dying to proclaim her good fortune and happiness to all the world. As nothing better was to hand, Lightning would serve.

"She's going to hand me a present of a swell gown, an' real silk stockings, an' shoes, an'—an' a fur-lined cloak. It's for the dance. An' she says I'll be the belle of the whole ball."

"Dance? What dance?"

"Why, the farmers' ball in Hartspool."

The old man's face was a study. His expression passed from astonishment and incredulity to frank contempt and disapproval.

"Ball? Say, Molly, gal, you ain't goin' to that bum hoe-down?" he cried almost desperately.

Molly's eyes widened with resentment at the man's contemptuous tone.

"It's not a hoe-down," she cried hotly. "It's—it's a swell ball, an' you know it. Sure I'm going to it. And the suit's forget-me-not blue, and the stockings are real silk—to match."

Quite suddenly the eyes of the old man hardened fiercely.

"How you goin'?" he demanded almost roughly.

Perhaps it was the tone. Molly was looking straight into the eyes of her loyal old friend, and a spirit of mischief prompted her.

"Why, Andy McFardell's going to take me. He's getting tickets."

There was a moment of deathly silence. Then Lightning thrust a gnarled forefinger into his mouth and hooked the chew of tobacco out of his cheek. He flung it on the ground and trod it underfoot. Then he hunched his shoulders and turned away.

In an instant contrition swept through Molly's heart.

"You haven't eaten, Lightning," she said gently.

The old man paused and glanced round.

"Eaten?" he echoed. Then he shook his head. "No, Molly, gal," he said almost dejectedly. "Guess I don't feel like eatin'—now."

CHAPTER XVII
A Golden Moment

ANDY McFARDELL'S drift was infinitely more rapid than appeared. The current of indolence was strong in him, and, to
a nature such as his, it was irresistible. Since the day of the visit
of Molly Marton to his homestead, and, later, the infinitely less
welcome visit of Lightning, not another rod of seeding had been
done, in spite of the week of perfect weather that had passed over
his head.

The simple truth was that Andy McFardell belonged to a type
to which discipline is an essential, to which it is sheer salvation. Robbed of the iron rule of the Mounted Police the man had
quickly degenerated to the condition of a storm driven, rudder-
less, derelict. Inclination swayed him like the yielding grass on a
wind-swept plain. The sturdy resistance of the forest tree was impossible to him. His moods impelled, and he drifted before them.

The drift had set for sheer and growing indolence where his
farm was concerned. The fierce enthusiasm which had first supported him, had died out like the fitful blaze of an unfed camp-
fire. And with its passing only the ashes of all that was best in him
remained behind.

Two purposes dominated him entirely just now. The one was
the thing which the shrewd mind of Lightning had suggested. And
the other was the storm of passion which Molly Marton had set
stirring in his selfish soul.

Molly's visit had served him with further excuse. It had served
him with another three days of respite from the work of his farm;
with another three days of Barney Lake's hotel at Hartspool; another three days of the allurements of its poker game and Rye
whisky. He had forthwith ridden into the township to obtain the
tickets necessary for the farmers' dance.

On his return home there was not the smallest pretence of
making up his leeway of neglected work. He was glad enough to
continue his drift. He had obtained the tickets. He must forthwith

convey the news to Molly and obtain her definite reassurance that she would let him take her to the dance.

He found Molly in her hay corral. She was at work in sun-bonnet and cotton overall, clearing the ground with rake and fork, and making ready for the new cut of hay, which operation was the next in the routine of the year's labours.

He had ridden hard. And when he drew rein at the corral fence the horse under him was pretty badly tuckered. It was caked with sweat and dust on the matted remains of its thick winter coat, and looked generally the mean thing that McFardell's neglect had reduced it to.

Had the rider been any other, the smiling eyes under the girl's sun-bonnet would have been full of serious condemnation. But with Andy McFardell's coming the girl's heart was beating high. She was concerned only with the portent of his visit, and thinking of the wonderful secret which lay between her and that kindly, generous, stranger-woman, Blanche.

"Why, Andy," she cried. "I just hadn't a notion you'd get along so soon. Is—is it all—fixed? The dance, I mean? You—you got the tickets?"

The man laughed as he slid out of the saddle. Molly was all eagerness.

"Doesn't that beat it?" he cried, in mock amazement. "Say, I've ridden hell-for-leather, worried to death guessing. You see, I'd paid for two tickets and hadn't definite word from you I was to take you along in to that dance."

He laughingly threw up his hands, and Molly came to the corral rail and rested her folded arms upon it. She was more than content.

Andy was good enough for any woman to gaze upon. In the saddle he had none of the horsemanship of Lightning, in spite of the latter's sixty years. But he had the military seat of the Police. He was clad in a loose cotton shirt, with sleeves rolled above the elbows. His breeches were the uniform breeches of the Police, with the yellow stripe removed, and they fitted closely over his sturdy limbs. His top boots, too, belonged to his police days. So, too, the heavy, rusted steel spurs upon his heels.

But it was neither his clothing, nor his horsemanship which concerned Molly at that moment. It was his good-looking face, the sturdy breadth of his shoulders, and the fine muscles of his arms which stirred her simple heart so deeply.

She ducked under the rail and came to him.

"Why," she laughed slily, "my mind was fixed directly I quit you."

Andy shook his head.

"But not before. You left me guessing," he said reproachfully. Then he glanced swiftly about him. "Where's Lightning?"

Never in her life had laughter more impelled Molly. She felt somehow she wanted to laugh all the time.

"Out on the ploughing," she cried. "He's breaking a new five acres."

Andy pulled an envelope from the pocket of his shirt. He opened it and drew out the contents. And the while he was watching the play of interest and expectancy on the girl's expressive face. He passed her the gaudily got up tickets, and waited while she read down the letter press.

"Fi' dollars!" she breathed in consternation, as she came to the price of the ticket. Then she looked up incredulously. "You paid fi' dollars for each? Fi' dollars for—me? Oh, Andy!"

The man laughed.

"Why not?" he cried, a hot light leaping into his eyes. "I'd do more than that any day. I'd hand out everything, if it left me without a cent in the world—for you. You see, little girl, I want to hand you a real swell time. Dancing don't mean a lot to me. With a girl it's surely diff'rent. Say, Molly, you just don't know the thing you've been to me around these hills. I'd never have got through or made good without you. Say——"

The man's words had come quickly. His tone rang with a sincerity which, at the moment, was completely real. And as he made a sudden movement towards her, a movement which there could be no mistaking, the passion in his dark eyes was an expression of the stirring of his whole manhood.

The girl stood like some simple, defenceless, fascinated creature. And only a wealth of rich colour dyed the soft roundness of her cheeks, and a shy responsive gladness lit her big eyes. Coquetry was impossible to her. So, too, was any girlish, unmeant denial. The passion of love she had nursed ever since her great realisation well-nigh suffocated her. It completely robbed her of all power for connected thought and speech.

For Molly the next few moments were filled with a wild rush of confused emotions, and unutterable happiness. It seemed to her that life could never again afford her a moment of delight comparable with that through which she was passing. She hardly knew; she certainly did not pause to think. For one wild moment she was caught and tightly held in the arms which had never failed to stir her admiration. She seemed to feel, in the delirium of it all, the strong beating of the man's heart against hers. Then came those kisses upon her lips, her cheeks, her eyes, her forehead. And as she abandoned herself to them her young heart was driving fiercely to make return.

Then—then—it was over. She had released herself, and she knew not how or why. Her returning senses revealed to her his passion-lit eyes gazing down into hers. Her bosom was heaving in a tumult of emotion, and every limb of her body was a-shake. But happiness, supreme happiness that was well-nigh exaltation, thrilled her. Life seemed at the very pinnacle of its amazing beauty.

In that brief, delirious moment of spiritual expression Molly's whole world had somehow become transfigured. Everything was changed. Her whole life had changed out of the even, unemotional calm she had hitherto known. It seemed as if a great new light were shining somewhere deep down in her soul, diffusing wonderful rays to the uttermost extremities of her being, lighting a path of unspeakable joy down the channels of her senses. The golden sunlight of the day about her had intensified. It had become doubly brilliant and more full of meaning. The old homestead, so full of the calm beauty of her childhood's sheltered happiness, the very trees and hills about it, all these, everything, had doubled the depth of their concern for her innocent mind.

Then the man with his passionate eyes, his strong arms, and sturdy body. He, too, had shared in the transformation. No longer was he the struggling object of her girlish pity; no longer was he a creature who had played the cruel rôle of fortune's shuttle-cock. All that was wiped out. It was all brushed away by the gilded artistry that had re-adorned her vision of life. He was the golden superman of her soul, crowned with the sublime halo of her young love.

They both stood speechless. Then at last it was the man who broke the silence.

"You—aren't mad with me, Molly?" he asked, still holding her by the hands that were so soft and warm in his. But his tone was without the doubt his words implied, and his smile was full of confidence.

Molly shook her head. Then she released her hands which moved in a queer little gesture that told so much.

"Oh, Andy!" she cried. And the exclamation seemed to set

loose the tide of her surging feelings. "Mad with—you? You? Oh, no. How could I be? I—I love you, Andy. Why," she added with innocently widening eyes, "I guess I've loved you right along always, just always."

The man's gaze had been averted as though something of the girl's innocence abashed him. But in a moment it came back swiftly, hotly. His hands were flung out, and he caught Molly up again in his arms. He held her crushed closely to him, and talked between the kisses which he rained upon her up-turned face.

"I just know, little girl," he cried thickly. "I surely know it all. I been through it. It's been the same here, right from the first, when you happened along with me opening out my clearing. I haven't ever been able to forget. I didn't want to anyway. I——"

He broke off in a fashion that startled the girl in his arms. And a sudden twinge of alarm shot through her senses. She looked up into the face she loved, and realised that the whole expression of it had changed. The eyes were cold and hard, and they were searching the distant bluff round which the grass-trail to the ploughing skirted.

It required no second thought to tell her the meaning of the change. Besides, there was a sound upon the warm air, the sound of the rattle of chain harness and plodding hoofs.

"It's Lightning," she said, recovering herself.

Andy's arms fell from about her. And together they stood searching the bluff. Presently they beheld Jane and Blue Pete appear from amongst the tree-trunks. And Jane's capacious back was bearing the grotesque burden of the old choreman with his guns. He was sitting sideways on her vast expanse of rounded breadth, and his heavily-booted feet were dangling.

Molly spoke quickly, anxiously.

"It's just dinner, Andy," she said. "You'll stop around an' eat?"

She knew Lightning's antagonism, and she wanted to make sure before the old man came up.

But Andy shook his head unsmilingly.

"I just can't stop around, little kid," he said quietly, his eyes still on the team with its queer burden.

"Why?"

Molly was disappointed, and her disappointment found expression in her monosyllable.

Andy shrugged. Then he moved over to his horse and busied himself at the cinchas of his "condemned" police saddle. He spoke over his shoulder.

"No, sweetheart," he said quietly, but decidedly. "It's no use. I got to get right back to work. If I stop around to eat the day'll be gone before I make home, and ther's the—seeding. Besides——"

"Yes?"

Andy indicated the choreman who was crossing the open towards them. Then, quite abruptly, he turned from his saddle and held out his hand in farewell. He was smiling, and his smile told Molly that his action was for the benefit of the man who was observing them as he came.

"No," he said, in a tone intended for Lightning's ears. "I won't stop around to eat. You see, I just got along to fix things with you, and tell you I'd got the tickets for the dance. There's a week. Just a week for you to fix your party frock in. You'll fix it good, eh?" he laughed. "You see, we hill folks need to show the town dames. I fancy you being a real show-up to 'em."

He had swung into the saddle, and Molly laughed happily. He had said the one thing that gave her the opportunity she needed. In spite of her feelings and emotions of the moment the memory of Blanche's visit, Blanche, with wonderful generosity for all she was a stranger, still stood out in her mind a matter of tremendous moment. Her femininity was abounding. Nothing in the world, it seemed, was left that could add one tittle to her happiness.

Her eyes were dancing as Lightning came up, and the great team halted of its own accord. The old man remained where he was on the mare's back, while some form of greeting passed between the home team and the stranger. He barely even responded to Andy's nod of greeting.

"Don't worry, boy," Molly cried airily. "I'll sure be fixed right. I'll be wearing a swell gown. I certainly will. When's the day?"

Lightning spat out a chew, and took a fresh bite at a fragment of plug he drew from his hip pocket. But his hard old eyes remained fixed on the other man's face as though he were reading him down to the depths of his very soul. He uttered no word. Not a single word.

"Thursday. I'll be along with the spring wagon."

Lightning's jaws chewed harder as Andy made his reply. There was not the flicker of an eyelid to indicate that which was passing behind his stony regard.

Molly was becoming uneasy at the old man's silence. She wanted to force him into speech. But she refrained, fearing the result.

"So long, Molly."

Andy raised a hand in salutation, and his horse stirred as he lifted his reins. "Thursday—sure."

Molly gazed smilingly up into the man's face under the cold gaze of the silent Lightning.

"Thursday—sure," she responded. "So long, Andy."

The horse moved off, and Andy McFardell glanced round at the choreman.

"So long, Lightning. I'm going after that matter—after Thursday."

But the old man still made no reply. He sat there on his old mare's back stolidly intent and watchful. His unfriendliness was adamant. And Molly became completely alarmed.

Andy rode off. His way took him up past the barn, and he disappeared beyond it, round the lean-to workshop, and headed eastwards for his home.

The moment he had passed out of view Molly turned on Lightning who had slid down from Jane's broad back. A flush dyed her pretty cheeks, and an angry sparkle lit her eyes.

"I—I won't stand for it, Lightning!" she cried, stamping her foot on the hard, dusty ground. "It's mean. It's so mean I can't believe it. He's been right into Hartspool and paid five dollars for my ticket. He's paid that for me! Just to hand me a swell time. I——"

"Don't 'ee do it, Molly, gal. Just don't 'ee do it."

Lightning was transformed. All the stony light of his eyes had changed to one of humble pleading as he stood before the child he loved better than life itself. His lean face seemed suddenly to have become more deeply lined, and his tatter of whisker looked more than usually grotesque and pathetic. His hands were outheld in appeal.

"Fer the love o' yer dead father, Molly, don't 'ee go fer to do it," he went on. "He's bad. He's rotten——"

"Don't dare say it, Lightning! Don't ever dare say it. He's not bad. He's—oh!"

Molly broke off with an exclamation of supreme disgust and helpless indignation. And she fled headlong towards the house as though Lightning's very presence were something she could no longer endure.

The old man gazed after her. Then the yearning in his eyes gave place to an expression which no thought of Molly could have inspired. He turned to his team, and it was the comfortable, gentle Jane he led, and addressed, as he moved towards the barn.

"It ain't no use, old gal," he said, with a shake of his grizzled head. "I'll sure jest hev to do it one day."

He hunched his shoulders in the fashion peculiar to him.

"Guess I ain't blind yet, an' my nerve's dead steady, an' I'm surely glad that's so."

CHAPTER XVIII
The Spy

AS Andy McFardell rode home from the Marton farm two definite channels of thought preoccupied him. And curiously enough that which had his passionate infatuation for Molly for its inspiration made by far the lesser claim upon him.

Perhaps it was the result of his confidence. Had Molly been more difficult, had she been less of the simple child she was, had she had knowledge and experience of the world of men, or realised something of the physical charm she exercised, doubtless she could have transformed his confidence into an agony of doubt, and plunged him into a vortex of maddening suspense that would have made any other interest impossible to him.

As it was his dominating concern had become the obvious antagonism of Lightning. He had left the farm under no misapprehension on the score of the old choreman's regard. The cattleman had displayed his displeasure at his intrusion without any attempt at concealment, and, deep in his heart, McFardell understood the reason.

The reason of it left him undisturbed. And he smiled to himself as he wondered what the man's attitude would have been had he been witness to that which had taken place just before his return from work.

But the attitude of Lightning brought back to his mind that other matter, when the old man had been at such pains to seek him out, and impress upon him the opportunity held out to him. It looked to McFardell like a foolish bluff in the light of Lightning's unvarying antagonism. Yes, he felt sure it was a bluff—in a way. The man was anxious to be rid of him. He was anxious and worried to death about——

He laughed softly to himself. Then of a sudden his mood became deadly serious. He dismissed Lightning's purposes from his mind. It did not matter a thing to him what the cattleman's object might be. Molly and he understood each other, and—— But he knew that every word Lightning had said about Dan Quinlan was right. He had heard all the talk in Hartspool. And Hartspool was very much given to plain speaking on matters concerning cattle and grain.

He had told Lightning he would look into the matter after the dance in Hartspool. But long before he reached his home his mind was definitely made up. Quinlan's was thirty-five miles or so away up in the hills from his place. Well, it would help to fill in the week before the dance if he outfitted himself for a few days on the trail. He would pay his promised visit to the queer Irishman and spy out the land—before the dance. In fact—right away.

So it came that two days later McFardell found himself on the trail, or—as he preferred to think of it—on patrol. It was useless to make pretence that he was anything but the police officer he had always been. He was on patrol, that work he had always loved in the days before his disaster. And as he rode the tangled country of the foothills his spirits rose, and he found himself almost thankful to the old man who had prompted him out of his own secret purposes.

It did not matter a thing. Lightning was old and well-nigh decrepit, and his antagonism need make no difference. He, McFardell, would do the thing he contemplated just as it suited him. And meanwhile the hills around Quinlan, and Quinlan's place itself, would be investigated very thoroughly before he returned on the day of Hartspool's dance.

* * * *

The watcher moved stealthily through the forest. Eyes and ears were alert. They were tuned, by long years of training, to the hush of the woods. He was afoot. And his movements gave out no sound as he passed amongst the myriad of bare tree-trunks, supporting their well-nigh impenetrable roofing of sombre foliage. His feet were moccasined, and they padded softly on the rotting carpet beneath them.

Far down the aisles of the forest he could see a sunlit clearing beyond. And the voices of the cattle came back to him something muffled by the intense forest hush. The sharp barking of dogs left no other doubt in his mind than that of the chances of his own discovery through canine scent and inquisitiveness. That, however, was in the lap of the gods. He was not unduly concerned. He was moving up against the wind, which in the shelter of the forest was almost indistinguishable, and his position he felt to be more than favourable.

As he neared the forest limits the wide expanse of the clearing opened out to his astonished eyes. And so his progress slowed down and finally ceased altogether. There was no need to go farther. He had no desire to court disaster. Besides from where he had halted he could see all that he needed and study it at his leisure.

It was an amazing sight. He had looked for the squalid hiding-place of a secret cattle camp, where the thief could secret and re-brand the beasts he had stolen. He had looked for the ordinary thing which Police work had taught him to expect. But that which he discovered was altogether different, and left him impressed and—disappointed.

There were corrals whose extent astounded him and left him metaphorically rubbing his eyes. They were stoutly built and of a permanent nature, and they were literally teeming with cattle amongst which a large number of men were busily at work. Beyond the corrals were other buildings. There were log shanties, and barns, and all the equipment of an extensive ranch. The place was literally a hive of industry, and bore no resemblance whatever to that which he had looked for.

The human figures amongst the cattle interested him deeply. At the distance he got the impression that they were mostly Indians, or, at least, half-breeds. But without doubt there were white men amongst them, and two particularly caught and held his interest.

One was a powerfully built man clad in typical buckskin, while the other looked to have very little relation to the hill country at all. Furthermore, judging by the mass of snow-white hair he discovered under the brim of his prairie hat, he was an old man. But clearly these two were supervising the activities in progress.

He remained where he was until the last detail of the thing he was gazing upon had been well photographed and tabulated in his mind. Then he withdrew. He would have been glad of a closer view of the two white men, but caution deterred any further approach.

He moved away and presently again became swallowed up by the shadows of the forest. And the direction of his going was southerly, where he looked for a view of the valley below.

When he reappeared again it was at a break where an undergrowth walled the limits of the woods, and he pressed through it till he came to the final screen. He held the foliage apart while he peered out beyond. Below him lay the valley of grass and woodland bluff, and it was alive with grazing cattle.

Now his interest quickened. It was not the sight of the cattle. That had been expected. There was something of even greater importance within his view. Away to his left on the sloping, hither side of the valley, and, he judged, somewhere adjacent to the clearing he had recently overlooked, a wide field of building operations looked to have been just begun. There were the cuttings ready for the foundations of a big barn or house. There, too, lay a wealth of hewn logs hauled ready for building. And even as he watched a four-horse team appeared from the woods, farther down the valley, skidding a load of freshly hewn lumber. He drew a deep breath.

Lightning was wrong. So, too, was Hartspool. All the tittle-tattle going on in that place was miles wide of the truth. Here was no cattle thief's encampment. The extent of the organisation he had been so secretly observing could have only one meaning. How it had been achieved was something beyond his understanding. Where Dan Quinlan had obtained his capital to invest in such an enterprise it was impossible for him to suggest. The one outstanding fact remained. Here, away up in the heart of the hills, was a great and thriving cattle industry, and Dan Quinlan was the man who had created it.

* * * *

McFardell's discoveries at Quinlan's were a source of bitter disappointment to him. They were the shattering, the complete shattering of his dream. He cursed himself bitterly that he had listened to Lightning's suggestion, and the idle talk of Hartspool. It was always the way. Folks jumped to absurd conclusions out of suspicion of anything that was beyond their understanding. He knew he had been thoroughly fooled, and since Lightning had helped in his befoolment most of his bitterness was directed at him.

But his long training in the Police had deeply impressed his mind. And, furthermore, the idea of somehow blackmailing his way back into the force had taken desperate hold of him. His inclination had been all for returning home and letting Lightning know the fool he had made of both himself and Andrew McFardell, but his training prevailed.

He asked himself the meaning of Quinlan's rise to fortune, and determined to see the thing through to the end. He would explore to the limit of his time, and look for any other secret these hills might discover for him. So he went back to his camp, deep hidden from all chance discovery by Quinlan, and planned out his further campaign.

* * * *

Andy McFardell was returning home after complete failure. He was moodily contemplating his wasted effort. He had done everything possible; he had left nothing unexplored, sparing neither himself nor his horse; and now there was nothing left but to return again to the life which he had learned to hate and detest.

His way lay down the same valley where recently Molly had sought and found her missing cows. He was travelling over almost the identical ground which her pinto had covered. He had found the same water-hole, and his weary horse had refreshed itself at the same stream that came down from the cold recesses of the far-off hills. The day was hot, and the air swarmed with flies and mosquitoes. But these things made no impression upon him, and only his horse suffered.

The net result of his five days' work was a final conclusion that his chance of buying his way back into the Police was practically nil. The whole position was clear enough. While he could discover not a tithe of evidence that the Irishman and his band of Indians were on the cross, yet there was much that needed explanation. The renegade was no longer the white Indian, simply existing in his miserable home in the hills by trap and gun.

No. That may have been his original case. But it was so no longer. He was ranching on a big scale. And furthermore his stock was mainly highly bred Pole-Angus cattle, the numbers of which suggested a capital value running into anything over fifty thousand dollars. Where had the money come from? But more important still, how had that industry grown up without other outside evidence than the sale of young stock in the Hartspool and Calford markets? In spite of the shattering of his dream of getting back into the Police Andy McFardell felt that the position was still not without possibilities.

Moving down towards the creek his horse flung up its head in a startled fashion. He was riding over the stretch of blue grass, at the very spot where, so short a while since, Molly had finally discovered her cows. Ahead lay the bush-clad banks of the stream. And away to the left of him the slope of the valley opened sharply into the gorge where Molly had parted from the man she called

Silver-Thatch.

McFardell was concerned at once. He knew the meaning of his horse's pricked ears, and the faint sound of its whinny. Another horse was somewhere in the vicinity, and, since the Marton farm was something less than five miles on, he searched the direction of his horse's gaze for a sight of Molly. To his mind it must be she. Lightning would be likely to have moved out from his work on the ploughing.

There were only a few yards of the open left and he bustled his horse on. The beast moved with eagerness and passed into the bush. Then, in a moment, Andy flung himself back in the saddle and jerked his horse to a standstill.

He was face to face with a horseman on a superb black beast with the small broad head and diminutive ears of a thoroughbred. But he at once became absorbed in the rider. He was the white-haired man he had seen in the clearing up at Quinlan's.

The stranger had drawn rein. He sat quite still, contemplating the dishevelled appearance of McFardell and his tuckered horse. Then a slight, inscrutable smile lit his eyes, and he nodded. The next moment he lifted his reins, and the eager creature under him moved off like a flash and disappeared into the bush ahead. It was almost uncanny. Not a word of greeting had passed; scarcely a sign. The man had smiled, that was all, and—vanished.

Andy stared after him where the bushes had closed behind him. He made no attempt to follow. His dark eyes were frowning with heavy thought. And it was not till the last sound of the hoofs of the stranger's horse had completely died away that he bestirred himself.

Then it was that he suddenly became transformed. His eyes blazed with a fury of excitement. He lifted his reins and jammed his spurred heels into the flanks of the beast under him, and rode straight at the bush where the other had disappeared.

"God!" he muttered. "It's Jim Pryse!"

CHAPTER XIX
The Moment

LIGHTNING was squatting on a box beside the doorway of the bunk-house that had sheltered him for years. The dawn was just beginning to break. A low, yellow tinge was spreading over the eastern horizon, and the sky was cloudless. The stars were still shining to the west, and south, and north. But their brilliance was past, and they were fading slowly before the dawn.

The chill of the hills was in the air, but it made no impression on the tough old body of the squatting man. Like everything else in Nature he was indifferent to it.

The man's lap was spread with a grease cloth. On the ground beside him lay the belt that was usually about his waist, with its holsters, two long, three-strapped open holsters. One of his two guns was in its place in its holster. The other was lying in pieces in his lap.

The old man's mood was one of content. His night had been long and wakeful, but with the first streak of dawn he had crawled from under his rough blankets and sought the sure solace of his present occupation. He was cleaning his beloved guns, handling them with something of the mother love for her child.

The contemplation of these priceless friends of his early days never failed to lull him into a quiet, assured confidence and content. When trouble beset they were his whole resource. And just now trouble was looming heavily.

It was the dawn of the day of the farmers' ball in Hartspool. So he saw to it that his guns were ready. Their carefully filed hair-triggers needed little more than a breath of wind to release, the beautifully adjusted ivory sights were without blemish, and the seven chambers contained not one single speck of rust.

With these things so, ease relaxed the tension of his troubled thought. He hated the day that was dawning. He hated the folk who had designed the farmers' ball. But more than all he hated, with all his untamed soul, the man who had stolen Molly's peace of mind and transformed her into a woman.

"Two-gun" Rogers snapped his second gun to. He opened it again. And again he closed it. Then, with a deep, satisfied breath, he stooped over and replaced it in its holster. Then he folded the grease-stained cloth and thrust it into his hip pocket, and, stooping again, picked up his belt. He stood up from his box, tall, and lean, and vigorous. And the process of adjusting the belt about his waist preoccupied him.

A moment later he turned and stared out at the golden prospect of the sunrise. The sun had cut the horizon and its fiery rays rent the heavens with slashes of furious fire. It was almost intolerable to gaze upon. Yet the man stood before it with the unflinching gaze of an old eagle.

He kicked the box he had been sitting on back within his doorway. And, with a hunch of his shoulders, he moved on quickly in the direction of the house. The cook-stove was waiting his attention. In all his years Molly had never been permitted to light it.

* * * *

The cook-stove remained unlit. Lightning had not yet passed into the house. He was standing just outside the door, and his eyes were gazing down upon something which seemed to bar his way. It was two securely lashed sacks bulging with their contents, and the old man's gaze was speculative as he studied their contours, their lashings, and the loose attached labels which gave them the appearance of having been delivered by mail.

After a profound study, which could not possibly have yielded enlightenment, Lightning resorted to the next most obvious procedure. He bent down and examined the labels. There was one to each sack. They were addressed in a clear, bold handwriting to "Molly" at "Marton's Farm." But they gave no indication whence they came and the old man was left to his own resources.

For awhile these looked to be distinctly barren. Then, slowly, a change of expression heralded inspiration. After a few more moments he gingerly stepped over the mysterious bundles and passed into the house.

* * * *

Molly's week had been passed in excited anticipation and growing anxiety. And in the end anxiety supervened over every other emotion. At first happiness had well-nigh intoxicated her.

134

Life, the simple daily life of her farm, had been transformed with everything else. The labours that were her routine were accomplished in something like a dream, a dream wherein the good-looking face of a man was always near to her, looking on, encouraging, and smiling his approval of her efforts.

In her the great love that had swept into her young life was no sickly, unwholesome sentiment. It inspired her. It supported her. It gladdened every moment of her day, and stimulated her spirit. She dreamed her dreams as she went about her simple duties. She dreamed, in the fashion of every other woman, of the home she would make for the love with which she had crowned her man. And the home which Molly contemplated was the home she had always known. She had yielded her love, and with it went all she was, all that was hers. There were no reservations. No less than her farm could be the setting wherein her love should find its home.

Every day she looked again for the man without whom the meaning of life would be completely lost to her. She did not expect him, but she looked for him. She knew. She understood. It was spring, and he was far too good a farmer, she told herself, to neglect the season. No, she did not expect his coming, but she looked for it, and her yearning was deep, and full of a profound content.

Then there was that other. Each day with her first waking moments expectancy leapt. Her trust was without question. An assurance, whithersoever it came, was an assurance. A promise would be fulfilled, or why should it be made? Life for Molly had no deceit. So each day she looked for the coming of Blanche, or of her messenger.

She yearned for the coming of Blanche's promised party frock as she yearned for nothing else in life. Blanche had promised that she should be adorned as no farmer's wife in Hartspool could possibly be adorned. And adornment, at that moment, meant something to her it had never meant before. It was for the eyes of her man to gaze upon. It was for the added attraction she might possess for him. It was that he might be proud of, and pleased with, the love she had so abundantly yielded him.

So each day she looked for Blanche's fulfilment of her given word, and with the passing of each she reassured herself of the morrow. And so came the night before *the* day, and the promise still remained unfulfilled.

That night the climax of her anxiety smote her. She said not one word to Lightning. She uttered no word of complaint. But the smile was less ready in her eyes; there was a curious, deep sinking of her buoyant spirit, and, for the first time, she contemplated the possibilities of the non-fulfilment of the promise she had relied upon.

She had prepared to retire to her bed that night in a dejection of spirit which Lightning was swift to realise. And for all his hatred of the thing the coming day meant, his manner of parting from her was infinitely gentle.

"That swell dame couldn't lie," he declared spontaneously. "Ther's surely eyes you ken look into, Molly, gal, an' see right through to the truth back of 'em. Her's was that way."

And as he prepared to take his departure for his bunk-house, his hand rested encouragingly upon the girl's soft shoulder.

When Molly entered the living-room at sun-up the next morning, and found Lightning completing his task at her stove, she was without her customary greeting for him. Lightning glanced up from his labours and discovered the anxious searching of her gaze. He smiled. It was a curious, twinkling smile that never got beyond his eyes. But those it lit in a fashion that must ordinarily have seemed impossible.

"Say, Molly, gal," he observed, with a studied contortion of his features intended to express physical pain. "Guess the rheumatiz's got my left hinge some. I'd take it kindly fer you to dump the ash bucket for me."

He finished up with another fierce contortion as he rose from his knees before the stove. And, in a moment, Molly was all sympathetic concern.

"Why, I'm sorry, Lightning," she cried. "I'll fix the hoss oils right away. You haven't had a touch of that a whole winter. It surely is the ploughing. The flat's damp with the spring freshet. I'll fix a good bottle before I eat."

She seized the bucket of ashes standing ready as the crackling of the wood in the stove developed into a roar of flame up the iron stove pipe.

She moved towards the door, and Lightning's voice followed her.

"Them iles is mighty good dope, but I don't guess them's my need. It's the saddle. It's the saddle I was raised to. And I bin weeks on my feet. The saddle'll fix it better'n hoss dope."

The girl had flung open the door to pass out, but she stood stock still where she was, the heavy bucket firmly grasped in one

136

hand. The old man watched her, and his eyes had strangely softened. He beheld a flush of excitement break out upon her soft cheeks, and then—and then the bucket fell to the ground and overturned its whole contents upon the immaculate floor.

"Lightning! You knew!"

* * * *

The living-room was littered with the ravishing contents of the carefully packed bundles. The ashes had been swept up by the willing hand of Lightning, while Molly's deft, excited fingers dealt with her treasure. Gone for the while was all thought of the breakfast that should have been in preparation. Gone was every other consideration, swept out of mind by that supreme moment of gladness.

What else could matter? Two great bundles in their waterproof wrappings, enclosed in stout sacks. The contents? Ah, those wonderful contents. The fairy godmother had done her work with due regard for the conventions of magic. She had waved her wand, and transported her burdens to the sheltering storm doorway of Molly's home in the night. That was understood. It was clear enough to the simple minds of these two children, the one so far travelled on the journey of life, and the other standing at the very threshold of the age of joy.

The messenger, whoever he was, had travelled with a pack horse. That was clear enough. And his instructions must have been very, very definite, and carefully considered. Clearly he had been admitted to the secret of it all. He must arrive in the night, when the world was wrapped in slumber, with only the twinkling eyes of the stars to see, and the full moon smiling down her beneficence. He must steal upon the silent house and deposit his friendly burden all unseen. Then in the morning, then—then—— In her heart Molly felt that only Blanche could have planned so heavenly a surprise.

It seemed well-nigh impossible that the sacks could have contained all that wealth of delight. The first of the two to be opened was given up to the afterthoughts of a generous mind. It was a delicious collection of creature comforts that had nothing to do with apparel. It was food delicacies such as no ordinary store in Hartspool could have provided. And here again was shown the consummate purpose of the sender. The whole thing was designed without a hint of charity. It was a present of only those things which no money could have provided out of the stock of a prairie

137

store. There were candies that must have come from some big city. There were bottled fruits of a quality Molly had never seen. There were foreign preserves in wide variety. There were sauces and flavourings for preparing food. Even Lightning's appetite was whetted, and he forgot the occasion of it all. No, there was no charity in it; only a supreme kindliness.

Then the second bundle, softer and infinitely lighter than the first.

The girl's cheeks reflected an almost painful excitement as her fingers fumbled with the fastenings. When the last of the covers was torn aside Molly drew such a breath that Lightning forgot the amazing display of luxurious garments that lay revealed. He watched only the hungry eyes devouring greedily all the beauty of tone and texture which the girl's fingers were moving amidst. The whole thing was beyond him.

Molly looked to be in a sort of trance. The beautiful fur wrap she almost ignored. It was fur, something she understood, something, in however inferior a quality, that had long since entered her life. Beneath it, enfolded in tissue paper, lay the party frock. It was gauzy and diaphanous, and of such a colour and material that was quite beyond her wildest dreams. Molly raised it gently, tenderly. It was so slight, and so—so delicate. It seemed to her her hands, those hands that were used only to her work, must inevitably crush and completely ruin it.

But with its removal a quick intense exclamation broke from the girl. Beneath it lay something that held her completely spellbound. It was several layers of garments of the most exquisite silk and crêpe-de-chine. They were those delicious things which are the dream of any and every woman's life, whatever her station. Something so irresistible that, once possessed, life becomes impossible without. And the warm fingers, accustomed only to the homeliest materials, moved amongst them, fondling them, and telling the old man looking on an emotion which was utterly outside his crude understanding.

There was everything there, everything even to the shoes and those necessities of the girl's dark hair which the sender had deemed essential. Blanche's promise had been fulfilled, her pledge had been redeemed with a prodigal generosity that almost dazed the simple farm girl.

Molly sighed deeply. It even seemed to involve an effort to raise her eyes from the fascinating spectacle set out upon the well-scrubbed table.

"I can hardly believe, Lightning."

The girl's words came scarcely above a whisper, and the old man watched her closely. In a moment his mind had leapt back to the meaning of it all. The smiling enjoyment of Molly's delight passed out of his eyes, and they hardened again to their natural glitter.

He remained without reply, and the girl roused herself. Quickly and deftly she replaced the garments and enfolded them in their wrappings. And she talked the while.

"Lightning," she cried, and the excitement of it all was still thrilling in her tones. "You got to help me. This is my day. My day," she repeated almost tenderly. Then she went on quickly and almost sharply. "You're mad about Andy. You're mad because he's my beau. Remember this, and get it good. I love Andy. I just love Andy with my whole heart. Whether you like him, or whether you don't one day he's going to be boss around this farm, just the same as he's boss right in—here." She pressed her hands over her gently swelling bosom. "Since father died I guess you've been real good to me. You been so good to me I just can't tell you about it. Well"—she drew a deep breath—"you aren't goin' to quit being good to me because of Andy?" She shook her head. "You surely aren't. You see, folks can't just help these things. I mean—I mean I—I love Andy. I can't help it. I wouldn't if I could. Won't you help me still? Won't you quit hating him?"

The suddenness, the earnestness of Molly's appeal almost caught the old cattleman off his guard. And he stood staring down at the refolded bundle she was about to remove to her room while he prepared his reply. Then, very deliberately, he shook his head, and gazed at her out of his framing of loose whisker and grey hair.

"Andy's your beau all right, Molly, gal," he said, in his harsh way. "The thing I feel fer that boy don't matter a' curse. You can't help the way you feel about him. Wal, I don't guess I'm no diff'rent. Leave it that way. I ain't no sort of archangel, or any pie-faced psalm-smiter. I got one notion in life. That's you. I'm goin' to see you fixed right if hell itself throws a fit and busts up the throne o' glory. If Andy's the boy that's goin' to fix you right I'm right behind him waggin' a banner, with a halo around my thatch, an' a pair o' dandy wings dustin' the sand out o' my eyes, an' talkin' pie like a Methody Meetin'. But if he ain't? If that boy sets you worryin', if that boy hands you a haf-hour o' grievin', why, I'm after him like a bitch wolf chasin' feed in winter. That goes, Molly, gal. Don't you worry a thing. Sure, this is your day,

139

gal. It's yours, all of it. An' I'm ready to weep around that boy's neck same as if I'd no more sense than a blind sheep at lambin' time."

* * * *

It was long past the midday meal that the sun of Molly's day reached its meridian. The afternoon was well advanced. Lightning had betaken himself to his labours, and the manner of his going had been sufficiently characteristic.

"Guess I'll quit you now, Molly, gal," he had said. "Ther's things in life as I see 'em it ain't no good trying to boost the way you'd fancy 'em. With your notion fixed that way ther' ain't no sort of sense 'cep' to leave 'em alone till they hurt you. Your Andy, boy'll get along, an' when he comes I don't guess you'll be yearnin' to hev the remains o' my life joinin' in your party. So I'll beat it right now to my ploughing. Hev a time, kid. Hev a real, swell time with them dandy fixin's, an' when you need me, why, I'll just get around."

So Molly had the afternoon to herself and the heaven of dreaming her young soul yearned for. She was more than content with Lightning's going. He was right enough in his estimate of her mood. There was nothing, and no one, must come between her and the wonderful thing that was hers.

From dinner to the time of Andy's arrival with his team and spring wagon was none too long for all Molly had to do. It was perhaps the most beautiful three hours in her life. For all that had gone before when the man had taught her her first meaning of love, these hours in contemplation of herself, and the beautiful garments that had been showered upon her by the generous hand of Blanche, were perhaps her real awakening to the meaning of her womanhood. The whole thing was so deliciously expressive of her ardent youth.

In her precise little way she had promptly decided there should be no half measures. Nothing but completeness could satisfy her. So it came that a great boiler was set on the stove, and the iron bath, in which her weekly laundry was done, was made ready. Nothing would have induced her to defile the precious finery with a body that had not been specially prepared.

Her bath was an expression of wonderful restraint, but she went through with it with a resolve that was quite beautiful in its self-denial. The whole time of it was one of infinite anticipation and yearning for the array of beauty laid out awaiting her in her bedroom.

At last the great moment came, and the joy of it all was beyond words. She lingered in a state of ecstasy over each detail of her dressing. Some of it was easy, even to her untutored mind; some of it was fraught with such bewilderment that she came near enough to despair. Inside out, wrong way round, the girl found herself well-nigh frantic through her lack of knowledge. But patience served her truly in the end, and her little mirror reassured her.

The transformation was complete. No Cinderella was ever more richly endowed. She gazed for minutes that swept swiftly on at the wonder which Blanche's wizardry had created. Her eyes shone with delight as they gazed at the beautiful picture they beheld looking back at her out of the old mirror. Blanche had judged rightly. Their figures were almost identical, so the delicate blue frock revealed itself in its most ravishing aspect.

Yes, the eyes gazing back at her were like twin stars in the velvet setting of a moonlit sky. Her carefully coiled hair, shining with satin-like sheen, was surmounted by paste brilliants which had been selected with such care and taste by the woman who had sent them. And the string of pearl beads about her soft, white throat were an adornment incapable of increasing its beauty. The straightness of the cut of the frock itself entirely disguised the soft contours of her youthful figure, and the arms, bare to the shoulder, were white, and soft, and round, with perfect formation of her trained muscles.

Then her feet, and the length of silk hose below the edge of the duly shortened skirt. The fascination of these things was something that left the girl almost bewildered at the change. The hose revealed the ivory tint of the flesh beneath and her diminutive feet, usually encased in heavy highlows, or gum boots or even buckskin moccasins that made them look broad and flat, seemed, in their beautifully shaped covering of silver tissue, utterly incapable of supporting the substantial burden for which they were designed.

The rattle of Andy's spring wagon pulling up outside her door sent the warm blood rushing into Molly's cheeks. Her moment had come, that moment for which for seven anxious days she had waited, and of which she had dreamed. Her inclination was to rush out and greet him, and so reveal to him the wonder of her physical transformation. But she denied the impulse.

Just for a moment a little smiling reflection looked back at her out of her mirror. Then she glanced round her bedroom. She left the fur wrap unheeded on the bed. No power on earth at that moment could have persuaded her to hide up her splendour beneath its folds. So she passed it by, and moved slowly and restrainedly out into the living-room, and, with all her woman's delighted vanity, she waited.

She heard his voice. He was talking to his team.

"You've a big piece to make before the night's through," he said. "Get that feed into you. You'll sure need it."

She heard him moving about. He was probably removing the horses' bits, and maybe easing the straps of the neck-yoke. Then his footsteps approached the door, and the girl's breath came quickly, and her colour deepened.

Then his voice came again. This time it was she to whom he was addressing himself.

"Ho! Molly!" he cried.

There was a pause. Just an instant's pause. Then the door was flung wide.

Andy stood framed in it. He was clad in a dark suit, with a light, thin raincoat buttoned over it. He made no attempt to cross the threshold. He remained just where the vision of Molly revealed itself to him, and abruptly bared his head. His dark eyes were alight with amazement.

"Molly!" he cried. Then, with a little gasp: "By Gee!"

The girl had her reward. It was truly her moment. It was the moment of her life.

CHAPTER XX
The Home-Coming

LIGHTNING resettled himself upon his box. He was leaning forward in an attitude of alert concentration, his arms folded across his knees, with an elbow grasped in the palm of each of his hands. He remained unmoving, except for the inevitable chew of tobacco which engaged the rusty remains of his teeth. His mind was correspondingly active.

Midnight had long since come and gone. The night was brilliant, and little enough was left for the shadows of night to conceal. The farm and its surroundings were in full view from where he sat. The bluff beyond the grass-trail was sharply silhouetted, a deep, black background to the south and west. Away to the right of him the corral, where the cows were peacefully slumbering on the accumulations of despoiled hay feed, was sharply outlined. So, too, with the hay corral, that stood nearly empty and ready for the new season's grass. The barn beside him rose sharply against the night sky, where its thatched ridge lifted above the sturdy log walls. And then, beyond that, the whispering tree-tops of the bluff stood up, where once the dead George Marton had confronted the emaciated figure of the starving fugitive from justice.

The air was cool with the threat of ground frost. But Lightning was no more concerned with temperatures than he was with the claims of a weary body. He was awaiting Molly's return from the party, and, if necessary, he would remain there until day came.

The drift of the man's thought went on without pause. There was speculation in a hundred directions. There was impatience. There was anger that was even directed at the girl he desired to protect. His mood was one of restlessness and disquiet.

A prowling coyote howled its mournful crescendo. Its melancholy cry died out. The man scarcely noted it. The deep bay of the timber wolf's reply, with its harsh threat, sufficiently impressed itself. In a moment it focused Lightning's mind upon the keen, dark eyes and narrow face of the man he felt to be something of a human wolf where women were concerned. He stirred and spat viciously.

He strove to dismiss the personality of McFardell from his thoughts. His understanding of the way things stood with Molly was all sufficient. He was logical enough, even temperate enough, to know he had no right to interfere. But he was equally determined that, at the first sign of what he deemed to be necessity, he would interfere. He would interfere in just such manner as his savage mind prompted.

A grim light shone in his cold eyes as they searched the moonlit scene. His barbaric ruthlessness was astir, contemplating a "short-circuit" of the whole situation as he saw it. If he permitted his guns, which he felt to be yearning to play their part for him, to execute their due mission, it would save so much precious time in preventing the disaster he saw lying ahead.

Molly—Molly would be broken hearted for awhile. Yes, that would surely be so. But he prided himself on his knowledge of women. He remembered the case of a woman in his Arizona days. He had contemplated piloting her through the shoals of life as a more than desirable companion. Tess. She was a swell creature—a real "upstander." Hair like black silk. A skin like satin. Then she'd those queer, big eyes that set any real man yearning for the trouble that ought to be lying around her anyway. Yes, that was a case in point. When Tug Lennox, her beau, got in front of his guns, and had no time to get away before they went off, what happened? Tess was nearly crazy for one day. Then she beat the trail across the border with Dago Pete, while he, Lightning, was getting over the elegant souse the boys had handed him for ridding Arizona of one of the worst toughs that ever shot up a peaceful township. Yes, Molly would be all in. He was sure of that, but——

He turned suddenly to windward.

No. It wouldn't last. Those things in a girl were like a summer storm, or—or horse colic, or something. Sunshine got busy and dried things up, and the colic passed swiftly, and left a horse feeling it hadn't eaten for two days. It seemed to him if he went after Andy McFardell with two guns it would be the best for all concerned. Certainly best for——

He stood up alertly, his sense of hearing directed to the hither drift of the night air. The intensity of the silence had again been broken. This was no skulking wolf or coyote. It had nothing to do with the frog chorus at the creek. It was a sound that came to him down the trail from the north-east. It was the familiar sound of the wheels and hoofs he had been awaiting.

He stretched his weary limbs. He yawned. Then he spat out his chew, and bit into a fresh one. Then he kicked his box into the doorway of his hut, and moved off somewhere in the direction of the house.

* * * *

Lightning waited. The murmur of voices came to him, but the words themselves were indistinguishable. He intended that to be so, but he hated the necessity. Driven by headlong impatience, he felt himself to be something like a traitor to the charge that was his. But for the life of him it was impossible to break in upon the scene he knew to be enacting in the moonlight at the door of Molly's home.

No, he must just stand by. He was yearning to drive the man headlong. He had the means to his hand, for all he was an old man and the other was in the full vigor of his youth. The savage in him was urging all the time. But even the savage was powerless before his love for the girl, and his reluctance to wound the heart that found happiness in the smile of McFardell's dark eyes. He was torn between head and heart. And so he stood waiting, waiting until the farewell had been said.

The spring wagon was drawn up before the storm door of the house. The man and the girl were standing together somewhere in the shadow of the doorway. They were standing closely together, and Lightning was maddeningly conscious of that which was passing between them.

He translated it in his own way, inspired by all that was human in him. He felt that Molly was tightly clasped in McFardell's arms. The girl was lost to everything, even to the wonderful finery which had set her nearly crazy with delight when she first gazed upon it. That was the way of women, he argued. No, she had no thought for anything or anybody but that—that—the man he hated.

There were moments of profound silence. Then there came moments when indistinguishable words passed between the two. Lightning wondered what they were saying, and would have hated to have known. Oh, he knew well enough. And as the sound of voices died out he understood that their words had been swamped by the passionate silence that fell so readily between them.

His witness of the scene was brief enough. Then, suddenly,

the tones of Molly's voice became raised, and something strident.

"You must go now, Andy," Lightning heard her say, and a thrill of satisfaction gladdened his heart. Then there was added urgency. "Oh, you must go. Please, please! I—I can't bear it. I sort of feel haf crazy. I don't know—I—— Oh, Andy, please, please go—now."

The appeal of the girl's tone drove the hot blood to Lightning's head, and his hands rested on those twin friends of his early days that lolled heavily at his waist. But he remained unmoving, waiting—waiting in desperate suspense for the man's reply.

He heard McFardell's voice, but not his words. They were low and persuasive, and they went on for some time.

Then the girl spoke again, and it seemed to Lightning that something akin to terror rang in her words.

"Before God?" she cried, and it sounded like an echo of that which McFardell had said. "Before summer's out? Oh, Andy! Sure? Sure?"

The man's low tones replied. And after that Molly's voice, full of excited happiness, rang out, so that no word was lost in the silence of the night.

"Yes, yes," she cried. "In Hartspool. At the Catholic church. Say it shall be the Catholic church. I was raised to father's religion. Oh, Andy!"

Lightning raised a hand, and his lean fingers raked their way through his grey hair as Molly's final exclamation died out. The snatch of talk he had been forced to listen to told him the simple truth. The thing he dreaded most in the world was to happen. There was only one interpretation possible to the thing he had heard—marriage. McFardell was to marry Molly before summer was out. Molly was to belong to that man before summer was out. Molly! A paroxysm of voiceless hate consumed him, and he moved a step forward.

But he got no farther.

"So long, little girl," he heard McFardell say. "It's just too bad." He laughed. "Why need I go? You're mine. Just all mine. We're—— All right, little Molly. I'll beat it. So long."

Lightning drew a deep breath. McFardell was going. He saw the man approach his team and pass around it. Then he saw him turn back to Molly, who had emerged from her doorway. The next moment Lightning saw him bend over her up-turned face. Then McFardell climbed into the wagon and the horses moved off.

Molly stood there in the moonlight clad in her beautiful fur wrap, gazing after the departing team. Lightning saw her hand raised in farewell. Then she turned sharply and passed into the house. And the door closed behind her.

* * * *

When Lightning thrust open the door he discovered Molly seated at the table. She sat there a ghostly little figure, still wrapped in her fur cloak, with the shaft of moonlight pouring in through the window falling athwart her. Otherwise the room was in complete darkness.

Lightning gazed at her in some alarm. Perhaps it was the moonlight that had transformed her. Her face was pale almost to ghastliness. It was pathetically drawn, and her eyes gazed up at him so wide, so helpless, so piteously. She had raised her head at the old man's intrusion, and something like reproach was in her silent greeting.

Lightning left the door open and came to the table. His eyes were smiling softly, and he stood for a moment regarding the queer, huddled figure, while his mind searched for the greeting that would not betray him.

"Guess you had a swell time, Molly, gal?" he said. There was no reply. The girl sat still—so still. Her elbows were thrust upon the table, and her small, clenched hands supported the oval of her cheeks that looked so ghastly in the moonlight.

Lightning moved up to the table. Then he glanced about him in the darkness beyond the moonlight.

"Best fix the lamp," he said.

"No, no!"

Molly's denial came almost fiercely. And instantly the man abandoned his search.

"You can't see to——"

Lightning's protest got no further. There was a cry—a cry such as the old man had never heard pass the girl's lips before. It was half fierce, half laughing. It was something that smote him deeply, for there was pain, horror, and despair in it.

In a moment Molly's bare arms were flung out full length on the table. Then they were spasmodically drawn up. Her head drooped forward, and her face was buried against her own warm flesh, and a flood of tears broke forth.

CHAPTER XXI
Out of the Past

"POOR little soul. Well, anyway, she's had her dance and all it means to her. And I guess that's quite a lot."

Blanche sighed as she turned from the verandah post, against which she had been leaning, and moved to the chair beside a squat-legged table. She flung herself into it, and smiled as she contemplated the white-haired brother spread out full length in the lounging chair in front of her.

The man withdrew his gaze from the scene of activity below him. The population of the ranch was preparing for work after an early breakfast. In the distance a horseman was riding towards one of the great barns. There was no mistaking that figure. Its flaming head of bright red hair stood out like a beacon fire in the sunshine. He would be up at the house shortly. There were other figures, mounted or afoot, moving among the corrals, the ploughings, the pastures. It was so in almost every direction. The activity of it all must have been pleasantly encouraging to the man responsible for it. Yet somehow the expression of Jim Pryse's eyes suggested no particular heartening.

For a moment he regarded his sister. She was full of that charm which had drawn the red-headed Larry Manford like a magnet to the heart of the mountains. Jim was by no means insensible to his sister's beauty, and even in that preoccupied moment he found it pleasant to gaze upon.

"It was last night, eh?" he said. "The dance, I mean? You know you're a good sort, Blanche," he went on, rousing himself. "I'll bet you fixed her right."

"Fixed her?" Blanche laughed happily. "It's a safe bet there wasn't a woman around that dance that didn't just about hate Molly Marton. It was a frock I hadn't had a chance of wearing up here, and the—— It was one I'd had made just before I quit New York. I guess it's out of date now. But it wouldn't be in Hartspool. What a child! Just a simple kid that you wouldn't fancy had a notion beyond her cook-stove and the farm. My, it makes me grieve to think about her. There she is, all alone, except for that queer old tough she calls Lightning. There's not a soul nearer than ten miles. Do you get what that means to a young girl, Jim?"

The man linked his hands behind his white hair, and gazed abstractedly out down the valley.

"It's tough, Sis," he said with a sigh.

Blanche shook her head.

"Tough isn't the word, Silver-Thatch, my friend," she said with a light laugh. "If you'd seen that little girl's face, if you'd watched her breath come and go as I talked 'frock' to her, I guess I'd surely have had a new sister-in-law in a week. You—you big, soft-hearted old thing, you couldn't have stood up to the pathos of it all for a half-hour. You'd have loosened your bank-roll right away, and whisked her off where there was life and such pleasure as that poor little kid has never known. I'm glad you owe her something, Jim. And I'm glad you're going to let me help you pay it."

The man nodded.

"And Larry did his share," he smiled.

"Like a jewel. Isn't it queer? He was most like a kid about acting a sort of Father Christmas. Oh, he planned the way of it. He planted my goods right in her doorway, and quit without a soul getting wise. It cost him a night and more from his bed, but he was glad enough to do it. And, anyway, I'd threatened him. But she was sore on you in her little queer way, Jim. I think she was feeling bad you'd quit her without handing her a name. But I had to smile at her name for you. I just love it to death. Silver-Thatch! That goes with me all the time."

Blanche laughed. Then her expression fell serious again and her even brows drew together.

"But you couldn't have risked your name with her. I know that. So it would have meant lying the same as I had to lie. Not about my name, but where I'm located. You know, Jim, it's a pretty terrible thing to lie to innocence like that. It's like lying to your own child. I've acted a lie once to that kid, and never again. I had to do it for your sake, old man. And I did it as I'd do most things for you. If we're going to help Molly Marton it must be done without lying. I'm sorry, boy. But I've been thinking it a week now since ever I first set eyes on that child. Now you want to think, and see how it needn't happen again. Maybe none of us can get through life without lying. I'm no better than anyone else.

149

I can lie all day to folks that don't matter. The whole world of society needs to lie, or things would break up in five seconds. But I can't have innocent child eyes looking up into mine, full of trust and truth, and know I'm lying."

Jim dropped his hands from behind his head, and one of them removed the empty pipe from his mouth.

"There'll be no need to lie any more," he said. "It looks to me it's only a matter of time before the whole game's up, anyway."

He looked up. There was an easy smile in his eyes that was no pretence, for all the significance of his words. Blanche was startled. She was a little terrified. The "game" being "up" could only have one meaning for her. It meant discovery of Jim's hiding. And discovery of Jim's hiding meant a movement towards the penitentiary to fulfil the sentence that had been passed on him.

"Hadn't you best tell me, Jim? All of it?" she said, and settled herself back in her chair.

The woman watched the man's fingers as they manipulated the tobacco into his pipe. But all her instinct, all her understanding and courage, were desperately alert. Where her men-folk were concerned these things were ever at their service. Larry Manford, with his flaming head, was her epitome of what manhood should be, but her brother Jim occupied a place in her heart that was very, very close to that which was reserved for motherhood.

Jim refolded his pouch and returned it to his pocket.

"Say, be a dear an' get me a match," he said easily. "And while you're gone I'll figger out how best to tell you. It's—amusing."

"Amusing?" Blanche stood for a moment. Then, as she moved off to do his bidding: "I'm glad," she said. "I hadn't thought it was that way."

When Blanche returned, she struck a match and held it to the man's pipe.

"Well?" she said. "We'll need to be quick. Larry'll be up along in a while. And food's nearly ready."

Jim spread out his hands.

"It won't take long," he said. "The police boys are getting around Dan's place."

"Why?"

"That's easy. Hartspool and Calford are worried. It's our sales of cattle. But it's not that. I've seen a—spook."

Blanche made a little impatient gesture.

"Cut out the spooks, Jim, and tell me the story quickly."

"Sure."

But Jim smoked on for a few moments longer.

"No. It was no spook. We can cut them out," he said at last. "What I've seen was real human flesh and blood. And it was the one person I wasn't yearning to see, or who should see me. I can't get his name. I only heard it once. But it was that police boy who was toting me along down for a rest cure in penitentiary when I made my getaway. I saw him two evenings ago as I was beating it back here from Dan's place. Yes. He wasn't any spook, but just the boy I recognised right away, for all he wasn't wearing uniform. And he recognised me, even though my hair's as white as a summer cloud. It wasn't near Dan's place either, so I can't say for sure he'd been along up there. But he was heading from that direction." He laughed. "Queer, eh? I mean the chance of it. We hit head on to each other right down there on the creek in Dan's valley. It was a few miles up from that little girl's farm, where we turn off up into these hills at the mouth of Three-Way Creek. If he'd been a half a minute before, or I'd been the same later, we'd have missed. And in these hills, too, where you could lose an army like nothing. Makes you wonder about Fate, doesn't it? Makes you feel like two cents trying to fix things the way you need 'em."

"Did you speak to him?"

"Nope." Jim's smile deepened. "But somehow the whole thing tickled me plumb to death. I just had to grin. I grinned into his queer dark face, and——"

"That's when he recognised you."

The man laughed outright.

"Maybe," he admitted.

"Of course it was." In spite of her anxiety Blanche was forced to smile. "Your silver thatch, as Molly calls it, wouldn't save you. It wouldn't save you if you were all covered up with the flowing beard of a patriarch. No one who's ever seen the grin on your foolish old face is ever going to mistake it again. And you think he'd been up around Dan's place? You guess he was a patrol? In plain clothes? And he was the result of Hartspool and Calford being worried?" She shook her head. "That doesn't sound good to me. I don't know much of the ways of the Police, but why would he be out of uniform? And why would they send the particular boy who lost you? And, anyway, why worry with Dan if there's been no cattle stealing going on around the hills? What could his place tell them?"

"Dan's place could tell them a deal," Jim protested at once. "You've got to see with their eyes. Dan's been known to be living a trapper life years. Suddenly he registers a brand. Then he starts in to trade stock big. He and I have talked this out. We've foreseen it. That's why we've started his building."

Again Blanche shook her head.

"You haven't answered a thing," she declared keenly. "You've got Dan's work on your mind. Look around outside it. The thing I'm looking at is the identity of that boy. Being the boy you got away from, I'd say he's more—a deal more—interested in—you. I'd say if he was looking for anything, he found it when he found you. Remember, you didn't find him up around Dan's. You found him at the start of our highway. Isn't that so? Has he discovered that highway, and is wondering who uses it? Eh?" Again came the woman's shake of the head. "The notion of Dan's place leaves me cold. There's no cattle stealing going on, no one to pass a complaint. Molly Marton is his nearest neighbour, twenty-five miles away. She's lost nothing. After her, another ten miles nearer Hartspool, comes that boy Andy, the new settler who took her into that dance. No, Jim, he was looking for you. And he's found you."

Jim removed his pipe from his mouth.

"This boy Andy?" he said inquiringly. "Andy—who? It's Irish, isn't it?"

Blanche laughed. She thought she recognised asperity in the man's tone, and interpreted it in her woman's fashion.

"Maybe. Scottish too, Andy's short for Andrew."

Jim started. In an instant his unconcern had fallen from him. He sat up, and his booted and spurred feet came down on to the woodwork of the verandah with a clatter. He swung round squatting on the side of his chair.

"Hold on, Sis," he cried. "Andrew? That was that police boy's first name. I got it now. And—it's given me the rest. Corporal Andrew McFardell. That's the name I've been yearning to get. And that's the man I saw," he cried in triumph, beating the palm of one hand against his forehead. "I wonder?"

"What?"

But Jim remained maddeningly silent. And it was not till a restless movement on Blanche's part finally reminded him of her presence that he looked up into her face with a dawning smile.

"It might be," he said. "It surely looks that way. I guess it must be. He wasn't in uniform. But his cloth riding-breeches looked like police breeches with the yellow stripe gone. Now, what would have happened to him after my getaway? Guess they'd sort of court-martial him. Sure. Maybe they'd 'fire' him. What then? He'd need to scratch a living some way. You can't quit the Police with a wad on the cents they get. That's it. That Andy is— Say, Sis, we got to locate that boy Andy, and get to know about him. You can do that. Molly can hand you his story. You——"

He broke off. Blanche's face had suddenly paled. A great apprehension was looking out of her eyes.

"I told Molly my name was—Pryse," she cried, aghast.

Jim laughed outright.

"That beats it," he cried. And Blanche suddenly felt like shaking him. "What a play! If our little Molly knows your name's Pryse he'll know it, too. If her 'Andy' is my 'Andrew' it won't have him guessing more than a year that Blanche Pryse has to do with one Jim Pryse, who's caused him a whole deal of trouble. And, having located Jim Pryse down at the creek, right by our highway, what then? It's easy. Maybe he's 'fired' from the Police. It doesn't matter a thing. There's a chance of getting back on the feller who's queered his job. Sis, we're going to get half the Mounted Police hitting our trail before we're many weeks older or—or I'm— No."

He shook his head decidedly. Then he flung himself back into his chair and gazed out down the valley. He raised his eyes to the eternal snows crowning the peaks which rose up in almost every direction about him. He scanned the dark glades of the forest which clothed their lower slopes. Then his gaze came back to the little world of his own creation. That shelter he had designed for erring souls, who, like himself, had fallen by the wayside of life. His amusement was dead, and he promptly negatived his hasty conclusion.

"No, Sis," he said. "We don't need to worry a thing. There's no police boys'll ever locate this ranch. Dan Quinlan chased these hills ten years before he lit on this valley—by chance. There's only you, and me, and Larry knows the way in and ways out of it. And there's fifty miles of hills, and gorges, and mountain streams, like a Chinese maze, for any feller who don't know what we know about Three-Way Creek before he can locate us. No. Don't worry. But things have changed. We need to reckon with that boy. We need to watch out. I'll have to put Dan wise. And you—why, you must keep tab on little Molly. I owed her father, and I'll need to pay his little girl. Nothing's going to stop that. You must see her as soon as you can. If you run into him, why, you'll not be worried losing him in these hills. And you'll be the best one to locate the thing he's doing. Here's Larry coming along with a big eat look written all over his freckled features. I'll have to tell him."

CHAPTER XXII

The Awakening

MOLLY was sitting up in her bed, with the grey daylight searching the night shadows that still lurked in the little bedroom that had known her from her earliest days.

Under the small window was the old drawer-chest that supported a painted mirror, before which the girl was accustomed to dress. Near by stood a home-made chair with a rawhide seat. In one dim corner of the room the folds of a cotton curtain hung down over the few garments of which her outer wardrobe consisted. And against the far wall, opposite the end of the bed, was a trunk, surrounded and adorned by a flounced covering of large-patterned cotton. The board flooring of the place had some of its bareness disguised by one or two home-made rugs. Yet, for all its bare comfort, the room had always contained for Molly a wealth of content and happy memory.

She was in her homely night apparel, with her knees drawn up under the well-worn bed-covering. Her arms were clasped about her knees, and she was staring hopelessly into the slowly receding shadows.

The silence was intense. As yet not even the wild-fowl on the river were stirring. And no sound of any sort came up from the slumbering kine in the corral.

Molly was alone with the dawn and her waking thoughts. She was alone with memory. And, strangely enough, never in all her life had she known such a profound dispiritedness. Slowly her eyes filled with tears. Her lips moved, quivering spasmodically. Then the storm of grief overflowed down her cheeks.

For some time her face was buried in the coarse sheeting of her bed. Then, with a quick movement, her head was flung up. She clad herself hurriedly in her working clothes. She bathed her face and hands, and adjusted her hair before the little mirror which reflected just sufficient light for the process. Then she moved to the chest with its floral-patterned cover.

For many minutes she moved about in her moccasin slippers. The lid of the chest was propped open, and her busy hands were at work folding and packing, bestowing inside it the delicate garments which only a short day ago had afforded her such delight. Somehow her mood was completely reversed. And there was not a moment in which she paused to contemplate the wonderful texture, the softness and delicacy, of the things she was packing. It was almost as if her work could not be accomplished with sufficient speed.

The last garment had been folded and bestowed. The silver tissue shoes had found their place in the chest. The cloak, with its fur lining, had been laid on the top of the others. Then the commoner garments, that had their ordinary home in the chest, were replaced on the top of all, and the lid was re-closed.

It was as though Molly's glory of yesterday was a thing repugnant to her; as though she were endeavouring to shut out the memory of it from her mind. As the lid of the chest closed, and the cover was re-set in its place, the girl stood for a moment before it with bosom heaving and a light of panic in her eyes.

The dawn had broadened towards full daylight when Molly at last turned away and passed out of the room.

* * * *

Lightning moved up to the house engrossed in thought. That which he had witnessed of the parting at the storm doorway had troubled him. The girl's subsequent flood of tears had shocked him out of all his confidence.

The earlier episode had been comprehensible enough. The disaster he had feared had happened. Molly had promised marriage. The man he felt he could never work for was to become the master of the Marton farm. For him, he knew, it meant the end of all things. And the thought that he would be driven to part from Molly froze his heart and left him groping helplessly.

It was Lightning's way to drive straight to the heart of things. But he was not prepared for the scene he discovered in the living-room. The cook-stove had been lit. The breakfast had been set. And Molly was at work frying the pork, and browning the beans.

Molly glanced round as Lightning thrust the door open, and he caught a glimpse of a pair of forlorn eyes darkly ringed as a result of hours of tearful wakefulness. Instantly the man's rougher mood melted. His desire to delve to the heart of things evaporated. A great wave of foolish sympathy set him yearning to say something, to do something, that would banish the look of trouble he beheld.

But inspiration failed him, and his greeting was a jarring complaint.

"Say, Molly, gal, I bin workin' around here since you was knee high, an' I ain't known the man or woman that set light to that darn ol' stove but me. It's a measly bet I can't set a lucifer to a bunch o' kindlin' for you the mornin' after your party night. What's got you, gal?" he went on, with a grin intended to help things. "Feelin' restless? Your fine fixin's got you worried they'd sort o' quit you come mornin'? I sure feel bad sun-up wa'ant early enough to light your stove."

Again the girl turned from her work at the stove.

"Does it matter, Lightning?" she asked, in a voice that lacked all its usual cheer.

"Come to that, I don't guess it does," the man returned on the instant, feeling he had no right to any complaint that could cause her distress. "You surely must ha' been plumb beat dancin' around at that hoe-down, though. Then ther' was all o' them fine fixin's. They'd get most any woman all worried to death with notions an' things. Ther' ain't nothin' like notions to get you so used up you can't sleep nor nothin'. Now I was reck'nin' to leave you sleepin' till noon. I'd figgered to fix my eats myself, an' hev you a real swell feed ready by noon. Then you'd get up an' around, an' hand me all the joy stuff your party showed you."

Molly dished out the beans, and set a layer of fat pork beside them on the platter which was to serve Lightning. The man's transparent kindliness was not without effect upon her. A ghost of a smile dispersed something of the woe which so distressed Lightning.

"You would figger that way," she said kindly. "That's you all the time. Well, this time I've done the figgering. I've figgered you need a breakfast right away. So sit around and eat, Lightning, and don't worry that I lit your stove for you."

The old man glanced at the heaping beans and bacon. Then he looked again into the face of the girl, who had made no attempt to help herself. He made no move to sit in at the table. He shook his head, and set himself to the task which he knew must be fulfilled without delay.

"You're goin' to marry him, Molly, gal?" he said abruptly.

Molly turned to the stove.

"I'm going to marry Andy—before summer's out," she said

in a low tone.

Lightning passed a hand over his unbrushed hair.

"Then I won't be needed—after harvest," he said, with a curious dullness.

Molly turned back on the instant. All the woe had passed out of her eyes. She stood up, tall and very pretty in her white waist and homely cloth skirt, and a gleam of hope reacted in Lightning's eyes.

"Lightning!"

Molly paused on her exclamation. Then:

"Lightning, you sure won't quit me, because—because of Andy?" she cried. "Oh, you—you just couldn't! You wouldn't! Why? Why? I'll need you more than ever. I shall. I could never do without you. You've been everything to me. You've—you've been father to me ever since—ever since father was killed. Want you? Oh, you don't know the thing you're saying. I know. You just hate Andy. And—and you want to quit me because of him. If you could only know the thing he is to me you wouldn't feel that way. You surely wouldn't. Say you won't quit me. Say you'll stop right along when Andy comes, just the same as—as now. Say that, Lightning. You must say it. You'll—you'll set me crazy if you don't."

Lightning's harsh voice jarred the silence of the room.

"Then he's comin' right here! That feller!" he cried. "He's comin' along to own this pore darn farm your dead father built right up fer—*you*! He's goin' to claim it all! He's goin' to claim—*you!*"

The old man's voice had risen almost to a shout. But with his final exclamation he seemed to realise whither his fury was driving him. And he stood silent, with his thin nostrils dilating, and with grim lips tight pressed.

Molly stared at him. Then, slowly, she raised her hands in mute but infinite appeal. There were no words, no angry retort, no argument. Lightning capitulated. He inclined his head in surrender, and the hate passed out of his eyes.

"Fergit it, Molly, gal. I'm crazy mad, sure," he said.

Then he glanced down at the steaming food, and a sound escaped him like a laugh of self-derision.

"Surely I'll stop around, little gal, with you needin' me," he went on. "If you need him here, you must have him. If you figger to hand him over your farm, you must hand it. If he's your man, then that's surely so, an' I ain't another word. If he acts right, an'

158

treats you right, may the good Lord be good to him, an' so'll I. If he don't— Say, I'll eat that feed right away, little Molly. An' I'll try an' remember I'm your hired man, an' fergit some day I'll hev to be his."

CHAPTER XXIII
Blanche Learns the Truth

IT was noon when Blanche rode up to the barn, to be greeted by a glance of genuine admiration which the old cattleman divided between the golden sorrel and its rider.

She nodded with great friendliness as Lightning bared his head. Then she lightly slipped out of the saddle, and looked up into the keen old eyes.

"Molly gotten back from her dance?" she inquired.

Lightning took possession of her horse. Stooping, he ran a comprehending hand down the creature's forelegs.

"She surely has, ma'am," he said. "She's by the house. An' I'd say she's most like a pore tired kid yearnin' for a play game she don't know about." He straightened himself up. "I'd say, them legs is clean as a gun bar'l, ma'am."

Blanche nodded. Lightning's downright love of horseflesh appealed to her.

"He surely is a gentleman," she laughed.

"A king, ma'am," the old man corrected. "I'll hand him a rub-down an' feed him good," he went on. "You'll be makin' the house right away?" His gaze passed to a thoughtful contemplation of Molly's storm doorway. "I guess you'll feel most like sayin' a piece that'll set Molly, gal, in sperrits?"

Blanche smiled into his earnest face.

"I surely will," she said, turning and passing on up to the house.

* * * *

The thing lying behind the old cattleman's words was soon made apparent to Blanche. It was there in the troubled eyes of Molly as she struggled hard to smile a warmth of real welcome.

Molly was at work. She had spent the morning in almost feverish effort. And it was an expression of a mind that was endeavouring to escape from itself. Molly was full of simple gratitude to this stranger who had so suddenly and even mysteriously, come into her life. And almost her first words were of thanks.

But the girl's appearance shocked Blanche. She was wholly unprepared for anything beyond the reaction of a glorious social adventure. Molly looked ill. And it seemed to Blanche that all the sunny enthusiasm, all the happy youth, of which she had carried away such a vivid impression after their first meeting, were entirely lacking. To her mind, if Molly had encountered some terrible grief rather than participated in the riotous delight of her first dance, her spirits and appearance could not have suffered more.

Her concern found almost instant expression.

"Why, child," she exclaimed, "you look like a little ghost." Then she shook her head. "The belle of the Hartspool ball never looked like that last night, I'll wager. Was the floor bad? Was the music a dirge? Did your frock get mussed? Tell me."

Molly denied with so much vehemence and endeavour to convince that she completely failed to allay the other's apprehension.

But Blanche had come there with a very definite purpose in her mind. She had come to learn all she could from Molly of the man who had taken her into the Hartspool dance. But she was too much a woman for that to be the whole object that had entailed many miles in the saddle over a territory that was without trail or track of any sort. No. Her visit was for the girl's sake, too, and for the sake of the gossip and happy chatter of the glorious time she had helped to provide her with.

But Blanche was foredoomed to disappointment. Molly's dispiritedness was so intensely real that she became more gravely concerned than she knew. It was not that Molly was not ready to talk of the dance. On the contrary she talked of it almost too eagerly. It was not that her smile was lacking. But to Blanche neither her talk nor her smile were such as she had looked for. There was no spontaneity in either. They were both the result of obvious effort. They lacked all naturalness. And all the time there was something looking out of the girl's eyes that intrigued and troubled her, and left her wondering.

Blanche was again sitting in George Marton's chair. She was sitting up in her neat riding-suit, with her hands held out to the warmth of the stove in spite of the summer heat. Molly was preparing the midday meal for her guest, neglecting nothing, meticulous in her care that the meal should be the best she could provide for her new friend.

"Is this Andy of yours a good dancer, Molly?"

161

Blanche was observing the figure bending over the stove. She was watching, with the closest interest, the girl's care in her work. When she put her apparently casual question she saw the bending figure start. Then, as it straightened itself up, she realised that the hand grasping the pepper-box, with which she was seasoning the jack-rabbit stew was trembling. Instantly a mental reservation warned her where lay the key to Molly's grievous mood.

The girl steadied herself with an effort. Then she laughed a little uncertainly.

"Why, I guess he's no sort of dancer," she said. "But then," she added quickly, "I wouldn't know the diff'rence. You see, I haven't learnt any swell dancing. I just sort of know the things you do at 'sociables.'"

Blanche's laugh came readily.

"I guess you don't need to be a swell dancer to have a time. If your boy's right, and you're looking good, and the folks are all in to enjoy things, the dancing doesn't matter a deal. This Andy—you didn't say his other name to me—he's a farmer like you?"

There was a moment of hesitation before Molly replied. It almost seemed as though she had forgotten the stew on the stove. She was still grasping the pepper-box, but a far-away, unsmiling look was in the sad eyes, that were turned upon the sunlight pouring in through the open window.

"He's your neighbour, isn't he? Ten miles east?"

Blanche was urging the girl in the gentlest fashion. At the sound of her voice Molly turned sharply back to her stove. She bent over her work again and spoke rapidly, without even glancing in her friend's direction.

"Yes. He's Andy McFardell, and he's set up his homestead along down the creek ten miles east of here. I'm—he's going to marry me. We'll be married—before summer's out."

There was just the shadow of a break in the girl's final announcement. Blanche noted her attitude, and a wave of pity she could not account for stirred her deeply.

"You're engaged? You're going to be married? Why, Molly, you hadn't said a thing. Tell me. Just tell me all about it. I'm surely dying to know. Is he a good-looker? Has he a swell farm? My!"

Blanche was acting. She condemned herself for it. Her enthusiasm was sheer pretence. She remembered that the man Molly had said she was going to marry was—Andrew McFardell.

The girl's reply came with a rush. It came with all the spontaneity which Blanche had missed before. And all the time Molly was talking Blanche felt that every word she was speaking was in some measure defensive, not against her, not against any individual, but against some feeling, in conflict with some emotion of her own.

"Maybe you won't understand," she cried. "How could you? Nobody could understand the way I feel. I guess I just love him to death." She laughed a little meaninglessly. "I love him so he could beat me, so he could walk all over my fool body. I just can't think what things would be without him. The thing he says goes all the time, and when I hear him I can't even think for myself. Do you know how I mean? Of course you don't. It's love, I guess. There isn't a sun in the sky to compare with his smile. With him around I just want to sit an' listen, an' do the thing he says. Oh, Blanche, it's awful, just awful, when you feel that way. I think it sets you crazy. Yes, yes. That's it, plumb crazy. If he said he was goin' to kill me I'd be glad. If he said I was a fool girl I'd know I was. It wouldn't matter what he said or did—so long as he didn't quit me. Oh, I want him, and—and he's goin' to marry me before the summer's out. Think of it, Blanche. When summer's through he'll be along here. I'll have him with me always. Every day I'll wake to find him near by, to listen to his voice, to see his eyes smile deep into mine. It—it'll be heaven—just heaven. Oh, how I'll work around to make this farm a home to him! His homestead's a poor sort of place. He's been working lone-handed. You see, he's only had it come two years, since he quit the Police. He hasn't had a good time. No. They've surely been cruel to him. But it don't matter now. I'll make that all different. Think of it, he'll be all mine to work for, an' to make happy. An' this farm's good, and some day he'll be well fixed. And—and I'll have helped to do that for him."

She drew a deep breath and stood up straight. And Blanche saw the wonderful light shining in her eyes.

"It's—it's all just wonderful to think that way, Blanche," she went on. "It makes me feel—it makes——"

Suddenly the light in her eyes faded, and she turned again to the stove in some haste, and went on with her work.

Blanche made the response she felt she must make. She had listened to the outpouring of the soul of the girl. She had been invited for one brief moment to peer into the inner recesses where the fires of simple human love burned fiercely upon the altar of sacrifice. And her responsibility burdened her.

163

She simply dared not pursue the matter in the light fashion she had intended. Then there was that feeling that the girl had been pleading in her own defence. And it was a feeling she was powerless to shake off.

It was not until food had been prepared and set ready on the table that Blanche found it possible to shake off the weight which the girl's confession had heaped upon her. But at Molly's invitation to "sit in" her lighter mood returned. The change was wrought by the change which her confession seemed to have brought about in Molly. The girl seemed easier in her mind. Her smile was less forced, and talk came more readily.

They talked through the meal, and as time went on Blanche's constraint passed altogether. They talked of everything that interested, and by the time the meal was finished Blanche felt that Molly had actually benefited by her visit, and she herself had learned all, and far more than she had wanted to know concerning the man who had once been Corporal Andrew McFardell.

When the time for her departure came, Lightning brought her horse to the door of the house, and stood apparently engrossed in his admiration of the golden creature.

Inside the house the two women made their farewell.

"May I come again, Molly?"

Blanche's smile was full of warmth. And Molly's eyes widened at the superfluousness of the question.

"Why, Blanche, I'm crazy for you to come along all the time. Next to Andy I want you most."

Blanche shook her head admonishingly.

"Say, my dear, some day I'm going to be married myself," she said, and her manner was very, very gentle. "I love the man I'm going to marry with all my foolish heart. He's not a good-looker like your Andy. And he's got a mop of scarlet hair and a bunch of foolish freckles. But I'm not going to let him set me crazy. It's not good to get too crazy that way. I—I may come to your wedding if I'm around here when the time comes?"

Molly nodded, and her smile was one of sheer exaltation.

"Surely, Blanche," she said. "It wouldn't be right without you."

Blanche took the girl by the shoulders and kissed her on both cheeks.

"Good. So long, Molly," she said.

* * * *

Molly was standing at the open doorway. Blanche had ridden away. She had long since vanished round the bluff where the grass-trail followed its outline in the direction where her father had been in the habit of hewing his cordwood. Lightning had been into the house for his meal. He had eaten it and returned again to his work. Molly had seen him moving out with his team, heading for the hay slough. Her own work was awaiting her.

The last shadow of her smile had passed. And the cloud of dispiritedness had resettled itself in the pathetic depression of her brows. The interim of relief had passed with the going of her mysterious friend. Once more she had fallen back into that distressing mood which had inspired the cattleman's appeal at Blanche's coming.

CHAPTER XXIV
At Haying Time

JANE and Blue Pete were doing their best. Their massive bodies were a sumptuous feeding-ground for the swarming mosquitoes, which transformed their cheerful roan coats into something drab and dismal. The air was hot and heavy in the depths of the slough, but the grass was luxuriant, and the hay cut was heavy.

Perched on the iron saddle of the mower, Lightning had no complaint to make against the conditions of his work, or the result of his labours. The heat, and the flies, and the mosquitoes, left the man unheeding. The toughened pores of his skin refused to exude a perspiration that could cause him discomfort. As for the flies, they made no more impression on him than if he had been a brass image. Even the blood-lust of the mosquitoes was little enough likely to obtain satisfaction from his hardening veins. But his temper was more than usually uncertain, and it found expression in a wealth of invective which he hurled at the heads of his devoted team. He sat there like some ragged, bewhiskered vulture, lean, aggressive, alternately cursing and coaxing. Lightning was worried. He was irritated. He was desperately unhappy.

Lightning's ill mood had been steadily growing for three weeks, ever since the night of Molly's party. It seemed like an eternity to the old man since that night which was only three weeks ago. He seemed to have lived through an age of disquiet and anxiety. And the depression of it had long since passed the stage when explosive blasphemy could afford him any relief.

With Molly's unremitting assistance he had been cutting, and hauling, and stacking hay for days. But he had found in the work none of his customary satisfaction. In happier times each accomplished item in the round of his seasonal labours signified something achieved in the interests of the girl. Every detail of improvement in the progress of the Marton homestead had been a source of complete satisfaction to him. But that was when he knew it was all for Molly. That was before the thought of Andy McFardell had become the disturbing element of his intolerant mind.

But now that disturbing element had given place to something a hundredfold worse. It was Molly who had become his gravest anxiety. Again he knew that it was the man who was the source of the trouble. But it was in a different fashion. Hitherto Lightning had deplored and hated the man's presence anywhere near the farm. Now he was desperately concerned at his absence from it. Andy McFardell had not been near the farm since the night of the party.

The change in the girl immediately following the dance had been bad enough. Whatever his regard for Andy, Lightning had felt that the girl's distress, her obvious unhappiness, was altogether wrong and unaccountable. She was going to be married. It was her own choice. She was crazy about the wretched man. Well?

The first day had passed without relief. But with the second day it seemed that the work of time and youth would surely tell. Molly's silence was less unbroken; her work was carried on less feverishly; even a shadow of her smile returned. Then came the moment when he discovered her returning from the trail by the creek, and he knew she had been there watching for the coming of her lover. His relief developed into something like joy, and he was amazed to find the contemplated coming of Andy McFardell could so affect him.

But the man did not come. Neither the next day, nor the next, nor the next. And now three weeks had passed without his having put in an appearance. Each day the old man had seen the girl move out down the trail looking for his coming. And each day the time she remained seemed to lengthen.

The change in Molly had become almost calamitous. She rarely left the house except at Lightning's express call for her assistance. She laboured silently in the hay corral when the old man brought in a load of newly-cut hay. But she always returned to the house the moment the work was finished. Her eyes had the look of sleepless nights. Her cheeks had lost their happy roundness, and a pathetic down-drooping of the corners of her mouth told the troubled old man their own tale of dreary unhappiness.

Then came that memorable night when Lightning had recklessly ventured. Molly had eaten little at midday. She was eating less at the supper she was sharing with him. He had been observing her closely while he noisily consumed his hash with an appetite wholly unimpaired. Molly was gazing out of the window, her food scarcely touched, watching the play of the evening sunlight upon the foliage of a distant bluff. It was realisation of un-shed tears in the girl's eyes that robbed the old man of his caution, and flung him headlong.

"Ain't you eatin' your hash, Molly, gal?" he asked kindly, al-though at the moment his own mouth was filled to overflowing. "It's real good," he went on, with a smack of his lips as he swal-lowed. "You surely hev got the onions good in it. You didn't eat at midday. An' you ain't eatin' now. There's a heap o' work around this layout needs swell muscle, even in a gal like you. Best eat."

Molly shook her head without withdrawing her gaze. And Lightning could restrain his impulse no longer.

"He ain't been round, Molly, gal," he said. "Ain't you lookin' fer him to come along?"

Molly sighed pathetically. Her gaze was studiously held to the window. Lightning realised the struggle she was making. Then, when she spoke, her voice was low and unsteady.

"I guess he isn't through," she said. "He'll be haying, too. He'll surely be haying. You see, he's such a boy for getting back of his work."

Lightning could have shouted blasphemy when Molly spoke of her lover's devotion to work. But, instead, his voice came very gently.

"Sure, he'll be haying. That's so. That's why he ain't been around. You couldn't want him to get around when the grass is ripe, and the season's good. Say"—he passed his plate for anoth-er portion of the hash he approved—"why not get your pinto out an' get a breath of good air, gal? You sure need it. I guess it won't worry me stackin' the grass I haul. Beat it over to that boy's place an' see the way he's makin' out."

Lightning needed no better reward than the look that respond-ed to his grin. He watched Molly pass to the stove to replenish his plate. And as she passed it back to him, he listened to the reacting hope which sounded in her voice.

"I surely could do that," she said eagerly. "Maybe it would help him, too. You see, he's alone. It isn't the same with him as it is with us. You don't need to haul to-morrow, anyway. Just cut. That way I could ride out and——"

Lightning felt he had really done a wonderful thing.

"Don't say a thing, Molly, gal," he cried. "I'll fix all that. You get your pinto an' ride over to-morrow mornin'. Guess you'll tickle that boy to death comin' along. An', say, quit this foolish-ness with your food, gal. You got me so worried I don't feel I could swaller a mouthful right. An' ther's Jane an' Pete worried about it, too," he grinned. "That's it," he cried, as Molly made a serious attempt to obey him. "You don't know the thing you're missin' in this darn hash."

That night had been the one bright spot in the whole of the three weeks. But it was only the forerunner of darker days. Molly went off the next morning. She went off in spirits she had not displayed for a week. She returned in less than three hours. It was her return that brought Lightning's structure of hope crashing about his unfortunate ears.

He encountered her at the barn as she rode up. Her pinto was blowing, as though the tireless creature had been flogged every mile of the journey home. But all hope had fled at sight of the distracted girl, and his heart sank to zero.

"Wal?"

Lightning's voice had never rasped so harshly.

But there was no reply. It is doubtful even if Molly heard. Her mare propped to a standstill and she leapt from the saddle. The next moment she was gone. She had fled to the house, leaving the pinto to its own devices.

Since that time another two weeks had passed—two weeks of worry which the old man had hardly known how to endure.

After Molly's return he had contemplated having the whole thing out with her at the first opportunity. But the girl settled the matter herself that very night. She met him in the doorway as he went up to the house for his supper.

He was astonished and further alarmed at the sight of her waiting for him. Her eyes contained not a sign of that which had filled them on her return at midday. They were calm—quite calm—like the eyes of the dead father he so well remembered. But they had a coldness in them that utterly forbade the intrusion he had contemplated.

As he came to the door the girl spoke.

"You fixed my mare?" she said sharply. "That's all right," she went on, as the old man reassured her. "We'll get right on with the haying. The seasons don't wait around for any foolishness. Do you get me? There's going to be no more foolishness. Not a thing more, and not a word about it."

So the evening had been passed without any explanation. He was never likely to forget that evening. Molly seemed suddenly to have grown years older. She ate her food and went about her work silently, deliberately. When he spoke to her, she replied sufficiently, in unemotional fashion. She never once smiled. It seemed as if all her youth had gone from her, as though an icy coldness had frozen up the last drop of the warm springs of her young heart.

Now Lightning was engaged upon the last of the haying. He was also engaged upon something else. At long last he had determined to discover the thing that had happened between the lovers from the other end of the affair—that end where no delicacy or scruple need be displayed.

He was perfecting his plans. He had thought them out in detail, and the result, in his view, was all he desired. This was the last cut of hay. To-morrow he would announce to Molly that the team must be re-shod. He would take them into Hartspool, and, on his way, he would call in at Andy McFardell's homestead, and be prepared to deal with the man as he saw fit. He would certainly discover the thing that had happened.

* * * *

It was nearly noon the next day when Lightning drove his team into the clearing of Andy McFardell's homestead. He had had no difficulty in putting his plans into operation. Molly had agreed, after inspection of the lengthened hoofs of the team. So the old man had driven off, with his treasured guns carefully concealed in the wagon-box. Once beyond all chance of Molly's observation, the weapons were taken from their place of concealment and adjusted about his lean body.

He gazed eagerly about him as he dodged the tree-stumps at the entrance to the clearing. The thing he expected to find had never been clear to him. But that which he did find was certainly the last thing he expected. Andy McFardell's homestead was derelict. It was abandoned.

He drove his team right up to the miserable barn and got out of the wagon. The door of the building was nailed up. He stood for a moment considering it. Then he raised one heavily-booted foot, and launched it, sole first, against the crazy boarding. It gave on the instant, splintering and cracking. A second effort flung it open by the simple process of tearing it from its rusted hinges. He passed within.

A few moments later he returned into the full sunlight. Just for one moment he glanced at his drowsy team. Then he glanced round at the other buildings, all of which had been lightly boarded up. Finally he sought the hay corral. There was a small scattering of loose hay littering it, otherwise the place was empty.

He collected an armful of the hay. It was the best offering he could make to his team. He had tried the barn for feed, but had drawn a blank. So he came back to his horses, removed their bits, and, leaving them busily devouring the hay, passed on to complete his investigations.

He spent a full hour at his task, and when he returned to his wagon to water his horses, and feed them from the reserve of oats he carried with him, it was in the full knowledge that Andy's farm was abandoned for good.

There was not a living thing to be discovered anywhere. The man's horses were gone. His two cows. His spring wagon, harness, and even the wealth of implements he had acquired from the machine agent. There was not a spade, or fork, or axe, or saw, about the place. The house, too, was similarly bare. Such items of furnishing as the place had possessed had vanished. Blankets, pots, and crocks—all had been swept away. And the answer to it came to him without even an effort. The man had given up, and either sold up, or been sold up—the man who had promised to marry Molly before the summer was out.

He had fixed his team and seated himself in the shade of his wagon, prepared to eat such food as he had brought with him.

The full significance of the thing he had discovered slowly took possession of him. And he found in it the looked-for answer to the latest change in Molly. Oh, yes, it was clear enough to him now. The whole thing must have been in contemplation, even exactly planned, at the time when—yes, that was it. Molly had found the same as he had found. What did it signify? Was it that the man reckoned he would no longer need the place with Molly as his wife? It looked that way. Then why had he not shown up in three weeks?

The old man sat there eating, and labouring heavily with thought. He saw the whole thing in its own light. He contemplated it from the viewpoint of his own experiences of men. Deliberately, definitely, his mind fixed itself on the night of the dance, and his whole focus became preoccupied with the girl's breakdown after McFardell's departure on that night.

Why? Why? Why that flood of tears? All the rest receded into the background. That one detail stood out above all others. And as he considered it, as he translated it in the only fashion possible to him, a sickening horror took possession of him.

CHAPTER XXV
The Beginning of the Harvest

THE things Lightning discovered at McFardell's homestead and later learned in Hartspool instantly suggested headlong action. He wanted to fling everything to the winds and get after the "gopher police-scab" with his old guns primed and a supply of bullets in his pockets.

But there was something, some subtle claim that was infinitely stronger, holding him back. He felt he would be serving Molly better by remaining at her call on the farm. Since that hour or so of meditation in the shade of his wagon at McFardell's there had steadily grown up within him a conviction that, whatever his devotion might prompt in Molly's defence, his place must be near her all the time now. He felt that never in all her young life had Molly had so great a need of him.

The thing he learned in Hartspool of Andy McFardell while his team was being shod came from the township's best-informed gossip. Barney, at Lightning's first introduction of the subject, was only too ready to pour out an opinion that never at any moment brooked disguise. He nodded a toast at the old cattleman, at whose expense he was drinking, swallowed his modest "two fingers" of Rye, set his glass in the water-trough under the counter, and, leaning forward against the bar, with arms folded upon it, let loose his story.

"That junk?" he said contemptuously, with a laugh that failed to reach his shrewd eyes. "Wal, the only thing makes me feel good about *that* is he's stung McCrae, the implement boy around hyar, good an' plenty. That guy McFardell's a shyster. But it don't make me feel more bad about him that he's stung McCrae. I ain't no kind o' use fer the machinery bosses o' this country. It ain't I've a grouch against machinery. It's their ways o' tradin'. There's folk reckon to close down every darn liquor joint in the whole of this blamed continent. I tell you right hyar our trade couldn't harm a louse compared with the 'crop mortgage' system o' pushing machinery on to crazy guys o' new settlers who don't know better."

He shrugged his burly shoulders, and his eyes snapped. "He's lit out, as I guessed he would. An' he was slick over it, too. He drove in at dark, nigh three weeks back, an' his wagon was full up of his fool kit. I didn't see him, but I got the story good. He'd sold one of his plugs, an' his two lousy cows, an' his wagon, before he got in. He drew his stuff fer that. Then he held a sort o' auction amongst the boys he was used to playin' 'stud' with for his out-fit. The thing I make out is they acted white by him. They handed him better money than I would. Anyway, he got away with it, an' then wrote out a piece tellin' McCrae where to collect up the machinery he'd stocked him with, and he could snatch his land for the money owin'. That he passed in through the mail office. And come mornin' he'd quit Hartspool with his saddle-horse, an' he ain't bin around sence."

Lightning drained his second glass of Rye, and set it empty on the bar.

"Quit the territory?" he inquired simply.

"Maybe. Can't say." Barney was wiping glasses, which seemed to be a habit with him in the absence of any more amusing occupation. "He ain't bin around, anyway. An' seein' he's the sort o' shyster he is, why, I guess he'd be right here on the bum till his dollars ran out—if he was around."

"You reckon he's beat it," mused Lightning, fingering his empty glass. Then he looked up. "You best pass that bottle again. I'm feelin' kind o' mean."

Barney laughed with his twinkling eyes this time.

"I ain't ever known you to feel any other way when you blow along into this burg, Lightning," he said amiably. "Hev this one on me. You're the sort of boy I like gettin' around. You get an' elegant souse down your spine, an' quit. That's how a boy should take his liquor."

He filled up the old man's glass with raw spirit, and Lightning's feelings warmed towards him.

"Do I reckon he's beat it?" Barney went on, putting the bottle away. "Surely I do. An' if you ask me, I'd say he's begun the hoboe trail. It mostly starts that way. Dollars an' a hoss. Later, no hoss. Then the freight cars. An' when he can't 'jump' them he'll need to pad the railroad ties. That's him. A sure hoboe."

Lightning shook his head decidedly.

"Guess he won't finish that way," he said.

"How then? Penitentiary?"

Lightning drained his glass again, and the spirit stirred his blood and lit his eyes fiercely.

"No. It won't be penitentiary either," he cried emphatically.

Barney eyed the old man shrewdly.

"Guess McCrae ain't the only boy he's stung," he laughed.

Lightning moved away a little unsteadily.

"I don't know who he's stung," he retorted coldly, "but I'll need to sleep right here to-night. I'm pulling out come mornin'."

Barney nodded.

"That's all right, boy. Be good."

And he laughed at the old man's back as Lightning passed out on his way to the shoeing-smith.

Blanche had visited the farm in Lightning's absence. And the news greeted him on his arrival home. His return seemed to gladden Molly, in spite of herself. She told him Blanche's visit was in the way of a sort of farewell. She had come to tell her that she was not likely to visit her again for some time; that she would be up in the hills with her men-folk on a vacation, and did not quite know when she would quit them. Molly told him she seemed sad because she was going to be in the hills. But she said she would come again to see her when opportunity offered.

Lightning yearned to ask if she had confided her trouble to this woman friend, but discretion forbade. Instead, he asked other questions of a casual nature. Did she stop around long? And he learned that Blanche had eaten at the house and then taken her departure.

It was not until he was alone in his bunk-house that night that he realised a curiously significant thing about Blanche's visit. She must have passed him on the trail from Hartspool. She was living somewhere around Hartspool. She must have been coming to the farm while he was leaving it. Yet they had not met. He had not seen a sign of her. Then a further thought occurred to him. Why had he so completely forgotten her when he was in Hartspool? No doubt Barney Lake could have told him just who she was and all about her. It was idiotic that he had made no inquiry. And he fell into his customary deep slumber cursing himself.

But matters relating to Blanche quickly faded out of his mind. Molly absorbed his whole concern. There was no improvement in her. She worked from daylight to dark. She ate clearly because she must. Her laugh was a thing he had forgotten. She was so changed—so utterly changed.

Her attitude towards him was pathetic in its gentleness. Sometimes there was a display of submissiveness which literally distracted him. As the weeks passed he realised, too, that her strength was failing her. She grew weary so easily. The labours with fork and hoe, which had once been child's play to her, not only became effort, but effort she could no longer sustain. And he knew by the signs that she was steadily becoming sick, not only in mind, but also in body. Time and youth were no longer her allies. And he was haunted by the danger-signal, which, with every passing day, he saw drawing nearer.

Lightning had not the temperament to stand by indefinitely without making an effort. And so it came about that on one memorable evening, after a day of more than usual anxiety, just as he was leaving his bunk-house he precipitated things with his sympathy.

"Say, Molly, gal," he said, no longer able to restrain the impulse, "you ain't lookin' good. An', mebbe, you ain't feelin' good. I kind of see them pore mean cheeks o' yours gettin' thin like paper. An' you ain't got the grit you had for the work around the farm. The oats is comin' ripe. We'll need to be cuttin' come a week. Now, I bin thinkin'. The season's good. Ther' ain't no rain about. Ther' ain't no sort o' hurry. Wal, I don't see you need to worry with that harvest. You sure don't. I ken do it lone-handed easy. You lie up. You set around. An' when them cheeks has filled right out, an' the colour's got back to 'em——"

But the old man broke off, aghast at the result of his effort. Molly's reply came in the midst of it. It was a repetition of that breakdown on the night of the party. She burst into a flood of tears, and fled from the room.

* * * *

Lightning was feeling more content than the condition of things seemed to indicate. He was on the saddle of his binder, ruminating behind the stout quarters of Jane and Blue Pete while he cut the oat crop. There was something very satisfying to him in the operation. The season was good. The air was hot and bracing under a perfect sun. The straw was sturdy, and not too long. The ear was heavy. Then there had been no summer storms to "lay" the dancing grain that rustled about him. There were feed and seed to spare in the crop. There would be many quarters for the Hartspool market.

These things undoubtedly influenced him, but there were others as well. Molly had voluntarily fallen in with his suggestion.

She had left the oat harvest entirely to him. She had remained to look after the lighter affairs of the farm. Then, on this first day of the cutting, Blanche had arrived on her first visit in two months. He had left her now with Molly, and somehow he was hoping much from her visit.

She had ridden up to the farm more than usually early, having arrived just after breakfast. Now it was nearing noon, and a big cut of oats lay sprawled in sheaves to Lightning's credit. He meant to cut till eating-time, and spend the afternoon stooking. His temper was easy as the machine passed up and down the crop. Jane and Blue Pete were having a peaceful time, and seemed to approve. From the creek to the bluff, which shut them out of sight of their barn, they moved on steadily, comfortably encircling the ever-diminishing patch of standing grain.

He was nearing the woodland bluff when Blanche appeared. She came through the woods, clearly prepared for departure. It was also obvious to Lightning that she had come specially to talk to him. Were it not so she would surely have departed the way she had come, which way lay farther down the creek, where he had broken the new five acres earlier in the year.

He drew up his team as he approached the spot at which she was awaiting him. His eyes betrayed the question in his mind, and his first words displayed his anxiety.

"Mebbe you ken tell me, ma'am, now you've seen her," he said eagerly. "I'm figgerin' that pore kid's sick. Sick to death. An' I'm wonderin'. I feel like it's right up to me. An'—an' I heven't a notion of the thing I need to do. It ain't a case o' salts fer Molly gal's sickness. Mebbe her body's sick. I guess it surely is. But I sort o' feel it's her mind's the trouble, ma'am. An' I guess ther' ain't no dope merchant in Hartspool ken fix that. You're a swell leddy, with knowledge, an' I guess she's a woman like you. It's since ever that party, an' that skunk of a boy ain't showed up."

Blanche's eyes were grave as she looked down on the man from her saddle. She was observing him closely, looking for an answer to the many questions in her own mind. Apparently her observation satisfied her, for an indefinable expression slowly eased her gravity.

"She's sick," she said. Then she added: "She's more sick than you guess."

The full significance of what she said lay in Blanche's tone. And Lightning's old heart sank within him.

"Meanin'?" he cried anxiously.

176

Blanche shook her head.

"I've never seen such a change in anyone in so short a while, Lightning," she said gravely. "And I can't get her to say a thing. I just can't get a word out of her about herself. She laughs. And her laugh's the most tragic thing I've ever heard. Oh, she talked about anything but herself, and she laughed like—like a machine. Maybe she thought she was getting away with it. She wasn't. I could see the trouble lying back of it all like reading an open book. It's a bit dreadful. You see, I could see the trouble without being able to—recognise it. Tell me anything you can—all you know."

Lightning felt that his hope and faith in this woman had not been misplaced. She had asked him to do the thing he had long since made up his mind to do. He intended to tell her the whole story, and began at once.

He told his story with all the close detail which his anxiety had impressed upon his mind. He told it from the very beginning, when they had first discovered Andy McFardell was their neighbour, down to his latest discovery that the man had abandoned his homestead and disappeared. He lost no opportunity of impressing on Blanche his own dislike and distrust of the man, and of how he had urged Molly to cut him out. He gave her frankly to understand that his urging of Molly was chiefly inspired by his dislike of the man, but was not unsupported by the things he had learned about him in Hartspool. And Blanche, listening to the harsh voice and harsher language, felt that she was being admitted to the innermost thoughts and feelings of a man who is completely at the end of his resources. There was something almost terrible in the savage passion of his final words.

"Ma'am," he said, his body crouched on the binder saddle, his face raised to hers till the stringy flesh of his throat was drawn like tight-stretched parchment, his eyes alight and burning like coals of fire, "ther's no dirt a boy ken do like settin' a gal crazy with all the love in her, an' quittin' her cold, an' lightin' out to beat it from the thing he's done. That feller ain't a skunk, ma'am. He ain't even a yellow cur. Ma'am, ther's worse things than them. Ther's things so mean, so low down, that the only way you ken fix 'em right is to crush 'em, smash 'em, beat 'em to small pieces, so you can't rec'nise 'em for the muss they make under your feet. Do you get me? That feller just needs smashin' to small meat."

Blanche had never encountered such concentrated hate and merciless bitterness. It appalled her. But she was caught by it, and held by the sense of the primitive that inspired it.

"It's awful!" she cried. "It's—it's just awful! The man's a—a scoundrel! He's—oh, it makes me crazy mad to think of it. It's——"

She broke off. There was a start of alarm as a thought flashed into her mind. She turned away from the man who was waiting upon her words, and her gaze sought the distant hills to the south and west.

There had suddenly come to her a new interpretation of Andy McFardell's going. And it was an interpretation that had nothing to do with Molly. The man had gone, cleared out, vanished. He had not shown up again in Hartspool. Then, where—where had he gone? *Was* his going the escape from Molly they had been thinking it was? She had suddenly remembered that Andy McFardell had encountered and recognised her brother, Jim. And Jim was the cause of his original downfall.

"I must be going," she said awkwardly. Then, realising the abruptness of her manner: "I've stopped around longer than I reckoned."

"Are you a long piece up in the hills, ma'am?" Lightning asked uneasily. He was thinking of the possible needs of Molly, and of his own helplessness.

"Longer than makes it easy riding down here often." Blanche shook her head. "It's rough territory," she went on, "and there's no trail. I couldn't tell you so you'd understand it right. No. I'll come along, though, just when I can. I don't know. That poor child's sick—sick."

The sympathy deepened in her eyes.

"Yes, it's her mind, Lightning. She's troubled so she's right down sick. And I don't know what you're to do. You must watch her, sure. Oh, yes, you must watch her. And—and if she gets worse, you'll need to get right after a doctor, if you can get one in Hartspool. You see, she won't say a thing. I can't quite——"

"No?"

Lightning's interrogation came curiously. There was something suggestive in it, something that caught and held the girl, and sent a wave of panic through her heart.

"No," she repeated, a little mechanically.

Silence fell between them. The intentness of their regard was for the thought that was passing in each mind. Maybe even, ill-matched as they were, yet so bonded in the object of their sympathy, there was something of thought-transference passing between them. At any rate, there was no spoken word that could have inspired the sharp-drawn breath which accompanied the light of panic that had suddenly appeared in Blanche's eyes. She seemed about to speak, but no sound came. Instead, her lips closed tightly, sealing themselves over the thing that, in an unguarded moment, was almost escaping her.

She lifted her reins and turned her horse. And as the creature moved Lightning's voice came low and almost pleading.

"You'll surely come again, ma'am?" he begged her.

Blanche inclined her head.

"Surely," she said.

Lightning watched her go. He watched her until she had passed completely from view. Then he got down and unhooked his team.

CHAPTER XXVI
The Climax

LIGHTNING had just reached the barn with his team. His horses stood timidly regarding the thing that held the man aghast. Perhaps they were mildly wondering at the extraordinary situation that held them up just as they were about to pass into the barn for their midday feed.

But Lightning was no longer concerned for their needs. He was startled, horrified, and he stared in helpless wonder at the litter of hay sprawled at the entrance to the barn, and the prone figure lying huddled upon it.

It was Molly—the seemingly dead body of Molly. Her eyes were half closed. Her face was ashen, with that dreadful pallor that to Lightning looked like death. There was an abrasure on her forehead, a slight wound that disfigured her face and suggested the cause of the tragic thing he had discovered.

In the first rush of his horror Lightning believed the girl to be dead. And he stood and stared in a queer sort of daze. But it was only for a moment. All of a sudden he dropped upon his knees beside her, unable any longer to withstand the tide of incoherent pleading that broke from him.

There was no response to his pleading, nor to the tender chafing of her cold hands. And after a moment the man looked up and gazed about him. The heat of the sun was furious. The air was without movement, and alive with the hum of flies. There was not a creature to whom he could appeal for help. In that moment an agony of doubt assailed him. She was a girl. She was his young mistress. He was a rough uncultured creature, without knowledge or refinement. She might be dead. It looked like it. And then again, there might be something he could do to save her. What must he do?

Of a sudden his mind made itself up. He stood up. Then, bending down, he gathered the helpless girl into his arms and strode off towards the house.

As Lightning moved on to the house he remembered Blanche's urging. A doctor—if there was one in Hartspool. Yes. That was it. Of course, there was Doc Blanchard, the man he had years ago brought out to the farm at the time of another disaster. Yes. He would get him. He would get him right away. But first of all—first of all he must ascertain the worst.

So he carried the unconscious girl into the house. He passed into the living-room, where food was cooking just as Molly had left it. But his purpose did not end there. He moved across to the door of Molly's bedroom and pushed it open. Just for an instant he hesitated. Never in his life had he passed the threshold of that room, and the act of doing so now filled him with a queer sensation of sacrilege. But he thrust his feelings aside. It was no time for scruple. He carried his burden in and laid it on the neat white bed-cover.

Having plunged once, the nature of the man reasserted itself. He possessed no knowledge, but his sympathy was infinite. It was this that served him now. He went back to the living-room and obtained a towel and cold water. Then he went back to his charge. He propped the girl up; he unfastened the clothing about her soft white neck with clumsy, hesitating fingers. Then, with one arm supporting her, he bathed her temples and forehead with the water, and talked to her unconscious form like a half-demented mother crooning over her sick babe. It was everything his distracted mind could suggest.

His reward was far beyond his expectations. It is almost doubtful that he had any expectations at all. Nothing that he did or said was calculated. He was beyond calculation. The first result of the water was to wash away the ooze of blood upon the girl's forehead, and it became quickly evident that the wound was little beyond a scratch, and a disfiguring bruise on the soft white flesh. Then, in less than five minutes, he beheld a movement of those half-closed eyelids. It was only a flicker, but it was sufficient. His dread lightened. He almost smiled. And certainly his curious jargon as he talked changed its tone to one of something like jocularity.

"Why, Molly, gal, that's just great," he muttered, as he plied the cold water with renewed zest. "I guess cold water's the greatest proposition ever. 'Tain't all folk figger that way. Now, Rye seems to me to hev more snap to it. But I guess that must be jest a notion. I wouldn't guess Rye could bring life back to your pore body same as this darn water's doin'. Jest get it. You was dead a

181

minit back, an' now you surely ain't. Ken you beat it? An' water's done it. Darn cold water, that I'd hate to hand out to better'n a yeller dawg. Still, ther' it is. Now you get them dandy eyes right open. An' set a bit o' colour right into them cheeks. Why, I b'lieve you was handin' out a sigh, one o' them things you mostly hand out when you're grievin'. You ain't grievin' gal? You ain't grievin' I bin dopin' you wi' water?" He chuckled. "Say, that's fine. Ther's colour in them cheeks now, same as I told you 'bout. Now them eyes. Jest open 'em. That's it, sure," he went on delightedly, as the eyelids were slowly raised, and Molly stared straight up into his face with just a dawning of intelligence. "My, but we'll hev you right in awhile. Then I'll go get right after that blamed Doc."

He laid the girl's head gently back on the pillow and stood up from the bed. Somehow he wanted to get out of that room. He hated the thought that he had sort of forced his way into it. Now that Molly was coming round he felt shame at being there. Besides, he wanted to be off for the doctor.

But he knew he dared not leave her yet. He must hear her speak first. He must have her reassurance. He watched her for some moments, and realised her rapid advance towards complete consciousness. Then, quite suddenly, she struggled to sit up.

"Wha—what happened?" she demanded dazedly.

"You're sick, an' I'm goin' right off fer Doc Blanchard. But first you're needin' food an' tea. Mebbe that'll set you feelin' good, an' I ken quit you fer awhiles."

Without waiting for any reply, the old man passed out to the cook-stove, and he felt happier in his familiar surroundings. He set beans enough for a starving man on Molly's plate. He buttered some bread, and then he dipped out a mug of tea, which he duly sweetened. After that he returned to the girl's bedroom, careful to knock on the door before entering.

The girl was sitting up. She was still looking ill. But her fainting had passed, and she looked very little different from her usual self. She protested at his offer of food, but accepted the tea eagerly. Lightning set the rest on the chair beside her bed.

"You jest got to eat that, Molly, gal," he said, with a bluffness that was only a mask. "You surely hev. You're sick. An' you need food. That's so. Now, gal, you eat, jest to make me feel good. I'm going right along to fix things."

He took himself off before the girl could refuse him, and he knew his going was a cowardly retreat. He passed down to the barn and saddled his horse, and fed and looked to his team. Then he returned to the house to snatch his own food. He would go in and see Molly before he went. He remembered he had mentioned getting the doctor to her when she was still dazed, and he hoped and feared for the foolishness of doing so. He hated deceiving her, but he knew he must do so. If he told her now he intended to get the doctor she would in all probability refuse her sanction. Blanche had warned him of the necessity. So his mind was irrevocably made up, and he approached her again with considerable trepidation.

Molly's food was untouched. The girl was sitting on the side of her bed when Lightning entered the room. She had re-fixed her waist where the old man's fingers had loosened it. And when he appeared she looked up and shook her head unsmilingly.

"I'm all right, Lightning," she said quietly. "Guess it must have been the sun. I don't know. Anyway, don't worry for me. You've been so good to me. I—say, I'll fix these things. I'll——"

She passed a hand wearily across her forehead. It was a gesture of mental rather than bodily weariness.

Lightning saw the gesture. He saw the weary spirit looking out of the tired eyes, and his heart bled for her.

"Then I'll get along, Molly, gal," he said eagerly. "You won't be needin' me in awhile. I'll get along in to supper. Ther' ain't a thing else you need, sure?"

"Not a thing."

Lightning left her with a readiness that seemed unusual. But again it was a retreat. He feared for his purpose. And his fear remained with him until he was safely in the saddle and beyond the possibility of recall.

* * * *

The moment Lightning had withdrawn Molly started up and began to pace the narrow limits of the room with nervous, uneven strides. Once she paused before her little mirror. But it was only for a moment. She turned away sharply, as though her reflection were repugnant to her, and continued her agitated pacing.

At last, however, she halted before the plate of food which Lightning had provided for her consumption, and the needs of the moment seemed to force themselves upon her. She picked up the plate and her tea-mug, and passed out into the living-room.

She set to work with a will. The energy she threw into clearing up the midday meal seemed wholly unnecessary. It was almost as though she dared not stop, or permit herself to think. When the work was completed she looked about her to see that nothing had been undone. Then she passed out of the house, her head enveloped in a linen sun-bonnet. Lightning was harvesting the oat crop. There should be no more weakness. She would go out to him and do the stooking it was her work to do. But first she would do those chores that needed doing.

She hurried down to the corral and loaded her arms with new hay, and returned to the barn. And as she passed in through the open doorway she was greeted by the gentle whinny of the great team that should have been out cutting oats.

Molly stood for a moment staring at the two great roan bodies. Lightning had gone to his work more than an hour ago. Then why were Jane and Blue Pete still here in the barn? Why——? She passed up into the stalls and filled the mangers. Then she left the beasts, and glanced down at the other stalls. Her pinto was there. But where was Lightning's saddle-horse? It was gone. So was his old saddle, and his bridle.

The girl passed out of the barn and into the sunlight. She stood for a few moments gazing about her. Then, on a sudden impulse, she went back into the barn and looked again at the stalls, as though to reassure herself. Then she sat herself on the edge of the iron corn-bin, gazing at the huge bulk of the team.

She was thinking furiously. She was struggling with memory. Lightning had taken his saddle-horse and ridden off somewhere. Where? She had some sort of feeling he had been talking when she awoke to find him beside her in her bedroom. She seemed to remember he had been talking of going somewhere. What was it he had been talking about? Where was he going? He was going to fetch someone. He was——

A cry broke from her. She started up from the corn-bin.

"Doc Blanchard!"

She remembered. Yes. That was it. He said he was going to get Doc Blanchard. He was going to bring him to see her. Her! Doc Blanchard! He—he—— She dared not see him! She would not see him! Oh, God! And Lightning had gone to fetch him! What could she do? Where—where——? Her pinto! Yes! That was it! Her mare! She snatched her saddle and flung it on the little creature's back.

CHAPTER XXVII
Blanche's News

"**I**'VE got to get Jim right away."

Blanche had just stepped on to the verandah, and the startled Larry Manford leapt out of his chair. He had been dozing prior to his final evening round of the bunk-houses, and had failed to observe her approach.

Blanche had hurried up from the barn, where her horse had already been stabled, and urgency was the keynote of her greeting. Larry recognised the situation in a flash. But he gave no sign. He dragged his chair, so deep and capacious, so inviting, farther back into the shade, shook up the cushions, and stood smiling indicating it.

"You've had enough, Blanche," he said solicitously. "Come and sit right here and tell me about it. Jim's away."

But Blanche made no move to avail herself of his invitation. She remained where she was, regarding the freckled face and flaming head of the man she intended to marry. "Where is he? Dan's?"

Larry nodded.

"Surely."

"He didn't say a word to me."

"He didn't know."

"Tell me, Larry. You're a most provoking creature."

"Not while you're standing, Blanche." The man laughed to hide his concern. "You're all in. You've had a long day. You're just tired to death. Sit; and I'll talk all you want."

Blanche took the proffered chair and spread herself out in it, while Larry propped himself against a verandah post the better to observe the face he was never tired of gazing upon. He bit off the end of a cigar and lit it.

"Shall *I* talk first?" he inquired, with that smiling calm of which he was a master under any provocation.

"Of course. I want Jim—in a hurry."

Blanche understood the red-headed creature. His smile had no power to deceive her. She knew there was something unusual lying behind his bald inquiry. And more than likely there was something unpleasant. She thankfully rested herself. She was hot and saddle-weary. She was yearning to change out of the riding-suit she was wearing.

"We got an 'express' from Dan," Larry began quietly. "The boy got in right after you'd started for the Marton farm. There's things doing between his place and this valley. It looks like there's some sort of bunch chasing up the trail we pass our cattle over. There's folk getting around looking for things that don't concern 'em." He shrugged. "We didn't get the details. Only an 'express' asking Jim to go right along over. The boy who brought it didn't know more than Dan was getting worried because folk were nosing around."

He laughed, and his laugh was calculated to allay Blanche's possible alarm.

"It was one of his crazy neche brothers-in-law. Jim set out right away," he added.

"Did he go by the Gateway?"

Larry shook his head.

"Passed out south, over the cattle-trail. It's out of the way, but he reckoned it best so."

Blanche looked out down the valley in the direction indicated. She was thinking rapidly.

Larry, watching her, realised the seriousness of her preoccupation. He interpreted the slight pucker of her brows unerringly. He knew she was more, much more than saddle-weary, and wondered what news he had yet to obtain from her. He felt that events were crowding rather rapidly and something unpleasantly. He felt that something of that which he had always foreseen was disturbing the peace which he had never failed to regard as artificial. He had things of his own still to tell, and he wondered if he were justified in imparting them. Finally he decided he was. Blanche was no silly girl. She was keen, unusually quick, and full of an immense courage.

"There's a flutter in the dovecotes down there," he laughed, with a jerk of the head in the direction of the ranch buildings. "The boys are worried to death. You know, Blanche, I'm not really bright, and I've no sort of gift looking through stone walls and things. Still, I guess I can see most all the way if there's nothing in between. The thing that beats me is the sort of wireless these crooks seem to know about, and use. Will you tell me how it is the boys have got wise there's someone chasing up their hiding-hole?" He shook his head. "It beats me. That 'express' came straight up to this house. He only spoke to Jim and me. And Jim rode straight back with him. He didn't have a chance to spread the gospel to a soul. But the boys know there's trouble around, and they're restless, and worried to death, and talking ugly—some of them. One guy figgered to me they were a bunch of rats in an elegant proposition of a trap. One or two are guessing half the Police are knocking at our doors. I had a bunch come to me at dinner-time. They wanted to know the thing we were doing, and what we knew. They talked getting out, and I surely told them they could beat it just as fast as hell would let 'em if they fancied it. We weren't holding them, and only handed them shelter. We sent two of them off south, across the border. And when the others saw them go they weakened right away, and remained. I showed them, in passing those boys out, we were holding dead to our contract. But I'll surely be glad to have Jim along back, and get his story."

As the man talked, the knitting of Blanche's brow smoothed out, and the old familiar smile returned to her eyes. It deepened and culminated in a low laugh. But the laugh passed at once, and Larry saw the shadow of trouble lying behind it.

"Then Jim won't get back till to-morrow," she said. "He can't make the double journey in the day. What is it by the cattle-trail? Sixty miles?"

Larry shook his head, and replied without removing the cigar from his mouth.

"Fifty, I guess. Maybe if he reckons there's need, and he rode in the night, he could make back about breakfast to-morrow. Beelzebub would do it without a worry. But I don't figger he'll be along till to-morrow evening."

"Which way will he come? The cattle-trail again?"

"No. He expressly told me he'd come by the Gateway. He reckons no one could locate us that way. He guesses there isn't a police boy, or anyone else, who could read the riddle of Three-Way Creek, or a soul but those who know it who would attempt the tunnel of the gorge. And I guess he's right."

Blanche sighed.

"I'm glad. The cattle-trail's our weakness," she said. Then she started up in her chair, and her eyes warned her lover that he was about to hear her worst news.

She gazed at him for some moments. His calm amused the

girl. But it irritated her as well.

"You're the most outrageous creature, Larry," she cried at last. "Do you know the way I feel? Why, you set me crazy to get you by your two big, foolish shoulders and shake you up into a hurry. I'm going to tell you the reason I want Jim. And it's a reason that ought to set you worried to death. But it won't. I'm going to tell you that that boy Andrew McFardell Jim encountered awhile back is Molly Marton's beau. Does that fix you? No. I'm going to tell you that ever since he located Jim, and recognised him, he's lit right out from his homestead—sold it up—and taken to the trail. Well? Does that set you in a hurry? No. It doesn't. Do you know what the sense of that is? It's easy to me, anyway. Andy McFardell hasn't shown up in three months, and now Dan's worried someone's trailing the hills around his place. Someone's hit on the connection between Dan's place and Jim. And I only need one guess who that is."

Outwardly Larry's display was of frank admiration. Of anxiety there was never a sign.

"I'd never have thought that way, Blanche," he said, with an appreciative smile. "Sure. That's Dan's trouble right enough. And, come to think of it, I guess Jim must have thought that way, too. I remember when that boy told us Dan's worry, and said there were 'folks' getting around, Jim shook his head. He said, 'No, only one.' But I don't see you need Jim in such a hurry."

Blanche stood up. She smiled into his face, and laid her hands upon his shoulders.

"I do, Larry," she said. "And I'm going to ride out to-morrow morning to meet him. You wouldn't see it my way. Jim's not your brother."

In a moment the man's cigar was flung from his mouth, and his arms caught up the slim figure.

"Sure he's not," he cried, holding her close to him. "But you're Jim's sister."

And somehow the argument seemed to satisfy them both.

CHAPTER XXVIII
By the Wayside

THE horses moved along together in friendly rivalry. Pedro gave way not an inch to his black friend. He displayed no sign of the fatigue of the double journey of the day before. There was no leanness about his flanks. There was no droop of his crested neck. The spirit of the thoroughbred was abounding. The powerful body was tireless.

Blanche had carried out her purpose. Early morning had found her on the trail again with her untiring horse. Her anxiety for her brother was something approaching weakness. There could be no peace of mind for her until she was assured of his safety, and he had learned all she had to tell him. So she had set out soon after sunrise, taking the trail of the Three-Way Creek in the hope of intercepting him on his way home.

She had discovered Jim at the water-hole on the creek that flowed through the heart of Dan Quinlan's valley, where Molly had first met him. Her relief was intense. It was as though a great weight had been lifted from her shoulders. And as they rode on together down the valley on their way home she heard the story of Dan's trouble, and eased her own anxiety by imparting to Jim the whole of the story which Lightning had told her.

Jim's comment at the conclusion of her story was characteristic. The threat to himself, and to his enterprise in the Valley of Hope, did not seem to concern him at all. He brushed it aside as unworthy of serious consideration. But the story of McFardell's treatment of Molly, and of her apparent ill-health and grief, stirred him profoundly.

"You know, Sis, folks like us don't have to worry for the thing the other feller's doing," he said, with a seriousness which hinted at the depth of feeling she had stirred. "It means nothing against you, and nothing against Larry. And as for the boys we've passed shelter to, we can get them all clear away before the worst McFardell can do could begin to hand us a nightmare. What's left?

There's only the tug between me and him, and the thought of that makes me glad."

Jim's eyes searched ahead, where the forest broke, giving way to the grass flat which he remembered to have been the grazing-ground of Molly's truant cows. And Blanche watched the cold, hard light take possession of them.

"No," he went on. "It's not our show that worries me a thing. It's that little girl, with her eyes as innocent as a child's. It's the thing you tell me of her. It's the thing that cur has done to her. Don't you see, Sis? She's her father's daughter, the man who helped me when all help seemed impossible. But that's not all. I want that little girl for myself. And I—I feel like making a break for her place right now."

"What could you do, Jim?" Blanche asked anxiously.

She was troubled at the mood which she recognised lying behind the man's manner. Jim shook his head.

"That's the trouble," he said almost moodily. "What could I do that would help her? You see, she loves that skunk. It seems queer, Sis. There's just nothing I wouldn't do to help her, and I'm helpless as a babe. Half the time it's that way with things. The real opportunity to help is the rarest thing in our lives. Out of some sort of generous, fool impulse we jump in and act, and it's only once in a century the thing a feller does that way is real help. Look at this, now. There's that poor, lone girl. She's grieving and sick. Money? It's no sort of use to her. It's unthinkable. She's not looking for that help. Can I pass her back her man? Not a thing. And she's sick in body and mind. Is there anything I could do, or say, that would heal those? It sets me crazy to think the way I'm fixed. Her father's always in my mind. So are that kid's pretty eyes, and her figure, that's so like yours. Say, she's a babe—a babe of these hills; and I can't pass her the hand of comfort I'm yearning to."

Blanche was closely observing, and she read the depths of emotion that were driving him so hard. His grief was all unconcealed. The sorrowful regret in his tone and words hurt her.

"But do you make it that he really has deserted her?" she asked, seeking the best she could find in the darkness of it all. "You don't think he's taken to the trail for the while, looking for you? It occurred to me it might be so. And when he was through he'd get back to her. For obvious reasons I couldn't say that to either Molly or Lightning."

Jim shook his head again.

"If you think that way, Sis, you don't know men," he said quietly. "But you don't think that. I guess you think the way I'm thinking. You're trying to find hope for that little kid, and there isn't a cent's worth that way. A boy can hate another good. He can yearn to avenge an injury all the time. But, even so, the girl that boy loves is first turn, surely. Certainly it would be in this case. Where's the reason in not telling her the thing he's doing? If he's to spend months chasing me up, why not tell Molly, and save her grieving? Why quit his farm? Why sell it up? Why a mystery? He's quit her. He's quit her cold, Sis. He was crazy for her; she was crazy for him. Yet he quits her cold, without a quarrel, right after that dance. That boy needs gun-play."

They rode on in silence. They had crossed the blue grass flat. They had re-entered the woods. And now their way carried them into the mouth of the gorge of Three-Way Creek.

It was Blanche who finally broke the silence. It was as if her words were literally wrung from her.

"Oh, Jim, it's just terrible," she cried, in a storm of distress she could no longer hide. "I've been thinking, thinking. I can't help it. Maybe it's awful of me. But—but I believe—I know."

The man glanced round sharply. There was a fierce, hot light in his usually smiling eyes. For an instant Blanche felt herself compelled as her horrified gaze met his. She felt he was reading through and through her, seeking the hideous thought that prompted her distress. Then he turned away, and his only response was a deliberate inclination of his head.

* * * *

They had ridden miles up the gorge of Three-Way Creek. And then—and then, as they came in sight of the smiling waters of the lagoon-like pool which formed the headwaters of the creek, the whole of the tragedy was revealed.

Molly's pinto mare, Rachel, was grazing peacefully on such rank grass as grew amidst the confusion of rocks. The little creature was saddled and bridled. But the saddle was empty, and the mare was free to stray as her mood inclined her.

It was Blanche who first beheld her and cried out. She flung out a pointing hand.

"Jim!" she cried. "Look! Molly's mare! There! Ahead by the water. What is she——"

But her words were lost as her horse leapt forward. And Jim followed hard on her heels.

As she came to the edge of the lagoon Blanche flung herself

191

out of the saddle. She had moved on searching amongst the boulders. There was no doubt in her mind, none whatever. Molly's mare saddled and bridled as she was, had not strayed into the gorge. She had been ridden there. Molly must be there, too.

Jim was left to round up the mare.

Blanche's discovery came quickly. There it was, huddled and still, lying under the lea of an up-standing rock, perilously adjacent to where the rippling surface of the lagoon lapped against the stone. She dropped upon her knees. She set her arms about the poor limp body, and raised it so that she could gaze into the ashen face of the girl she had come to love so deeply. It was Molly. It was Molly looking like death, and wholly unconscious.

What had happened? Why was Molly here at these headwaters, so far from her home? Had her pinto fallen with her? And what had she been doing here at the water's edge?

Blanche glanced up at the sound of Jim's approach over the stones.

"I'm not sure she isn't—dead," she said, in hushed tones.

"Not—dead!"

There was that in the man's voice Blanche had never heard before. In a moment he was kneeling beside her, studying the death-like face. The eyes were half closed, and looked fixed and utterly lifeless. The lips were without colour. The gently swelling bosom was still—so ominously still.

"There's a bruise, but no cut," he said, indicating her forehead, and shaking his white head. "That wouldn't have killed her. No."

He picked up one of the girl's limp arms. He raised it. Then he laid it down again with infinite gentleness. Again he shook his head.

"She's not dead," he said emphatically.

"No."

Blanche's reply came mechanically. She was struggling with the fear that possessed her. Then her courage seemed to return. She drew a deep breath, and relinquished the girl to the man's support while she sat back on her heels.

"She's badly crashed, anyway," she said. "She's been thrown or fallen from her pony. But—why here? Why at the edge of the water? What was she doing here, anyway? My!"

She watched Jim's movements. He was gently stroking the broad white forehead, removing the loose hair which had fallen over it. He laid his finger-tips upon the girl's temples. Then, very

192

carefully, he endeavoured to raise an eyelid. After that he laid her gently back on the ground.

The next moment he was on his feet, and Blanche too, stood up. He stared about him at the dark scene which the sun was endeavouring to lighten. And for awhile he remained lost in thought.

He was gazing up at the western hillside, where the mouth of a great cavern yawned, and out of which a shallow stream cascaded down over a tatter of rocks to the lagoon below. It was the same on three sides. Towering hills surrounded a narrow amphitheatre, that was darkly forbidding by reason of the immensity of height that crowded it, and the pine woods which edged the lagoon. The waters reflected the gloomy scene, and the sun, slanting its blaze of light, transformed the clear depths into a mirror of dancing light.

The place appeared to be a sort of dead end. To any who knew nothing of the tunnel exit it literally was a dead end. There was no apparent outlet other than that which the flowing waters had made for themselves down the gorge. For the rest, a barrier stood up, shutting it off from the mountain heart beyond.

There were three streams, which, pouring down the hillsides, fed the lagoon, and subsequently the creek. There was one to the north, one coming down the southern hillside, and that which tumbled headlong out of the mouth of the cavern set so far up on the face of the western hills.

The whole place seemed to be a barrier designed by Nature in her most secret mood—a barrier which was the whole salvation of those who lived in the world of hills beyond it. But the passage was there. It was there through the yawning mouth of the cavern. And it was approached by a long inclined path set on a narrow ledge, which rose diagonally from the foot of the southern hill and made its devious way across its precipitous face.

At last Jim turned from his contemplation of the splashing water pouring from the cavern mouth. He glanced across at the three horses tethered at the edge of the surrounding forest. Blanche urged him.

"We need to act quick," she said, her troubled eyes gazing down at the object of their pity. Then: "What—what are we to do?"

"Do? Do?"

A great light was shining in the man's eyes. It was a smile of hope such as Blanche had never known in him. It was as though the tragedy they had discovered had furnished him with something he had never looked for, as though a great overwhelming desire of his had been suddenly fulfilled.

"She's going right up the valley. That poor little kid isn't dead. She's just sick to death. Do? Why, she needs all the help we can hand her. It's my chance. It's the thing I've dreamed. I'm going to pay her father through her. And I'm going to pay with both hands."

* * * *

Jim Pryse's purpose was carried out without regard to any consequences. His impulse was irresistible. Blanche had protested half-heartedly, but her protests had been swept aside. She had warned him of the danger to himself and to others in the thing he was about to do. And he had laughed. She had reminded him of Lightning, and Molly's own home. And again he had only laughed. Then he had displayed that forethought for which Blanche had given him no credit.

His plan was simple, as his plans always were. He had thought out the whole thing at the express speed which was ever his way. His purpose alone mattered. All objections that might fairly be raised against it were only things to be ignored, and, in a few moments, the whole thing had been agreed between them. In the end Blanche gladly enough undertook her share in the work.

It was arranged that they should change horses, for two perfectly sound reasons. In the first place, Beelzebub was the fresher of the two, and he was high strung and nervous, and would be difficult when asked to carry that which looked so like a dead human body. So it was decided that Pedro, the infinitely more steady, should carry Molly and Jim up to the valley.

The change of saddles effected, Blanche assisted in lifting Molly across the front of Jim's saddle. When Jim had mounted, and raised her into his arms, and, supporting her, had set off up the queer ledge path to the cavern mouth from which the sparkling waters cascaded, Blanche watched him, confident but anxious. She watched the graceful, docile sorrel plod its way up the familiar path. She saw it pause for a moment at the entrance to the tunnel, while Jim shifted his burden to a position of greater security. Then the beast stepped into the shallow flood, and splashing its way up the stream, became swallowed up by the darkness out of which the waters leapt.

With a sigh of relief she turned to Beelzebub and sprang into the saddle, to carry out her part in the arrangements. There were some twenty-odd miles of the gorge before she got back to Dan Quinlan's valley, and after that a few more miles to the Marton farm. Her day had already been long, but she gave no thought to her own comfort. She was determined to do her utmost for Molly and for her brother.

Molly's pinto was willing enough to be led back to its home, so she removed the little creature's reins, hanging over the horn of her saddle, and, linking her arm through them, set off downstream in quest of Lightning and the farm.

CHAPTER XXIX
Lightning's Despair

LIGHTNING had never made the trip into Hartspool at such a speed. His horse had understood the thing expected of it at the moment of setting out. The savage Mexican spurs on the old man's heels had told the willing creature all and more than it wanted to know, and Lightning had raced into the busy township. He had ignored every familiar stopping-place. He wanted none of them. He rode straight on to Doc Blanchard's house.

The doctor was away—gone for a prolonged holiday to the east. Lightning blasphemed, as was inevitable. But the hired man who informed him could give not a glimmer of hope. The Doc, he assured him, wouldn't return in weeks, maybe months. It was a medical conference of very great importance. And in the end the old man was forced to return home, disappointed, hopeless, helpless.

His journey home was no less rapid. His outward journey had been inspired by his desire to obtain help. His homeward journey was inspired by his desire that Molly should lack no help that he could render. And as a consequence Barney Lake never even obtained a glimpse of his faithful customer.

But Lightning's return home afforded him one of the worst moments of his old life. Within half an hour of his arrival, at an hour when supper should have been preparing, and everything should have been snugged down for the night, he learned something of the extent of the disaster that had befallen. Molly had disappeared. She had completely vanished, and, apparently, with her had gone her pinto mare.

For a brief while the old man thought she had possibly ridden out for some form of pastime, perhaps feeling that the evening air and a good gallop would help to restore her after that which had happened at noon. But a close scrutiny of the state of things generally quickly convinced him that something desperate was wrong. The team had not been fed. The cows were standing at the corral fence waiting to be admitted and fed. And in the house there was not a sign of any preparation of supper. It was this, to him, amazing state of things that stirred within him the full sense of disaster.

He set to work feverishly to repair the neglect. He fed his team and the rest of the horses; he saw to the cows and hayed them. He raced through his round of chores, even to hauling water for the house. Then he bestowed such food as his pockets would contain, saddled a fresh horse, and set out, determined to ride till darkness defeated his search.

It was long after darkness when he turned. And as he came to the farm again he looked eagerly for a light shining in the window of the living-room. There was none. The house was as empty as he had left it, and the pinto's stall at the barn was still waiting the return of its occupant.

After a long, wakeful night Lightning set out again. This time he prepared for all eventualities. He turned the horses out into the fifty-acre pasture, which, in Molly's dreams of the future, had been ultimately intended to come under the plough. The cows, too, were turned loose. Fortunately they were no longer in milk, and their need could be easily satisfied with the grass feed, and the waters of the creek. Then, with a mind at rest so far as the farm was concerned, and with his guns slung about his lean body, he set out to scour the countryside, determined to continue his search until the worst was known.

His first search lay in the direction of McFardell's homestead. It was a natural instinct that prompted him. His crude mind indicated that as being the most likely direction. But disappointment awaited him. The place was still deserted. It was precisely as he had left it once before, even to the broken doors which his heavy boots had destroyed. From the homestead his course radiated over the surroundings of hill and forest. He searched with every instinct alert, and with eyes that never in his long years had been keener for such a task. But every hour only added to his disappointment; every moment deepened his despair.

Noon came and passed. He ate and rested his horse. Then he continued as he had planned. His next effort carried him back beyond the farm into the valley of Dan Quinlan. He meant to ride till night, return to the farm to sleep, and, with a fresh horse, set out again on the following morning.

He had scoured the woods along the creek. He had sought every rising ground that could afford him breadth of view. He had searched as never in his life had he thought to search in that amazing wilderness. And more than half the afternoon had spent itself when, utterly dispirited, he turned and crossed the creek at the water-hole. There was nothing left him but to retrace his steps and search the far side of the valley.

At last he reached the opening of the gorge of Three-Way Creek. His old body was weary and his heart was sick. Yet he drew rein at the edge of the water just above its junction with the bigger stream and contemplated the wide-flung entrance to the western gap. It was not that it interested him deeply. He had always known of its existence. But never in all his years on the farm had he attempted to explore it. Now, however, he wondered. Now he gazed at it with a new interest. Yes, nothing must be left to chance. To-morrow——

He turned an ear alertly. Every nerve was on edge, and nothing escaped him, sight nor sound. Now, though probably indistinguishable to ordinary hearing, there came to him, clear, and beyond all question of doubt, the plodding sound of hoofs. He waited well-nigh breathless while he decided the direction in which the hoofs were travelling. And a sigh escaped him. The hoofs were approaching—rapidly.

He lifted his reins and turned his horse heading for the gorge. He urged the wary beast through the bare-trunk aisles of the twilit woods. Just ahead of him there was a wide patch of sunlight, and he made for it. And as he came to the edge of the clearing a rider, mounted on a coal-black horse and leading a familiar pinto pony, broke from the wood directly opposite him.

CHAPTER XXX
Lightning Passes the Barrier

B LANCHE knew better than to make any mystery of the situation when she encountered Lightning. She knew it was a moment when frankness alone was possible. For the old man laid bare his soul to her in the words of his greeting.

"You got her mare," he had cried, at sight of the pinto, in tones that were unforgettable. "Wher' is she? I want her, that pore, sick kid."

Blanche replied without hesitation as she reined up her horse.

"That's why I'm here, Lightning," she said gently. "We've got her. Found her lying all of a heap up this gorge. My friends have taken her back to our camp, where there's a doctor man."

"She ain't—dead?" Something like terror looked out of the man's eyes, and again Blanche realised his burning devotion.

"She's bad, but I don't think she's dead," she replied. "Will you come with me?"

"You ain't—lyin'?"

"Why should I lie?"

The man remained for a moment without speaking. He was striving to read behind the eyes of the woman who had no desire to conceal the truth.

"We'll go right now," he said at last, and bestirred himself.

"This pony?" Blanche demurred. "Can we leave her at the farm?"

Lightning shook his head decidedly.

"She'll need her," he said. "We'll take her along." Then his manner softened. "Maybe you'll tell me things, ma'am," he said. "You can tell me as we go."

It was then that Blanche became mistress of the situation. She was determined that no chance word of hers should hurt her brother. And she had no fear of this man, for all his manner and the ugly guns he carried.

"No," she said. "I've told you the simple truth. We found poor

Molly badly smashed. She's gone where the right help can be found for her. And I'll take you to her at once, if you like. You must trust me."

And Lightning agreed. Whatever suspicions Blanche's refusal might have inspired they remained unexpressed. For the time he seemed suddenly to have frozen up.

Now they had ridden the miles of the gorge together, right up the headwaters of the creek, only speaking just sufficient for the needs of the journey.

At the foot of the inclined ledge, over which the ascent to the cavern mouth had yet to be made, Blanche turned to the cattle-man. Beelzebub, with head haughtily raised, gazed disdainfully upon its more lowly companions.

Blanche indicated the path, which, for all its indefiniteness at the start, carried prompt conviction to the practical mind of Lightning. He observed the marks of usage at once. The lank grass was obviously hoof-trodden.

"Will the pinto trail behind on your rope?" she asked. "There isn't room for two ponies abreast. If it won't travel that way we'd best leave it right here. You can pick her up going back."

Lightning shook his head. His eyes were unsmiling.

"Molly needs her," he said shortly.

"Well, it's up to you," Blanche said with a shrug. "Look up there at the mouth of that tunnel, where the water's pouring down the rocks. This path rises on a ledge, and makes its way to that cave. We're going to pass right inside it. It's a tunnel; and the walls of rock meet overhead for several hundred yards. After that they open out, and we pass into the higher hill country. Do you feel good about it?"

"You said Molly's at the end of our journey, ma'am," Lightning said quietly. "The things by the way don't matter a curse."

Blanche smiled as she listened. Her heart warmed towards this queer creature with his ragged whisker, and his long guns with their many barrels.

She inclined her head, and turned Beelzebub to the path.

"Then keep close on my trail," she said, and lifted her reins.

The procession started. Beelzebub moved confidently. The creature was familiar with every foot of the path, and seemed to rejoice in the rapid dropping away of the gloomy lake-shore as he mounted the sometimes almost precipitous incline. Lightning came hard behind him, and beyond him trailed the pinto on the end of a rawhide rope.

There was not a moment of hesitation on the part of the horses new to the ascent. Lightning was a master in the saddle, and his horse had the added encouragement of the black quarters directly in front of his nose. The pinto, behind, knew her stable companion, and was more than content.

The path quickly became a rocky ledge about four feet wide, with the wall of the hill sloping back from it. It mounted sharply and then flattened; and, a few yards farther on, it rose sharply again.

Lightning seemed quite unconcerned with its vagaries. He seemed to disregard its turnings and twistings, and its width at no time gave him a moment of unease. He once or twice glanced below as the precipice deepened, and the flash of sunlit waters caught his eye; but his chief concern was the well-clad woman's figure, ahead of him, and the thing that had already passed between them.

Half-way up the mounting path Beelzebub dislodged a small rock, which clattered as it rolled over the precipice and hurtled to the depths below. The horse gave no heed to it, but its rider was startled. Lightning saw her movement of sudden apprehension.

"Leave him his head, ma'am," he warned. "He's got elegant nerve."

It was not his words so much as the sound of his voice that instantly restored Blanche's confidence. She eased her hand, and the horse continued the ascent.

They had passed the sharp angle where the ledge cut on to the face of the western hill, and mounted the last lift which terminated at the tunnel entrance. The black pressed on eagerly towards the tumbling waters, and Lightning was close behind. The clatter of hoofs became lost in the turmoil of breaking water. A light spray was floating in the air, moistening it, and tempering its heat to something pleasantly cool and humid.

Far below them the lagoon, with its surrounding of forest, looked strangely small and distant. And the creek itself, beyond that, looked nothing bigger than a glistening silver thread. In his watchful fashion Lightning had made an estimate of the height they had climbed. He knew it could not be less than four hundred feet.

As the black came to the edge of the little watercourse Lightning held up his horse. He realised the sharpness of the turn the creature ahead of him had to make. He gave the beast room, and Beelzebub passed swiftly into the water and into the tunnel.

The waiting man was about to follow on. He lifted his reins, but on the instant checked his horse. He turned about in the saddle and sat gazing far down the gorge. He sat there still and watchful until the muffled tones of Blanche's voice encouraging him came back to him from the tunnel. Then he urged his horse, and followed her into the yawning archway.

For awhile, as the darkness engulfed him, only the light from the mouth of the cavern behind served Lightning with any idea of the nature of the tunnel through which he was passing. At first he was aware of dripping walls set nearly twenty feet apart. The roof, too, was dripping, and his horse was wading a shallow stream whose depth was no greater than sufficient to cover its fetlocks. But the sound of the movements of the horse in front came back to him, and he was satisfied. Wherever the woman led he was unafraid to follow. The pinto behind him was less easy than its stable companion. It had no rider to encourage it, and its equine terror was in full play. Once within the broad cavern, however, Lightning drew it up alongside him, and persuaded it, and soothed it, with voice and hand.

The light from behind died out, and black darkness completely engulfed him. Only was there the splash of the water underfoot to afford any sort of guidance. But this phase of the passage was little more than momentary. Almost at once, it seemed, the pitchy darkness gave way to a faint twilight that made progress possible. The light came from above, and Lightning promptly discovered that the cavern had passed, and, in its place, he was moving up the course of a stream flowing through a deep cleft in the mountain. He gazed up, searching for a sight of the sky above him, but there was none. The light percolated down through the rift, but the rugged facets of rock hid its origin.

As he rode on the light steadily increased. The rift was widening. Now Lightning could clearly see the outline of the horse and rider ahead of him. And the walls were falling back, and the bed of the stream was widening. Presently the woman and her horse passed out of view, and the watchful man understood that the passage had taken a bend to the right. He could clearly see the sharp, dark line of the wall directly ahead, and on the opposite wall was an increase of light.

He came up to the bend. He passed it. And, in a moment, he beheld full daylight. He drew a deep breath. It was an expression of that relief which never fails the human on returning to the daylight which has been denied.

* * * *

The journey was nearing its end. For two hours or more Blanche and Lightning had been riding the wilderness of forest, and hill, and valley, since leaving the dark precincts of Nature's secret postern.

It was a world whose might was nothing new with which to impress the mind of Lightning. The hills were, perhaps, more sublime in their magnificence; the forests were, perhaps, more deep and dark than those amongst which his life was passed. The towering crests, spread with the sweep of eternal glaciers, affected him no more than did the sparse grass under his horse's hoofs, and the beds of treacherous tundra which had to be so carefully avoided. He was preoccupied to the exclusion of everything in Nature. One thought, one purpose, alone actuated him. Blindly he was permitting himself to be led to the only goal desired. Somewhere in these hills Molly was lying sick, possibly to death, and the woman beside him was conducting him to the haven with which her friends had provided her.

They were moving up an incline which mounted to a saddle between two lesser hills. There were great sweeps of forest on either hand, and with a break between them of barren, rocky highway that was without a vestige of vegetation. Away to the right, far across a valley, a mountain reared its head, and plunged it deep into the heart of the summer cloudbanks. To the left of them lay the upward sweep of forest, which only terminated where the snow-line cut it off.

"We've come more'n fifteen miles since we quit the headwaters," Lighting said, in his ungracious fashion. "How much farther?"

Blanche turned at the sound of his voice. She smiled as she took in the hawk-like profile of the man. She realised his intensity of feeling. She warned herself of the trust he had placed in her. And she forgot completely his ungraciousness, and remembered only that phrase with which he greeted her: "I want that pore sick kid."

"You'll see the camp from the 'saddle,'" she said quietly, raising an arm and pointing ahead. "It's right below the Gateway."

"The Gateway?"

The old man was staring round at her.

Blanche nodded. Her smile had deepened, but it elicited not a shadow of any responsive smile.

"Yes. The Gateway of Hope," she said. "It's a wide-open Gateway, that's never closed to those in trouble—simple human trouble. And beyond it is shelter, and help, and—peace. Molly's in trouble, and—she's passed in through that Gateway."

Lightning leant and spat beyond his horse's shoulder. Then he raised a hand and scratched the unbrushed hair under the wide brim of his hat. He stared incredulously into the woman's eyes.

"Say, ma'am," he suddenly exploded, "you ain't crazy?"

* * * *

They had halted at the highest point of the saddle. Blanche had permitted the cattleman to reach the summit first. It was he who had made the halt. And he sat there in his saddle, gazing down on the thing that had seemed to him so unbelievable.

There was the Gateway—two sheer, barren cliffs rising out of the forest which grew about their feet. They were wide, so wide, and towered to a height that was amazing. They formed a clean-cut gateway, as though set up by some giant hand, for the silver streak of a placid river that flowed in between them. Behind them and about them lay a wilderness of wooded hills. They had none of the darkness of the greater forests they had hitherto encountered. They were softly green and gracious in their many hues.

But Lightning ignored these things. His concern was for that which lay beyond the Gateway. It was the splendour of the valley which had captured Jim Pryse during his long imprisonment in it, and the handiwork that had since been achieved.

It was a wonderful picture in the light of the setting sun. And it stirred the old man's pulses with something of the hope of which Blanche had spoken. The woman was not crazy. No. Molly was down there, somewhere there in the shelter of that ranch-house, with its wonderful pastures, and corrals, and barns, and——

Lightning turned from it all. He sought the woman's face and realised her smile. Then he turned an ear to windward.

"Are you satisfied I wasn't fooling you, Lightning?" Blanche spoke almost joyously. "Molly's down there in my house by now, and maybe the doctor's already fixed her."

"It's your house, ma'am?" Lightning said, with an ear still turned.

"Mine and my brother's. Shall we get on down? We've more than two miles to go."

"Sure, we'll get right on down. Say——"

The old man broke off as the horses began the descent. As

he made no attempt to add anything further, Blanche spoke, and there was something thrilling in her tone.

"He built all that," she said. "He built it for a notion. A queer sort of crazy notion. And I sort of feel his dream's coming true. You're a cattleman, Lightning. There are cattle down there that'll make you feel good. There's the sort of grass you dream about, and the life you know. You're the first from the outside that's ever seen it."

"You're sure that's so, ma'am?"

Blanche searched the eyes that were looking into hers.

"There's only Molly else," she said. "And maybe she's not seen it yet," she added significantly.

"You got folk outside them gates?" Lightning asked, pointing at the headlands.

"Not a soul."

Lightning suddenly drew rein, and turned about in his saddle. He gazed back over the way they had come.

"Then I guess ther's a stranger chasin' up," he said sharply. "We're follered, ma'am."

CHAPTER XXXI

Lightning Becomes a Friend

"LIGHTNING thinks we've been followed, Jim."

Jim Pryse surveyed the lean figure that suggested nothing so much as a bare frame strung with whipcord. He knew Lightning well enough from his sister's account of him, and from the talk of Molly on their memorable ride together. But this was the first time he had set eyes upon him. And from his head to his heels the old cattleman became an object of the keenest interest.

Lightning gave no sign. And somehow the whole poise of the man suggested to Jim something of his boyhood's ideas of the calm of the Red Indian. There was even more than that in the likeness—the man's face and high cheekbones, the aquilinity of his nose, and the thinness of his capacious mouth. Only were his eyes, and the foolish tatter of his chin-whisker, anachronisms.

They were standing on the verandah, and Lightning was studying the white-haired man with no less an interest. The two men were taking each other's measure.

"We were."

Lightning corrected the doubt in Blanche's statement with cold assurance. Then he went on, quite undeflected from his purpose.

"I come fer Molly," he said. "I got her pony to take her back."

There was a negative movement of Jim's head. He turned to Blanche.

"You'd best get right into the house, Sis," he said. "Doc Lennox is with her now. Poor little kid. She woke right up as we rode up to this verandah, and I guess I was never so crazy at the sight of a pair of wide-open eyes in my life. Right up to then I was scared she was dead, for all I couldn't believe it. But she wasn't. No. And she's going to get right. But you get right in and hand Doc the help he needs. There's something else worrying, and—I need to make a big talk here with Lightning."

Blanche was glad enough to hurry away to Molly. And Jim waited until she had passed in through the open French window. Then he smiled as he indicated a chair to the man he had determined to make his friend.

"Will you sit, Lightning?" he said. "You and I are no use to her in there. Doc Lennox is a real, smart doctor man. And my sister's crazy for that little girl of yours. You and I can do better talking."

There was a moment of hesitation, while Lightning seemed in the throes of making up his mind. Then, quite suddenly, his coldness seemed to melt, and he nodded.

"I don't get things, an' I want to know," he said, as he sat himself in the lounging chair.

"And I want to tell you," Jim replied simply.

Jim took another chair, which he drew up and set facing the cattleman. He was sitting with his back to the valley, which the verandah overlooked. Lightning had a full view of everything—the ranch, with its many buildings, and the range of the whole valley, with its surroundings of forest and mountain. Jim offered a cigar, but Lightning shook his head.

"Guess I'll chew," he said, and the other kicked a cuspidore towards him.

Lightning fumbled a piece of chewing plug from his hip pocket. He bit deeply into it, and Jim watched him. He knew he had a difficult talk before him, and meant to make no mistake.

"It's queer, Lightning, how we can be rubbing shoulders with folk and not know about it," he began. "That's how it is between you and me and Molly. I've been in this valley a longish spell. I've been around outside quite a lot. But it wasn't till more than three months back I knew of Marton's farm, and of you and Molly. And yet ever since I've been around here I've had in mind a great big hope that some day I'd locate a boy called George Marton, who had a daughter, and pay them both good for the help they once gave me. It was the sort of help a man can never forget. It was something that could never be paid for right. George Marton saved my life. He saved me when few would have wanted to save me. It wasn't only my life he saved. It was something more than that. Sure enough, if it hadn't been for him my body would have been poor sort of feed for timber wolves. But he saved me

207

when he hadn't a *right* to save me. And it was Molly's hands that provided the food that kept my body going."

Lightning stirred in a chair that left him feeling a queer sense of mental discomfort. He tried to lounge back in it, but sat up again at once. He ignored the cuspidore, and spat beyond the verandah.

"I ain't pryin' secrets," he said, in his harsh way. "I'm jest lookin' to get Molly back to home. This talk ain't——"

Jim nodded.

"It's all to do with her being here," he said quickly. "We—Sis and I—knew where she came from when we found her down at the water's edge on Three-Way Creek. There wasn't a thing to stop us riding back with her the moment we located her. But we didn't do that, because——" He spread out his hands. "I meant to bring her right along up here, and do my best to help her some way. You see, Lightning, it was the chance I'd been yearning for. She was sick. She was badly hurt. Then there was that cur McFardell, who'd set her crazy for him, and—quit her cold."

The old man's jaws worked violently at the mention of McFardell's name. His eyes snapped. Jim interpreted the signs he beheld unerringly. He inclined his white head.

"Sure, we'll come back to him in awhile, Lightning," he said. "Now I just want you to listen. I'm going to hand you a story. I'm going to put myself right into your hands. But it doesn't worry me a thing. You've just one idea in life, and so have I. It's Molly. We're both looking to do the same thing from different ends. Well, we've got to get on common ground. To do that I want you to know me, and all about me. When you know that I'll be good and satisfied, if you feel that way and Molly's yearning to go, for you to take her right back to her farm. Will you hear the story first, boy?"

In a moment the hardness passed out of Lightning's eyes, giving place to a smile like a sunbeam breaking through the grey cloud of winter. He gripped the arms of his chair.

"A friend to Molly, gal, is sure a friend to me, mister," he said. "Mebbe that story's your own, and I'll sure take it as told. That pore gal's eyes is full of sadness, an' her innercent heart's clear froze over. I'm grievin' fer her, an' that's all. An' if you're out to pass her help I can't never hope to, why, I'm all in it with you."

But Jim shook his head.

"That's not my way," he said. "Sit right back and let me talk."

Jim told his story with care for the detail of it. He began it at the point where he had once saved his brother from the consequences of shooting his wife's lover. He told of his frustration of the Police; of his ultimate trial and sentence. Then he passed on to his journey down to the Calford penitentiary, with Corporal Andrew McFardell as his escort. He smiled over the incident of his escape in the snowstorm. Then came to the story of his battle for life, and his arrival at Marton's farm. He told of his appeal to the farmer, and its amazing result. And it was at this point that the old cattleman nodded and interrupted him.

"I get it now," he cried. "That feller set you in the workshop. You slep a night ther'. An' you beat it at daylight. He warned me to keep clear o' that shack that night, and didn't hand the story of it. Then he asked Molly fer food come morning, and that day we was a saddle-hoss short. It was you that was ther' that night. An' it was you he passed on next morning. Gee! He was a swell feller."

"He was more than that," Jim replied, and drew a deep breath.

Then he continued rapidly. He told of his wanderings in the hills till he found Dan Quinlan's place. And the story of Dan Quinlan, and of his ultimate shelter in the Valley of Hope, held the cattleman's deepest interest. Dan Quinlan! The man he had despised! The man he had believed to be a cattle thief, and anything else that was sufficiently unworthy! Then he came to the story of the valley as it was at present.

"You see, Lightning," he went on, "Dan's got his share in this enterprise. I've given him a share, and a good one. He's got, or is getting, a swell home, and all he needs for himself and the bunch that he's father, mother, and brother to. It's something of a return to him, but nothing like enough for what he did for me. I built this place up for one big notion. I'm a rich man, with more dollars than I need, but I tripped up badly. There's not a moment of my foolish life but I'm liable to go down to do five years in penitentiary. Well, I figure there's many folk fixed that way—folk who're not a deal more to blame than me. This is a shelter for such folk. They can come here, and work, and hide, just as long as they fancy. But they can only come on our terms, and live by our rules.

209

And we aren't a harbour for real criminals. They need to be folk who've tripped up. That's all. There it is, boy. It's maybe a crazy notion. But it's a sort of thanksgiving, and I got it right in my bones. And now my chance has come to pay something of the debt I owe Molly and her father. And you've come right along here to tell me you're going to let me pay it and help me. Isn't that so? Yes. I guess it is."

Lightning's answer was there in the thrust of a hand that reached out towards the man opposite him. Jim gripped it, and wrung it, and as their hands fell apart the last of his smile vanished.

"We'll get right back now to McFardell," he said, and his face hardened.

"You ain't through with him," Lightning interjected.

"No. I don't want to be either."

Lightning turned his gaze upon the valley below him, where the passing of the evening sun had softened the far outline of the forest-belts. The life of the place was settling for the night, and the lowing of cattle came up to him, and reminded him of long past days.

"We were bein' trailed on our way here," he said significantly.

Jim shrugged.

"McFardell's been trailing us weeks," he said quietly. "He and I met down near Molly's farm, and he's been trailing me ever since. It's not that worries me. If it did, I'd only need to have the folk beat up this territory till we'd run him to earth. And he wouldn't get a dog's chance to do the thing he reckons to do. It's not that. It's Molly I'm thinking of."

Lightning stirred uneasily in his chair. He watched the setting of Jim's jaws. He observed the abrupt change in the eyes he had seen so full of kindliness. So he waited.

But Jim seemed in no hurry to continue. He was measuring the queer creature that bore so deep a hallmark of the uncouth manhood that had served him in his sixty years of hard life. He was wondering. With an almost crazy disregard for consequences he had put into Lightning's hands power to undo for him all the labours of the past years. The reason he had done it was the better to be able to help Molly, whom he knew now needed all the help he could give her. He needed this man's complete trust and he believed he could inspire it. Now, dared he tell him the rest? Dared he?

Yes. Molly must remain where she was. It was absolutely imperative. Therefore there was only one course open to him—the truth, the simple truth.

"No," he said at last, "I don't want to be through with that feller yet. The longer he hangs around spying these hills the better."

"Why?"

The word was jerked at him.

"We'll know where he is," Jim went on. "We'll be the better able to get our hands on him."

"Why?"

Again came that swift interrogation.

"Why?" Jim glanced out over the evening scene below them. Then his eyes came back with a steady look into the cattleman's lean face. "Because, if the thing Doc Lennox guesses is right, we'll need him. I'd say we'll know when my sister gets back to us."

"What d'you mean?"

Lightning was leaning forward crouching in his chair, his hands gripping its arms as though he were about to spring. His eyes were shining with the cold fury of a tiger. His jaws were still, the worn remains of his teeth gritting.

Jim realised the storm lying behind his question.

"Why, there's swine of men in the world, Lightning," he said, "who're always ready to take advantage of a woman's weakness when she falls for the love that's just bursting her heart. And—and—he's one of 'em."

"God! I'll kill him!"

Lightning's words came with a shout. He had risen to his feet, and stood for a moment unmoving. Then he came to the edge of the verandah, and his eyes were on the hills, as though they were already searching for his victim. Jim watched him. And as he watched the man turned slowly.

"If—if he's—"

"The Doc reckons someone has."

Jim's coldness matched the other's. Lightning raised one clenched fist. And the movement was an expression of irrevocable purpose.

"It's him!" he cried. "I know it! Sure I know it! I knew it right after that party night. An' I've seen it in her pore face ever sence. Man, that skunk's goin' to get it!"

CHAPTER XXXII
Lightning Borrows a Horse

OUTWARDLY the life in the Valley of Hope had undergone no change. The atmosphere of peace and well-being remained. There was not even a ripple to be detected on the surface of things. Yet a change had developed—a definite, significant change, which left a feeling of unease, a question in the minds of those responsible for the enterprise.

Daylight had found Jim Pryse and Larry Manford abroad. And their work lay in the pacification of the fears which assailed those for whose safety they held themselves responsible. A shudder of real apprehension had found its way through the heart of the valley. How it had done so no one seemed able to tell. Yet it had dated from the moment of the arrival of Dan Quinlan's "express." It had to be dealt with promptly, and Jim Pryse had set about it in thorough fashion. It was this that preoccupied him at daylight on the morning following Molly's arrival at the valley.

Meanwhile the tragedy of Molly's life was being enacted under the roof of the home on the hillside. And those who were witness to it were the skilful, diminutive Doc Lennox, and the woman whose heart was racked with grief for the wantonness of the girl's calamity.

The day broke calm and still. The valley was alive with the goodliness of the season. There was the morning song coming up from the river, and the sounds of stirring, eager life echoing through the corrals and pastures. Great banks of summer mist enveloped the slopes of the upper hills. Sunrise was at work upon them, and the flood of brilliant light was fast rolling them upwards towards the cloud-line.

Jim and Larry paced over the dew-laden, sun-scorched grass on their way to the house where they would eat the breakfast waiting for them.

Jim's eyes were on the verandah ahead of them, for his concern for that which had been passing within the walls of his home was infinitely deeper than for any of his more personal anxieties.

"We've got to be rid of those boys before sundown," he said, reverting to the matter on which he was engaged. "You were right, Larry," he admitted. "There's no real scare in them. And they're using the scare of the others for a play of their own. They're a tough bunch, and they mean mischief. I'm standing for no crook work here. Despard's got them tabbed. I figgered on three. But you reckon that new fish, Jack Pike, is on the crook, too. Well, he'll have to go with 'em."

Larry laughed quietly.

"It's good you've got it at last, Jim," he said. "I'll be tickled to death to see the last of Dago Naudin and Slattery. That Soapy Kid's worse. And as for Pike—well, I guess the rest, with them clear across the border, will be like handling a Sunday school. I've no sort of illusions. They'll be double blindfold when they go, and I'll pass them over myself."

"Maybe I'm losing one or two of my own tame illusions," Jim said, with a laugh that failed to change the look of anxiety with which he was regarding the two figures on the verandah ahead of them. "But I mean to play the hand out to the last card. I promised those boys to clear up their scare for them, and I must make good. There needs to be no let-down."

"You mean—McFardell?"

"I certainly do."

Larry shook his head. His inclination to laugh had gone. He saw the difficulties, which, to his mind, short of murder were insurmountable.

"How?"

His interrogation came with a sharpness that made Jim look round.

"There's none of those boys who've relied on my word are going to find trouble through McFardell," he said deliberately.

"Which means, one way or another, an end of this show."

Larry's bluntness left the other unaffected.

"One way or another, maybe," Jim agreed. "You see, boy, there's that poor little kid up there now, and it's made a difference—a hell of a difference—to the way I see things."

"See here, Jim," Larry replied sharply. "There's two clear things I see. McFardell's got to be fixed so he can't do the thing he wants, or you've got to close right down here and get out. That's the situation as I see it. Lightning reckons he was followed here, which means McFardell's located the tunnel. He's no doubt locat-

213

ed the valley by now. Well, what next?" He made an expressive gesture. "The game's up—right up. Unless, of course—— No, Jim, boy, the other's not for you, even for this kid, Molly Marton. You belong to us—Blanche and me. There's better than that waiting on you. McFardell deserves anything he gets, but don't let it come from you. Close down this outfit and make a break for a new world. Blanche and I are right with you. We'll stick by you with the last ounce in us."

The man's freckled face was deadly serious, and his manner was urgent. But, for all their apparent effect, his words might have remained unuttered. Jim raised a hand, pointing at the verandah they were approaching.

"The Doc's waiting on us," he said.

Further protest or appeal was useless. Larry knew too well the headlong recklessness that governed this impulsive brother of the woman he was to marry. He felt he had said all, and perhaps even more than he should have said. He even felt that if he left well alone his protest might actually bear some measure of fruit. At any rate he had made it, and now he could only watch and wait, and, in so far as lay within his power, do his best to protect this absurd creature from his own loyal impulses.

As the two men approached the verandah both became absorbed in the thing that was awaiting them. The dark-faced, quick-eyed Doc Lennox was there. So was the overshadowing figure of Lightning. The latter regarded them in the unseeing fashion of a mind oblivious to the things he beheld.

"Well, Doc? Is it good news, or—bad?"

Jim stepped briskly on to the verandah, while Larry remained below. Jim removed his broad-brimmed hat and flung it on the table. Then he ran his fingers back through his white hair.

"It's a question of point of view." The doctor's reply came without encouragement.

"How?"

There was a curious blankness in Jim's monosyllable.

The doctor's quick eyes snapped as he looked up into the other's face, and all his professional attitude seemed to fall from him.

"If I'd a golden throne among the fool angels, who don't know better than to sit around doping over their harps," he cried, without a shadow of a smile, "I reckon I'd feel like weepin' hot tears over news as bad as human news can be. But, seeing they don't keep my size in haloes lying around up there, I'd say it's—the best. That poor kid's going to pull round in no time at all," he went on, with quiet confidence. "She's young, and she's strong. She's full of physical health. It's nursing she needs, and your good sister don't need showing a thing that way. But she's had a bad shake-up. I mean mentally. I can't figure how bad it's been. It sort of seems she came darn near ending everything—whether by design or accident, God alone knows. But I want to tell you the same as I've told him," he went on, indicating Lightning. "There's some feller around who needs lynching."

His final pronouncement encountered a profound silence. Then it was Jim who spoke. And his words came haltingly.

"Then—it—was so?"

The eyes of the doctor flashed. His face flushed, and the whole of his diminutive body seemed to bristle.

"Man!" he cried fiercely. "I've told you folk I'm no sort of darned angel. I've lived too long in a profession where you see most of what's rotten in human nature to hug swell notions to myself. But if I'd a shadow of right to protect that poor, innocent kid, I'd get right out after some guy with a whole arsenal of shooting machinery, and I wouldn't quit his trail till I'd shot him to death, if it was the last crazy act of a foolish life."

* * * *

Lightning had not moved from the verandah. He was sitting on the edge of it. He had been sitting hunched there all the morning, and now it was nearing noon.

He had been steadily gazing out upon this new world of busy life without a shadow of the interest which Blanche had prophesied for him. It almost seemed as if nothing could ever again interest him in his surroundings. He saw the coming and going of the men, whom he knew to be fugitives from the law, who did the daily work of the ranch. He saw the droves of cattle being dealt with and handled, however inadequately, without a single uncomplimentary mental reservation. He was content to remain where he was, with the thoughts that were his.

The doctor had passed on down to the bunk-house, to employ himself again in the new life he had adopted. He had given his verdict; he had told of the reality of Molly's calamity; he had exercised all his undoubted professional skill on her behalf, and spread the glad news of a coming quick bodily recovery. Lightning had no further interest in him.

Jim's cordiality was a thing that had left him cold. Jim had told him that the whole valley, his house, everything that was his, was at his entire disposal. Lightning had thanked him briefly and continued to chew his tobacco in stony silence.

Larry, too. He had been no less solicitous of the old man's welfare. He had referred him to Despard for anything and everything for his convenience and comfort. The old man had watched both men depart. But he—he had remained precisely where they had left him, a sort of grim, silent sentry, standing guard over the helpless girl who was the idol of his half-savage heart.

But Lightning's vigil meant more than that. Whatever the old man's shortcomings, whatever his failings, lack of decision and the energetic prosecution of purpose were by no means amongst them. As he sat there at the edge of the verandah, with a sub-tropical sun pouring down its merciless rays upon his hard old head, never was his decision more irrevocable, never was his energy more ardently concentrated.

He was waiting for one thing—for one thing only. Sooner or later he felt certain that Blanche would appear. And it was she for whom he was waiting.

The end of his waiting came with the approach of noon. The rustle of a woman's skirts somewhere within the French window behind him warned him of Blanche's coming. Instantly his whole attitude underwent a transformation. He glanced swiftly down in the direction of the ranch buildings. There was no sign of the return of the men-folk to the house. So he straightened his body and stood up. And the face, with its tatter of whisker, that turned to greet Blanche was smiling!

"I sure take it she's feelin' good, ma'am," he nodded. "If it wa'an't that way I don't guess you'd be gettin' around to breathe the swell air of midday."

There was no responsive smile in Blanche. Her whole expression was grave. There was sadness in the down-drooping of the mouth that was accustomed to respond so readily to her smile.

"She's going on well," she said. Then, with a sigh: "Poor little Molly."

That expression of pity came near to undoing all Lightning's carefully calculated pose. A furious desire to blaspheme, and hurl malediction upon the author of the girl's trouble, drove him hard. Perhaps Blanche read something of that which was passing through his mind, for with the passing of his smiling greeting she went on.

"You know, Lightning," she said gently, "we mustn't let ourselves grieve too badly. She's going to recover, and—and things might have been worse."

"Worse?"

The old man's eyes rolled, and his tone was full of scorn.

"Yes. They might have been—much worse," Blanche went on quickly. "She might have died. She might have—— She's going to get well. She'll be her old self again. Time will see to that. And maybe she'll have forgotten—him. Yes, I think that's so. She's a girl of character. And—and I sort of feel she'll never, never let him come near her ever again."

"No."

Lightning's monosyllable was significant. He glanced down at the bunk-houses. Then his gaze came swiftly back to the woman's face.

"I was waitin' around fer you, ma'am," he said simply. "The Doc said his piece. He said it right here to us all. But it wasn't the thing I needed. It was your word I was waitin' on. I had to get it from you that Molly, gal, was goin' on right. So I jest waited around. Now I guess I'm ready to beat it back to home."

Lightning's manner was never so supremely simple, and Blanche was wholly deceived.

"You're going to quit here? You're going home? You're leaving Molly?"

The woman's astonishment was not untouched by disapproval.

"Sure. Right away, ma'am," he said. "I got to. An' it's fer Molly, gal. Ther's the cows, an' the hosses, an' then ther's the harvest. It's all Molly's, ma'am, an' she'll need it."

Blanche's disapproval was completely dispelled.

"I'd forgotten. Of course. You'll surely have to get right back. And when Molly's feeling good and strong again I'll bring her right home to you."

Lightning nodded.

"That's how I'd figgered."

His gaze drifted away in the direction of the barns. It was almost as though he found it difficult to look the woman in the face.

"I need to get right away now," he said with a shrug, "only I don't feel like settin' saddle on my plug fer the trail of that canyon, ma'am. He's mean. He's mean as hell, ma'am. It was diff'rent beating it up here. He'd your black to foller, which was everything. I surely don't guess I'd get him to face that crick through the canyon in the dark. Still, I got to get right back anyway. I'll sure need to make a break fer it."

217

The old man's regret and anxiety were perfection. It was quite impossible for Blanche to resist it. Her smile broke forth at once.

"Why, you don't need to worry that way," she cried. "It certainly would be a tough proposition facing the canyon with a scary horse. You go saddle up my Pedro. He's right there in the barn, and he knows that path and that tunnel like a child knows its prayers. You can have him and welcome, and you can treat him the same as if he was steam driven. You go right on. And while you're fixing things for Molly down there, we'll be fixing things for her here. And between us, with God's help, there'll be little amiss with her when she gets right back to you and at her home."

* * * *

As Lightning moved down towards the barn his manner had undergone a complete transformation. He hurried with long, rapid strides. Somehow his lean body looked straighter and taller. Energy and something like youth seemed to bristle in every movement. Even his eyes had lost their recent expression. They were alight now. They were alight with a sparkle of almost unholy joy. He felt that at long last the great test of his manhood was about to begin.

CHAPTER XXXIII
Night in the Valley

IT was late in the evening. Jim Pryse and his sister were alone in the apartment where Blanche loved to sit in company with her men-folk. The stove was radiating a pleasant warmth, for the summer evenings, so high up in the mountains, were chill with the breezes that came down off the fields of snow. Blanche was still enveloped in the overall of her domestic labours, and Jim was lounging in his favourite rocker, clad in utility garments of his day's work on the ranch.

A shaded lamp cast its mellow light over the room, and found reflection in the polished walls of red pine. But its light was mainly focused upon those sitting about the stove. Blanche's busy hands were at work upon her sewing. The door of the room stood ajar, and while she talked, and listened to the deep voice of her brother, there was never a moment when her attention could have missed any sound that came from beyond it. She had left the sick girl asleep. She had left her in the full conviction that her reassurance that noon to Lightning was more than being fulfilled. Now her anxiety was allayed, and she was enjoying the rest she was more than entitled to.

Larry had not yet returned from the work of deporting the four men who had become something more than troublesome to the peace of the valley. He might return that night. On the other hand, he might not return till late next day. His movements were of no particular concern. He had his own methods of dealing with an exodus from the valley. Despard was with him, and one or two others, who were part of his official staff, and the whole thing would be completed with that effectiveness which gave no opportunity for any trickery.

Blanche glanced up from the tangle of silks in her lap. She surveyed her brother, who was sitting with his head inclined forward till his chin pressed deeply against his cotton shirt.

"I'm glad you gave Larry his head about those boys, Jim,"

she said. Then she smiled indulgently. "You know, Jim, I'm beginning to think Larry's pretty bright. He's got a rare way of sizing men up. He laughs and says things, but there's always a deal lying back of what he says. He was talking to Lightning after I brought him along last night. I guess I got mad with him for it. I'd seen him looking at the old man in that queer, half-smiling way of his, and wondered what he was thinking. I got it all later." She laughed softly. "He said—you know his ridiculous way—'Do you know what you've done, heart of my heart? You've brought into our perfect haven of purity a tough that would sooner murder than eat. Maybe your friend Lightning's all you believe him. I haven't a doubt. But I'd like to tell you he's a whole lot more. I'm eternally grateful to the folk who figure out the luck of a red-headed guy that I didn't get across his trail that night you sent me down to the farm as your express-man.' I wasn't going to stand for that, and told him it was a pity he hadn't."

Jim's gaze remained on the stove.

"He's a type," he said, without real interest.

"What d'you mean?"

The man bestirred himself.

"Oh, he's a cattleman, bred and raised in the toughest school of a trade that flourished when he was a youngster. Look at the guns he carries. Never moves about without 'em. They're prehistoric, but, I'd guess, in his hands mighty effective. It's always so with his kind. But Larry used the wrong word. It should have been 'kill,' not 'murder.' Lightning couldn't murder. But he'd kill like a real gentleman."

Blanche felt her superiority over these men in her understanding of Lightning.

"You're both wrong by miles," she said. "You're judging him, like Larry did, by the outside show. Men are mostly like that. You don't know the Lightning I know. You don't know the kindness, the affection and loyalty of the man towards little Molly. And I couldn't begin to tell you about it. Why, even with her lying here sick, his queer practical mind was worrying for her future. He was crazy to get back to the farm to see to her interests, her stock, and the harvest. No. Lightning's a swell bluff as a 'bad man.' Why, he was scared to face the tunnel on his own horse, because the beast was as scared as he was. I had to lend him my Pedro to get him home."

Jim was looking up. His preoccupation had gone. He was grinning ironically at the confident woman.

"Lightning borrowed your Pedro to make that trip home?" he asked incredulously. "It's a—joke, Sis. It's——"

He broke off. And his irony fell from him, leaving a sudden frown on his even brows.

"Why is it a joke?" Blanche had become aware of the man's change of expression. "What—what are you—guessing?" she asked.

Jim shook his head.

"Just nothing," he said, with a shrug. "Only—— Maybe, you're right, though. That tunnel and the ledge are difficult when you think about it. A scared horse might easily get into a fix. And it's certainly important that Lightning should—carry on the work of Molly's farm."

After that they remained silent. Somehow Jim's explanation failed to convince, and Blanche had an uncomfortable feeling. But she refrained from pursuing the subject further.

Jim was thinking hard. Why had Lightning borrowed his sister's horse? Why not use his own? The idea of Lightning being afraid of facing the tunnel on his own horse was absurd. Inspiration promptly supplied him with all he wanted to know. Pedro! Blanche had told him of the cattleman's admiration of the beast. He knew the merits of the creature himself. Pedro was capable of anything in the world that a horse of his class might be asked to do. Why should Lightning desire the loan of such a horse? There could only be one reason, and he sat on in silence, staring at the polished sides of the stove, contemplating the tremendous thing that had suggested itself.

Blanche went on with her work. The tangle of silks seemed to cause her no inconvenience. Once she passed out of the room to visit her sleeping patient. It was only to return again to her sewing with a word of reassurance.

The evening slipped away. Blanche began a conversation. But its failure to flourish left her no alternative but to abandon the attempt. And in place of it her woman's mind made play to itself between her preoccupied brother and the girl lying ill in another room.

Jim bestirred himself at last. He sat up, and shocked his sister into amazed attention.

"I want to marry that little kid, Blanche," he said, without preamble. "I'm going to. Do you think—I guess you know your own sex—do you think she's going to want that boy when she gets well?"

With the passing of her first shock, Blanche wanted to laugh. But her desire was not inspired by the thing he had said. It was the curious synchronising with it of the thoughts that had been passing through her own mind.

"If she does, Jim, she's not worth any good man's thought," she said promptly.

Jim was sitting up. His chin was propped on the knuckles of his clasped hands, and his elbows were set upon his spread knees.

"You were right, Sis," he went on. "I laughed at you when you said it, but I knew you were right even then. When I first saw Molly the thing got hold of me. And it wasn't just gratitude to that boy, her father, that made me think and feel the way I did when I looked into her child's eyes. No. Say, I carried that little kid in my arms right up to here. You can't ever know what carrying a pretty kid like her in your arms means to a man. It just sets him crazy with pity and—love. It wasn't my gratitude to her dead father made me do it. When I said to you the thing I meant to do, it was all dead fixed in my mind. I'm just crazy to death for that little girl, and I want to have her my wife. Oh, I know. I know it all. I'm only worried she won't have learnt to hate that boy the way he deserves. And there's the thing that's always hanging over me. Would I dare, Sis, if she'd learned to hate that way, with the shadow of penitentiary always around my heels? Would it be right? Would it be honest? Sometimes I reckon it would, and sometimes I reckon I'd be little better than the skunk who betrayed her. I don't know." He smiled a little pathetically. "It seems I can't think right about it. Tell me, Sis; you're wise to these things. You see, you're a woman."

Blanche bent over her work, and spoke without looking up. This brother of hers, this strong, reliant man, seemed more like a child to her than ever.

"It's all so simple to me, Jim," she said, without a moment's hesitation. "The world surrounds the business of marriage with a lot of stuff and notions that have no right to any place in it. A boy loves a girl, and she loves him. There isn't a thing matters to them beyond the love which is pure, and good, and as natural as God Almighty intended it to be. What matters, to a girl feeling that way, if a human threat is dogging the man she loves? Doesn't it make it sweeter to her to care for him, and think of him, and worry for him? Sure it does. Then think of her. A boy doesn't love what has been, only what is. He loves her. Well? Folk say this, folk say that. Who cares what folk say? It doesn't seem to me that they matter in the least. Their approval wouldn't help in the hour of need. And their disapproval wouldn't rob folk who love of one moment of their happiness. When the time comes, Jim, just be yourself. Tell Molly all you think. Make her your wife if she loves you. And if you two are to get the happiness I wish for you there'll be one, anyway, whose approval will do its best to help it along."

* * *

The first of the dawn had lit the valley with its twilight. Blanche was passing out of Molly's sick-room. It was her last visit for the night. Three times she had left her own bed to assure herself of the girl's well-being. At each visit she had found Molly sleeping calmly, and without a sign of fever. Her satisfaction was intense.

She was about to return to the warm comfort of her own room when the sound of a spurred footstep on the verandah broke upon the silence of the house. The meaning of it came to her instantly. It was Larry returned from his journey. And she knew that he must have ridden something like a hundred miles in fifteen hours. She drew her dressing-robe closely about her, and passed out on to the verandah to meet him.

She found him sprawled in a big chair gazing into the twilight of the dawn. The air was chill, but it signified nothing to her. That great, red-headed creature was the man of her woman's dream, and her gladness in him rose above any thought of discomfort.

He raised a pair of astonished eyes as she appeared through the French windows.

"For goodness' sake, child, you haven't been sitting around waiting for me to get back?" he cried, springing to his feet.

Blanche laughed at the half impatient, wholly solicitous greeting. It was so characteristic of him.

"I guess worry for you wouldn't keep me from my bed a minute," she cried. Then came the inevitable touch of affection. "It's only for an incompetent a woman needs to worry."

She came close to him and smiled up into his face. In a moment Larry's arm was about her yielding body, and they stood together gazing out on the broadening of the dawn.

"Dear old Blanche," he said at last. "Worry or no worry, I'm glad to get back. You know, kid, I'm sick to death of these toughs. I feel like a sort of penitentiary guy, who needs to go around with automatic shooting weapons and a club to make things sure he'll

223

eat his next meal right. If it wasn't I'm guessing I can see the end of this crazy notion coming I'd have to get out on the hillside and holler. But it's coming, kid. I've shot that bunch out, and the junk we've got around now couldn't commit crime enough to set the police worrying after 'em. I've a notion I've been figuring on. It's a good notion. This ranch gets me all the time. So do the hills and the air—the whole darn thing. I'm herding Jim along a road that'll leave this place just what it is—a swell mixed farm run right, and the crook shelter can go hang. The only thing that's got me scared is the thing Jim may get doing to that gopher, McFardell. How's the little kid?"

"Sleeping like a child. I've just been in to her. That's when I heard your big feet out here."

A great spread of yellow topped the eastern hills, and Blanche watched it grow.

"If things go right, Jim won't need much herding along that road, Larry. I don't think you need to be scared for him," Blanche went on confidently. "He's fallen for Molly, and I'm going to help things along all I know. Think of us in the old days back in New York," she laughed. "Then think of us here. Think of me trying to fix things up with Jim and this poor little soul of a farm girl, who's hit the biggest trouble a woman can strike. Does it make you want to laugh or weep? No. That's right. Shake your disreputable old head. And so it is with me. I don't want to do either. This is our valley of a big hope—hope for Jim and hope for that little girl. Well, old boy, time will show how things are to go. It just can't go on as it is with that boy McFardell on our trail. Something's going to break for us. It's got to be a get-out one way or another. Molly, maybe, is the whole answer to the problem. Meanwhile I'm getting my death standing around making love to a boy who doesn't know enough to get quick to his blankets after a hundred miles in the saddle."

CHAPTER XXXIV
A Burdened Heart

THERE was no sound in the room but of the rustle of the sewing upon which Blanche was engaged. It was a blazing afternoon. Beyond the open, mosquito-netted window the nature-sounds added to the sense of general drowsiness. There was not a breath of air stirring amongst the hill-tops to temper the summer heat.

For a moment Blanche raised her eyes from her work. They were gravely contemplative as they surveyed the face of her charge, who was occupying her own luxurious bed. Molly was half sitting, propped up against a number of ample pillows, and her eyes were closed, while her face was calmly reposeful.

The pallor of her brow and cheeks robbed the girl of none of her prettiness. Her surroundings perhaps even enhanced it. Her dark hair was hidden under the embrace of a lace cap, which set a sweet framing about her rounded features. Then the ravishing dressing-jacket, which concealed her night apparel, had been carefully selected for her from Blanche's wardrobe. Its sleeves were wide, and terminated at the elbows, which left her forearms fully exposed as they lay helplessly on the coverlet of the bed.

Blanche was more than satisfied. The child, she told herself, was sleeping easily. And it needed no word from Doc Lennox to tell her the value of such restful sleep.

It was Molly's third day at the ranch. It was the third long, anxious day since Jim had passed her safely through the wide-open Gateway of Hope. And Blanche understood that the worst of the child's physical trouble was over. The thing that concerned her now was that other—that psychological reaction which she knew could so easily undo the rest. As she sat guard over the girl's slumbers she pondered deeply the possibilities of disaster.

Blanche possessed no narrowness in her outlook upon life. Tolerance and generosity were the very essence of her nature. Human disaster never failed to wound her. And her sympathy went

225

out without measure in response. Condemnation never entered her thought. It was the same for Molly as it had been for her own brothers. Eddie was far away beyond the reach of the penalty to which the laws of man entitled him, and she was satisfied. Jim was in hiding, no less a victim of human law. She made no excuse for either of them. She saw no need for excuse. These things were the disasters which afforded her the opportunity of indulging her devotion.

She realized something of the tremendous nature of Molly's lonely struggle. She knew well enough that the girl could have taken the easier course of selling out at the time of her father's death. She could have gone to a city, and taken her chance in life with others similarly situated. But she had done no such thing. And the courage of it all had caught her imagination and enlisted her sympathy. Molly had accepted the big battle for which her youth and sex found her so unfitted.

Then at the back of everything else lay the knowledge of her brother's desire, and the memory of the thing which George Marton had done for Jim in his extremity. And so she had taken Molly to her heart like some young sister who needed the mother-care she had been so long deprived of.

Molly had spoken so very, very little, and Blanche understood. The girl's reticence was not the result of weakness, of sickness. She had spoken her thanks for every kindness without hesitation or effort. But she had set up a barrier beyond that which forbade any intrusion upon the suffering it concealed. Blanche had made up her mind that that barrier must be removed. And if the girl herself failed to remove it, then she must do her best to break it down. Otherwise she knew that the girl's recovery could never reach that completeness she desired for her.

The afternoon wore on, and the hour for tea approached. The sun had shifted its position, and its beam fell athwart the bed. Blanche rose from her seat, and gently drew a curtain to shut out the offending light. She returned at once to her sewing. Resettling herself, she glanced over at the bed. Molly's eyes were wide open.

The older woman smiled.

"Did I disturb you, dear?" she asked, in that low, hushed tone so quickly acquired in a sick-room.

For answer the lace cap moved in a negative shake of the head.

"Why, no," Molly said. Then, a moment later: "I guess I wasn't asleep."

Blanche raised an admonishing finger.

"Foxing, eh?"

The smiling eyes were inviting, and Molly drew a deep breath. Blanche waited for her to speak, but the girl closed her eyes again, as though seeking to avoid the sight of the things about her.

Blanche went on with her work.

"Blanche!"

The summons came with an energy that startled the girl at the window. She looked up, and rose from her chair, and, laying her sewing aside, came swiftly to the bedside.

"Yes, dear?" she said gently.

"May I—I want to talk to you," Molly raised herself on her pillows.

Molly's tone was almost pleading. It was the humility of it that troubled the other most.

"Sure," Blanche said. "Talk all you need. But you haven't to tire or excite yourself. You see, dear, I'm your nurse, and you've got to do as I say."

It was all very gentle and almost playful. It was intended to soothe. For Blanche had detected at once the excitement lying behind the girl's eyes. She felt that the moment had come when the barrier must be passed, and she knew that on the manner of its passing depended the whole of Molly's future. But the girl gave no heed. Her eyes were fixed on the other's face, and it was more than doubtful if she realised the words so solicitously intended.

"You see," she cried in a tone that was slightly strident, "you couldn't ever be like me. You couldn't ever feel the way I do. You don't need to. You haven't done— But I've got to talk. I've got to tell you. I've got to say it all, or I'll go crazy. You see, Blanche, I just loved him. I sort of loved him to death. We were fixed to be married before summer was out. And then—and then I—I just wanted to die. I—I wanted to kill myself. I tried. Oh, if I'd only had grit enough. But I hadn't. I got scared. I thought of father. I thought of the priest in Hartspool, and the things he used to say when father took me in to Mass. I got scared worse. Then the water was so black and deep, and I knew I hadn't the grit. And then—and then—something seemed to happen, and I didn't know anything any more at all."

"You were worn out and ill, dear," Blanche said soothingly. "You'd been in the saddle hours and hours. I guess you'd been in the saddle all night. Lightning told me. You dropped in a faint at the water's edge. But do you want to talk of it? Will it help you? Won't it bring back all your sorrows and trouble—that don't need ever to hurt you again? You see, Molly, I think I know it all. I think I know all you felt—all your trouble. You loved Andy Mc-Fardell, and—and that's the whole of it."

Molly gazed long and fixedly into Blanche's face. And the older woman realised a swift hardening in her eyes. It was curious, subtle. They were so unfitted for such an expression.

At last the sick girl drew a deep breath, and the fixity of her regard passed. Her gaze fell away, and sought the carefully-shaded window, where the sunlight shone about its edges.

"I couldn't tell anyone else," she said, all the sharpness gone from her tone. "But you—you understand, Blanche. You're not blaming me? You—you don't feel badly for those who—who—— Oh, Blanche, I loved him. Why did God make us like that? I didn't think. I didn't care. He seemed to me the whole world. So fine and strong, and so kind to me. No one else mattered a thing. Lightning was nobody. And even you. But—but it's diff'rent now."

"Different?"

Blanche watched. Just for an instant a tinge of colour dyed the girl's cheeks. It mounted even to her brows. Then it receded, and her eyes had become hard and cold, and, to Blanche's imagination, merciless.

There was a movement of the head. It was a quick, decided inclination.

"Yes, quite diff'rent," Molly said, in a voice that was without emotion. "Have you ever hated, Blanche?" she went on quickly. Then she shook her head. "No, you haven't. You couldn't. It's only girls like me can hate. Girls who've been wicked. Girls who're bad. I loved Andy. Oh, I can't say all I felt. He made the world so good to me. The sun never shone so fine as when he was around. Hope? Why, Blanche, I just didn't need to think of hope. Life was a swell garden, and work looked like real playtime. Then I had it all figgered. The farm should be his. And we'd build it right up into a swell proposition. And it was all for him—just him. And then I'd raise his children, and they'd surely be boys like him. And they'd have dark eyes like his, not pale things like mine. Then their laugh would be his, too. And I'd nurse and love them for him, and there wouldn't be a moment in life that I didn't know real happiness. Oh, I dreamed it all fine. I reckoned we'd have our troubles. I figgered on set-backs that would need grit to face. But

I was glad to think of them. It would make it so I could show him the grit I was made of. It was a dream—just a fool dream. Maybe most girls have dreamed the same, and then wakened up the same as I have. Blanche, I'm bad. I'm wicked. He's made me that way. I hate him. I hate him as bad as once I loved him. Never, never, never as long as God makes me live will I ever see him again. If he came near me I think I'd—kill him."

The girl's final words came in a fierce whisper, and Blanche's decision was taken on the instant. There was much she could have said. There was so much her inclination prompted her to.

"That's the way I'd feel," she said quietly.

She sat herself on the edge of the bed and took possession of one of Molly's hands. Her eyes were smiling as they looked into the startled face of the other.

"Why not?" she went on. "Love and hate run side by side. There's nothing in between that's of any account. Dear, you reckon you've been wicked. You reckon you're bad." She shook her head. "You're neither. You're just a good woman who's loved as God made us capable of loving, and I thank Him with all that's in me that the waters were so dark and deep that they scared you. Maybe there's folk would say, don't hate. But I'm not one of them. Hate him, Molly, if you feel that way. I should. And no good man or woman will ever blame you. But, dear, there's something better. Forget. The man who could do as he's done is a poor sort of creature. He isn't good enough to be a villain. He's just a mean thing, that's only fit for a woman's contempt. Don't let him stay a day longer in your mind than you can help. Forget him utterly, and remember only that God moulds our disasters as well as our happiness. Remember that He fashioned all things for His own purposes. Out of this terrible experience and grief with which He's afflicted you happiness may yet come. It will come. I'm dead sure. Forget, dear, and sure, sure, you'll come to a greater happiness for the courage with which you sweep your disasters out of your mind."

Blanche felt the responsive pressure of Molly's hand as she finished speaking. She knew that she had won her complete confidence. Then she saw tears gather and slowly roll down the pale cheeks.

"Oh, think of it!" the girl cried out in a choking voice. "Think of it, with all my life ahead."

Blanche stroked the hand she was still holding.

"There, there, dear," she said caressingly. "It's just great to

229

think you have that life before you. But we've talked enough for now, sure. We're going to do no more. I'm here all the time, and when you feel things beating you down, why, just pass them on to me. Forget, child. Forget as hard as you can. And remember the folk who're looking after you just love you all they know. Now, don't worry while I fix your tea."

She leant over and kissed the tearful face, and with a final squeeze of the hand, she rose from the bed to depart on her mission. In her wisdom she knew that the thing she desired would be accomplished.

CHAPTER XXXV
Molly Comes Back

THREE days later Blanche's labours had borne that ample fruit she had looked for. She had known that Nature would fulfil her good work if only she could uproot the mental tares that threatened to grow up in the fruitful soil of Molly's mind. After the first break through of the barrier of the girl's reticence Blanche had laboured incessantly, with tact and imagination. She had given the girl no excuse for further unhealthy brooding on the disaster into which her love had plunged her. And Molly's natural courage had been her staunch ally.

Had Molly been weakly sentimental, had she obtained her early schooling in anything less rugged than her mountain world, the task might well have been more difficult. But Molly was of the very essence of the mountains. Her emotions of love and passionate resentment, and even hate, were strong, and as irresistible as the torrential mountain streams. Her love knew no bounds. Her generosity was no less. And, equally, when stirred to passionate anger, her mood was without mercy. Now her anger and hate were as deeply stirred as had been her love for the man who had betrayed her. And her salvation in those early days lay in the tremendous reaction of it all, and in the manner in which Blanche's sympathy convinced her that her girlish weakness, however to be regretted, was no crime in the eyes of God and humanity.

So the nurse realised the girl's swift return to health. And the last concern remaining to her was the final achievement she looked for. Her own work was Molly's complete recovery with her fresh young heart unburdened. She knew that the white-haired brother she had given up so much for must accomplish the rest.

It was Molly's first day in the open mountain air she loved. For nearly a week she had lived in the shaded bedroom which Blanche had instantly given up to her. For all that time she had seen no one, and spoken to no one but Blanche and the little doctor who had stumbled on the devious road of his professional life.

Now, as she gazed out from the verandah, she felt that the world had again opened its doors, and she wondered and feared for the reception awaiting her.

She dreaded the daylight that she felt to be searching her soul. She smelt the sweetness of the mountain air, and felt that in its very purity it must be condemning her, and mocking her. She longed for the saddle, that she might hurry home to the farm, where she could hide herself from the eyes of the world, where she knew that no word of blame would ever pass the lips of the savage old Lightning. It was a moment of intense panic when Blanche helped her to a capacious lounging chair, and set a light rug about her knees and ankles.

Blanche smiled encouragingly as Molly gazed up at her from the depths of her chair.

"You know, dear, there's no time in the world for a woman like her first appearance from a sick-room with men-folk around. They just stand around saying fool speeches that aren't true, and pass her all the help she doesn't need. It's the man in them try-ing to be kind, and, if I'm a judge, they mostly succeed. In awhile Larry'll be along, and he'll be talking to you as if he wanted to marry you instead of me. Then Jim'll get around, with his white hair—he's only a year older than me—and you'll sort of feel you've known him all your life. That's his way."

"I—I wish they wouldn't come."

Molly's voice was full of her panic.

"My dear, don't say that," Blanche expostulated, her eyes full of laughter. "Why, do you know, I've had to fight them both to keep them out of your sick-room? I almost had to threaten Larry I wouldn't marry him before I could get him to do the thing I said. And Jim—why, you see, it was Jim who carried you right here to this valley. And it was hard stopping him. Jim's like some big kid to me, and is just the most foolish best fellow in the world. He'd never forgive me if he couldn't come along and see for himself you haven't died and been buried in the dead of night."

Blanche saw the trouble fade out of Molly's eyes.

"Why has—Jim—got white hair?" she asked abruptly. "I sort of knew he was only a young man that time I saw him away back."

Blanche looked out down the valley, where the cattle were roaming the pastures, and the workers were busy in the crops. The scene was one of calm industry, lit by a sun that was powerless to rob the mountain air of its freshness. There was no sign of the men-folk she had spoken of, and so she turned, and, drawing up a chair, sat herself close beside her patient.

"There's a story to that," she said seriously. "Shall I tell it you? His white hair is partly the meaning of this place—this ranch. Partly. The rest is to do with the quixotic heart of a brother I'd follow to the ends of the earth if he needed me."

Molly's eyes lit. And she leaned back in her chair, waiting for the story, the promise of which intrigued her.

Blanche began her story in a low, even voice. And as the story proceeded there was no shadow of lightness that could lessen the impression which its teller desired to make. She was talking of Jim, whose personality was something sacred to her. She wanted to reveal him to this girl in the light in which her own eyes beheld him. Jim had told her he wanted to marry Molly. So she left out no detail of the narrative that could display her brother as she saw him.

When she told of Jim's defence of his brother against the Police, and the penalty he suffered for his unquestioning loyalty, the girl's cheeks flushed deeply, and the shining light of her eyes was something which filled the older woman with delight.

"It's a shame!" Molly cried, with swift, passionate indignation. "Oh, it was cruel! Think! But he got him away. Eddie had done no wrong. No. He did right. And then—and then—they punished—Jim?"

Blanche smiled.

"No," she said. "He escaped."

Molly sighed, and Blanche went on to tell of the escape. The girl listened with a further deepening of interest as she came to the moment of Jim's desperate straits. It never occurred to her to question the identity of the man from whom Jim had escaped, and Blanche scrupulously withheld his name.

Then came the moment of Jim's approach to her father's farm, and Molly became even more deeply absorbed. And at the end her eyes lit with excitement.

"I remember," she cried. "Oh, yes. I packed his wallets with food. Think of it! Just think! It was your Jim, an' I fixed his food! Tell me."

And so the story went on to Jim's meeting with Dan Quinlan, and of his sojourn in the Valley of Hope. It told of how Dan had fed him, and how his privations turned his hair white. It told of how, in those long winter months he conceived the idea of helping, through the agency of that great valley, others who, like himself, had stumbled on the road of life. It told of his ultimate safe return to civilisation, and of the help he had sought from her, Blanche, in setting up this refuge. And it was not until the story reached its close that Blanche, with keen instinct for her purpose, concerned herself with McFardell's place in it.

"Do you know who it was that Jim escaped from on his way to penitentiary?" she asked. "Can you guess? Sure you can if you think awhile."

For a moment Molly gazed at her blankly. It was as though the interest, the wonder, of the man's story still held her. Then of a sudden her eyes hardened like grey granite, and Blanche realised the completeness of the thing she had achieved.

"Andy McFardell," she said, in a low, hard voice.

Blanche nodded.

"Yes. And Andy McFardell has discovered Jim's hiding-place here, and hopes to regain his place in the Police by betraying it to them. Even now he's working to send Jim down to the penitentiary."

The girl sat up in her chair.

"But he won't succeed—you won't let him succeed?" Molly cried, in an agitation she made no effort to conceal. "It's just too crazy that he can get away with it. Andy? Oh, no, no! Tell me it won't be. Tell me Jim's too clever. Tell me, promise me, you—you won't let that wretched man succeed. It's—it's awful."

Blanche shook her head. And her confidence was reassuring.

"Now, don't scare yourself, dear. There's no Police could get Jim in this valley. There's a hundred ways of making a getaway. Nature didn't set up these mountains for a trap for folk like Jim. I've a big conviction that Andy McFardell can't get away with this play. If I didn't feel that way I wouldn't be sitting around with you now without a worry. I trust Jim as I never trusted any human creature in my life. I—— But here he is himself, coming along up on the rush from the barns. Maybe he's located who's sitting around."

Blanche rose from her seat and waved a greeting to the hurrying man, and Molly remained where she was, a victim of an overwhelming return of that panic which Blanche had done so much to dispel.

 . Jim bared his white head as he came. His smile was one of frank delight.

At that moment Molly's one desire was for flight. She yearned that the earth might open and swallow her up. Never in her life had her shame seemed so great a thing. This good man, it seemed to her, could have nothing but contempt for a creature like herself. And yet his eyes were smiling, the clean-shaven mouth was so generous, and his whole expression so tremendously kind. Then his voice as he greeted her!

"At last," he cried. "Why, this is great!" He laughed delightedly. "You know, Molly, Sis here has been all sorts of a terror to us fellers. The best we could get out of her was you were going on right. Larry implored and even threatened her. I—why, I'd have promised her anything in the wide world for a sight of you. But——"

"Promised, yes," Blanche laughed.

Jim nodded at her indulgently.

"Anyway, you're around at last, Molly, and I'm God thankful that's so. These hills'll soon set colour in your cheeks, and in a day or so you'll be racing down this old valley of ours in the saddle. Why—— Oh," he cried, as he took possession of Blanche's chair, "Sis has beat it. Well, we'll sit around and yarn."

He glanced round at the open French window through which Blanche had retreated. Then, for all his promise of talk, he gazed out down the valley and remained silent.

Molly made no attempt to reply. She was beyond words, completely overwhelmed by the presence of this white-haired man whom she had learned to know only through his sister. At last, however, a single remark from Jim set a great peace sweeping through her troubled soul.

"God Almighty's pretty good, Molly," he said, in a voice that rang with sincerity. "I've just lived for the day when I could pass a hand to those who helped me to the life that looked to be passing right out of me. You were part of that bunch."

For the first time the girl dared to look into his face. But it was with a mist of tears that blurred her vision that she stumbled out her reply.

"I—I'm—just glad," she said.

And after that talk came easily, and they sat on talking, talking, with the intimacy of a great friendship.

And so Blanche found them later, when she deemed it the moment to exercise her authority as nurse. She took Molly back to her room with a feeling of great thankfulness at the amazing change Jim had wrought in her. The girl was transformed.

CHAPTER XXXVI
Nemesis

THE hills were wrapped in the hush of the close of day. The sun had long since dropped behind the skyline of mountain-tops. And now the heavens, which had flamed out in a glorious wake, were faded to the thin, cold yellow which the purple of evening was deepening every moment. In a short time the lesser glory of a myriad night-lights would embark upon its brief, triumphant reign.

Night was already in the heart of the great forests. The last of the twilit distance had been swallowed up by the advance of hungry shadows. Now, with darkness reigning, the hush was crowded with the strange pianissimos of invisible life, and the uneasy creak of tree-trunks, stirred by the cold breath from the glacial heights, that was insufficient to do more than provoke a chill shudder down the stately aisles.

A camp-fire was smouldering comfortingly at the feet of the man squatting over it. He was a queer, crouching figure, with hands clasped tightly about his drawn-up knees. His somewhat sunken eyes looked to shine with a desperate gleam as they caught the ruddy reflection of fitful flame. A single revolver was strapped about his waist.

His clothes were sufficiently scant for the chill of the night. They were rough, and worn, and looked to be loose on a body that had lost some of its wonted robustness. The pipe thrust between his jaws was unlit, empty. From the crown of his loose-brimmed prairie hat, drawn low over his head, and his lean cheeks, with their stubble of black beard and whisker, right down to his long, heavy boots, he looked unclean, unkempt, something of the "mean-white" so despised by the manhood of the outworld.

But Andy McFardell's appearance at the moment did him less than justice. It was the result of a long, weary trail. The man was wasted, underfed, hard driven. His life for many days had been little better than that of some forest beast, for his way had lain unmapped, unscheduled. He had been moving blindly, searching a region where the only humanity he was likely to encounter must be avoided. Careless of himself, careless of everything but his task, now with hope soaring high, now with despair wringing his heart, he had moved on and on with tireless purpose.

Near by a rifle lay on the ground, and a few yards away his horse was tethered at a place where the only possible feed was the green foliage of a low-growing shrub. The beast was in no better case than its rider. Even in the uncertain light of the camp-fire the sharp angles of its quarters were plainly discernible, and the dejected droop of its whole body was pitiful as it slumbered standing. Close at hand, as near to the fire as safety permitted, the man's blanket was lying ready for the moment when sleep over-took him. But that moment was not yet.

He had no intention of slumbering for hours yet. Sleep just now was the last thing that concerned him. He wanted to think. He wanted to plan. He desired to map out to the last detail all that was yet to come. He was in that condition of mental exaltation when physical needs and comforts had no place in his consideration. It was sufficient that he had lived for this moment—this great mo-ment when he saw the man who had been the first cause of his downfall held absolutely at his mercy.

Mercy? He knew no such word. There was no mercy for Jim Pryse. There was no mercy for any one. He was fighting for some sort of worldly salvation for himself. It was the only sort of salva-tion he understood, and furthermore, he realised that it looked to be within his grasp.

He bestirred himself, hardly realising his purpose or the thing he did. He released his knees and stood up. He moved over to a small pile of deadwood fuel, which was his whole store. He brought an armful back with him, and recklessly flung it on the fire. Then he squatted again upon his haunches.

He sucked at his empty pipe. He had nothing with which to refill it. But it gave him the taste of tobacco, and, in his present mood, it was sufficient.

He smiled as he watched the leap of the flames which so read-ily devoured the dead, resinous wood. It was a smile of fierce de-rision—an ugly smile that played about his loose mouth. What fools those folk were to have given him such a chance. He would never have found the place. He could never have hoped to do so.

The smile died out of his eyes as he thought of the prolonged labour of his search. The weary days, probing, seeking, in a hill country whose confusion was sufficient to madden the bewildered human mind. The days of blistering heat. The nights of cheerless solitude. The weary dispiritment of it all to a man who has given up everything, staked all upon the chance of things, relying only upon his endurance and the skill acquired in a police training. No, he would never have discovered Jim Pryse's hiding-place but for the folly of those associated with him. And yet—and yet—there it was, so easy to arrive at. The way was practically a direct trail from the Marton farm.

His smile returned. He recalled the vision of Lightning as he had halted at the entrance to the valley of that queer creek. For himself he had only narrowly escaped the man's observation. The old man's attention had been held in another direction, or surely his discovery must have been inevitable. Then had come that woman on her black horse. How he had strained to discover the talk that passed between them. But it had been impossible to hear from his shelter in the woods. He could see. Oh, yes, he could see. And when they moved up that queer creek together he was as close on their heels as safety from discovery permitted.

Then had come the arrival at the lagoon and the three-way source of the creek. And then—and then he had watched from a distance the ascent to the mouth of the cavern out of which the waters cascaded. Even now, in his mood of tremendous elation, he found the mystery of that weird inlet into the heart of the hills something profoundly absorbing.

He continued thinking of it all. He wanted to do nothing else. He remembered his own ultimate passage of that tunnel, and the revelation beyond. And he wondered how it came that Pryse had first discovered it. Yes. It certainly was no wonder that the police patrols sent out in pursuit of the man had returned to report complete failure. No police patrol could have found it; could ever have hoped to find it. No trained policeman would have admitted that that cavern mouth could by any miracle be the entrance to another, higher valley. But they would learn the facts now surely enough. Oh, yes.

He reached out a foot and kicked the fire together. Then he glanced over in the direction of his horse. After that he turned an ear to the sound of the breeze in the foliage overhead. It had increased. And the chill of the night had increased with it.

He turned again to the fire and shook his head.

No. He would tell them nothing but the fact that he could lead them to the hiding-place of Jim Pryse, who was due for five years in the penitentiary—with hard labour. He passed his tongue across his lips with intense satisfaction. Yes. He would tell Leedham Branch that. And his price for the man's recapture would be very definite.

He hugged himself gleefully, for he knew that nothing could be more sure than that his price would be paid. If he knew the Police it certainly would. There would be no preliminary payment. But on fulfilment of his part it would be different. A cold word of approval. A word to the Sergeant-Major. A regimental order. Reinstatement. And then his final triumph. He would beg to be allowed to convey the prisoner to the penitentiary.

He laughed audibly as he wondered if the old kit he had returned into store would come back to him again. Perhaps.

Oh, it was fine. It was the happiest dream he had dreamed since he had set out. But it was more than a dream. It was a certainty—a whole, complete certainty, of which nothing short of death could rob him. With the first of to-morrow's daylight he would set out for Calford. He should make it in two days. His old horse could do it. It would have to do it.

After awhile he rose again from the fire and replenished it with the remains of his fuel store. It was his final precaution. Then he rolled his blanket about his tough body, and, using his saddle for a pillow, stretched himself out as near to the fire as safety permitted. Far into the night he lay there, wakeful and thinking. But finally he slumbered with the dreamlessness of complete weariness.

Not for one moment had a single thought been given to the girl whose love he had so wantonly betrayed.

* * * *

The trail lifted gently out of the valley. It was a trail Andy McFardell knew by heart. In one direction it led to the pleasant purlieus of Barney Lake's hotel in Hartspool. In the other it lost itself somewhere behind him in the foothills he had learned to hate so cordially.

Somewhere up there, at the top of the incline, where a dense bush country reached out towards the wide undulations of the prairie beyond, the trail forked. And it was of that fork that the man was thinking, for the right-hand trail led to Calford, which was just now his whole object and purpose in life. He wanted to look once more upon the city from which he had so long been banished. He wanted to look on it with the eyes of a victor. For days now he had been living through a succession of wonderful anticipations. They had grown into almost grotesque proportions. He felt that his approach to Calford was in the nature of a triumphal progress.

His only anxiety now was for his horse. There was nothing else that could hold up the plans he had so carefully made. He had no sympathy for the well-nigh foundered creature. He cared not a jot that the poor thing was terribly saddle-galled. It meant nothing to him that its ribs looked as though the wind must blow through them, and its quarters were so lean and shrunken that the bones looked to be about to burst the skin covering them. He wanted to reach Calford. He intended to reach Calford. And his anxiety was for how the poor, wasted brute was to negotiate that last fifty miles still remaining. His mood was merciless. The horse would have to carry him till it dropped. After that? Well, after that, he would walk. That was all.

The dishevelled outfit topped the valley slope at last, and passed into something of shade from the brazen light of the sun. The road had entered a luxuriant spruce bluff that was wholly inviting, and stirred even the jaded spirits of the horse. The creature broke into a shuffling amble which by no effort of imagination could have been regarded as a lope.

The trail went on in its own peculiar winding fashion along the line of least resistance, and there was not a moment when the horseman could obtain a view for more than fifty yards ahead. But that was of no consequence. The road was perfectly familiar. Andy McFardell knew there was less than half a mile to the fork, and then——

The ambling horse stumbled. The man flung himself back in the saddle with a shout of blasphemy. With all the strength of arms and body he sought to keep the falling creature on its feet. It was a vain effort. The beast was too utterly weary to help itself or be helped. It had tripped badly over some unseen obstruction, and pitched headlong.

For the second time in his life Andy McFardell found disaster in the fall of his horse.

The man sprawled clear of the saddle. He was unhurt, and, on the instant, made to spring to his feet. But he never got beyond a sitting posture. He was held there motionless and something dumfounded. As once before, a man was standing over him with a levelled gun. A pair of stern, merciless eyes were looking down into his. The face of the man was lined, and burnt to a deep bronze. It was old in years, but alight with cold purpose. Even the grey hair and the tatter of the whisker could not lessen the significance of the hate which shone so frigidly in his sunken eyes.

It was the last man Andy McFardell had thought to encounter. It was Lightning.

CHAPTER XXXVII
By the Light of the Aurora

THE northern horizon was alight with a splendid aurora. It was still evening, with a prevailing sense of great peace. The two men and two women on the verandah were absorbed in the magnificence of the heavenly display. It was nothing unusual. There was nothing new in the magic of its movement. But its interest and beauty were a source of never-failing attraction, even to Molly, who had known its splendour from the days of her earliest childhood.

The yellow lamplight, shining through the window, lit the intimate little scene. It was the hour before supper, an hour of complete rest after the day's work. Jim and Larry were lounging luxuriously in rocker chairs. They were smoking, and meditating over the long, cool drinks with which Blanche had provided them.

Molly was seated close beside the older girl. She had laid her sewing upon the table before her, and, with elbows resting upon it, she remained with her chin supported in the palms of her hands, staring thoughtfully out at the ceaseless movement of the heavenly mystery.

Blanche was talking. It was her way when her men-folk were present. She made no secret of her weakness, she even laughed at it openly.

"Isn't it good to be right here sitting around on such a night?" she asked generally, turning almost reluctantly from the radiant night sky. She laughed a little self-consciously. "I can surely guess the thing Larry's thinking in his queer red head. Maybe he's wondering when I'll get something new to scare him with. But then he hasn't a soul for the beauties around him," she added, with pretended regret. "There, Molly, look right down there at the barns and bunk-houses. Look at the lights winking out at us. Don't they stand out like—like jewels? Then look down the valley into the darkness and shadows. See the mists gathering along the creek. And listen to the croaking chorus of the frogs, that never seem to get tired of their queer chatter. And the air, and the stars standing out overhead. It's—it's all glorious," she breathed contendedly. "It's so quiet and peaceful, and—and it makes you feel that God never meant us folk to build drab cities and things. It makes you think we were all meant to live in the open——"

"Till winter gets round. Then you guess again, and yearn for the Dago janitor who can fix the steam heat right."

Larry chuckled amiably as he buried his nose in the glass of whisky that had been prepared for Jim, and caught Blanche's smiling, censorious glance. Jim laughed outright in the depths of his chair.

"That's the way they always go on, Molly," he said, to the girl at the table. "If Blanche reckoned it was Tuesday, Larry here would assure her it was Broadway, New York, or something equally foolish. But Sis is right," he went on. "She certainly is. There's a peace around this valley that makes me feel good." He laughed. "And it's a peace that's not a thing to do with stars, or northern lights, and not even frogs." His smile died out. "I made a trip down to your farm to-day."

Molly was startled out of her contemplation of the valley. She sat up, and her eyes were shining as she gazed at the white-haired creature who had brought her to this haven of rest and human kindliness.

Blanche's efforts had succeeded far beyond her best hopes. The girl was daily growing stronger. She was no longer sick and ailing. But, best of all, her recovery, both mental and physical, was complete. The men had watched the progress, and applauded the nurse. But Blanche understood the reality of the thing that had happened. She knew that the last of Molly's childhood had passed. The days of her child-dreaming were over. She was a woman now, with all the rest lost in the passionate storms that had swept over her. A real understanding of the hard things of life had come to her, for, in her agony, her eyes had been widely opened. The hate to which her love for Andy McFardell had turned was an act of Providence which had brought about the rest.

"Then you've seen Lightning?" she asked. "He'll be harvesting."

There was eagerness in Molly's tone. It told of a mind that was again full of the affairs of life that had always been hers.

A quick glance passed between brother and sister. The man was questioning, and Blanche inclined her head. Jim leant back in his chair. He knocked out his pipe in a fashion intended to rob any words of his of unusual significance.

"No," he said, "he wasn't there."

A moment passed before Molly spoke again. Blanche was observing her closely, and wondering. The red-headed Larry turned his freckled face in the girl's direction.

"He—he wasn't there?"

The question came with a curious little gulp.

Jim shook his head, which the lamplight transformed to something like burnished silver.

"I didn't see him," he said smilingly. "No, he wasn't there," he went on definitely. "It didn't seem he'd been there since he came up here with Blanche, chasing after you. The harvest was standing in fine ear. Your team and cows were out at grass. There wasn't a sign at the house, or his bunk-house, that he'd been around."

Larry hastily devoured the remains of his drink. Jim was lighting his pipe. Blanche had forgotten the beauties of the night, and laid one hand gently on Molly's shoulder.

"He borrowed my Pedro," she said. "He left his horse here, down at the barn."

Molly turned in a flash.

"You hadn't told me," she said sharply.

"No," Blanche said. "You were sick."

Molly drew a deep breath.

"Why did he borrow your Pedro?" she asked.

"He said he was scared to face the trail of Three-Way Creek with a horse that didn't know it right."

Molly's eyes widened.

"He said that? Lightning?" she asked incredulously.

"Yes. He said that."

"And you—you believed it?"

"I did—at the moment."

Molly turned to Jim with disconcerting abruptness.

"Did you believe it, too?" she demanded. Then she looked over at the freckled face of Larry Manford. "And you?"

It was Larry who replied. He shook his fiery head. And his words came with a short laugh.

"I certainly didn't," he declared.

Molly looked into his keen eyes for a moment. Then she turned to Jim.

"And you?" she persisted.

"No."

Jim turned himself about, and sat facing the girl whose whole

244

manner had undergone so complete a change. Her eyes were alight. There was excitement and apprehension in them. There was something else. The men failed to recognise it, but Blanche had no illusion. The girl, like Jim and Larry, had read through Lightning's subterfuge.

Molly shook her head. She was exercising a rather desperate control. She was striving for a calmness she found almost impossible.

"No," she said, in a low voice. "How could you believe it? Lightning would ride his horse anywhere." Her tone became less quiet. "Oh, I could laff if I wasn't scared," she cried. "You folk don't know Lightning. I guess I know him through an' through. Lightning didn't loan your Pedro to make home on. He was looking for a beast that could make a big trail. He's gone after Andy."

Her manner was headlong. Her breathing had quickened. Her agitation was growing. Suddenly her hands clasped together. Then they fell apart in a movement of wringing. She turned on Blanche.

"Why—why did you lend him your horse, Blanche?" she cried. "Why—why did you let him go? Oh, it's awful! If—if you'd told me I could have stopped him easy. He'd have done as I said. Don't you see? I do. Oh," she went on, turning again to Jim, "I know what you mean, talking of the peace of this valley. You reckon Lightning has headed Andy from getting the Police around. Ther's only one way for Lightning when it comes to fixing things. If he's after Andy McFardell he means to kill him. He will kill him. And it won't be to head off the Police from this valley either. Oh, it's all crazy. It's terrible. It'll be murder, and—and Lightning's done it. He's a reckless, crazy-headed savage. He's the whitest, loyalest friend. And they'll take him, and hang him, for—murder. I know," she went on, in a surge of emotion. "None of you know, or can ever get the things lying back of Lightning's head. He cares nothing for himself. Nothing for anybody but—me. He's gone to kill Andy McFardell, and he'll never quit till he's done it."

Molly stared out hopelessly at the winking lights which had seemed so beautiful, so peaceful, such a brief while before. Now everything was changed. Tears gathered unheeded as she yielded to the dread thoughts which her vision had conjured.

Jim stirred helplessly in his chair. He was yearning to take her in his arms and undo the mischief his words had brought about. But somehow he felt he had done right. And it was with Blanche's knowledge and approval he had acted. He looked over at Blanche. She was calmly watchful. All that had happened she had foreseen. And, as certainly as it had happened, she knew the effect would swiftly pass.

It was left to Larry to break up the silence. It was left to him to distract Molly's mind from the shock of her own feelings. And he did it in no uncertain fashion. He sprang from his chair and passed to the verandah post, and stood leaning his big body against it.

"Is it murder to shoot a wolf?" he cried hotly. "Is it murder to kill a foul, stenching skunk? Not on your life. If Lightning's killed that swine, I'm out to see he makes a right getaway." Suddenly he broke into a queer, short laugh. "Say, folk," he cried, with a humour that was irresistible, "I was never so glad of this valley, and this crazy layout of Jim's, as I am right now. Don't worry a thing, Molly. Don't you drop one of those dandy tears. We're men on this ranch, not saints. And there isn't a soul among us but says Lightning's right—dead right. My only worry is that Lightning shall kill that feller good an' plenty."

Without pausing for the result of his utterly immoral approval of murder, he stepped off the verandah. But he turned at once at Blanche's smiling challenge.

"Where now, Larry?" she asked gently.

The man made a little gesture of impatience.

"Why, to fix my horse right. I pull right out after supper. There's going to be no darn hanging for Lightning."

Blanche shook her head.

"No, boy," she said, with decision. "You men are all mostly foolish when your heads get hot. You're going to stop around here to see no hurt comes to the woman who doesn't know better than to marry a man whose head Nature intended to get hot. Lightning doesn't need your help. He borrowed my Pedro. And—he'll bring him right back here. I know that. And I guess Molly knows it, too. She and Jim here can ride down to the farm to-morrow. She'll ride her own pinto that Lightning insisted on bringing up for her. Maybe Molly's quick eyes'll see things Jim isn't likely to."

Then she turned to the girl beside her. She took possession of one of her hands, and caressed it between her own soft palms.

"Then you'll come right along back here, dear," she said. "You can't quit us till you're well and strong, and feel good for the work you belong to."

"But you never told me Lightning brought my pinto along up," Molly exclaimed.

Blanche smiled.

"Didn't I?" she said. "Guess I must have forgotten."

The two women looked into each other's eyes, and the girl squeezed one of the hands caressing hers.

"I guess you're right, Blanche," she said, with a little sigh. Then her smile began to dawn again. "I—I think you're most always right. Sure I'll go to-morrow. The harvest must be fixed, and—I guess Lightning won't fail me."

Blanche sighed contentedly.

"No," she said, "Lightning won't fail you."

* * * *

Supper was over. At the girl's request Jim had gone with her down to the barn where her pinto was stabled. She wanted to see her little mare again, that creature that was almost part of her life. Larry and Blanche were alone on the verandah. They were standing together where the others had left them. One of the man's arms was about the woman's shapely shoulders, and she was drawn close up to him.

"You're all wrong, Blanche, sending that little kid down there to look at the show where all her trouble happened," Larry said, with a wise shake of the head. "Jim ought to've bucked right away. What sort of good are you looking for? Look at the way she broke up over Lightning. You're taking a hell of a chance. And if I'd been Jim——"

Blanche laughed softly.

"Oh, you boys," she said. "You're all so—so wise, and strong, and brave, and big. But you're just big foolish kids when it comes to—women. The only chance I've taken is that Jim's no fool. And I don't guess he's that way."

The red head turned quickly and looked down into the fact that was laughing up at him.

"But you know Lightning's not there," Larry said. "You know as well as we do he's gone after that miserable skunk. You know as well as that kid does he'll kill him sure. Why not let me get out to pass him a hand, and you keep Jim and Molly right here? Say, there isn't sense in the thing you've fixed. There surely isn't."

"Isn't there?" Blanche sighed happily. She raised a hand to her shoulder and clasped it about the muscular fist she found there. "Of course I know all those things, Larry," she went on. "All those things are so. It's man's way, so it's Lightning's. Molly's right. He'll never leave McFardell alive. He'll follow him and kill him."

The man felt her shudder, for all the calmness with which she spoke. "Maybe I'm all wrong. Maybe I'm callous and wicked. But I'm not interested in anything but Jim's happiness—Jim's and Molly's. Molly's fallen for Jim. I know. You see, another woman can see these things. Well, to-morrow's Jim's opportunity. On the way down, before she sees for herself that—— Oh, psha! anything might happen. She's impulsive. Lightning! If she thought he needed her help, good-bye everything else. Jim must fix things on the way down. And I'm wicked enough, vicious enough, to hope that Andy McFardell comes by his deserts."

Blanche felt the squeeze of the man's hand.

"There's nothing wicked to you, Blanche," he said. "I'm with you that McFardell gets his med'cine good an' plenty. But say, kid," he cried eagerly, "you'll let me pass a hand to Lightning? I want him to kill that skunk. I do so. It's queer. I got this place in my bones." He laughed boyishly. "I just hate it I'm the only feller around this outfit that doesn't need to worry in the daylight."

Blanche's laugh came low and full of humour. She glanced up at him slily.

"Oh, Larry," she cried, "you are—you certainly are a crazy—— And what about me? Do you reckon I'm going to marry you to be toted along on the run from justice?"

The man remained quite undisturbed by the threat. His arm tightened about the girl's slim body and his eyes lit mischievously.

"Why not?" he asked, with a grin. "I haven't heard that Jim had to ask you twice, with him on the run."

"Yes, but Jim needed me."

"Well?"

Blanche's eyes shone in the darkness. She reached up and tenderly kissed the freckled face she loved.

"Neither will you, Larry, boy," she said, all her love shining in her eyes. "If Jim fixes things with Molly so he no longer needs us here, why, I'll beat the longest trail with you you can figure out, just how and when you want me. Yes, and you can do all you fancy for Lightning."

CHAPTER XXXVIII
Lightning's Triumph

FOR the third time in his life Beelzebub was in the company of Molly's pinto mare. The little creature was above herself. She was full of oats, and bored to extinction with the luxurious monotony of a barn to which she was quite unaccustomed. So she danced her way through the Gateway with a frivolity unbecoming her years, and her splendid companion looked on in dignified unconcern.

The morning was fresh. There was a nip in the air, which was calm with the promise of a later blazing day. The sun was rolling up the night mists, and with every passing moment fresh vistas of forest, and valley, and crag, were appearing through the thin grey of the lifting veil.

Molly had waited for nothing. She had risen that morning with the dawn, full of an intense yearning for the home that was hers, and the queer, disreputable old servant and friend for whom she entertained the gravest fears. Her anxiety was real. It was even a little more desperate than Blanche cared to see. So the older woman had urged her brother promptly.

Once beyond the barren crags of the Gateway, Jim and Molly were swallowed up by the forest. And somehow their earlier talk died out in harmony with the hush of their surroundings.

Jim's whole thought was for the girl beside him. The meaning of their journey in his mind had little enough to do with Lightning, and the life or death of Andy McFardell. He knew well enough that they would find the farm to-day as he had found it yesterday. He had no hope that it would be otherwise. The trip in that respect was useless. It was worse than useless in so far as Molly's peace of mind was concerned. Then it might undo so much that had already been accomplished. No. He felt it was all wrong. Yet the appeal of it was irresistible.

Molly wished to visit her home. Then Molly should do so. Molly desired to retake her place in those affairs of life which concerned her. So it must be. She was troubled. Well, his greatest desire was that he might be beside her to help her, to comfort her, to make clear to her that she was no longer alone, to face the life that had already treated her so hard; that, whatever chanced, whatever might befall the old man to whom she was so devoted, his own whole future was hers. He was hers—body and soul.

So he watched the girl as they rode through the shadowed forest beyond the Gateway. So he spoke ready words of comfort when her fears threatened to overwhelm her. He laughed her nightmare to scorn, and by sheer effort of will forced the return of her smile to her eyes. And through it all he knew he was fighting for himself as much as for her. Through it all he knew he was acting a lie. For, whatever Blanche believed, he had little enough hope that any of them would ever again set eyes on the grizzled creature, who, he felt certain, had set out on one final act of devotion.

They had long since breasted the hill overlooking the Gateway. At the summit Molly turned to gaze back on the blessed haven that had come to mean so much to her. And as she gazed a doubt flashed through her mind. Would she return to it? Would it be possible? Would not she be held at the farm to succour the man who was ready even to kill for her?

In that tense moment she cried out:

"Oh, I wish I could get it into my fool head I'd find him there cutting the harvest when I get home."

"Don't think about it, Molly," Jim said gently. "There's things no wish or act of ours can alter." He smiled. "I guess Lightning's one of 'em."

Molly lifted her reins, and her impatient mare moved hastily on.

The last of the hill mists had been swept away. The great August sun was scorching the grass and woodlands with its brazen rays. It was a wide, rugged world, encircled by hills whose snow-capped summits reached up to the very clouds. It was a glorious arena, miles in extent, with lesser hills and stretches of forest littered throughout its length and breadth.

They kept to the bank of the creek which flowed eastward. They hugged its course over a trail that had become almost marked by the traffic of their horses. And an hour's riding brought them to the point where they must leave the soft, springy soil of the creek bank and take to the bed of the stream itself. It was here that the whole nature of the country abruptly changed. It was the beginning of the gorge, which only terminated at the dark passage of the tunnel.

Molly hesitated as Jim indicated the water.

"It's easy," he said, with a smile. "I guess your pinto knows it, if her memory's good. Maybe you don't. Those grey eyes of yours couldn't see a thing, Molly, when I carried you up this stream."

Molly gazed downstream at the narrowing hills that lined it on either side. She shook her head.

"No," she said quickly. "And I sort of don't want to remember." Then, in flat contradiction, she asked: "You—you carried me along—this?"

"Sure."

"My!"

Molly's eyes were smiling. For one moment her nightmare had left her, and a soft light shone in her eyes.

"I must have been mighty heavy," she said.

Then, almost at once, she frowned. Again the purpose of their journey flooded her mind.

Jim ignored the frown and laughed.

"Mostly feather-weight," he said easily. "You see, I'm not old. I got white hair, but I wouldn't say there's many years between us. Say, Molly——"

But that which he would have added remained unspoken. Perhaps Molly guessed. Perhaps her little mare's eagerness was real. At any rate, the pinto recklessly took to the shallow water of the creek, and its chill set her sporting with apparent delight.

There was a moment in which Beelzebub watched her curiously. He stood on the bank with his head raised and his nostrils a-quiver. Then he moved. He stepped down into the water, which covered little more than his fetlocks, and his manner was completely dignified. But the gallant creature knew what was due to his sex. He went ahead of the mare and led the way.

* * * *

They were at the mouth of the cavern, gazing down at the waters of the lagoon. A few yards ahead of them the stream hurled itself, tumbling and splashing, to the depths below. The full light of the sun blazed athwart the cavern entrance, and the rugged beauty of the valley of Three-Way Creek lay spread out in full view.

The pinto had drawn abreast of the black. And the two creatures stood together like statues. They stood with ears pricked and heads thrown up, and their soft eyes were far gazing, while their sensitive nostrils quivered with a scarcely expressed equine greeting.

It was neither the cascading waters, nor the beauty of daylight after the darkness of the tunnel, nor the mysterious depths of the waters of the lagoon, that preoccupied the riders as well as their horses. Molly and Jim were startled into complete silence, while their horses apparently regarded that which they beheld as a revelation of the intensest interest. A big sorrel horse, saddled and bridled, was down there beyond the waters of the lagoon, searching amongst the boulders, cropping hungrily at the green, ripe tufts of grass that grew about them.

Even at that distance there was no mistaking the identity of the horse; its size, rich colour, its short, staunchly-ribbed body. It was Pedro. And he was roaming free, even though he remained saddled, and it looked as though his bit had not been removed from his mouth.

It was Molly who drew attention to the latter detail. Perhaps Jim was less observant. Perhaps his mind was more deeply absorbed in the significance of the apparition. At any rate, he had given no sign from the moment he reined in Beelzebub and permitted Molly's mare to come abreast.

"Do you see?" the girl asked, in a low, hushed tone, as she raised a hand, pointing. "Pedro's tight cinched, and his bit's still fixed." She shook her head. "That sure isn't Lightning. Lightning doesn't set a horse grazing that way. Where is he? Lightning? Do you see him—anywhere?"

For some moments Jim made no reply. He was searching in every direction for a sign of the man who should have been there with his horse. There was none that he could discover.

"I don't see him around," he said. "I don't see a sign of a noon camp." He drew a deep breath. Then he added, with a decision that was unforced: "But he's there, sure. He's right down there—somewhere."

He glanced round at the girl beside him as he spoke, and discovered something of the effect which the sight of Pedro had had upon her. She was deathly pale in the sunlight, and her eyes had widened with a look of deep concern.

"You think that?" she cried. "You guess he's—down there? Then," she went on, as Jim inclined his head, "something bad's happened. He's—he's sick, or it's a fall. Maybe—he's—— Oh, say, Jim, we can get right down there? Yes, sure we can. I know. Oh, let's get right on down. Maybe he's hurt. Maybe——"

But Jim waited for no more. He had caught the infection of Molly's fears. To Molly it seemed that Lightning must be sick. It was even possible he had had a fall. To Jim it was neither of these things which had left Pedro still saddled and bridled, grazing free. Surely there was more lying behind their discovery. And it was the thought of grave possibilities that set him hastily moving on to the descent to the lagoon.

* * * *

Lightning stirred uneasily. A muffled sound escaped him that terminated in an almost soundless, choking cough. The weak movement of his head and chest, as the fit went on, had utter helplessness in it. But it ceased at last, and his lips were dyed with crimson, and a trickle of blood had found its way to the corners of his mouth.

The cattleman was sprawled in the shade of an up-standing boulder. He was propped against it, with his long legs spread out towards the lapping waters of the lagoon, which were almost within reach of the hand that lay palm upwards on the bed of stone upon which he was lying. It was the identical boulder that had once sheltered Molly.

He looked to have slipped down from the sitting position he had originally taken up. Now only his shoulders rested against the water-smoothed sides of the stone. He was lying over, almost on his side. His grizzled, bare head was lolling forward, till his tatter of whisker was pressed down on his blood-stained shirt. His eyes were closed, and his sunken cheeks were ghastly. Then, too, his lower jaw was slightly sagging, in the grievous fashion of a creature whose last will-power is exhausted.

But, whatever his appearance, exhaustion of will was not yet. The shattered body was living in a soul that refused to yield. Lightning was near enough to death. But the work he had designed was not yet completed, and so he battled to hold together the dregs of his life.

The flies were swarming, lured by the sanguinary ooze from the man's two wounds. But their aggravation left him indifferent. His remaining purpose was too precious to permit of irritation from so small a thing. Molly was somewhere up there in the hills. He had yet miles of difficult trail to make before he reached her. He must reach her. He must reach those who were caring for her. There was that splendid horse he had borrowed. Then there was his news for the men-folk. Faint with bodily exhaustion, gasping and choking at intervals, he pondered these things.

He had ridden so far since—since—— Yes, and he had no intention of failing in the rest. He would lie where he was till his breathing got better. Then he would get up and ride on. Yes, he would get up. Of course, he would get up as soon as his breath got better. It was nothing but darn laziness, lying around with work still to be done.

It was a great thought he was going to see Molly again so soon. How long was it? Yes, it was days. And somehow he couldn't count them. But it didn't matter—now he was going back to her. He guessed she'd be well by now. But he wouldn't tell her about—about—— No. It was good news, but he best not tell her. He wouldn't unless—unless she forced him to.

But he would tell the others. Oh, yes. He would tell Jim Pryse. Jim Pryse would need to know, because he hadn't a thing to worry about—now. He was a bully feller. A great boy. It was queer his hair was white. But it didn't matter. A feller who could act the way he had for a brother was the boy to see Molly right.

Something broke in on the man's disjointed thought.

He stirred uneasily. A far-off sound had startled him. It was the sound of voices that broke through his misty comprehension. He wondered dully who it could be talking. Who could be around? But he made no attempt to move. He made no attempt even to open his eyes. There seemed to be no need. And then he could think better, and hear better, with his eyes closed. Darkness seemed to help him. He wanted to think clearly. He wanted so badly to think of—Molly.

His movement again bestirred his helpless coughing, and he forgot all about the voices. Then again, with the passing of his agony, his thoughts went back to other things. The farm again came into his dazing mind, and he thought of the harvest he meant to begin cutting as soon as he had taken Molly back home.

It was a swell crop. The ear was long and heavy. And there had been no early frosts to damage it. What a bunch of money Molly would collect for it in Hartspool. Yes, it was Hartspool. A queer name for a prairie town. But it was fine now that she was free of that—— She mustn't work too hard. No. She'd been sick. Of course she'd been sick. He'd almost forgotten about it. And she was feeling bad. He wondered why she felt bad. There wasn't need. Not now that—that——

Ah! What was that? That was his name. Lightning? Of course it was his name. Who was calling?

A moment passed while he summoned his will. Then his eyes slowly opened.

"Molly!" he cried.

Lightning made a tremendous effort. By sheer will-power he lifted himself and made his dying body obey him. He sat up. He drew up his knees and clasped his lean hands about. Only a moment before they had lain limp and inert upon his stone bed. But the cost was great. Greater than he knew. He paid for it in a terrible fit of that hideous, soundless cough.

Jim Pryse was standing over him. His pitying gaze was for that grievous, unkempt figure. He saw the blood-stains on the shirt, and on the stone on which Lightning had been lying. He beheld the ooze dying the corners of his hard old mouth. And he knew. There could be no mistaking the sign. Death was very near. The man's superb courage alone supported him and carried him through the fierce effort he was making.

Molly was kneeling on the stone beside him. Already one of her arms was flung about the lean shoulders of the dying man. She, too, understood. And her action was less a support than a caress.

In that supreme moment Lightning looked to need no support. He squatted on his old haunches in a fashion so familiar. His lower jaw was no longer sagging. His head was erect, and a queer sort of smile looked back into the girl's passionately troubled eyes. It was the moment of his life.

"I was comin' right—along—up," he gasped. Then a queer look replaced his smile. "You hadn't need to—butt in—Molly, gal. I ain't needin'—no sort o' help," he complained.

Molly looked into the dying eyes; she saw the blood ooze at his mouth, the poor, sunken cheeks so ghastly. She wanted to cry out. She was swept to her soul by passionate pity.

"But you're hit, Lightning," she cried. "You're wounded. Oh, God? You're wounded to—death."

A flash of storm lit the old man's eyes.

"Ther'—ain't—no—feller," he gasped, "wi' the guts to shoot up 'Two-gun' Rogers. You're—wrong, Molly, gal. I ain't—shot up. He couldn't—shoot up a—buck louse. I left him feed for the coyotes. I ain't—shot—up," he cried obstinately. "Jest grazed. That's all. It's this—darn cough."

Molly looked away. Her agony of mind was terrible. The sight nearly broke her heart. She gazed up at Jim in helpless appeal, and the man dropped on his knees beside her.

"Isn't ther' a thing we can do?" she cried. "Oh, Jim, tell me. Can't——"

"Cut it—out, Molly, gal," Lightning mumbled, as his body rocked. "Ther' ain't goin'—to be—no bleatin'."

His choking attacked him again. It was ghastly. Then came the blood ooze afresh, and the poor old creature gasped out his words through it. His eyes were on Jim. And their eagerness suggested that anxiety was pressing.

"You're—clear—of—him," he spluttered. "I shot him cold at the fork—o' the Calford trail. I gave him a chanct—that was no—darn chanct. We stood up at fifty—wi' two shots each. He dropped—cold. I come along up—to—to tote Molly, gal, home. Guess—I won't make it, though. This darn cough——"

Again Lightning choked. And it was moments before he recovered sufficiently to go on. When he did, however, his hands had parted from about his knees. He would have fallen heavily back against the stone but for Molly's support.

His eyes were half closed now, but they still gazed urgently up at the white-haired man.

"Say," he cried, with a spasm of dying energy, "it's up to—you." He gasped. Now, curiously, his cough made no return. "You'll fix—her right? Guess I'm—failin' through. She ain't got no one but me. An' I guess—I'm—done. You will? You're clear o' that skunk. So's she. You'll——"

Jim nodded. In that moment of the old man's agony he was glad enough to help him. But he knew that, even at the moment of death, the old creature was contriving another service.

"Lightning, old feller," he said earnestly, "you don't need to worry a thing for Molly, gal. I'm crazy to marry her, if she'll have me. And I'll make good for her, too, same as you'd have me do. Don't go, old feller," he said, thrusting his arm about the dying man for added support. "Just ask her yourself. Then you'll know."

There was a moment without response. The cattleman's eyes rolled ominously. But finally they found Molly's face, and remained looking into it.

"You'll—mate—up with him?" he mumbled, in a faint whisper.

The girl was powerless to hold back the flood of tears which rolled all unheeded down her cheeks. But she steadied herself to reply.

Her simple "Yes" came in a low tone no louder than the old cattleman's whisper. And, though her face was deliberately turned from the man beside her, it reached his keenly intent ears.

But, alas, it fell without meaning upon the dead ears of the faithful Lightning.